A Stranger's Thoughts....

"Freeze your soul forever, Dorian gran Grannel," Kay shouted into the garden. She'd never dared saying such a thing while he was still alive, but she felt braver knowing she'd never see his face again. "You're a disgrace to all Avatars. I'll never understand why Winter chose you, but I pray He replaces you."

Kay ava Seltich, that's a cruel thing to say. Who are you to question the Four?

The voice—a woman's—seemed to speak inside her mind, but Kay wasn't linked with Gwen or any of her other sister Avatars.

She whirled around, but no one else was in the room.

"By the Four, what was that? Who was that?" she whispered, tracing the compass rose of the Four over her chest.

Kay? Can you hear me?

Now the voice seemed to come from behind her. She faced the open window. Even though she was inside, she grabbed the breezes, ready to push the intruder through the window and down into the courtyard.

She still couldn't see anyone, but as she peered at the snow-flakes, she noticed a blank spot that they avoided. It was shaped like a human figure, similar in build to Gwen or Ysabel. The figure reached toward Kay as if inviting her to link. Then a sheet of snow gusted through the window, drowning the figure.

Summon the Seasons

Book Five of the Season Avatars

Sandra Ulbrich Almazan

Solar Unicorn Publishing

Sandra Ulbrich Almazan/Solar Unicorn Publishing
www.sandraulbrichalmazan.com

Publisher's Note: This is a work of fiction. Names, characters, places, and incidents are a product of the author's imagination. Locales and public names are sometimes used for atmospheric purposes. Any resemblance to actual people, living or dead, or to businesses, companies, events, institutions, or locales is completely coincidental.

Book Layout © 2017 BookDesignTemplates.com
Book Cover by Maria Zannini of Book Cover Diva

Summon the Seasons/ Sandra Ulbrich Almazan. — 1st ed.
ISBN 978-1-944437-05-3

CONTENTS

Grandmother of Stories

The Grandmother of Stories had never left the Hidden Archipelago, but She knew the world in a way no other deity did. Every country had its own story, as did every inhabitant of those countries, and She had the weaving of all of them. So many of those stories had the same themes of wanting love or wealth or power. The Fip Empire in particular was greedy for power. Like a starving child, it gobbled up every country in its path. It wouldn't take long before it discovered Her people's hidden chain of islands. Grandmother shuddered to think what would happen to them if She couldn't distract the Fips or others bent on conquest.

Fortunately, there were lands in the Fip Empire that would divert them from Her people. Centuries ago, the Fips had conquered a country called Challen, neighbor to the Dead Land where absolutely nothing lived. While most countries had only one or two Gods or Goddesses, Challen had four. Each of Them had taken a new name, calling Themselves after the four seasons Their country experienced. Each of the Four chose three Avatars to bless with Their magic. Spring gave Her Avatars healing; Summer, plant

magic; Fall, animal magic; and Winter, weather magic. By forming quartets with one of each type of Avatar, the Four planned to
ensure prosperity for Their people.

Then Salth, ruler of the Dead Land, picked a quarrel with an
Avatar's husband. Grandmother admitted that killing Salth's
magic-dependent son, even accidentally, was sufficient cause. Extending Salth's quarrel with Kron and Bella to the Four, however,
was risky, even for a demigoddess. Salth added insult to injury by
using her time magic to mix up the seasons the Four loved so.
Restoring the damage caused by the unpredictable storm occupied
the Avatars as they were reincarnated over eight hundred years.
The Four were bound by the World Covenant not to interfere except through Their Avatars.

Finally, after centuries in which the Avatars had increased their
skills, they were ready to face Salth. Salth had converted one of
them to her side, but Grandmother suspected this would backfire
on her. Soon this tale would come to its end, and She planned to
be there as it unfolded. A few rewrites to this story, and the deities
in the world would be too distracted by the Dead Land to care
about the Hidden Archipelago.

CHAPTER ONE

The King Is Displeased

Two days ago, Kay had been brought back to life after being killed by ancient creatures. Now, she knelt in front of the king of Challen while he scolded her quartet of Season Avatars. In some ways, he scared her more than the animals had.

By the Four, I'd rather be facing that flying reptile again. Kay smoothed out the white silk of her mourning gown. *At least I could blast that with lightning without worrying about committing treason. Jenna's plant magic and Ysabel's animal magic are just as useless here. Let's hope Gwen's noble upbringing gave her a tongue skilled enough to save us all.*

"Avas, as happy as I am to see you all safe, it would make me even happier to have you abandon your Grand Tour of Challen," the king said. He didn't give them permission to rise from the hard marble floor. "Those strange creatures that destroyed the absent Spring Avatar's grave could reappear any heartbeat. I know you can handle Chaos Season best from the One Oak, so you should stay there in case the animals return."

Ysabel, kneeling next to Kay, looked up. "I doubt that they will, Your Majesty."

"Can you be certain, Ava?"

The four of them—Gwen, Jenna, Ysabel, and Kay—exchanged glances. Salth and her son Sal-thaath had already tested Gwen, Jenna, and Ysabel. Kay knew she was likely to be the next target, especially now that Dorian, the previous Winter Avatar, had joined forces with Salth. Telling the king that wouldn't reassure him.

"Your Majesty, we haven't finished honoring our predecessors yet," Gwen said. "That was why we decided we should perform a Grand Tour in the first place."

Kay admired Gwen's ability to keep her expression unchanged as she lied. The Season Avatars had another reason to visit the previous quartet's graves besides honoring them. They still needed to retrieve bones from three more Avatars: one from the quartet immediately before them and two from the quartet before that. That would complete the full set of twelve Avatars and allow them to face Salth, possibly ending Chaos Season forever. But like the Challens, the Fips believed in leaving the dead undisturbed. They couldn't tell the king they were robbing graves. No matter how privileged Season Avatars were, that crime wouldn't go unpunished.

The king let out a heavy sigh. "Perhaps you can find a better time to perform that duty, say, after a season or two of calm." He turned his gaze directly onto Kay. "Surely that isn't too much to ask, Ava?"

Terror squeezed her throat. For a moment, Kay was a seamstress again, confronted by some demanding customer who expected perfection yesterday. *I'm the Winter Avatar,* she reminded herself, *chosen by the God of Winter centuries before the Fips conquered Challen. I control the weather in Challen, not the king. I was born into a poor family so I could learn how to help them. I can't let the king's rank scare me. He can't carry me into the air, after all.*

The reminder of her recent experience gave her courage to answer. "Your—Your Majesty, there's never an end to Chaos Season. Even in winter, Salth disrupts the way the weather should be. We can't let Chaos Season stop us from doing what we need to do. Besides, we need to—" she hastily changed what she had been about to say. "We need to finish the Grand Tour before the winter solstice." Since the God of Winter was also God of the dead, His day would be the best time to contact the eight dead Season Avatars so all twelve could face their ancient enemy together.

"Ah yes, of course, so you can return to Wistica in time for the soltrans at the Temple. Though I hear this new Delns Avatar that's joined with you can take you anywhere you need to go in an instant." The king scowled. "He should offer that service to me."

Ysabel must be grateful her intended hadn't been included in the king's summons. If the king was foolish enough to imprison them, Kron would find them and help them escape.

Gwen boldly raised her head, her blonde chignon so tightly pinned that not a hair moved. "Your Majesty, Kron Evenhanded has been a great asset to us. With his help, we can return to the One Oak any time it's necessary." She paused. "And we can leave at will."

"Yes, you Season Avatars have always been difficult to control." Now the king grinned. "But what about your wards? The Summer Ava's child, the Fall Avatar's siblings?"

Kay and the rest of her quartet exchanged uneasy looks.

"I've sent royal soldiers to your household," the king continued, "ordering the children sent to Wistica. Not to your house, but to mine. And if you continue to disregard my wishes, I can have them shipped to the Fip mainland before nightfall."

"What?" Ysabel cried out. Lathtin hissed, his ears flat as he stared at the king. Although Lathtin had been reborn as Ysabel's cat, he'd originally been her brother. Any threat to Ysabel's other siblings affected him too.

"You'd separate a mother from her child?" Jenna rose, fingers twitching as if she wanted to grab a fighting stick and square off with the monarch. She'd never get the chance, but Kay would have placed all her chals on Jenna.

"I assure you, Ava, no harm will come to my nephew—if you simply follow my order. It's best for Challen, and we all want that, don't we?"

Gwen carefully laid a gloved hand on Jenna's arm. She didn't curl her fingers around Jenna's wrist; ever since she'd brought Kay back to life, she'd lost use of her hand. Only an observant person or someone who already knew her secret would notice, however.

"We'll follow the Four's wishes, as we always have," she said quietly. "Your Majesty, if you'll permit us, we need to pray to Them in Their Temple."

"Of course, of course." He smiled as he waved a hand at them. "My honor guard will accompany you."

Kay copied the others as they curtseyed before leaving. Guards flanked them on both sides as they left the throne room. They couldn't plan anything out loud, but their four-fold link allowed them to exchange thoughts as long as they were touching each other. Gwen kept both hands at her sides, as if to demonstrate she wasn't causing trouble. Kay and the rest copied her example.

As they climbed into their carriage, one of the guards scrambled up to the coachman's seat. Kay hoped he didn't plan to take over the drive from their coachman. Another guard tried to follow them into the carriage itself, but Gwen stopped her with a smile and the words, "I'm afraid there's no room." Lathtin sprawled out between Ysabel and Gwen. Jenna and Kay spread their skirts out to cover their seat. With a scowl, the guard left.

Gwen extended her good hand, signaling a link. As soon as they had all joined hands, she sent to them, *First, we find out for certain if the king made good on his threat.*

And then we rescue Robbie—and Ysabel's brothers and little sister? Jenna asked.

Kron will be able to track them. Ysabel sounded confident despite her worry. *All he needs is a single piece of clothing, and he can build a finder tuned to the owner. Even if the king sends them to Fip, he'll bring them home, sure as he loves me. And if the king tries to stop Kron...*

The children might be safer in Fip, where Salth can't find them, Gwen said. *But either way, we have to slip out of the king's reach before he figures out another way to bring us under his thumb.*

That should be easy enough, Jenna said. *We step through a portal...*

To someplace the king isn't expecting us to go. But how long can we keep a season ahead of him? We foolishly informed all of Challen about our plans to visit the graves, so he'll know where we have to go.

Gwen sighed. *I wish I'd been able to find pictures of the graves so Kron could portal us there. It would make this task so much simpler—and let us travel faster than the Watch.*

The carriage halted. "Avas, we've arrived," the coachman said.

Despite her useless hand, Gwen insisted on descending to the street without help. Once they were all gathered in front of the Temple, Gwen raised her head and led the way up the worn stone steps. Jenna and Ysabel followed, leaving Kay to bring up the rear—as always. She was the youngest, and her season, Winter, came last in the Challen year. A few pilgrims to the Four's Temple recognized the Avatars and approached Gwen for blessings. Although a couple of them turned next to Jenna and Ysabel, none of them came to Kay, as if they associated her not just with Winter's control over the weather, but death itself. She sketched the sign of the Four for them anyway. A heavily dressed dark-skinned foreigner chanted in a lilting language. He seemed to direct his words at Kay, and that bolstered her spirit.

I'm a Season Avatar as much as Gwen or Jenna or Ysabel, she reminded herself. *I've served as many lives as they have. Besides...* She laid a hand over her bosom and felt the raised scars Gwen's magic hadn't removed. *I know the Four Gods and Goddesses want me to live, even if it's just to keep our quartet intact.*

Kay smiled as she entered the Four's sacred space. A statue of one of the Four dominated each quarter of the main room of the Temple. She faced the God of Winter, an old but hale man with white hair. The sculptor had shown Him with an open mouth, puffing out the wind. Of course, the Four Gods and Goddesses were more than human, so these statues were only what people imagined the Four to be like. The Four were too glorious to be limited by human forms or human thoughts. That was what Kay loved about Them so. When she prayed to Them, she could leave behind her shortcomings and dwell on Their perfection.

Her faith would carry her through this mission. She was sure of it.

As she stared at the God of Winter's face, her vision wavered. Superimposed over the God's face was the image of Jon, the railroad fireman and engineer she'd loved for several years. She rubbed her eyes, but the vision didn't fade.

By the Four, I must be dreaming. Or more tired than I realize. Did something happen to my eyes when I was in the God of Winter's domain?

Gwen would have known if Kay was in less than perfect health. Was this vision a product of her over-stressed mind, or a sign from Winter? If the latter, what did it mean?

***

Kay forgot her questions as their carriage pulled into the courtyard of their home in Wistica. Four of the Watch, impossible to miss in yellow jackets, stepped in front of the gate as it closed. Their captain guarded the front door. He saluted as the Avatars entered, but the footman who answered the door wouldn't let him in.

"The butler told me he should wait outside, Avas." The young man bowed his head nervously. "He said he doesn't belong here."

"Indeed he doesn't," Gwen said. "Are there any letters?"

As she glanced at the cards arranged on a silver tray, Jenna darted up the stairs toward a private parlor Kron had transformed into a permanent portal between this house and the One Oak. She returned a few moments later, as Kay and the others sat down to an informal supper. "It's true!" Jenna's hair had come unpinned, and strands flickered about her face like wisps of flame. "I don't know how the king arranged things so quickly without his own magic, but he must have had a troop in place as soon as we left the One Oak. They swooped in and claimed all of the children. Nursemaids too. Freeze him forever!"

Ysabel drooped and pushed her empty plate away. Lathtin bounded up to push his head under her hand. "The forest animals didn't take much note of humans and horses entering and leaving the One Oak," she said. "I don't know if I'll be able to trace them."

"They're probably on a boat headed down the Chikasi River to Wistica." Jenna's green eyes gleamed. "We could be waiting for them…"

"Not yet, not yet," Gwen said. "We don't want to give away all of our tricks too quickly. Let the king think he's beaten us. Stay here a day or two and prepare our things." She grinned. "Then, when the guards are starting to think we've settled down, we send them to sleep and sneak out in the middle of the night."

Jenna and Ysabel nodded, though Ysabel said, "And then we fetch my brothers and sister?"

"We could have Kron rescue them at the same time," Jenna added hopefully.

"And then what do we do with them? Send them back to the One Oak so the king can capture them again? Bring them with us on our journey, when we have to travel fast and be inconspicuous?"

Kay felt obliged to point out, "We'll have to travel to the Dead Land once we have all the bones. Will Kron's artifacts be able to protect all of us?"

Ysabel shuddered. "Salth and Sal-thaath would delight in tormenting them. I hate to say it, but they'll be safer with the king."

Gwen nodded as she sliced open a still-steaming loaf of bread. "Very well. We'll have to hope Lex makes sure they're taken care of. Ysabel, where's Kron? I assume he'll come with us, so we need to make plans with him."

Kay touched a hand to her scars again. She hadn't had a chance to tell Jon what had happened to her. Was that why she'd seen his face earlier? Was it only her own longings talking to her, or was the sight a sign from Winter?

It has to be Winter trying to tell me something. At least, I hope it was Him. The Four know I haven't always worshipped Them properly, but I've never imagined Jon as one of Them before. Her cheeks grew warm, and she blew on her bowl of chicken soup to cover her blush. *I hope I'm interpreting this sign properly.*

She swallowed a spoonful of soup, then said, "I think we need to bring Jon along with us."

Silverware clattered as Gwen dropped the bread knife. All three of them turned to look at her.

"Jon?" Gwen asked. "Your intended? Kay, he doesn't have magic."

"I know, but...." Would they believe her? Even if they linked to see her memory, they might explain the vision away. "I think Winter gave me a sign at the Temple earlier."

"He did?" "What was it?" "Why didn't you say something sooner?"

"I'm not sure if it was real. Link with me and tell me what you believe."

She extended her hand to Gwen, then realized Gwen's closest hand to her was the one affected by the cursed shard—and Kay's death. Trying to push her guilt deep enough so the others couldn't share it, Kay rose and walked around the table to the other side of Gwen. Jenna and Ysabel moved as well so they could all share the link. Kay flushed again as she brought up her memory, but the others mercifully left her alone.

"Very strange," Gwen said as they broke apart. "It could have been a trick of the light, but I didn't notice anything unusual on Spring's statue." She glanced at Jenna and Ysabel. Both of them shook their heads.

"We shouldn't ignore it, no matter what the cause," Ysabel said.

Gwen sighed. "I suppose not, though I don't see how he's supposed to help us."

"The answer will come to us in the proper season," Kay said.

Some of the strain in Gwen's faced eased, but not all. "Then we'll have to arrange for Jon to meet us two nights from now. Perhaps Kron can visit him and create a portal from his boarding house to here. Ysabel, is it safe enough to use Lathtin as a messenger, or can you recruit a different animal?"

"Why can't I visit him myself?" Kay asked. "Does the king expect us to stay locked inside all season? How can we do anyone any good if we can't perform our normal duties?"

"She's right." Jenna reached for the soup tureen as if she'd just realized they needed food to fuel their magic. "We should be seen around town, praying at the Temple, maybe shopping for new clothes—"

"Taking care not to give our plans away," Gwen said sharply.

"But it would be natural for us to visit the University, wouldn't it?" Ysabel asked. "We've been there a couple of times already. Kay could meet Jon after one of his lectures."

"Very well." Gwen nodded. "You two visit the University tomorrow. Jenna and I can see to the supplies."

***

The Watch accompanied Kay and her sister Season Avatars when they drove out the next morning. However, when the carriage dropped Ysabel, Kay and Lathtin off at the entrance to the University grounds, only a single Watchman, stout and nearly sixty, came with them. Kay hoped Ysabel had a plan to distract him while they spoke to Jon.

They stepped through the frost-coated gate. No students lingered in the square of brown grass and bare trees. Ysabel shivered and drew her cloak closer around her. To Kay, the cold air was bracing.

"How long have you known Jon?" Ysabel asked.

Kay drew cold air closer to her cheeks, fighting her urge to blush. "I met him about four years ago, when the nightmares started and I tried to hide from my magic."

"You used to live in Wistica, didn't you? Why did you leave?"

Kay glanced back at the Watchman trying to eavesdrop; he fell back a couple of paces. "One stormy night, a vision of Dorian drew me out of the window and onto a nearby tree. The branch broke, I fell, and I was locked outside my home without so much as a hairpin. Nightmares convinced me I'd die if I used my magic, so I fled from everyone who knew I was an Avatar." Shame still heated her face whenever she remembered that cowardly decision. "The only good thing about that night was meeting Jon. He helped me escape from his supervisor and suggested I hide in Rainbow River. I stowed away on a westbound locomotive."

Ysabel studied the signs identifying the buildings before leading them to the main lecture hall. Kay suspected she was really searching to see what animals were in the area.

"How long was the trip?" Ysabel asked as she turned up the walk. "Did you have food with you?"

Kay shook her head. "I never had enough chals to eat my fill, let alone save some food for the journey. I hadn't planned that far ahead. All I knew was I had to leave Wistica as soon as possible." Ysabel's sympathy made her recall the terror of the trip, first worrying she would be crushed by cargo every time they rounded a curve, then trying to conceal herself every time they stopped, never sure how long the locomotive would remain at the station or even which town she was at. "It turned out Jon was on the crew for that train. He found me after about four or five stops. He shared his meals with me and found me a better spot to hide for the rest of the journey. Then, when we arrived in Rainbow River, he took me to a cousin. She introduced me to the seamstress I worked for until Gwen found me."

They passed through heavy wood doors three times Kay's height and discolored with age. Inside, a small lobby sheltered small groups of students. They paid no attention to Ysabel and Kay, but the two of them kept their cloaks wrapped tightly around them to hide their distinctive dresses. Ysabel held Lathtin tight despite a soft mew of protest. Closed doors to the main lecture hall muffled a speaker's voice. As they drifted closer, Kay caught snatches of "rock layers" and "sediments," but she couldn't catch enough words to follow the gist of the lecture.

Ysabel tilted her head toward the door, where the man from the Watch had just entered. The students closest to him eyed him warily. "We'd better find someplace quieter to talk."

"If we go back outside, I'll use the wind to carry our words away from our guard," Kay said.

The speaker inside the lecture hall grew quiet. After a few moments, the doors opened. Kay backed away as dozen of students streamed out. She craned her neck, looking for Jon. He was among the last to leave, walking with a Summersman and saying, "So, Dame K'linmin's experiments prove the land is many thousands of years old, much older than the country of Challen or the Fip Empire."

"But is the ground older than the Four?" the Summersman asked.

Kay waved to catch Jon's attention. He continued, "No one knows for certain. We only learned of the Four about eight hundred years ago, but that doesn't mean—" He turned his head toward her and broke off with a wide grin. "But here's someone who's an expert on the Four. Kay—I mean, Ava, it's a pleasure to see you."

She winced at his formality. Manners might require them to behave formally in public, but all she wanted to do was clutch him and plead for him to never let her go. "Master Stunstrug, a moment of your time, if you please?"

"Of course." He nodded to his companion, and Ysabel offered the Summersman a brief blessing before he left. The delay gave the Watchman time to intercept their group. "Where are you going, Avas?"

Freeze it, now what do we do?

Ysabel simply raised her head and swept past him without a glance. The action was so much like Gwen Kay couldn't help smiling as she followed. Once she, Ysabel, and Jon were outside, they lengthened their strides until they were nearly running. They garnered odd looks from other students, but the Watchman fell behind. Ysabel released Lathtin. "He'll keep the Watchman distracted."

"By the Four, what are you doing?" Jon asked.

"We need to find someplace where the Watchman can't overhear us. Where can we go?"

Jon thought for a few heartbeats. "The chocolate shop is always crowded, and the librarians don't like anyone talking in the book stacks...."

"It doesn't have to be inside," Kay said. "Some hidden place where I can keep our words from him will do."

"I have an idea. Follow me." Jon quickened his stride. Kay wanted to protest, but she was out of breath. Fortunately, Jon didn't lead them far. He took them between two buildings, where a series of four pillars had been built with carefully balanced stones. A few offerings of dead flowers lay at the base of the pillars. Kay glanced back the way they had come, but the Watchman wasn't visible. She considered creating fog to hide them, but that would only draw more attention to him. Instead, she sent great bursts of wind in both directions to keep anyone else from joining them.

"By the Four, Kay, what's going on?" Jon asked. He tugged the jacket of his second-hand suit into place. "I thought you and the other Avatars were on a Grand Tour of Challen and wouldn't be back for moons. Any why are you so worried about the Watch? It's not as if anyone would ever hurt an Avatar…"

He had no idea what she'd been through. The terror of being snatched up, of falling and struggling to control the wind, the pain and shock of seeing the God of Winter's domain—like a storm kept at bay too long, her emotions finally broke. "Jon!" She flew into his arms.

"Huh? Kay, we're not alone." Nevertheless, his arms folded around her, bringing the warm scent of his soap and the harsher smell of lye from the laundry. She snuggled against his chest, her head barely reaching his heart, and shuddered with cold she couldn't banish. Tears threatened to downpour, but she squeezed her eyes shut to hold the drops back.

You're an Avatar, she reminded herself. *You can control snow and wind, lightning and hail. You have three sister Avatars who brought you back from the God of Winter's domain.* She should feel secure enough to stand on her own without Jon, but she couldn't imagine facing Salth again without him.

"I need you, Jon." She tilted her head, hoping for a kiss. "Come with me."

"Where? Back to the One Oak?"

Ysabel shook her head. "We still need to finish the Grand Tour."

He hesitated. "I'm so sorry, Little Stowaway, but no."

Even his pet name for her couldn't calm the shock she felt.

CHAPTER TWO

A Sighting

"No?" Ysabel was the first one to speak. "By All Four Gods and Goddesses, why not?"

"I can't, Ava! I still have two more lectures this afternoon. Then after that, I have books to read and a paper to write and an evening as a doorman at a local pub to earn a few extra chals—"

"They're not important right now." Ysabel toyed with her glove. "How do you feel about my sister Avatar, Sir?"

Jon huffed. "She's everything to me! By The Four, why do you think I'm here when I could be on the railroad? If I'm ever to become worthy of an Avatar, I have to improve myself. She deserves better than me!"

Kay stared at him, stung. "I never said you were below me, Jon."

"No, you didn't." Now he reached for her hand. "But once the other engineers on the line found out who you really were, they gave me such grief that I couldn't work with them anymore. I wouldn't want anyone to think I was courting you for the chals or the power you have."

"Why would anyone think that when you're not a noble?" she said bitterly. "Ladies who insulted me one moon try to flatter me the next. The lords are no better. I'll have none of them."

"Stowaway, you're important enough to have whomever you want. But I'll only just be your consort. I'm not the kind of person who can lie easy in a soft bed and grow fat on chals I didn't earn. I have a strong back and arms. I have to use them to serve Challen and the Four, the way you do with your weather magic." His eyes took on a determined expression lit from within. "Maybe I can't tame Chaos Season like you can, but I still have to do something."

How could she not love him more after a speech like that? Worry squeezed her heart. He must be capable of doing something to help them end Chaos Season; otherwise, Winter wouldn't have graced her with a sign. Would that put Jon at risk?

Do I have to tell him about the sign? Will that change Winter's plans if Jon knows the God wants him? Kay glanced at Ysabel, who gave her a brief nod. Jon hadn't pledged himself to one of the Four the way she had. If he wanted to serve the Four, he deserved the chance to do so—but he had to know the cost.

"Jon, I had a sign from Winter Himself. I think the Four want you to come with us."

His eyes widened. "Are you certain, Stowaway? By All Four Gods and Goddesses, why? Why me?"

Ysabel checked their surroundings again before stepped toward them. "It's more than just a Grand Tour, but we can't talk about that here. It's not safe. Kay isn't safe."

"What do you mean she's not safe?" Jon asked. He glared at Kay as if she were the threat. She reminded herself Jon would never hurt her. "Who would dare even think about harming you?"

"Salth," she whispered. "She...she's the one who's been haunting my dreams. She tried to kill me."

"And she nearly succeeded, too," Ysabel said. "She did, technically. But praise the Four, They gave us enough magic to bring her back."

Jon gaped at Kay. He squeezed her hands, then patted her arms as if to reassure himself she was still alive. "You seem very much alive to me."

"It was real, Jon. It happened." She looked up at him. "Magic leaves scars Gwen can't heal. I can show them to you sometime when we have privacy. A great deal of privacy."

His eyes widened, but he clung to her hands and didn't let go. "What happened?"

Kay glanced at Ysabel for reassurance before saying, "You know the four of us were on a Grand Tour of Challen, traveling all over to share our magic with everyone." She lowered her voice to a whisper. "We also had a secret mission, to collect some items—" she didn't want to admit what they were— "that we need to defeat Salth and Sal-thaath."

"Who are they? Are they the ones who hurt you?"

"They're the ones who send Chaos Season to Challen. Actually, Salth does. She drained all the life from the Dead Land to keep her son Sal-thaath alive, and now she wants Challen's magic too."

"But you stop her, don't you," Jon said slowly. "You and the rest of the Avatars in your quartet." He nodded at Ysabel.

Ysabel stepped forward. "According to Kron, we need to reunite all twelve Avatars, living and dead, to defeat her."

"Is that why the older three Avatars died, so they could all be reborn?" Jon asked.

Ysabel shook her head. "We have another way to bring them back from the God of Winter's domain." She looked up and down the corridor again. "But this isn't a good place to talk about it. Kay, go on."

"I was trying to." She shot an annoyed glare at Ysabel. "A couple of days ago, while we were collecting what we needed for one of the Spring Avatars, Salth used her time magic to bring some very old creatures back to life. One of them attacked me. It flew off with me in the air, just like in the nightmares I've had for years. Then it dropped me. I used my weather magic to cushion my fall, but then Dorian's soul threw a fence post at me with the wind. It went right through my heart."

Jon's face turned ashen, and he gripped her even tighter. "Kay, Kay, little Stowaway…" He bent down and kissed her full on the lips. Ysabel sucked in her breath but didn't say anything, allowing Kay to drown in the taste of Jon's mouth. All too soon he pulled away, put his hands on his shoulders, and gave her a serious look. "Darling, if this task is so dangerous, perhaps you and the other Avatars should give it up."

"This is the only way to free Challen from Chaos Season!" Ysabel said.

"What if it doesn't, and one or more of you is hurt again? Challen can't risk that. If something happens to your quartet, who else will take your place?"

Kay traced the edges of her unfamiliar scar; Jon's eyes grew bigger as he watched her. She'd seen the absent Avatars' souls in the God of Winter's domain. They had stood in a group, staring at her expectantly. She wasn't sure what she was supposed to do about them, but she knew the Four had gone to a great deal of trouble to make she *could* do something. It would be ungrateful and impious of her not to try.

"No one can replace us, but I can't back away from this any more than I could use the wrong color thread for my fabric," she told him. "The Four have given me my life back, and now I must repay Them."

He stared at her for a few heartbeats. "What exactly do you have to do?"

"I have to bring the absent Avatars' souls back into the land of the living so all twelve of us can face our ancient enemy again," Kay said. "I don't know how yet I'm supposed to do that, but it's the only way we can stop Salth." Her scar ached, and rubbing it didn't help. "Jon, I've lived in fear of her for years, but she can't do anything worse to me than what she's already done." *As long as she doesn't steal my soul the next time, the way she did Dorian's.* Her throat threatened to close, but Kay continued, "It's time for me to face her, but I can't do it alone. I need my sister Avatars, of course, but Jon, I also need you."

He smiled sadly. "By All Four Gods and Goddesses, Kay, why? I don't have healing or plant or animal magic like an Avatar, and I certainly can't control the weather the way you do. I'm just an ordinary train engineer. I shovel coal, I control the engine, I can even fix it if necessary. Yes, I'm trying to make something better of myself, but all the books in the University won't give me magic or any other skills that would make me equal to who you are. All I can do for you is carry your trunks or help you find a train, and you don't need me for that."

"Winter says we need you," Kay said. "I saw your face in the Temple. We think it's a sign you should come with us."

Jon shook his head, only stopping when Ysabel nodded confirmation. "You can't be serious," he said.

"By the Four, Jon, after everything we've told you, you still don't believe us?" Kay snapped.

"No, I just can't believe a God would send me with you...."
He sighed. "But if it's true, I don't want to anger Him—or risk
losing you again."

Kay's annoyance faded. Her sister Avatars were gifted, but
they couldn't reassure her with a solid presence the way Jon could.
This part of the trip would be easier with him by her side.

Lathtin streaked over to Ysabel. "The Watchman is heading
this way," she said as she scooped him up.

"Why are you avoiding the Watchman?" Jon asked.

"The king doesn't want us to resume our Grand Tour," Kay
replied. "We're going to sneak off tomorrow night. Where should
we meet?"

"I can come to you," Jon said.

Ysabel gestured them toward the other end of the alley. "We're
guarded day and night."

"Then how will you escape?"

"We'll find a way," Kay said. "Just meet us by the gate of our
house at midnight."

"I will." Jon reached for Kay as if to kiss her, but when the
Watchman appeared, Jon drew back, bowed formally, and turned
away.

"By All Four, Avas!" The Watchman huffed as he caught up
to them. "You mustn't leave me like that."

"Do you expect the Ava Winter to speak with her beau in front
of the entire University?" Ysabel said.

"It'll be all over Wistica by tomorrow. Are you done here,
Avas? We shouldn't stay here too long."

"We may as well." Ysabel imitated Gwen being haughty.
"There's nothing for us to do here."

Kay nodded agreement. She should be happy; Jon would be
with her on the rest of this journey. But as she followed the others

back to the entrance, she wondered what dangers the two of them would face—and how someone without magic could survive them.

* * *

Once they reunited with Gwen and Jenna in the carriage, they linked to form their final escape plans. Gwen would disguise herself as a scullery maid—Jenna wagered a chocolate pastry she wouldn't be able to carry it off— then pretend to be performing a chore and send the Watch to sleep. Once they were taken care of, Kron would create a portal to the carriage house, where they would meet up with Jon and Kron and drive off.

Is harnessing horses anything like hitching them to a wagon? Jenna asked. *Or will we have to kidnap a coachman too?*

We'll manage it somehow, Gwen said, *though I don't know how much help I'll be with my useless hand.*

Never useless! Jenna protested with enough passion to make Ysabel and Kay want to withdraw from the link.

What do we do after we harness and load the carriage? Kay asked.

Gwen raised her eyebrows. *Why, we leave Wistica and travel to the nearest grave, of course.*

But we won't be able to leave the city at night. There'll be more Watch members guarding all the roads in and out of the city.

By All Four Gods and Goddesses, why? Gwen snorted. *Who's going to attack the Fips in the middle of the night?*

It's a tradition going back to the founding of the Fip Empire, Jenna replied. *Lex told me the monarch's city is always guarded at night, to make sure rebels don't attempt to overthrow the government.*

If only Kron could portal us to the gravesites, we wouldn't have to worry about this, Ysabel said wistfully.

I know, but we haven't been to any of the sites and don't have any pictures of them.

Then maybe we should have Kron create a portal to someplace outside of Wistica, Kay said.

That's it! Gwen sounded as triumphant as if it had been her idea. *Kron can enchant the carriage door into a portal, so that should work. We can go someplace where the Watch won't be looking for us, so they won't know which road to watch. I'll ask him if my absent aunt's house will work. I have a sketch of it somewhere.*

We should disguise ourselves too, Jenna said. *There aren't that many groups of four young women, each wearing yellow, green, red, or blue, in Challen.*

I look forward to wearing something besides yellow, Gwen said. *Very well, then. Tomorrow we'll have an open house for those who need our magic. Afterward, we can have an early dinner, plead exhaustion, and go to our rooms to pack and change. Remember, keep our plans from the servants. They can't be punished for what they don't know.*

As they broke the link, Kay hoped the servants would be loyal enough to hide their escape from the king and the Watch for as long as possible.

* * *

The next day dragged on forever. Kay's weather magic wasn't needed in the city, so she didn't receive any petitioners. All she did was link with Gwen to share her magic as necessary. Gwen tried to hide her useless hand from the petitioners, but she struggled with every healing. Despite the link, she pled exhaustion and ended the session by mid-afternoon. Kay tried to appear calm, as if nothing more pressing bothered her than mending clothing for the poor. Her stitches were uneven, so she was glad when the sunlight faded.

The Avatars weren't receiving anyone tonight, so there was no need to dress for dinner. Kay's short hair didn't need to be rebraided or pinned up, but she readjusted the blue headband that held her hair back from her face. She washed her face and hands, then looked over the carpetbag she had packed with spare clothes and other necessities. Her sewing kit went in there as well. There was nothing left to do before dinner than pray to Winter and the rest of the Four.

Kay opened a window to let in fresh air. The view looked out into the small garden. As cold air brought in the smell of dead leaves, Kay glanced around, searching for something she could focus on while she prayed. Blankets in the Four's colors draped the bed, and a silver basin and pitcher rested, empty, on the dresser. The paintings were all of the One Oak at different times of the year. She studied the winter one for a few heartbeats, moving closer to see it better. A board squeaked underfoot. She glanced down at it, and something sparkling by the edge caught her attention. Curious, she squatted to examine it. It looked like a diamond, possibly part of an earring. Wondering why no one else had found it sooner, Kay pried it out of the crack with a couple of needles from her sewing kit. No larger than a bead, the jewel was pointed on one end. Kay wrapped it in a scrap of silk for safekeeping. She was about to tuck it into her sewing kit when a gust of freezing air straight from the depths of winter blew in through the window.

Kay tensed. The previous Winter Avatar, Dorian, was dead, but according to Gwen, his spirit hadn't crossed over into the God of Winter's domain. Some incidents during the last few Chaos Seasons made her wonder if he'd joined forces with Salth and Salthaath, even though the pair had been enemies of Challen for centuries. Maybe Dorian was behind this breath of winter. By the Four, would he never leave her alone? What did she have to do to be free of him?

She crossed to the open window and glanced out of it again, taking care not to risk herself. A dusting of snow graced the dormant garden, but no snow was visible elsewhere. This couldn't be normal weather, but further proof Dorian was still haunting her.

"Freeze your soul forever, Dorian gran Grannel," Kay shouted into the garden. She'd never dared saying such a thing while he was still alive, but she felt braver knowing she'd never see his face again. "You're a disgrace to all Avatars. I'll never understand why Winter chose you, but I pray He replaces you."

Kay ava Seltich, that's a cruel thing to say. Who are you to question the Four?

The voice—a woman's—seemed to speak inside her mind, but Kay wasn't linked with Gwen or any of her other sister Avatars.

She whirled around, but no one else was in the room.

"By the Four, what was that? Who was that?" she whispered, tracing the compass rose of the Four over her chest.

Kay? Can you hear me?

Now the voice seemed to come from behind her. She faced the open window. Even though she was inside, she grabbed the breezes, ready to push the intruder through the window and down into the courtyard.

She still couldn't see anyone, but as she peered at the snowflakes, she noticed a blank spot that they avoided. It was shaped like a human figure, similar in build to Gwen or Ysabel. The figure reached toward Kay as if inviting her to link. Then a sheet of snow gusted through the window, drowning the figure.

CHAPTER THREE

Escape

"By All Four Gods and Goddesses, Kay, you must have imagined a spirit." Jenna spoke lightly, but she gave Kay a concerned look as she ran a hand over her newly shorn hair, now as short as Kay's. Even more shocking were her clothes: grey riding breeches and a violet jacket. Jenna must have strapped down her bosom, but even so, it was still hard to think of her as a man—or Jules, the name they were supposed to call her while they were travelling.

Kay blinked a couple of times to focus on their conversation. "Link with me once we're on our way, and I'll prove it wasn't my imagination."

"We'll have to wait until Gwen is done." Even though Gwen had urged them not to draw attention to themselves, Jenna drew the drape aside and peeked into the courtyard. Heartbeats later, she pulled away. "Freeze it, we have a visitor!"

"This late at night?" Ysabel asked. "Who is it?"

"It must be Jon." Kay came forward to look for herself. To her disappointment, the visitor had come on horseback, so it couldn't be Jon. Gwen wasn't in sight; she wondered if her sister Avatar was hiding. Then she glanced again at the visitor as he crossed under a light. "By the Four, it's the War Avatar!"

"Lex?" Jenna reached for her trunk. "He didn't send word he was coming!"

Ysabel bit her lip. "I don't suppose we can have the butler say we're not at home."

"But I want to see him! It feels like it's been forever! Only..." Jenna looked down at herself. "I suppose I'd better find a dress. He'll know immediately we're planning something if he sees me like this."

"We all better put on different clothes." Kay gestured at her own gray dress, then at Ysabel's brown one. "Or at least ask Kron if he can change the colors back to their normal ones."

"I hope he hasn't encountered Gwen yet. Even with her disguise, he might recognize her." Ysabel crossed the room to open the door for Lathtin, who bolted as though shot from a bow. "Lathtin will find her and tell her what's happening."

Jenna narrowed her eyes. Since Ysabel's anilink had regained human consciousness, he'd also been able to mentally communicate with them in the link and privately with Gwen. Kay thought Jenna was jealous of him, or maybe she thought a Selathen in a cat's body wasn't good enough for Gwen. Couldn't she see how the worry faded from Gwen's expression whenever Lathtin was near? It was like what Jon did for her. As Kay waited for Kron to return her dress to its normal blue, she hoped Lex hadn't seen Jon either. While Jon had every right to call on her, it would be suspicious and scandalous if Lex spied Jon's luggage.

Jenna raced down to the parlor to greet Lex as soon as he was announced. Kay, Ysabel, and Kron followed more slowly, giving them a few moments of privacy. As Kay entered, Lex, his hands on Jenna's shoulders, turned to study Kay. He seldom paid much attention to her, and she blushed. Was he only comparing hair styles, or did he suspect they were planning to leave Wistica without notice?

"Kay has such an easy time caring for her hair, I thought I'd copy her," Jenna said brightly.

Lex raised an eyebrow as he turned back to her. "I didn't know you tired of your long hair. Or was this a surprise for me, my warrior maiden?"

"Speaking of surprises, have you seen Robbie? Or Ysabel's family?"

Lex scowled. "I only found out what my brother had done this evening. Nothing but foolishness and jealousy drives this desire of his to force his control on Avatars. I reminded him our duty is always to our chosen deity first, even above the emperor and his monarchs." He turned to regard Kron. "Though I'm still not sure where you stand in that hierarchy, Artificer."

"Hopefully outside of it," Kron countered.

Ysabel stepped further into the room. "Avi, have you seen Tal, Lin, and Francie?"

"Those are the names of your siblings? No, I haven't seen them yet. My brother assures me they're still in Challen, but he refuses to tell me exactly where. Incidentally, I thought you had another sister. Where is she?"

Ysabel thinned her lips. "With my father on the other side of Challen."

Gwen finally entered the parlor. Like the others, she had changed into a dress of the formality and color she would normally wear at home. However, it hung askew, as if it hadn't been buttoned properly. Habit from long years of helping others made Kay curl her fingers, wanting to take her aside and make her more presentable. Gwen didn't appear to be discomfited by her untidy appearance, though. She gave the War Avatar a brief curtsey—

even after his betrothal to Jenna, Gwen still preferred keeping Lex at arm's-length—and said, "Your Highness, as much as I'd like to believe you're here simply to see Jenna, I know you're too much of a strategist for that."

Lex rewarded her with a small smile. "Correct as always, Ava." He looked at each of them. "The time for you to face Salth grows near, does it not?"

Kay took a deep breath and spoke. "The winter solstice. That's when we must face her."

"Not just any soltrans, but the one for Winter, Who controls both weather and death in Challen? Interesting. Very interesting."

Instead of feeling reassured, Kay worried she'd given the War Avatar information he could use against them. He served Fip's God, not one of Challen's. Even if he claimed to be their ally in this fight, it wasn't for the same reasons.

If Gwen shared those doubts, she didn't link with the others to share them. "Kay is correct," she said to Lex. "But we're not ready to face Salth yet. Your brother's insistence on protecting us and our dependents is hampering us. Can't you persuade him to leave us alone and let us do what we need to?"

"I wish I could, Ava, but as I told the rest of your quartet before you arrived, my brother likes to think he can control Avatars the same way he does ordinary people."

"And what will happen when it turns out he can't?" Gwen asked softly. "Will we be safe? Our families?"

Lex broke away from Jenna and paced across the parlor, weaving around the unoccupied seats and tables. "War isn't a kind God, Ava. Many must suffer in the cause of war."

"The Four Gods and Goddesses are here to relieve suffering," Gwen said. "They reign supreme in Challen, not War."

"This isn't a war," Kron said. "Chaos Season is Salth's revenge on me and my beloved."

Lex scoffed. "Revenge so strong it imperils an entire country? I think you underestimate your importance, Artificer, as well as the violence needed to end this Chaos Season. Nonetheless, War is willing to have me aid you. Simply tell me how."

Gwen and Kron exchanged glances. Finally, Gwen turned to Lex again. "We don't know that yet ourselves, Your Highness," she said. "But if you can intervene with your brother and let us take care of our business without interference, it will make our task much easier."

He gave her a short nod. "I'll do what I can, but I can't promise anything either. Good evening, Avas, Artificer. Jenna." He squeezed Jenna's hand, then left without further word.

For several minutes, no one spoke. The silence was deep enough for them to hear the wood in the fireplace pop and floor-boards creak in another part of the house. Finally, Ysabel said, "He's gone."

Everyone let out their breaths and collapsed on the furniture.

"Should we still go ahead with our plan?" Jenna asked.

"We'd better," Gwen replied. "Only the Four know how long it will take to retrieve the rest of the bones."

"But, shouldn't we wait to see if Lex can call off the Watch?"

"It doesn't matter." Gwen absently reached for a neglected mug of chocolate. "I'm not going to let the king delay us any longer."

"But our families?" Ysabel wrung her hands.

"We'll find them, darling," Kron told her.

"But first, we escape." Gwen drained the chocolate, then rose. "After we change yet again."

* * *

Two hours after Lex had departed, they were finally ready to leave Wistica. By now, only a couple of servants were awake, so Gwen had no problem slipping out, ambushing the Watch, and opening the gate for Jon. She and Kron crept out to the carriage house, and he created a portal so they could shove their trunks through it and next to the carriage.

"How many outfits are you bringing with you?" he asked as he attached painted feathers to the corners of each trunk.

"We brought four dresses each. Except Jenna. Are you going to dress as a woman at all on this trip?" Gwen directed the last part to Jenna.

Jenna shrugged. "I brought one in case it was necessary. Hopefully I won't need it. I must say, breeches are easier to manage than skirts." As if to prove her point, she climbed to the top of the carriage. Kron levitated the trunks to her, and she arranged them. The last item was a pot containing a small sapling created from her oak tree. She hugged it as if it was a dear to her as her son.

"Four dresses each?" Kron sounded surprised. "Are you sure that's enough?"

At last, Kay felt she had something to contribute. "Jon always said to travel as light as possible."

"What's light for a woman is heavy for a man," Jon said as he entered with a carpetbag. He gave Kay a quick hug and a kiss on the cheek. For him, that was daring with so many others about. "But ladies, especially Avatars, have different standards to maintain."

"We can't travel as Avatars," Gwen said. "We shouldn't even act like nobles. The more ordinary and forgettable, the better."

Jenna smirked. "I can't help being unforgettable."

Gwen shook her head. Turning to Ysabel, she asked, "Are we ready?"

"Almost." Ysabel made a few last-minute adjustments to the harness. It was a tight fit hitching a team of four inside the narrow building, but her touch helped keep the horses calm and cooperative, despite the late hour.

"By the Four, we just need to get through Kron's portal, Ysabel. Once we arrive at my absent aunt's house, we'll trade this for something more common."

"I might be able to transform the outside," Kron said.

Gwen nodded. "Good. Let's get going, then."

Jenna remained on top of the carriage, while Ysabel scrambled up to the coachman's seat and murmured at the horses to keep them calm. Jon helped Gwen and Lathtin into the carriage before swinging Kay up and climbing in after her. Kron didn't join them. Instead, he pulled a sketch out of his satchel and studied it for a few heartbeats. Then he pressed it against the center of the big carriage door, where it stuck without glue. Kron took some enchanted chalk out of his satchel and drew a line on the door frame. When the frame stretched out of reach, he released the chalk and gestured upward. Without breaking the line, the chalk rose upward like a feather floating on a gust of warm air. Kron guided the chalk to the top of the door, across, and down the other side until he could grasp it and finish drawing the line himself.

Jon gaped as he watched him. "How does he do that? I thought he isn't one of the Four's Avatars."

"Kron was born hundreds of years ago, before Challens even knew about the Four," Ysabel replied. "People back then were sometimes born with their own magic."

"Does that mean he's a God too?" Jon asked.

Kay frowned. "The Four are the only Gods and Goddesses Challen needs." Although Kron had spoken of the Four occasionally, he'd never claimed to be one of Them. He'd been there when the Four first blessed Their Avatars, eight hundred years ago when Wistica was much smaller, called Vistichia, and built out of long-crumbled mud bricks. The only building old enough to have stood in both cities was the Temple. All other traces of Vistichia had disappeared, except as relics eagerly sought by rich collectors and the University.

Kron completed his portal, and everything inside the chalk drawing faded away. Replacing the door was a country house as big as the apartment building Kay had grown up in. Surrounding it was a small orchard and a garden. How was it that one person could own so much and others so little?

Kron climbed up to sit next to Ysabel. As she guided the horses through the portal, he said to Jon through an open window, "I'm not as powerful as the Four, but I'm more powerful than I used to be."

"How is that possible?" Jon asked.

"I gained more magic—or should I say, it chose me." He frowned. "I wonder sometimes if I'd taken more magic at the time, we wouldn't have to worry about Chaos Season today." He softened as he looked at Ysabel. "But I made the best choice I could."

They drove onto a road leading up to the house. Night creatures fell silent at their approach. Kay watched the house, wondering if the inhabitant knew they were coming.

"My aunt was afraid of Chaos Season," Gwen said, "so she kept her storeroom well stocked in case the harvest failed. We can pick up supplies here in case we need to avoid the inns or can't find one. Then we can drive southeast until we reach the forest where the oldest Summer Avatar is buried. Ysabel, is anyone else here besides your mother and my aunt's servants?"

Before Ysabel could answer, clouds passed over the crescent moon. Lathtin yowled.

"Chaos Season," Ysabel said.

Kay pushed at the carriage door, trying to get out. Jon reached over to assist her. She hopped out, and Ysabel and Jenna climbed down in time to help Gwen. The four of them linked. Kay probed the storm. It was still gathering strength, so she hoped she could tame it before it grew too big. The air around her grew cold, and hail the size of hens' eggs clobbered them.

Ow! Jenna almost broke the link to rub a sore spot on her head. *Sometimes, being the tallest isn't fun. Hurry up and melt these stones before we're all hurt.*

Gwen sent Kay a boost of magic to help her get started. Without sunlight, it would be harder to warm the air, especially since it was naturally cold enough for frost. Kay stretched far across Challen to pull in as much heat as possible. She warmed the air surrounding them so it was like a shield stopping the hail. Then she pushed the warm air up toward the clouds to break them up. The clouds drifted slightly away from them until they threatened the house. Kay followed them with the warm air. A few hailstones split shingles and broke a couple of windows.

How dare she damage my aunt's home! Gwen said.

Kay tried a new strategy. Instead of spreading out the warmth, she collected it into as small an area as she could manage, forming it into a spear-like shape. She thrust it upward, past the house, past the tallest trees, up to the clouds themselves. Before the spear could strike, she spilt it into several rays. All of them struck home. The clouds spun away into nothing, but she grabbed the magic that had gone into them. She searched for additional signs of Chaos

Season before allowing Gwen to pass the storm's magic to Ysabel and Jenna. The weather was calm in their immediate location, but Kay found additional smaller cells of Chaos Season: one to the north and one to the west.

That's my family's farm! Jenna exclaimed.

And the lo Havil estate. Gwen's mental voice took on a more determined tone. *If Salth thinks she can deter us with personal threats, she's very much mistaken.*

Kay seized the closest storm—the one over Gwen's family estate—and drained the magic from it before realizing their families might not be the only ones in danger. Salth knew Kay's own family lived in Wistica. A storm there could affect thousands of people.

In the link, thinking about something automatically shared it with the other three. They agreed Wistica had to take priority and shifted their attention to the city. The bulk of the storm's energy was in the Salt Waters Harbor. Winds battered sailors and ships alike, and the waves tossed them all like dice in some cruel game. Kay had more experience dealing with land storms than hurricanes, but she'd spent much of her free time as a girl studying the harbor. She knew the locations of all the docks and where the deep and shallow areas were. Plus, most of the magic driving Chaos Season was in the wind, and that she knew well. She tamped the winds down, ended a snowstorm over the Winter Quarter, and cooled down the unseasonably warm temperatures in the Spring Quarter. Jenna and Ysabel followed in her wake, restoring the plants and animals. Still bolstered by the magic she'd absorbed, Kay stretched her consciousness to check all other areas where there was a trace of Chaos Season and mercilessly dampened all the local outbreaks.

There. That should show Salth we can handle her.

Kay hoped Salth would stop sending them Chaos Seasons, at least long enough for them to recuperate.

Gwen broke the link. "The servants at the house will recognize me, unless Ysabel's mother has dismissed them all for some reason. But we'll be able to eat, get some rest, and set out in the morning."

That seemed like a good plan, so Kay nodded with the others.

Kay conjured a few small lightning balls to help them find their way to the main entrance. As Gwen had predicted, the old man who answered the door smiled at her. "Lady lo Havil! I mean, Ava now. A pleasure to see you in these troubled times."

"Thank you, Ferdinand." Gwen led them into the foyer, too small to hold all of them. "I'm sorry we weren't able to send notice, but we need food and a place to spend the night. We'll be gone in the morning."

"What about the Fallswoman?" the butler asked hopefully. "Will she be leaving with you?"

Ysabel pressed forward. She'd had to deal with the horses and had therefore entered last. "Why should my mother come with us? I'd think she'd be happier staying here and composing her music."

Ferdinand sniffed. "According to her, the absent Lady lo Havil's pianoforte is inadequate for her needs. But the real problem is the Selathens spying on her."

CHAPTER FOUR

A Selathen Ambush

"Do you think they're watching her, waiting to see what she does, or checking to see if we'd come here?" Gwen asked sharply.

"They haven't been here long," a woman's voice answered. Ysabel's mother, draped in a red wool robe, entered the room. "I only noticed them in the last day or two. By the Four, what's going on?"

"Mama!" Ysabel rose and opened her arms as if to embrace her, but her smile faltered. "Did you know Bethany was spying on me for Father? And that he might be dying?"

"What? What?" The Fallswoman glanced down at her arm where her marriage tattoo used to be. "Well, I knew something wasn't right with the Honored Lathatilltin, but he never bothered to tell me how serious it was."

"He wanted extra time from Salth. That's why he wanted to trade me to her." Ysabel trembled. "Oh, by the Four, what if I made a mistake sending Bethany away? What if he sacrifices her to Salth in my place?"

"I don't think that's likely," Gwen said. "Bethany's not a Season Avatar. Salth wouldn't gain much magic from her. Besides, didn't you say your father was already youthened?"

Ysabel shrugged.

"I was hoping Kay could create a fog in the morning so we could escape without notice," Gwen said. "Now we may have to capture a Selathen and question him."

"And then what do we do with him?" Jenna pounced on a tray of bread and cheese. "He'll only be a nuisance if we bring him along, but if we release him, he'll let everyone else know where we are."

She left unsaid the obvious: to hurt or silence him would be counter to the will of the Four.

"But we still need to know why they're here and what they're planning," Gwen said.

Lathtin sat up straight and stared at his sister, then paced to the door and looked back at her.

"He's offering to eavesdrop on the Selathens for us," Ysabel said. "He's certain he can do it without being noticed."

Gwen sighed. "Very well. Please tell him to be careful, Ysabel. In the meantime, we'd better get some sleep. Dame s'Ivena, may we spend the night?"

"Of course, Ava. This place still belongs to your family, doesn't it?" Ysabel's mother pulled a bell cord. "There's not much in the way of beds or spare bedrooms, but we'll manage."

Kron and Jon settled down in the parlor, trying to curl up on loveseats too small for them. Jenna's disguise didn't fool Ysabel's mother, who gave them all her room—or Gwen's aunt's room. "I can work on my symphony and catch up on my sleep later," she said. "I'm used to be being up at odd hours."

The bed was wide enough that they could all fit, providing no one needed to turn over. Luckily, Kay found herself on the end. She stared at the ceiling, wondering if the ghost would return—

What ghost? Gwen thought at her.

Too late, Kay realized their fingers were touching. She ought to be sleepy, but the excitement of the evening still flooded her body. So she replied, *I thought I saw something strange before dinner.* She showed the memory to Gwen. Other details sprung up in her memory. It hadn't been cold enough for snow, and the air had been too dry. Magic had been involved—but it hadn't been hers.

Where's that gem you found? Gwen asked. *Do you still have it?*

It's in my sewing kit.

Why don't you fetch it while I share your experience with Jenna and Ysabel? This might be important.

Kay didn't want to leave the cozy bed, but she did so and dug around in her sewing kit until she found the scrap of cloth with the gem. She carefully unfolded the cloth. Her sister Avatars sat up, and Jenna lit the candle next to the bed.

Kay brought the gem over. "Is this real?"

Gwen held out her good hand. "Let me test it."

She studied the gem for several heartbeats. A gold stem had broken off on the less polished side. Gwen reached for her necklace, a gold chain with a pink crystal suspended inside of a heart. She turned the crystal over and scraped the pointed end of the clear gem on it.

Ysabel leaned over to examine it. "By All Four, it's scratched."

"A jeweler could perform other tests," Gwen said as she passed the gem back to Kay, "but I'd say this could be a diamond."

Ysabel's eyes grew larger. "Whose was it? Any idea?"

"We'd have to ask the staff who stayed in that room recently. Most likely, this could have been one of Sophia's earrings, or Margaret's."

Margaret and Sophia, Ava Spring and Ava Fall respectively, had been members of the Avatar quartet before them. Kay had only met Sophia, since Margaret had gone to the God of Winter before Kay's quartet had come together. Sophia had worn partial white in mourning for her sister Avatar, but she had never worn diamonds, only rubies and rose topazes similar to the one Gwen currently wore.

Ysabel shook her head, as if she shared Kay's thoughts. "This isn't the color gem a Spring or Fall Avatar would normally wear."

"Dorian wore full white for his wife," Jenna said. "This gem would match his clothing."

"True, but do you remember him ever wearing jewelry? I don't. And while that backing could have been part of a cufflink instead of an earring, it's more likely to be an earring."

"Maybe it didn't belong to an Avatar at all. It could have been a guest." Jenna rebuttoned her man's shirt. "Does it matter if we don't know whose it was? We have far more important things to worry about than returning lost property, no matter how much it's worth."

"True, but I can't help thinking it's connected to that shape Kay saw," Gwen said. "Maybe the gem belonged to her—assuming it was a woman, that is."

"And she came back from the God of Winter's domain to claim it?"

Gwen shrugged. "I know it sounds impossible, but we've already experienced so many other impossible things in this lifetime. We could live a century and still not see more strange things than we have already." She took a deep breath. "Anything unusual could affect our mission."

Jenna yawned. "Could we maybe talk about this in the morning, after we're on our way? I'd rather get some sleep than talk to a spirit."

Ysabel's eyes widened, showing off the green-and-gold flecks in them. "By the Four, do you think she'll return tonight? I won't be able to sleep for thinking of it!"

"I can take care of that," Gwen said.

Ysabel shook her head. "Best not, if we have to leave early."

Kay put the gem back in her sewing kit and climbed back into bed. Jenna blew out the light. Judging by her snores, she was the first to fall asleep. Gwen and Ysabel soon copied her, leaving Kay to stare at the ceiling and wait for a ghost. Surely the spirit would tell her what they were supposed to do next. But she didn't appear, and neither did Lathtin.

***

Kay awoke as Lathtin jumped onto the bed. She slid out and stretched stiff muscles. One by one, the others roused, with Jenna last. Ysabel frowned as she rubbed her brother's fur dry with the blanket.

"There are three of them watching the house, two at day and one at night," she said. "Their orders are to capture Mama and bring her back to Tradetown for flogging."

"Flog her? Why?" Gwen asked. "Just because she's your mother?"

"They suspect she's been stirring up trouble. By the Four, they don't know the half of it!" Ysabel made a fist. "Fall won't stand for that, though, and neither will Her Avatar."

Jenna raked her fingers through her shorn waves. "Are you going to invoke Fall against them?"

"I can only do that if they actually attack Mama."

"Or us," Gwen said thoughtfully.

Kay wasn't ready for planning after so little sleep. She splashed some cold water on her face from a basin left on the dresser. Even that didn't give her the insight she needed. "I thought we were supposed to travel incognito. Wouldn't showing them we're the Season Avatars cause problems?"

"Fall protects all women, not just Avatars," Ysabel said.

"But would they attack ordinary visitors?"

"They might, if they thought we were up to something." Gwen wiggled the fingers of her good hand. "Let's link. We can plan more effectively that way."

They postponed linking until they'd all had a chance to wash their faces and change into their day dresses—or jacket and breeches. As the window brightened with the dawn, they joined hands. Ideas flowed among the four of them like water. Jenna wanted to subdue the Selathens and drop them off in Midpoint with the local Watch, but Gwen pointed out that that would not only make them detour, but bring them to the Watch's attention. She would have been content to send the Selathens to sleep or let Ysabel send animals to harass them.

But they'd still be here to bother my mother, Ysabel said. *I wish we could take her with us.*

That's it! Gwen's excitement burst through the fog Kay was trying to gather to hide their escape. *No, we don't want to sneak away,* Gwen continued. *One of us could disguise herself as Ysabel's mother and get into the carriage with us. They'll follow us, and we can get them lost, send them to sleep, and then leave them behind, unable to follow us or figure out how to return here. That would also give the Fallswoman time to flee somewhere else if she chooses. Maybe Father would let her stay at our estate for a while, since she was a friend of my aunt's.*

They all mulled over the plan, trying to find weaknesses.

If the Selathens saw us arrive, they know how many of us are in the party, Jenna said. *They'll notice if there's one less of us.*

Kron might be able to create an illusion of my mother. For once, Ysabel seemed doubtful of her intended's abilities. *None of us resemble her closely enough to impersonate her. I suppose I could try it—*

No, I think you should talk to the illusion as if it were your mother as we depart, Gwen said. *Let's ask Kron before we decide.*

They broke the link and headed downstairs for a breakfast of porridge, pork sausages with sage, and chocolate. Jon and Kron trailed in a short time later, and Gwen asked him if he could create an realistic illusion of a person.

"How realistic does it have to be?" he asked, reaching for more sausage. "Sight and sound are easier to fool than touch."

"We want to fool the Selathens watching the house," Ysabel replied. "They've been creeping around the edge of the property, near the road. I doubt they'll come close enough to touch my pretend mother unless they're foolhardy enough to think they can capture our entire group."

"They might try it if they have those revolvers," Kron said darkly. "By the Four, I hate those things. Ysabel, are they carrying any magic with them as well?"

She frowned as she pulled a glowing ruby pendant out from under the neckline of her dress. "I felt it growing warmer last night when we tamed Chaos Season. I think it detects our own magic as well as outside magic."

"Freeze it. Pass it here." He clenched the pendant in his fist for a moment before handing it back to Ysabel. "There. It'll ignore my magic and Avatar magic."

She brought it over to the window and held it in front of her. "It's still glowing, Kron."

"If they have time traps, that complicates matters." He mixed maple syrup into his porridge and ate silently for a few moments. Kay forced herself to eat as well, in case her fog proved to be necessary after all.

"I can create an artifact to disable the time traps," Kron said when he was done, "but I would have to get close to them, practically touching them. The only way to draw the Selathens out is to have a real person wear the illusion of Dame Lathatilltin. That would be more lifelike than an artifact."

Kay and her sister Avatars exchanged glances. Ysabel had to talk to the actress, and Gwen's paralyzed hand would interfere with the illusion. Jenna was taller than the Fallswoman and already in disguise. That left only Kay.

"Could you use me for the illusion?" she asked. Since she was thinner and younger than Ysabel's mother, she didn't know if Kron's illusion could change her shape too.

Kron studied her for a few heartbeats, enough to make Jon, sitting next to her, tense. "If my future-mother-in-law is willing to lend me one of her gowns, yes, I can manage it."

"Won't someone notice if Kay is missing, though?" Jon asked.

Jenna devoured the last sausage on her plate before Lathtin could snatch it. "If all of us have to impersonate someone else, we might as well just bring Ysabel's mama with us."

Gwen laid her fork down so softly it didn't clink against her plate. "If we say Kay has taken ill, or that we have to take Dame s'Ivena to the Ava Spring right away, it would sound plausible."

A final round of glances, and everyone nodded.

"Are you sure you want to do this?" Jon whispered to Kay. "You'll be putting yourself at risk."

"Only until we're in the carriage," she replied. Her stomach suddenly felt too full. Kay hoped she could keep her food down. "Once the Selathens can no longer see me, I can remove the disguise. Besides, I can still use my weather magic even with it on."

Jon sighed. "Yes, you're all so much more gifted than I am."

"Your love is magic enough, Dearest."

"It'll have to be," he muttered.

Gwen eyed the pair of them as she slipped a piece of sausage to Lathtin, but she didn't comment or offer to link. Kay would have to handle her beau on her own, without advice from her sister Avatars. Perhaps that was for the best.

While the maid and the cook packed a luncheon and any food that could be spared from the household, Kron altered a gray day dress of the Fallswoman's. Kay grimaced as she watched him pull a needle and white thread out of his satchel. "That doesn't match the fabric, Kron!"

"It doesn't need to," he replied calmly. "Just a few stitches here and here…" He darted the needle in and out of the neck, both sleeves, the waist, and the hem. Kay wanted to chide him on his technique, but he was done before she could put thoughts into words. "There. Try it on."

Rather than argue with him, she took the dress back to her room and changed. No white thread was visible, and when she slipped the dress on, it fit as if made for her. Kay looked in the mirror and gasped. Although she still had dark hair, it now had gray sections and was pinned into a bun. Her light blue eyes were now green, and heavy jowls broadened her face. She even seemed taller, but when she held her hand at the top of her head, it rested lower than the reflection's hand in the mirror.

"By the Four!" Her voice had changed too. Shuddering, Kay turned away and hurried downstairs.

"Don't forget your ward!" Kron called after her.

Her ward? Oh, the artifacts Kron had constructed for each of them to protect them from Salth's time magic. Kay hadn't expected to need it this deep inside Challen, but she pinned the brooch to her dress anyway.

The cook intercepted her. "Dame, should we give the Avatars the mincemeat pie?"

She nodded, not trusting her disguised voice. Pie was always welcome, even if it was mincemeat.

"The pie?" It took Kay a few heartbeats to realize she was hearing Dame s'Ivena's real voice. "Not the mincemeat pie, Gayle! I wanted that for my own supper...oh, By the Four." She put her hand on her ample chest. "Ysabel told me what you had planned, but seeing your own double, it's uncanny!" She shivered.

Kay shrugged, unwilling to use another woman's voice if she didn't have to.

"Anyway, I think everything else is packed." Dame s'Ivena drew closer. "Thank you for taking this risk for me, Ava. You're the Ava Win, correct? I'll say an extra prayer to Fall for you."

"Thank you." A Fallswoman's prayers would mean something.

Ysabel's mother guided her to the front door. A carriage was waiting outside. With faded red paint and all the gilt decorations gone, it looked nothing like the carriage they had liberated last night. Kay hoped Kron hadn't done anything to make it fall apart on their trip.

As Ysabel's mother retreated, Ysabel came forward to take Kay's arm. Perhaps it was coincidence, but Ysabel's arrival made

Kay realize how silent it was outside. Shouldn't birds be singing when a Fall Avatar was in their neighborhood?

"The Selathens crept closer to the house during the night," Ysabel whispered to a spot above Kay's real head. "My magic-sensing pendant feels warmer now. Be prepared for anything."

Kay nodded and twitched her fingers. If she needed lightning, it would form. "Can your father use magic?" she whispered back.

"He's not an artificer like Kron, but perhaps Salth enchanted one of his watches. I think that's how he obtained the time traps in his shop." Ysabel raised her voice as the butler opened the door for them. "Now be careful with these steps, Mama. You know you're not as spry as you used to be."

By the Four, how was Kay supposed to respond? No one had discussed it with her. Maybe no one had even thought about it. Kay clung to the railing, suddenly nervous. She didn't have to act to take the steps slowly.

"Thank the Four you're here, daughter," she said in Dame s'Ivena's voice again. "I don't know what I'd have done if you hadn't come along."

She reached the bottom step. Something arced toward her, a silver-and-black watch that landed right in front of her. The butler called something, but his words cut off. Rustling branches froze in a way that had nothing to do with winter. Three men, garbed in black and with mufflers wrapped around their faces, rushed toward them.

Ysabel raised her hand and scowled. Any animals that would come to her defense must have been caught in the time trap. It would be up to Kay to stop the men.

Although lightning twitched on her skin, she created ice instead. She cast it at their feet to make them trip. Two fell, but the

one farthest back managed to stay upright. Ideally, Kay would en-
case him in a thin layer of ice, but the air was too dry for her to
pull that much water from it. If she could just take care of his lower
body...but that didn't work either. Even water droplets were
caught in this time trap.

Lighting would have to do, then. Kay tried to shoot a thin bolt
at the watch. Again, her weather magic didn't work properly
within the range of the time trap. It did, however, make the man
halt. His gaze burned through his masked face.

Kay conjured a lightning ball above her palm. Thank the Four
that worked. "Come any closer, and I'll fry you like a slab of
meat." She winced as the older woman's voice shook. Nonetheless, all three assailants—the other two having regained their
footing—stepped back. The farthest one brought out a revolver—

"None of that," Kron said harshly as he stepped out from behind the carriage. The revolver cracked in two. Its wielder yelped,
dropped the pieces, and ran off.

Ysabel spoke to the assailants in Selathen. As she did so,
Gwen, Jenna, and Jon emerged and surrounded them. The men
stared at each of them in turn, as if trying to decide who was the
worst threat—or perhaps the weakest. Kron took advantage of
their hesitation to toss an orange handkerchief into the air. "Kay,
could you be so kind as to float this onto the time trap, please?"

It only took a small breeze to make the handkerchief flutter
over the watch and settle in place. The silk melted as the time trap
let off smoke and the odor of burning metal. A murder of crows
cawed near the road.

"I say!" the butler finished exclaiming.

The two Selathens glanced at each other, then said something
in Selathen. They raised their hands to their mouths and bit on
large silver rings each of them wore.

"No, don't!" Ysabel said in Challen. "Gwen, they're killing themselves for Salth!"

Gwen dashed forward. She stretched out her arms toward each of the men, but the hand with the shard remained limp. Frowning, she turned to the closer man and touched him. It took her several heartbeats, and her scowl deepened as she inspected the other man. "Too late for him. It was a fast-acting poison. Ysabel, did your animals catch the runaway?"

"The crows are attacking him," she reported. "He doesn't have a horse, but some two-wheeled contraption similar to what Kron used the night we saved him from that fanged lion."

"He's too far away for me to reach with my magic," Kron reported.

"Which way is he headed?" Gwen asked.

"West."

Gwen faced the others. "Should we follow him?"

Kay was a little shocked when the others stared at her. Then again, perhaps she shouldn't be. Thanks to her new spirit magic, she was going to have the most important role once they'd collected all the remaining bones and faced Salth. With that thought, she knew what her answer had to be.

"He's not as important as our mission from the Four," she said, grimacing at her magic-altered voice. "We have to head to—to our next destination."

Gwen nodded, then turned to the butler. "Sir, perhaps you could secure this man, and send the Watch after the other one? Only, please tell the Watch that the Selathens were pursuing Dame s'Ivena over some domestic matter. For the love of the Four, don't breathe a word of us being here."

He bowed slightly. "As you wish, Ava."

"Thank you." Gwen climbed into the carriage, managing it surprisingly well despite her useless hand. The others followed her into their positions from the previous night. Within moments, they were off.

"I can't believe that man chose to take his life rather than yield to us," Jenna said after a few moments.

"Lathtin says Ysabel wonders who will claim his soul: Winter or Salth." Gwen stroked Ysabel's anilink. "I hate to think it would be Salth. Who knows what she could do with a soul freely given to her?"

Kron scowled. "She certainly doesn't need any more."

Gwen sighed. "Let's hope we don't run into any more Selathens on the way to Summerwood."

"Kron, is it safe to take the enchantment off this dress now?" Kay asked.

With a smile, he reached over and pulled a few stitches out of the hem. Kay sagged with relief to see her hands return to normal.

In some ways, the first part of the Grand Tour went more smoothly than this, she thought. *I hope we don't have more people blocking our way at every gravesite. If we're doing this for the Four, why don't They make our path easier?*

Winter didn't send her an answer.

CHAPTER FIVE

Summerwood

Journeying back toward Summerwood, the forest where the Summer Avatar Frederick min Jole was entombed, was almost easy enough to convince Kay the Four had decided to aid Their Avatars after all. Ysabel managed the horses as well as if she'd spent a previous life as a coachman. She coaxed the most distance she could from them every day and tended to their needs every evening, keeping their hooves strong and making sure they rested well overnight. The group passed through several villages where they could purchase more food after they devoured what they'd brought with them. The first couple of evenings, they were able to find rooms in taverns or farmhouses. Kron pretended to be the uncle of Jon and Jules, Kay and Gwen the intended brides of the two younger men, and Ysabel their driver hired to take them to the Hall of Records in Wistica. While their hosts asked them for news and made jests about the weddings, they seemed to take the cover story at face value.

Best of all, there was no sign of Chaos Season while they were on the road. It was enough to make Kay feel as if she was an ordinary person, not the Winter Avatar in charge of the weather. She sewed when the roads were smooth enough to allow it, stretched her legs by walking with Jon during their rest breaks, and allowed herself to hope that Salth, Selathens, and the Watch would leave them alone.

The third evening, Ysabel took them to the edge of Summerwood. Kron created a shelter from blankets. He also removed cushions from the carriage and turned them temporarily into mattresses. It wasn't as cozy as her bed at the One Oak, but at least Kay didn't dream about Salth, Dorian, or dying. In the morning, they restored everything as quickly as they could, ate a slightly burned meal of porridge, and set off toward Frederick's tomb. The road wandered along the edge of the forest. The trees were all bare by now, allowing them to see the flash of deer or birds bold enough to seek the Fall Avatar before disappearing. It reminded Kay of the spirit who had sought her out several nights ago. Who was she, and what did she want? Why hadn't she returned? Was she part of their mission?

The road swung between the trees. Clouds blew in, promising rain. The group's collective mood grew somber, or perhaps nervous.

"Do you think anyone or anything is waiting for us at Freddie's tomb?" Jenna asked.

"Did you know him well enough to be so familiar with his name?" Gwen countered.

"It's not like he's around to object, is he? Besides, I hear other men talking like this all the time. I just want to blend in."

Gwen rolled her eyes and stroked Lathtin one-handed. "Ysabel has the best magic to scout ahead. Lathtin, could you ask her to check, please?"

Jenna stared at her, suddenly serious. "And you're familiar enough with Ysabel's anilink to use his first name too."

"I can link with him. When you've been introduced mind-to-mind, titles and surnames are far too formal."

Kay wagered there was more going on than Gwen cared to admit. Gwen and Jenna had centuries of history between them, and a single lifetime when they were both women wasn't going to erase that, even if Gwen refused to pledge herself as a Fallswoman. Jenna would marry the Avatar of War someday, but who would give Gwen the heirs she needed for her family estate? Lathtin couldn't.

Gwen fumbled with the window leading to the driver's seat. Once she managed to slide the window open, Lathtin squeezed through. A few heartbeats later, the carriage slowed, then halted. Ysabel peeked inside. "There are men and horses blocking the road ahead."

Gwen turned to Ysabel. "What kind of animal is telling you this? What other details can you make out?"

Ysabel closed her eyes for a few heartbeats. "Birds—woodpeckers and nuthatches, since there aren't any hawks close by. There are five men. They don't look like Selathens, but the birds noticed lots of shiny metal on the men's clothes. Maybe they're from the Watch or the Fip Army."

Jenna sighed. "Too bad Lex isn't here to order them away."

"We don't need him," Gwen said harshly. "Our own magic should be enough."

Jon shifted uncomfortably next to Kay. She hoped what she had to offer wouldn't upset him, even though it was the obvious thing to do. "I could create a fog and hide us," she said out loud.

Gwen leaned closer to the window. "Good idea, Kay. The fog shouldn't hide the soldiers' auras from me, so I can sneak up on them and send them to sleep."

They climbed out of the carriage so Kay could be out in the open. Even Jon and Kron came out to watch. Self-conscious, she closed her eyes and tested the air, examining how much water it held. Not enough for what she needed. Perhaps instead of creating a fog from scratch, it would be easier to coax a cloud to come to her. The closest clouds that were dense enough for her purposes were several miles out over the Salt Waters, at the edge of Kay's influence. She summoned a wind to blow them closer to her, but it slipped out of her control.

"I need more magic," she said, trying to push down her embarrassment. All of them needed an extra boost from time to time; she just didn't like admitting it when non-Avatars, especially Jon, were present.

"It's all right." Gwen offered Kay her hand. Jenna and Ysabel took hold of her as well. Power surged into her, then through her to the wind. Within heartbeats, the cloud drifted toward land. The wind blew so strongly it threatened to blow the cloud apart. Kay diverted some of its force into the waves. Meanwhile, she encouraged the cloud to pick up more moisture from the Salt Waters. Dimly she was aware of the light fading and the temperature dropping, but she barely felt it.

Once the cloud was over Challen, Kay's control of it increased. As it approached her, she encouraged it to descend, shifting the weather constantly so the cloud wouldn't break up. Soon her face, the only part of her exposed to the weather, felt covered in water. She opened her eyes. Surrounding all of them was gray mist so thick she could barely see her sister Avatars next to her, let alone the men farther away.

"Wonderful. Now all we have to do is avoid getting lost or separated ourselves," Jenna said.

"You can sense where all the trees are," Gwen said, "so you can keep us from running into them. Ysabel can borrow animals' senses to guide us through the fog."

Jenna glanced at Ysabel. "You'd better wake some bats."

"Some of them are already hibernating. I don't want to disturb them."

"You'll disturb the guards if you don't lower your voice," Gwen said. "Are we ready to go? For that matter, are we all going?"

"Of course," Jenna sounded as confident as if the others had given her permission to speak for them. Kay would have preferred to remain behind, but not by herself. It wasn't safe for any of them to be alone.

"Then let's join hands," Gwen said.

"All of us?" Jon asked. "I'd only get in the way. Maybe I should stay behind and watch the carriage. Or at least stay next to it. I can't see my hand in front of my face."

Kay took advantage of the privacy to reach up and kiss his cheek. "We appreciate your help." She hoped she left him with a smile.

Ysabel, with Lathtin perched on her shoulder, and Jenna led the way. Gwen and Kay clung to them, and Kron took up the rear. Kay tread softly, trying to muffle her footsteps. Dead leaves crunched under her boots. Dark columns of trees loomed before them, but Jenna turned them away before they ran into one.

"We're nearly there," Ysabel whispered. They weren't all touching each other, so she had to speak out loud.

"Let's get off the road," Jenna suggested. "They'll be peering through the fog at the road, not at the trees."

"Unless they're worried about deer," Kron muttered.

Gwen squeezed Jenna's and Kron's arms until they were silent.

Kay peered at the fog and decided to thicken it some more in this area so they'd be even harder to see.

Jenna turned them off to the right, twisting and turning until Kay knew she'd never find the road again on her own. The ground here was uneven, causing them to stumble. While Jenna tried to hurry them along, Ysabel halted, pausing before taking each new step. Maybe she needed more information from her animal spies to scout the ground, not just where the soldiers were. No matter how much Jenna tugged, Ysabel refused to travel any faster. It would have been funny if this whole affair wasn't so serious.

They heard the soldiers before they saw their shapes silhouetted against the fog. Three of them seemed to be facing the road, while two hung back, watching the woods. They called to each other: "Nothing this way, Sir!" "By the Four, I swear this soup is getting thicker!" "Thicker than the grub they call soup back at the barracks." "Probably tastier, too."

"Keep watching, Privates!" the officer in the center of the road said. "Brace yourselves for a possible Chaos Season."

Gwen pulled away from the others and motioned for them to stay where they were. She crept toward the closest soldier, one watching the woods. Soon the fog swallowed her up.

Jenna whispered, "We'd better follow her in case she needs our help."

"She wants us to stay here!" Ysabel said. "If we leave this spot, how will she ever find us?"

"If she can see ordinary people's auras in this, ours ought to stick out like the first red leaf on a tree."

Jenna seemed to be making the wrong choice for the right reason. "How can Gwen see anything through this?" Kay asked. "Can she make her vision sharper?"

"She can make it as sharp as any human's, but not like an animal's," Ysabel replied.

"Assuming the death magic trapped in her hand doesn't interfere with her own magic," Jenna muttered.

Kay glanced down, trying to find her boots. Again, she'd made things more difficult for her sister Avatars. Gwen had shown her nothing but patience, and this was how she repaid her. Perhaps she ought to lift the fog so Gwen could see. Of course, if she did it too soon, the soldiers would see her as well.

Kay huddled there for several moments, imagining the worst, before a few footsteps warned them someone was approaching. Kay tensed, balling her hands to summon hail, while Jenna groped around for a fighting stick. Only Ysabel remained calm. "Are you finished, Gwen?"

"There you are! By the Four, the fog distorts auras more than I expected. Keep talking so I can find you."

Gwen sounded a little annoyed, but she was no longer whispering. She must have found all five of the soldiers, then. Kay raised her head, relieved. "Is it safe for me to lift the fog?"

"Just thin it a little, please."

Accomplishing that was harder than simply sending the cloud away. There wasn't enough heat or sunlight to evaporate the extra water, so Kay allowed some of it to settle out as dew. Bit by bit, the fog cleared, allowing them to see each other. Gwen had wandered off the other side of the road.

Jenna gasped. "Gwen, move away from those plants! That's itchy ivy."

"Is it? It doesn't bother me." Despite her words, Gwen hurried over to them. "The first three were easiest, but by the time I got to the last two, they knew something had happened to the others. I couldn't touch both of them at once, so I had to take care of the private first, then dodge when the officer shouted and waved his rifle about. He made so much noise I was able to creep up behind him and take him out."

"But the road is clear now," Jenna said. "We can slip past them, take a bone, and be gone well before they wake."

"By the Four, I hope so." Gwen gestured for Jenna and Ysabel to proceed. "We'd better stay together so we don't get separated or trip over one of the soldiers."

Kay wondered privately—clothing prevented the link from forming—why Gwen worried about the soldiers waking up too quickly. As the Season Avatars' leader, she ought to have full control of her magic. Maybe her cursed hand was interfering with her magic more than she cared to admit. Or maybe Gwen was just worried something else would go wrong. Nothing could be worse than their visit to the Spring Avatar's tomb. The fog made Kay feel like one false step would send her falling through the air again....She clutched Ysabel harder, hoping her sister Avatar wouldn't mind.

At least they did seem to be moving faster now that they were on the road. Jenna and Ysabel drifted to the side a couple of times, but they managed to correct themselves before they left the path. As they advanced, trees closed in, lining the path like an honor guard.

"I think I see it!" Jenna said.

Unlike the Avi Spring's grave, which had been surrounded by an iron fence, this one was inside a white mausoleum. The only way Kay could distinguish the building from the fog was by the solidity of the structure. She peered through the fog, but she couldn't tell where the door was. The entire building was white.

"How do we get in?" Jenna asked.

Kron released Ysabel and stepped forward. "I can open the door with my magic—"

He stopped as something whizzed at them. At first, Kay thought an insect had survived longer than it was supposed to, or that Chaos Season had triggered its birth moons too early. Then Kron staggered, his hand on his shoulder. Blood spread past his fingers.

"Kron!" Ysabel gripped him. "Are you all right? What happened?"

"I did," a strange female voice said. "And the rest of you have ten heartbeats to leave before the same thing happens to each of you."

CHAPTER SIX

The Tomb

A dark-clothed, slight figure slipped around the mausoleum. She carried a rifle with as much confidence as if some God or Goddess had made her an Avatar of modern weapons. Kay hadn't faced a rifle before, but she knew their bullets traveled incredibly fast. The only magic that might stop the soldier before she hurt someone else was Kay's lightning. However, the God of Winter hadn't given her that magic to kill Challens. Only someone as selfish as Dorian would use magic that way, and Kay didn't want to do anything that reminded her of him.

Gwen had to focus on healing Kron, not dealing with this unexpected guard. Jenna might be next oldest after Gwen, but her temper ran too hot to treat with people diplomatically. Ysabel reached out to link with Gwen, keeping her other arm wrapped around Kron. Her priority would be helping Gwen heal Kron. That meant Kay had to do something, anything, to keep the situation from getting worse. She thickened the fog around the shooter until she was barely more than an outline. Hopefully that would be enough to spoil her aim. In case it wasn't, Kay readied a ball of lightning behind her back. *I won't toss it directly at her, O Four; just close enough to make her flee.*

Jenna stepped forward. At some point she'd found a stout branch, which she wielded like a fighting stick. "Leave us alone, whoever you are. We're on the Four's business."

"Freeze it, you slug! This is the final resting place of one of the Four's Avatars. They want him left undisturbed."

Jenna shook her head—not that the other solider could see her. "I dare say we know the Four's business better than anyone else."

"Jen—Jules, careful!" Gwen whispered. "She'll know for sure who we are!"

"Then she can't hurt us, can she?" Ysabel asked.

"She could still have us brought back to Wistica under guard. Or the king could ship our families off to the Fip mainland. Keep her talking, just don't reveal too much!" Gwen laid her hand against Kron's neck, on the side closest to the wound.

Keep her talking...dare I try? Kay never liked having to speak in public for the soltrans or any other ceremony. Maybe it would be easier since she couldn't see the other woman.

She called up a breeze to help blow her words to the sniper. Then she stepped forward, past Jenna. Jenna raised her eyebrows but didn't comment. Kay realized she was making herself the easiest target for the solider. She bit back a laugh. She'd already died once, so what else could happen to her? The Four wanted her to live, so she hoped They would intervene again if necessary. Thinking of the Four sobered her up enough to send Them a quick prayer: *O Four, please help me find the right words to make her leave us alone.*

"We mean no harm," Kay said.

Jenna cupped her hand behind her ear, as if she couldn't hear Kay despite standing so close to her.

Kay closed her eyes, trying to remember what it was like performing in the soltrans. She hadn't had a chance to participate in this life, but she'd done so countless times in other lives. While she hated having to recite lines in front of hundreds of people, she had learned how to project her voice so they could hear her. She drew on that knowledge now, standing up straight, drawing her breath fully into her chest, and facing the solider.

"We mean no harm. We honor all the Season Avatars of Challen—" *except one*— "and the Four Gods and Goddesses. We truly are on the Four's business. Please, won't you let us pass?"

"I have orders to let no one pass."

"From whom?" Jenna challenged.

"The king himself, passed down through the Grand General of the Challen Army."

"His Majesty—" Kay worked up courage to say the next words— "His Majesty is not the supreme leader of Challen. Neither is the Fip Emperor. The Four Gods and Goddesses are, and They have commanded us to come here and perform a task for Them."

"So, you are the new Avatars?" the solider asked.

"Don't confirm it," Gwen whispered.

"We've already given ourselves away by using magic, Gwen," Jenna said.

"Or it could be the Four choosing to work a miracle." Gwen didn't sound very hopeful about that. "If we tell this solider our names or titles, then that's evidence a judge can't dismiss."

"I'm getting impatient, intruders." The solider made some sort of mechanical sound—Kay didn't know how else to describe it— with her weapon.

Instead of answering her, Gwen glanced at Kron. He nodded. Now Gwen stepped forward, past Kay. "I assure you, solider, we aren't people you should harm. In fact, you'll find that your rifle is now broken."

"That's impossible. I checked it myself before going on shift." The solider did something to her weapon again. This time, even Kay could hear something grinding like sand inside the rifle. "Chaos!" she screamed. "Captain, I need backup!"

"The other soldiers can't hear you—"

With a shout of rage, the solider charged, boots pounding on the stone road. Gwen and the others, including Kay, faded back to the side. Kay raised her hand, wondering if she would need lightning after all. Before she could direct it at the solider, Jenna, fighting stick raised, came forward to intercept the soldier.

"Jules, no!" Kron shouted. "That's a bayonet!"

As the soldier closed in on Jenna, she lowered her rifle. Something long and pointy gleamed on the end.

Jenna whirled her fighting stick to block the bayonet. The two of them unleashed a flurry of blows at each other. Kay lowered her hand. The fighters were too close together to risk lightning. Hail, maybe? She doubted she had control fine enough to keep Jenna from being hit.

Half-a-dozen crows dove onto the soldier, followed by more. Some of the boldest flew at her face, while others settled on her bayonet. Jenna took advantage of the distraction by swinging at the soldier's head. The birds dodged, but she didn't. As she collapsed, Gwen ran forward to examine her.

"I hope she's not a Fallswoman," Ysabel said.

Gwen pushed up the sleeve of the soldier's uniform. "No tattoos of any kind." She pressed her fingers to the soldier's close-cropped hair. "Freeze it, Jenna, she's bleeding. I hope you didn't seriously harm her."

"She wanted to do all of us harm," Jenna countered. "By the Four, she shot Kron."

Kay watched Gwen tend to the soldier's wound, then realized she would be of little help unless Gwen needed to draw on her magic. Kron moved stiffly, and Jenna twisted her wrist gingerly, as if she'd injured it. Ysabel was distracted, going back and forth between Kron and Gwen. Kay was the only one available to examine the mausoleum and retrieve the bone they needed.

Since the fog would be of no further use now that all the soldiers were unconscious, Kay let the cloud thin out to nothing. She listened for signs of more attackers, but when birds started to chirp again, she let out her own sigh of relief.

The mausoleum, about the size of a shed, stood at the end of the road. It was surrounded by dead flowers that probably looked lovely in the proper season. Now they reinforced the dismal atmosphere. Kay circled around to the back, looking for the entrance. It was secured by a metal bar with a chain and padlock holding it in place. She rattled the door with her limited strength, but it barely budged. Everything appeared to be well-maintained, making their task more difficult. There were no windows allowing the living to spy on the dead. Even animals would be hard-pressed to force entry. Other than blasting the mausoleum apart with lightning—something she didn't want to do—she wasn't sure how she could help here. Unless—she squinted at the padlock again. When Kay was a child, one of her neighbors had taught her how to pick locks. She didn't carry hair pins with her, but she did have several long needles and sewing pins.

Kay selected her longest needles, wincing at having to ruin them, and set to work. It was more difficult than she had anticipated to bend her needles into the appropriate shapes. Then she braced the padlock so none of the pins would move. Once she eased the pressure, she had to test all of the pins inside the padlock to figure out which one needed to be moved first. When that pin clicked into place, others froze. She reminded herself this was a slow and steady task, just like keeping her stitches even.

As she was working on the final pin, Kron asked right behind her, "What are you doing, Kay?"

Startled, she bent her needle too much and snapped it. "Freeze it!" She inspected the broken tool, tempted to throw it away.

"Save it. I can fix it later." Kron reached past her to put his hand on the padlock. Naturally, for him, it snapped open in a heartbeat. He unwound the chain from the bar and dropped it, scuffing the links with his boots.

"That was a good idea you had to pick the lock, even if you broke your needle," he told her. "Whoever investigates later will think ordinary thieves and vandals broke in, not Avatars."

His praise made her blush. To think that such an unusual skill would be almost as useful here as her weather magic. Perhaps the Four had better prepared her for this task than she realized.

Kron eased the bar away, revealing another lock. This one resisted him for a moment before yielding. He pushed the door open. Dust covered a few withered garlands and the coffin, still intact.

"Are you going to break it open too?" Kay asked Kron.

He sighed and leaned against the wall, rubbing dust onto his clothes. "I must admit I'm struggling more with my magic now than I have since—since your life as Caye, when I first met you." He smiled wryly. "Spring hinted that the star magic made me...more than human, but less than the Four. I suppose I'm not as immortal as I thought. Gwen stopped the bleeding and forced the bullet out, but she couldn't completely heal my shoulder thanks to the frozen shard she bears. I'd rather save my strength and find another way to open the coffin besides magic."

Kay nodded for a few heartbeats, halting when his words sank in. "Immortal? Star magic?"

Kron gave her a serious look, then lowered his voice. "How much have the Four told you about Themselves?"

Thrown by the shift in topic, she struggled for a reply. "They came to help Challen."

"That's it? Nothing personal about Themselves?"

"Personal? They don't even have names besides the seasons."

"I've always wondered why."

"What do the Four's names have to do with retrieving Frederick's bone?"

"Nothing. Nothing at all." Kron studied the coffin. "Maybe we should just smash it, complete the picture of robbers. What do you think?"

"No!" She shrank against the wall of the mausoleum, trying not to touch it. "What we're doing is damaging enough."

"Then I need to coax a couple of planks loose." Kron shuffled forward, leaving a trail in the dust. He touched the coffin. Kay wished she'd brought rags to clean the coffin lid. Kron wiped his black-smeared hand on his jacket. A board from the side clattered as it fell on the floor. Yellow-white bones gleamed in the dim light.

He stepped back. "Since you're the Season Avatar, you should be the one to remove the bone. You have the right, not me."

Kay didn't think any of them had the right, but it was her duty to obey the Four, no matter what They asked of her. Before advancing, she offered a silent prayer: *Spring, Summer, Fall, and Winter, I pray this is truly Your will. If I must disturb an Avatar's rest, let it be for good reason. And Frederick, Summer Avatar, forgive us for disturbing you between lives. Aid us in our fight against Salth.* With her conscience appeased, Kay reached into the coffin and pulled out a couple of bones. They were a little larger than the fingertip bones they'd retrieved from five of the dead Avatars. A ring rolled onto the floor, but she left it there, unwilling to steal jewels from the dead. *Only two more bones to go.* She hoped they would be easier to obtain than this one.

Kay studied the marks they'd left in the dust. Would someone be able to trail them from this evidence? Even if their footsteps were too smudged to leave clues, the prints made the layers of dust more offensive. Time to clean all of it. "We need to leave," she told Kron, "but I have something else to do before we close the door."

Once they were both outside, Kay raised breezes to blow all the dust away. The wind couldn't scour the walls clean, but she didn't want to summon rain inside the mausoleum. Kron raised an eyebrow at her work. "Don't tidy up too much," he said. "No one will believe the Four hired maids to break into Avatar tombs and clean them."

"The coffin!" she said. "We didn't seal it back up."

"Maybe they'll see the ring we left behind and think we were tomb robbers." Kron closed the door and draped the chain back in place. He put the lock back but didn't bother repairing it. "There. I hope that will fool them. Did we leave tracks?"

Kay sighed as she looked at the ground. "I suppose I should make it rain." At least it wasn't too cold for that.

They hurried to rejoin the others. Before they could ask, Kay showed them the bones, then secured them in her reticule.

"I already had to put the captain back to sleep," Gwen said. "We'd better leave."

The trip back to the carriage was much faster now that they didn't have to worry about fog and could follow the main road. Jon came forward to meet them. "Kay, are you all right?" he asked.

She smiled, trying to reassure him. "I'm fine."

"Then what happened to Kron?"

Kron's clothes were ruined. The bullet had torn holes in both his jacket and shirt, and they were stained with blood. Even if the blood could be washed out, the jagged hole couldn't be mended invisibly. Ysabel still clung to her betrothed. "Gwen, I think he's bleeding again."

"Freeze it, I knew we were walking too quickly." Gwen halted. "Sister Avas, will you link with me? Some extra magic would be helpful."

By the Four, Gwen can normally heal that type of injury in a heartbeat. Kay stretched out her hand, eager to make up for the way her death was limiting Gwen. Jenna and Ysabel reacted at the same time. The three of them touched Gwen's arms, offering their magic. Laying her hand against Kron's wound, she reached deep into tissue and slowly healed him from the inside out, finishing with only shiny pink skin to mark where the bullet had entered his shoulder.

Kron moved his arm experimentally. "Much better, Gwen. Thank you." His expression relaxed, as did Ysabel's.

"Next stop, Bent Hook," Ysabel said as she climbed back up to the driver's seat. "Well, next destination, anyway. We won't get there before sunset. Which way once I leave Summerwood, Gwen?"

"North and west, only more north than west."

"I was hoping for more precise directions."

"If I had them, I'd give them to you."

Ysabel sighed. "Should I just hug the coastline?"

Gwen shook her head. "Then we won't get there until spring."

"By the Four, at least get us on our way," Jenna said.

Ysabel clicked her tongue, and the horses started off.

Gwen leaned against the back of her seat for a moment, then forced herself back into an upright posture. "I wonder how difficult it will be to retrieve Margaret's bone. Who do you think will be waiting there, the Selathens or the Watch?"

"I don't think the Selathens know anything about Margaret," Ysabel called through the window. "But I hope it's not the Watch again."

Jon shook his head. "The king can't have all the Season Avatars' tombs guarded, can he?"

"The Fips have to do something with all the soldiers in their army," Jenna said. "Just look at how many they had here. The next tomb will have a full platoon of them, mark my words! How will we deal with that?"

"You're all worried about the wrong threat," Kay said.

Rain pattered on the carriage, the only sound as her sister Avatars stared at her. She struggled not to shrink against the seat. As the youngest Avatar—though only by a few moons—she tended to say the least and let the others argue. But just as her season was approaching, so too was the time when she would be needed to do something extraordinary—even if she wasn't sure what that was yet.

"What do you mean, Kay?" Gwen asked.

She reached for her work basket. "Do you remember that Chaos Season that happened right after the fall equinox?"

"How can we forget it?" Jenna asked. "It attacked the One Oak itself! Thank the Four Robbie was in Wistica so he wasn't in the nursery. He could have been hurt!"

"There was something strange about that Chaos Season." As if anything could be normal about a magical weather storm that mixed up the seasons. "I felt as if Dorian was guiding the storm somehow."

"Even though he's dead?"

"Remember how he died," Gwen said. "I don't think he passed peacefully to the God of Winter's domain."

"He may have become part of the weather," Kay said. "If he remembers anything from his past life, it will be his love for Margaret."

"And we need one of her bones." As Ysabel spoke, Lathtin flattened his ears.

"Exactly." Kay was relieved someone grasped the import of what she was saying. "We may have to face an Avatar-guided Chaos Season to get it."

CHAPTER SEVEN

Bent Hook

Despite Kay's worries, the weather continued to be fine for the next few days of their trip. As before, they traveled far—between forty and fifty miles—every day without mishaps, thanks to Ysabel's and Kron's magic. The first night, they stopped in a village named Sweetwater, where the tavern owner lamented it was the wrong time of year for his signature roast leg of lamb. Gwen had to restrain herself from healing some of the other guests, a woman with a broken leg and a man with a burned arm.

"We need more portals to every part of Challen, Kron," she said before they retired to their separate rooms. "Then these people don't have to wait for a Grand Tour before I have the chance to heal them."

"And so we don't have to spend day after day doing nothing but sitting in a bumpy carriage," Jenna said. "I can't believe how dull it is!"

Boring or not, the trip seemed to tire out the other Avatars, for they slept soundly. Kay forced herself to stay awake so she could try contacting the woman's spirit again. It was hard to concentrate in a strange tavern with strange people talking in the room below them and the building creaking at odd times. Every gust of wind convinced her Dorian was going to stalk her with the weather. By midnight, she gave up.

Sweetwater was the last town they saw for the next two days as they passed through more forest. Their food supplies dwindled, so Ysabel and Jenna foraged at every stop. They slept in Kron's improvised tents again. Kay slept poorly the first night but roused before dawn to try to contact the spirit. The second night, she left the tent and stood staring at the stars for an hour or so, first becoming accustomed to the sounds of the shifting horses and nocturnal animals surrounding them. Next, she prayed to Winter for help before taking her gem out of her sewing kit. Then she waited. Nothing happened.

The next afternoon as they traveled, the trees thinned out, and the horses picked up speed as the road sloped downhill. The air took on a salty scent, one that brought Gwen and Jenna to full alertness. They had to be close to the Salt Waters and Bent Hook.

Ysabel knocked on the partition. "Another hour or so, and we should be there—"

Lathtin sprang to a standing position, his hair on end. "Chaos Season," Ysabel confirmed. "Right here."

Kay didn't need Ysabel to tell her the weather was changing rapidly. The rising wind outside taunted her, threatening in its wail to blow her away. Heartbeats later, rain pounded the roof of the carriage.

Ysabel halted the horses. Jenna grumbled as she searched for her waterproof cloak. "Can't we just tame the storm from here?"

"I'll have better control if we're outside, directly in it," Kay reminded her.

"I know. I'm just too stiff to move."

Gwen jabbed her; it didn't look accidental. "Freeze it, Lazybones. We're needed."

Kay, Gwen, and Jenna struggled into their cloaks, bumping into each other in the cramped space. Finally, they were ready. Kay unlatched the door and stepped out first, trying to create a gap in the rain to protect her sister Avatars. The storm refused to co-operate. By All Four, if she had trouble with such a little thing, how would she tame the storm, even with support from the other Avatars?

I am the Winter Avatar now, not Dorian, not anyone else. The weather must listen to me. Kay reached inside herself for strength. She was a pearl, with layers of knowledge and power from her previous lives. No storm could batter through her defenses. She pushed with her will, and the rain cleared out of her immediate area. Gwen and Jenna climbed out of the carriage. Ysabel passed Jenna's sapling to her before descending from the carriage. All of them gave Kay smiles of approval.

Then the rain returned with a will of its own. It turned colder, freezing, trying to coat her in ice. Kay remembered a time when Dorian had done the same thing. Coincidence, or evidence Dorian's soul was still controlling the weather?

Gwen and the other Avatars linked with Kay, sending her their magic. Dimly, Kay heard Jon shouting at her, but the storm demanded all of her attention. Normally, Kay would drain the magic from Chaos Season and share it with her sister Avatars. If Dorian was involved, he would anticipate how she worked and thwart her. She needed to do something unexpected.

Instead of dealing with the weather surrounding her, Kay reached farther, seeking the ultimate source of the storm. She moved west, following the storm clouds hugging the Challen coastline. She hesitated as the trail led into the Dead Land. Maybe this was a trap. If she ventured any farther, Salth might snare her soul. Kay couldn't risk it, even with the link to pull her back.

She retreated and surveyed the storm's path. A wide peninsula would allow her to blow the storm over land and weaken it. The northern coast of Challen offered many ragged harbors and protrusions, but none of them were big enough to break up a storm of this size. However, she did find a stretch of cliffs tall enough to present a challenge to the storm's winds. She set up several crosswinds in the area. It required more magic to force them in contrary directions, but by pulling energy from this section of Chaos Season, she was able to turn the storm's strength against itself. Part of the storm flowed inland. She harvested its magic until she felt as stuffed as if she'd eaten an entire cow by herself. Gwen pulled magic from her and gave it to Jenna and Ysabel, who set about restoring the plants and animals. Gwen reserved some magic for herself and swept the area for injured people.

Kay remained tense as she watched the sea. If Dorian was guiding this Chaos Season, he'd let them think they were done with it, maybe allow them to drop the link, before sending another wave at them....

Kay, birds are migrating north instead of south, and insects are hatching moons too early, Ysabel said.

They think it's spring? she asked. She always hated having to reverse nice weather, as people complained more about that than when snow covered their doorstep in heartbeats.

Thank the Four there aren't any maple trees up here, Jenna said. *It's hard sending sap back down once it's started to rise.*

Kay sighed and reached for more magic. The storm retreated southward, still active, as if taunting her to follow.

We'll keep you linked and safe, Gwen promised.

Gwen had kept her word before, so Kay hurried after the Chaos Season, trying to outflank it before it traveled across the entire country. She pulled on its magic—and it pulled back on her.

By All Four Gods and Goddesses! Kay struggled, not just to keep her own magic from feeding the storm, but from being drawn into it so deeply she lost herself. Her panic subsided as Gwen and the others anchored her. If they had brought her back from death, they could bring her back from this. They trusted her to handle the weather, no matter what it did. She couldn't disappoint them.

I have just as much experience with Chaos Season as Dorian does, she reminded herself. *There has to be a way to tame this Chaos Season. All I have to do is find it. Maybe looking at it from a different perspective will help.*

Kay let her soul soar above the clouds so she could study the entire weather system. Warm air currents from the south were mixing with cold northern winds to feed the storm. Dorian would expect her to attack Chaos Season from the north, closest to her physical location. Kay therefore needed to disrupt the southern part of the storm. If she cooled southern Challen—not enough to cause frost or harm plants and animals—then the warm winds would lose energy and stop feeding Chaos Season. From there, she should be able to tame it as normal.

She gathered heat from the southern winds and spread it across the rest of Challen. She hoped people would appreciate the break from the normal fall weather. The additional heat would buffer the effects of Chaos Season.

As the main storm lost strength, it spun off smaller, weaker storms. These she was able to tame easily. Each one increased her magic. Normally Kay would have shared her reserves with her sister Avatars, but she held the magic back, waiting for Dorian to make a move.

As she expected, Chaos Season surged south, toward what Dorian now perceived was her location. This time, she was ready for the way the storm surrounded her, trying to swallow her soul. She allowed it to flow into her, then into Gwen, who shared the magic with Jenna and Ysabel. They worked diligently to restore the plants and animals caught in the storm, undoing whatever damage they could. Kay didn't stop draining Chaos Season until it shrank away to nothing.

There, I've done it. Challen was finally safe. She and the others could break the link, then eat and rest before retrieving a bone from Margaret's tomb.

Well done, Kay, Gwen said. *I agree it's time to rest. Now I understand why my Aunt Gabri hated traveling so much.*

Kay let her awareness drop back into her body. Hunger stabbed her belly, and her eyes burned as if sand grains had blown under her eyelids. The others felt the same way. Gwen pulled away, leaving Kay alone with her bodily miseries. She blinked several times and stretched herself.

"By the Four, I'm glad that's over," Jenna said.

It should be, shouldn't it? Kay probed the weather in their immediate area. Everything was still, unnaturally still. Dorian had a final card to play in this weather game.

"Everyone take cover," she ordered as she cast about for the source of her disquiet.

"Freeze it, Kay, there can't be any magic left—"

"I wouldn't be so certain, Jenna," Ysabel said. "Lathtin hasn't settled down yet. Neither have the horses."

Where could Dorian summon another Chaos Season from so quickly? Kay had cut off the weather storm stretching from the Dead Land, and they'd used up all the weather magic in Challen. Of course, there was still the Salt Waters. Water storms normally developed on the east coast of Challen, not this far north. She extended her senses over the water, just to make sure. Her range was more limited over the Salt Waters than it was over land, only a few miles. It was far enough for her to tell that the air pressure was sinking like a stone. That would cause more strong winds—and they seemed calculated to come from right behind her, where the carriage and its nonmagical occupants waited. Including Jon.

Despite her fatigue, fear for Jon gave Kay new strength. As the wind rose, she pushed back to control it. *You can't harm me or anyone I love.* The wind lashed her hair. *Enough. Die down.* She created a region of calm air around herself and her sister Avatars. *Freeze it, Dorian is behind this—again.*

As if the dead Winter Avatar was still plaguing her, the carriage shook under the gale. The horses stamped their hooves. Ysabel must be hard-pressed to keep them from bolting.

Very well, Dorian, if it's a weather duel you want, a weather duel you shall have. Kay stepped forward, tugging her air shield with her. She advanced past the carriage and into the path of the gale, then drew more air into her shield. As the gusts struck the shield, it quivered, but Dorian's wind lost its force. Again and again the wind buffeted her, trying to disturb her shield and reach her. Distantly, branches and tree trunks cracked. Some limbs fell close to the carriage, and the horses neighed. Another person walked through Kay's shield toward them. It had to be Ysabel, determined to calm the horses no matter how much risk she took upon herself. If a branch didn't fall on her, the horses could panic and trample her. Kay extended her shield, gasping as her strength ebbed. If she failed this time, the entire quartet might perish with her.

Bells pealed from Bent Hook. Their notes were oddly timed, but the melody reminded Kay of an old song Ysabel's mother had played for them on the pianoforte. Tree branches stopped moving; perhaps they were listening too. The wind looped around, then snuffed itself out.

The ground came up to meet Kay. Before she could put her arms in front of her face, dirt and sand smacked her.

CHAPTER EIGHT

Margaret's Gem

Kay woke up in a strange bed. For a few heartbeats, the scratchy blanket made her think she was back at Rainbow River, hiding from Salth and her nightmares. Then she remembered the Chaos Season that Dorian had driven at her several times. Although her head and stomach complained for different reasons, she scanned the weather outside. Thank the Four it was calm, if chilly. She hoped her enemies were as exhausted as she was. *Who will recover first? Chaos Season always happens when it's least welcome.*

What was welcome was the sight of Gwen and Ysabel bringing her food. They each held a tray with a bowl, a hunk of bread, and a mug of ale. "It's not what we would dine on back at the One Oak, but Gwen assures me it won't kill us," Ysabel said as she set her tray down on the bed.

Kay sat up slowly and grabbed the bread. It was stale, and there was no butter, but she devoured it anyway. The stew was a little better, though the fish must have been from Kron's original era. She cleaned off both trays anyway.

"How much time has passed?" she asked once her hunger was satisfied for a few heartbeats. "And how much damage did the storm do to the area?"

"Surprisingly little," Gwen answered. "Another reason to think Dorian was behind this Chaos Season. He would spare Margaret's grave." She laid her good hand on Kay's. "You must be feeling better." It wasn't a question.

"I could use another night's sleep."

Gwen sent a burst of energy through her, clearing the cloud in her head. Details came back to her of the wind threatening the carriage. "Jon and the others...are they all right?"

"They're fine. As a matter of fact, your intended is worried about you." Ysabel gave Kay a knowing smile. "He's in the dining hall if you're ready to go down."

Kay splashed cold water on her face and smoothed out the wrinkles in her dress. Then she followed Ysabel downstairs. The dining hall was smoky, poorly lit, and smelled like fish. Jon, Kron, and a couple of locals sat next to the fireplace, playing a card game. It was hard to tell who was winning. Jon looked up, smiled at her, and put down his cards. He hurried over to her. Before he could speak, Ysabel put a finger to her lips. Jon drew himself up before he could use Kay's real name—or her title.

He reached for her, pulling his hands back at the last heartbeat. "Are you well?" His lips formed her name.

Kay nodded. She wanted to throw herself into his arms, kiss him passionately, and celebrate having tamed one of the most challenging Chaos Seasons she'd faced in this life. Where could they go in this strange small town for privacy?

Ysabel coughed. "The sky has cleared up most wonderfully. By the Four, I can see more stars here than in Wistica. Would you two like to view them with me?"

Kay nodded, eager to be out in the refreshing open air and worried that the damage had been more expansive than Gwen had claimed. "Where are we going? To the beach?"

"It's small, but it will do." Ysabel eyed her meaningfully. "Don't forget your shawl."

Thankful for the reminder to pretend she didn't have weather magic, Kay wrapped a gray wool shawl around her shoulders while Jon put on his coat. They followed Ysabel outside. She led them to a beach more stone than sand, halting at the edge. Kay and Jon stepped out farther, following the moon until the seawater lapped at their boots.

"At last, we're alone. We don't have to act as shy as nobles." Kay let herself fall against Jon, expecting him to embrace her. His arms did wrap around her, but heartbeats slower than normal. She looked up at him. "What's wrong?"

"Wrong? Nothing's wrong." Now he gripped her tightly. "I've just never seen you tame a Chaos Season before. Did you really turn aside that wind at the end?"

She nodded. While that wind had been a stubborn one, it hadn't been as challenging as taming a Challen-wide Chaos Season, as she and the other Avatars had done during the summer. Jon had lived in Challen all his life; he knew all about Chaos Seasons and how the Season Avatars handled them. But to show him her magic seemed unnatural. When she'd first met Jon, she'd hidden away the magic-using part of herself, and now that she was an Avatar, she'd spent much less time with him. How could she ever bring the two parts of her life together?

Jon chuckled awkwardly as he looked down at her. "By All Four Gods and Goddesses, I still have a hard time believing the wind won't blow you away."

Kay tamped down her irritation at his words. Dorian had said similar things about her, trying to make the other Avatars think she wasn't capable of doing her duty. No matter how many times she'd struggled with that idea, it hurt more hearing someone else say it, especially Jon.

His grip on her loosened, and his smile faltered. "I mean, you never so much breathed you were the next Winter Avatar. No one expects to meet an Avatar in their daily life. How could I have known who you were?"

"Would you have still felt the same way about me when we met?"

He sighed. "Ah, Stowaway, you looked so lost. You didn't need me to help you. You could have brought a farmer rain for food and shelter, or made your way to the One Oak—"

"That was the last place I could go." Kay broke free of him and dipped her fingers in the water. Even with her magic, it still felt cold, though she knew saltwater wouldn't freeze easily. "Dorian hated me. He would have hounded me as mercilessly as Salth— or worse."

"Is that why you didn't speak at his funeral?"

She nodded, studying the way the water rippled as it flung itself against the land. "Now we're here to take a bone from his wife's body. I'm sure he'll find some way to stop us, even if we're doing this to end Chaos Season." She shook her head. "He probably wouldn't help us anyway with that, even if he hadn't joined forces with Salth. He'd complain that without Chaos Season, Challen wouldn't need Season Avatars."

"That's nonsense. You and the other Avatars keep the land healthy and the crops bountiful, no matter how much time passes between Chaos Seasons." Stones slid under Jon's shoes as he came toward her. "Even if there's never another Chaos Season, farmers would still line up to have you water their crops. You're important. You can do something no one else in Challen can do, so important the Four wouldn't let you die." His voice trembled on the last word. "And I still can't believe you haven't found some handsome, rich nobleman to replace me."

"Of course not, Jon. I love you." *Though I wish you'd love me back the way you used to instead of always saying you're not worthy of me.* "It doesn't matter if I'm a seamstress or an Avatar."

"I only wish that was true."

"Then By the Four, prove it." Why did her voice sound so irritated? She attempted to smooth things over with a smile. "We have as much privacy as we can expect on this journey. Let's not waste time with talk." Kay gave Jon a coy glance over her shoulder, just like Jenna would have.

He hesitated, looking around and studying Ysabel for a few heartbeats before approaching Kay. He kissed her tenderly, as if she was still the timid Stowaway he'd first met. But she was more than that now: she was a Winter Avatar, with the songs of storms in her blood. Even if she and Jon weren't married yet, there were ways they could give each other pleasure. Granted, they had always done it indoors, but Jenna claimed she had lain with Lex under a giant rosebush. Why couldn't they do the same? There had to be a sandy place around here that would be more comfortable than the stones.

Kay tugged at Jon, but after a couple of steps, he planted himself so firmly she couldn't budge him. "No, Stowaway," he said gently, "this isn't right."

"We've done it before—"

"That was different."

"Then why did you agree to come with me, if you're going to treat me like I'm made of glass?"

He stepped back, eyes full of confusion and hurt. "Kay, what's wrong? I'm only trying to treat you as an Avatar deserves."

"I don't want to be an Avatar with you. I just want us to be Kay and Jon, the way we were before I was forced back to the One Oak."

He shook his head. "That's impossible. You know it as well as I do."

Freeze it, he was right. The king had ennobled her, along with Jenna and Ysabel, when they'd been officially recognized as Season Avatars. The elevation in rank was supposed to be an honor, but it only made her life more complicated with social conventions she was supposed to obey. The Four had sent her to a commoner's family so she could understand the needs of ordinary people. If only others would let her live simply and not try to persuade her to find a different match or make her intended behave as a different person.

I wish I could talk to one of my sister Avatars about this. Gwen was nobly born, and Jenna, though first married to a shopkeeper, planned to marry the king's brother. Ysabel was half-Selathen, and Kron had come forward in time; they weren't as bound by Challen rules as she and Jon were. None of the living Avatars could sympathize with her...but maybe a dead one could. Margaret had obviously come from a poor town. Some of her relatives had to live here still; maybe they could tell her how Margaret had adjusted to becoming an Avatar.

What can I learn from someone who loved Dorian? Kay thought sourly.

"Kay, I think we should return," Jon said. "People might start talking about us."

She would have preferred remaining outside longer, but he was right. They didn't want to draw attention. She stomped past him, not bothering to take his hand. Wouldn't it please everyone else if they came back to the inn separately? It certainly didn't make her happy.

Although she wasn't tired, Kay went straight to her room. Ysabel followed her before Kay could finish changing. She gave her a sideways glance as she unpinned her hair. "That didn't sound as if it went as well as you'd hoped."

Kay removed her dress and hung it on a wooden peg. "Men. I don't understand them. You try to convince them you haven't changed, only to go and find they have."

Ysabel smiled. "How odd. Kron and I had to work through that as well."

"That's different. You two first met eight hundred years ago, when you were in your first life as an Avatar."

"And he traveled to this time without dying. I'm not sure he can die. He's changed very little in the moons since we met him."

Kay pondered that as she put on a wool nightgown, so finely woven it wasn't scratchy. Kron and Lex were both extraordinary men with their own magic. Maybe it was easier for them to be betrothed to Season Avatars when they knew they were capable of great things. Jon had started educating himself but had to leave University to come with her. Was that why he was so distant with her? She'd hoped they would draw closer on this journey, but perhaps she'd been selfish in insisting he accompany her. She'd interrupted his chance to achieve something on his own.

I should tell him he could go back to Wistica and continue his studies. The thought left her stomach feeling hollow. Even if Jon wouldn't kiss her properly, seeing his cheerful expression always warmed her. Was it selfish of her to keep him with her for that? But what would happen if he returned to Wistica? Although they'd tried to be discreet, there had been a couple of mentions of them in the papers. If the Watch suspected the Avatars of robbing graves, the yellowcoats might take Jon in for questioning. Only the Four knew what the Watch would do to him then.

Before Ysabel could blow out the candles, Kay asked, "Ysabel, how did you and Kron work out your troubles?"

She grinned sheepishly. "I think it was more we decided we didn't want to be apart from each other. After he left the One Oak, I realized some of my complaints weren't as much of an issue as I thought they were." She sighed. "Though Gwen thinks he won't be able to give me children. Maybe we'll claim a few orphan babies as our own."

"I'm not ready for babies, my own or otherwise," Kay said. "Neither is Jon. I think..." she struggled for words, "I think he wants something of his own first."

"What do you mean?"

"Something that makes him equal to an Avatar, or close to one."

Ysabel let out a sympathetic laugh. "How can he do that? Being ennobled is difficult enough if you're not an Avatar. Earning chals isn't always enough. I know Selathen families richer than some of the old Challen nobles, but they haven't been able to add a prefix to their names, let alone a noblename."

Kay shook her head. "I know, but try telling Jon that. Once he gets an idea into his head, he rides it like a locomotive that can't stop for anything."

"Men worry about the strangest things sometimes. Isn't that right, Lathtin?"

Her brother narrowed his pupils to slits.

"Maybe it seems silly to us because we've never had to worry about it," Kay said. "Even when I was an apprentice seamstress, I knew I was doing useful work."

Ysabel gave her an odd look. "But you always knew you'd come back to the One Oak as an Avatar."

"I didn't know I'd survive dying," Kay snapped. "By the Four, I didn't expect to survive my first year as an Avatar." She shivered, remembering her death. "The hardest thing I ever did was let Gwen coax me into using my magic again. And now she's paying for it."

"Poor Kay. That was very brave of you to come back to us. And Gwen doesn't blame you for her dead hand. None of us do." Ysabel drew her into a motherly embrace. Kay held herself stiff for a moment, then let herself relax. Avatars were always supposed to present calm and confident faces to the rest of Challen, but it had been a very difficult year. With Ysabel's warmth enfolding her, Kay could release all of the fear and frustration she'd been holding inside for moons. Ysabel didn't say anything; she simply rocked her and hummed as if Kay was a child.

When Kay finished crying, she climbed out of bed and found a handkerchief to wipe her face. "Sorry about that."

"Don't be sorry." Ysabel smiled as if a wet shoulder didn't bother her. "We're sister Avatars. We need to support each other."

"Well, thank you anyway." Kay climbed back into the bed, the straw mattress offering little support. At least with Ysabel around, she wouldn't have to worry about bedbugs.

"If you ever want to talk, just the two of us, no linking with Gwen or Jenna, I don't mind. Sometimes it's nice just to be by ourselves and not have to share everything with them."

Ysabel blew out the candles, and Lathtin settled between them. Kay closed her eyes. Her problems with Jon and Dorian were still there, but maybe they could wait until the morning.

* * *

Kay woke, cold. She reached for the blanket, but it wasn't there. Ysabel and Lathtin had stolen it. She tried to tug a corner of it away from the cat when she realized she shouldn't be cold at all. Even when she was asleep, her magic should keep her warm. Was something interfering with her magic? Maybe Dorian had found another way to attack her. Sitting up, she cupped her hand to form a ball of lightning.

"You don't need that, Kay," a woman's voice said softly.

Kay whipped her hand around as she tried to probe the darkness. Her lighting, though white-blue, didn't penetrate very far. Shadows seemed to lurk within the shadows. She knew she didn't need to fear them, but they prevented her from learning what she needed to know.

"Who are you?" she whispered. "By the Four, where are you? How did you get here?"

"Where's the diamond? It will make our conversation much easier if you hold it."

"Just a moment." Kay slipped out of bed and hunted for her sewing kit. Someone had placed her trunk in a corner, and her sewing kit, along with a few other items she'd kept with her, lay on the lid. Kay released the lightning to hover overhead while she dug through the bag for the tiny gem. Just as she began to worry it had been lost, her fingers found it. *I should have this mounted in a piece of jewelry so I can keep it with me.* Wondering if she'd be able to find a jeweler on this journey, along with the time to have it done, Kay cupped the diamond in her palm and swung it about.

Light glinted through the diamond and diffused, revealing a woman's face an arm's length from Kay. The rest of the woman's body seemed insubstantial, like smoke caught in a shape for a heartbeat before the wind dispersed it. The woman could have been Gwen's older sister, or a cousin. While this woman had smooth skin, she stared at Kay with such world-weariness Kay felt the weight of her own previous lives drag her down. Memory stirred inside her. They'd never met, but she'd seen that face—or a fresher, more hopeful version of it—back at the One Oak.

"Margaret gran Garnell?" Kay whispered. "The Spring Avatar from Bent Hook?"

She nodded. "The same." She peered around the room curiously. "So close to the living again."

Kay noticed a sheen over not just Margaret's face, but the area around her, as if they were staring at each other through a window. Could that window be broken and allow Margaret to return in some form from the God of Winter's domain? Kay swallowed, hard. Did Margaret know why the Avatars were in her hometown and what they planned to do to her body? She glanced at the bed, suddenly worried Ysabel, who'd first thought of taking Avatar bones, would wake and expose herself to danger. To Kay's relief, both Ysabel and her anilink slept deeply.

"Why are you here?" Kay asked. "By All Four Gods and Goddesses, Margaret, *how* are you here?"

She smiled. "Winter's season is less than a moon away. Normally He keeps strict separation between our world and His domain, but with your quartet so close to facing Salth for the first time in eight hundred years, Winter is bending His own rules slightly in the hope that we can help you."

Kay exhaled. "Praise the Four. So, what are we supposed to do?"

Margaret glanced at Ysabel. "The bones won't be enough. Our magic doesn't reside in our bodies, but in our souls."

"Does that mean we don't need the bones?"

"No, you do. They will help us cross over."

Kay leaned closer to Margaret, despite the cold streaming from the barrier between them. "So, please, tell me what to do."

She looked embarrassed. "This is going to sound strange, but you have to take us inside—"

The window shattered, scattering glass inside the room. Kay created a wind to deflect the shards away from her and the bed, but since the air in the room was still, she couldn't raise the protection quickly enough. Cuts bloomed on her hands. Lathtin uncoiled and hissed at the window.

"Dorian!" Margaret said. "By All Four Gods and Goddesses, why are you doing this? Leave the girls alone!"

The wind outside howled. It stretched with greedy fingers toward Kay's hand—the one holding the diamond.

Freeze it. If this was an ordinary wind, Kay would be able to handle it on her own. With Dorian behind it, however, the weather became as cunning and unpredictable as he was.

Frustrated, she turned to Margaret. "Freeze it, he's your husband. You talk some sense into him! By the Four, what did you ever see in him anyway? He's never been anything but cruel!"

Margaret's gaze hardened, and Kay wished she could take her words back. Before she could apologize—or at least explain—Margaret's face disappeared. The unnatural cold faded.

Ysabel stirred, mumbling something Kay couldn't make out. Lathtin batted her face. It would probably take her a few moments to fully awaken. Even then, she wouldn't be able to boost Kay's magic without Gwen to help. Kay would have to face Dorian on her own.

How can he be so powerful when all that's left of him is his spirit? Is Salth sharing her power with him? That would explain why the storm earlier had come from the Dead Land. She thought she'd severed that connection earlier, but maybe she'd have to do it again…

The gusts intensified and brushed away the small shield she'd created. Ice formed around her fist with Margaret's diamond. If Dorian managed to take it from her, she'd lose the ability to speak to Margaret as well.

As ice crept between Kay's fingers, she approached the banked fireplace. A small, highly controlled lightning bolt rekindled a flame.

"Kay," Ysabel said from behind her, "what's going on?"

"Dorian. Tend the fire. It'll help me set up more air currents in this room."

Ysabel set her feet on the floor, then grabbed the blanket and draped it around her shoulders. "Is he why it's so cold in here?"

Instead of answering, Kay coaxed the warm air from the fire toward her, melting the ice around her fist. Her hand was so cold she couldn't tell where the ice ended and the diamond began. At least that wouldn't melt—

The ice vanished, leaving her hand dry. The outside wind stilled, letting the curtain fall back into place. Kay wriggled her fingers, then turned her fist over and stared at it in disbelief.

The diamond was gone. Kay expanded her lightning ball and searched the entire floor, even the cracks between the wooden boards. Ysabel and Lathtin copied her, but no one caught so much as a glimpse of the gem.

CHAPTER NINE

Return to the One Oak

"Dorian stole a diamond right out of your hand?" Gwen arched her eyebrows. "By the Four, what could he possibly want with it?"

They were gathered for breakfast downstairs, around a table that held more dried fish than bread. Lathtin, who'd polished off several portions of fish, basked in a slant of sunlight. The serving woman glanced at him from time to time as she swept, but she didn't comment. Hopefully she didn't know the current Ava Fall used a cat as an anilink. The Avatars could change clothes and disguise themselves, but it was harder to hide an animal, even one as intelligent as a human.

"Perhaps he wants to propose to Margaret again," Jenna said.

Gwen scowled. "Be serious, Jules."

"The diamond once belonged to Margaret," Kay said. "It allowed me to connect with her soul. Now that it's gone, I don't know how I'll be able to contact her again."

"Simple enough." Jenna grabbed the last piece of bread and wrapped it around a piece of fish. "This is where she lived. It ought to be easy to find something else she owned."

"Kron might be able to tell what would have the right magical resonance to link with her," Ysabel added.

"Finding anything might be a problem." Gwen reached for the teapot, holding it awkwardly in her good hand. Ysabel tried to take it from her, but when Gwen silently refused to give it up, Kay settled for holding the cup, shifting it to align with the trembling spout. Kay let out a sigh of relief when Gwen set the teapot down and continued, "If we can't tell anyone we're the Season Avatars, why would Margaret's family talk to us? We're strangers here."

Jenna swallowed the last of her fish sandwich. "We can tell them that we're here to pray at Margaret's tomb for Gwen's hand to be cured."

Kay grimaced. "The Four can hear our prayers wherever we are. They don't approve of treating past or present Avatars on a level with the Four."

Gwen met her gaze. "Then you don't think we should offer them a few chals for something that used to belong to Margaret?"

Kay hesitated. Bent Hook didn't seem like a prosperous town. Most families here probably wouldn't hesitate to sell someone's castoffs, or even a family treasure, for whatever chals they could get. "Did Margaret send chals back to her family? They might be well-to-do by now and in less need of our aid."

"They might not even live here anymore," Jenna added. "Did you check on that before we left Wistica, Gwen?"

She frowned at her chipped mug. "I didn't think we'd need to contact her family. The town started a special gravesite for her. They're supposed to plant a garden there next year too. From what I read, it's on the outskirts of town, so we shouldn't have any problem—"

Gwen broke off as a group of villagers entered the pub. They stared at the Avatars as if they had taken their favorite table, then moved to the table second closest to the fireplace. The serving woman called out a greeting, set down her broom, and hurried to the bar. Their new neighbors kept talking among themselves.

"You heard it from Old Salty?" a man said. "And you believed him? He was either still in his cups or clouding your mind."

A woman shook her head. "No, he didn't see it. Said the Widow Blackfin saw it and she told him."

"What was she doing by Young Maggie's resting place?"

Kay exchanged glances with the others at the table. Could they be referring to Margaret?

"Dame Blackfin wanted to give thanks there that her house wasn't damaged by yesterday's Chaos Season," the woman who'd spoken earlier said. "Even brought one of her husband's scarves with her to tie around the stone. Can't imagine what an Ava Spring would want with something so tattered, not even fit to pass down to an orphan, but that's Dame Blackfin for you."

"By the Four, Parly, tell us what she saw." The first man tilted his head back toward the bar. "You're slower than Sally here."

"Don't you have nets to mend?" The serving woman called back.

"How can I think of nets when I have your beauty to gaze on, lambkin?"

"I'm no more a lambkin than you're king of the Salt Waters, Jack."

The crowd at the other table laughed.

Gwen rolled her eyes and laid her good hand on the table. *By the Four, hurry up and tell us what happened at Margaret's grave,* she shared after they linked.

Don't be so harsh on them, Gwen, Jenna said. *This has to be the most exciting thing to happen here in moons. They'll be talking about this story all season long, turning over every detail like a farmer plowing a field.*

Well, we don't have all season.

I think they're getting to the good part now, Ysabel said.

Gwen broke the link, turned to Kron, and asked him if he thought it safe to travel. Kay didn't listen to his response. Instead, as she broke up a piece of too-salty fish, she, like the others, strained to hear the rest of the conversation. Fortunately, the woman at the next table didn't seem to mind sharing her story with the entire pub.

"So the Widow Blackfin packs up her scarf, grabs her cane, and sets out before dawn to Maggie's grave. Takes her an age to get there. By the time she reaches it, the sun is up. There's frost everywhere. But not on the grave."

Gwen gave up her pretense and leaned toward the next table.

"Was the grave covered with flowers?" The man asked. "The Avi Summer did that when he and the Ava Fall came up here this summer."

"By All Four, no. Just the opposite." The woman paused for a sip of beer, glancing around at her audience. Before Kay could spring from her seat and demand an answer, the woman said, "It was iced over."

"Iced over?" the other villagers said in unison.

"Aye." The woman grinned. "The grave, headstone, and the ground around it were covered in a block of clear ice."

"Maybe the Avi Win did it, he that married our Maggie," Sally said.

The man slapped her arm. "Freeze it, woman, don't you remember he died at the fall soltrans? They laid him next to her. You can still see the upturned dirt over him!"

Sally tilted her chin upward defiantly. "Then he had to have done it somehow, out of love for her. They say Avatars carry their magic from life to life, don't they? Then maybe they still have it after they're dead."

"They're both with the God of Winter now." The woman who'd told the story made the sign of the Four over her heart. "Maybe He did it to protect their graves."

"Maybe." The man nodded. "First Avatars killed by strange creatures at the Fall Soltrans, and now they can't even rest in peace without their graves being disturbed."

Gwen gestured for the rest of them to finish eating so they could leave. They halted outside the pub so Gwen could check if anyone was watching them before leading them down the street. "Which way to Margaret's grave?" she asked in a low voice.

Kay probed the town for abnormally cold areas. She frowned as nothing appeared on her first search. Dorian must be trying to hide his wife's grave from them. She created a moderate breeze to stir up the air currents, searching for areas where the air remained unnaturally still. They'd said Margaret's grave was outside of town, so she focused her attention there. Finally, she found a possible spot within sight of the ocean. "Northeast of here, about a mile away."

Gwen nodded. "Very well. Let's go."

They formed a line and walked down the main street. Weather-worn boards creaked underfoot. The dry goods store was a little smaller than the pub, with a tailor and a seamstress on either side. Kay glanced through the window, inspecting the stitching on the clothes. A carpenter and a blacksmith came next, with an herbalist at the end of the row. Ten or twelve houses clustered near the dock. Kay steered them toward the spot she'd discovered earlier. It didn't take them long to find the grave. Like the Avi Spring's grave in southern Challen, this one was surrounded by a fence, but made of splintered wood, not iron. Dried flowers, a faded scarf, and even rag dolls waved in the breeze. The grave itself wasn't visible.

"I wonder if we're supposed to bring our own offering," Jenna said.

"It seems wrong." Gwen sighed as she glanced down at her useless hand. "Though I've often wished I had a chance to meet her after I was able to use my magic. She might have helped me remove that frozen shard before it affected my hand."

Jenna scooped up Gwen's hand and studied the violet bracelet on her wrist. "Gwen, the flowers have lost their scent."

"I know." Gwen's mouth thinned.

Kay, like her sister Avatars, picked up the pace, as if obtaining a bone from Margaret might save Gwen.

As they neared the grave, they could see several villagers gathered around it. Even if Kay could remove the ice, they wouldn't be able to take the bone until they had some privacy.

An old man standing in front of the gate looked up. "Ahoy, strangers. Have you come to visit my daughter?"

They halted. "The Ava Spring was your daughter, good sir?" Gwen asked.

He chuckled. "Dama, you'll find no sirs in this town. Yes, she was." He looked over at the headstone. "My youngest child. Never thought I'd outlive her, what with her being able to heal herself."

"May the Four give her good sleep and gentle rebirth," Kay said. The others echoed her.

Gwen continued, "We heard in town there was a miracle here…"

Margaret's father smiled with pride. "Of course. Come take a look for yourself."

He beckoned them over, but the other villagers were reluctant to move and let them see for themselves. They came up to the gate one at a time to view the grave. Kay flinched as she realized the site was wide enough for two. One headstone—Margaret's—had already been installed, but Dorian's hadn't been put in place yet. Kay hoped her relief wasn't obvious. A block of ice covered both graves. It was clear enough for Kay to read Margaret's name on the headstone. She probed downward, trying to see how far the ice extended. Dirt wasn't her natural element, and it blocked her efforts to sense any ice below the ground. The soil here was colder than the surroundings. Ysabel looked at the group and gave them a tiny nod. She could feel little soil-living animals like worms and insects, so she might have learned something from them as well.

"By the Four, I've never seen anything like it." Gwen made the sign of the Four over her heart. "How long has the ice been here?"

"We just found it this morning," Margaret's father replied.

"Maybe it's left over from Chaos Season yesterday," another man said.

"Why would the Avatars leave that there?" a woman countered. "They normally clean up every last trace of Chaos Season."

Another woman shrugged. "Who knows? I hear this quartet doesn't act like all the others we've had."

"I've heard they're the ones destroying the Avatar graves around Challen," a third man said.

Margaret's father turned to look at Kay and the other Avatars again. "Are you from Wistica? Have you heard any more about the grave robberies?"

Kay's tongue felt frozen. Jenna shrugged and stepped forward. "Only what's in the paper." The pitch of her voice wavered. A couple of the women stared at her suspiciously.

"Do you really think the Avatars are doing it?" one of the women asked.

"By All Four Gods and Goddesses, why would they do that?" Gwen shrugged.

"Well, all we know is none of us are doing it." A man stepped forward, toward Gwen, scowling. "So we can't trust any strangers in town. You got business here, you do it and leave. Today."

Jenna stepped up next to Gwen, eyebrows drawn together. Gwen tugged at her sleeve awkwardly. "Of course, my good man. We don't want to cause any trouble." She glanced back at them, her gaze resting on Kay's. "We'd just like a few heartbeats to pray at the Ava Spring's grave. My hand's been troubling me lately."

The man didn't back down. He continued glowering at Gwen until a thin woman said, "Oh, come, Carl, let them pray. The Four would approve, and they look harmless enough, don't they?"

"That's what they said about the current quartet."

The rest of the crowd backed away, leaving the man standing alone. Gwen passed him and knelt at the gate, eyes closed. Kay copied the other Avatars as they bowed their heads. Instead of praying, she examined the ice. It was solid underfoot for two yards all around the graves. Hoping none of the people there sensed the ground warming up, she searched for a way to soften the frozen dirt. She could summon lightning to start a fire, but that would most likely injure someone and reveal she was the Winter Avatar. Instead, she parted the clouds so sunlight could bathe the area. It would take several hours for the heat to penetrate the top layer of dirt, and the light would lose strength as the day wore on and the sun moved.

Winter, let this work, Kay prayed.

"That's enough time," Carl said. "Now get your things and go."

Jenna sputtered, but Gwen absently made a sign of blessing as she turned to leave. Kay hoped no one in the crowd remarked on it.

"Frozen fool," Jenna muttered once they were well away from the grave. "It's still a crime to threaten us."

"Well, it is a crime to disturb a grave," Gwen replied. "Thank the Four they didn't suspect anything. We'll have to come back at night. The only question is where do we hide our carriage until then."

After a few heartbeats, Jenna said, "There's a clearing a few miles away that might work, but it might be difficult bringing the carriage there."

"Kron and Jon can manage that," Gwen said. "Kay, how deep does that ice extend?"

"Far enough that it would take a quarter-moon to thaw it."

Gwen shook her head. "We don't have time for that. Jenna, Ysabel, anything your magic can do to help?"

"Is the dirt frozen?" Jenna asked.

Kay nodded.

"Then it's going to be very difficult for plants to break it apart. If there are any seeds trapped in there, I can try to force-grow them, but it's the wrong time of year for that. I'd have to touch the dirt to give the seeds enough magic."

Ysabel said, "There aren't many wild animals in this area strong enough to dig up Margaret's grave."

"What about mice or other rodents?" Gwen asked.

"It will take a good dozen of them several days to break through." She glanced at Kay. "Assuming Dorian doesn't just re-freeze the ground—or the animals."

"Once we're settled, I'll thaw out the area as best as I can," Kay said. "There's already so much moisture in the air from the Salt Waters that it may be difficult to pull the water away."

Gwen sighed. "We'd best leave, then."

Back at the tavern, they explained their plan to Kron and Jon. The men grumbled about having to leave town, even if temporarily, but they soon started plotting ideas for removing the block themselves.

"Just don't damage the grave," Gwen said as Jon proposed using a steam engine to melt the ice. "We need to be able to use the bones when we're done."

"At least they'd be small and easy to carry if the men blow them up," Jenna said, prompting all of them to stare at her until she flushed.

As they drove the carriage toward the clearing Jenna had found earlier, Kay kept the day warm, but not unseasonably so. She coaxed breezes to stir the air around the graves. Dorian didn't interfere with them, but he kept every drop of water locked up in the ice. Kay worried her lip. They wouldn't be able to take a bone from Margaret until the ice was gone. How could she remove it when Dorian guarded it so fiercely? Maybe the men would have to pound the dirt with large hammers, as they'd suggested. That seemed like it would take too long and also attract the villagers. Was there a way to distract Dorian long enough for her to steal a bone?

"Kay, wake up," Gwen said, shaking her shoulder. "We're here."

"I wasn't asleep. I was trying to remove that ice block."

"Did it work?" Jenna asked.

"How long are we planning to stay here?" Ysabel scooped up Lathtin and stared upward at the bare treetops.

"As long as it takes." Gwen held onto the carriage door as she eased herself out. "So let's make ourselves comfortable first."

Jenna scrambled to catch the luggage as Jon handed it down. "Why bother? Once we link, the four of us should be able to overpower Dorian's magic in a heartbeat."

"I don't think it will be that easy," Kron said, pulling out a stack of blankets. "Remember, he's allied with Salth and Salthaath now. Their magic supply is much vaster than ours."

Kay nodded. "I could feel that during the most recent Chaos Season. It was like a thread reaching all the way to Selath."

"If we could just cut that thread somehow...." Gwen murmured.

"If we could, we wouldn't have to worry about Chaos Season to begin with." Jenna huffed as she set a trunk down.

Kay unpacked a pot and a bag of beans. If she warmed the water while they soaked, she could cook the beans tonight. Kron spread out more blankets, joining them at the edges and stiffening them so they formed a shelter. Jon helped Kron place them. Jenna gathered fallen branches while Ysabel unhitched the horses. Only Gwen stood apart, idle, watching the others as she covered her dead hand with her good one.

"Gwen, just because you were born noble doesn't mean you're above doing chores," Jenna said. "Especially since this was your idea."

"By the Four, I'm not sure what I can do with one hand." Gwen glared straight at Jenna. "I have trouble enough buttoning my dress in the morning."

"Why don't you gather firewood? You can drag it over there."

Gwen scowled, but she grabbed a big branch Jenna had ignored.

"That one's still too green," Jenna said. "It'll make the fire all smoky."

"Very well." Gwen dropped it. "I'll set up the shelter." She stalked inside the house of blankets.

Kay grabbed the skillet and searched for water, glad for an excuse to get away from her bickering sisters. When she returned, Ysabel released the horses and came over to her with a bag of grain. "We'd better do something to calm them before they start fighting in earnest," she whispered.

"You're much better at it than I am," Kay whispered back.

"I still have to feed the horses and start flatcakes. Can't you try it?"

Kay winced, unsure how to refuse. "What do you think I should say?"

Ysabel scooped out some of the water before Kay could add the beans. "Remind them we shouldn't be fighting each other when Salth and Sal-thaath are our true enemies. We have to work together if we're going to retrieve Margaret's bone."

Kay nodded. That sounded reasonable. As for whom she should approach first, Gwen was the less volatile of the two.

Kron had built the shelter off to the side of the clearing. Inside, it was so dark Kay stumbled on a corner of a rug. She righted herself and created a ball of lightning to hover in the air. Gwen sat in a corner, half-heartedly sorting belongings.

"I wonder if Kron can make beds for us too," she said.

Kay examined the materials Gwen had brought out, mostly extra cloaks. Kron could put objects to many strange uses or change their size or shape, but he'd never changed one thing into something completely different. "Do you really think he can do it?"

Gwen sighed. "Probably not. It would be lovely if we dared portal back to the One Oak or Wistica, though I suppose there's nothing in either place that will help us remove that ice."

Kay squatted next to her. "If all of us work together...."

"Against Salth and Dorian combined?"

"But if we can cut off their flow of power, or distract them...."

"The only one who could possibly distract Dorian would be Margaret herself," Gwen said bitterly. "How are we going to connect with her if we have nothing to draw her to us?"

"There must be something around here we could use," Kay said. "Or even someone related to her."

"How could we use a relative without telling them what we were doing? Unless we managed to buy a souvenir from someone..." Gwen peered into her trunk and let the lid fall with a loud thump. "By the Four, my brain must be frozen. There are other things of Margaret's left at the One Oak or in Wistica. Probably items belonging to all of the other absent Avatars as well."

Jenna, still in men's clothing, entered the shelter, grabbed some moonflow rags from her trunk, and left, all without speaking to either of them or even looking at them. Kay, like Gwen, watched her silently. It didn't matter that Jenna had cut her hair or changed her wardrobe; her posture and carriage still remained feminine and confident, unmistakable. Gwen's paralyzed hand also made her distinctive, as did Ysabel's Selathen complexion. Of all of them, Kay was the least likely to be noticed, and she remembered very well what it was like to have to act meek and let someone else give her orders, something neither Gwen nor Jenna would tolerate.

Kay searched through her trunk for her plainest dress, then pulled a torn apron from her workbasket. "Kron should be familiar enough with the One Oak to create a portal anywhere in the house, yes?"

"The public rooms, but not our suites," Gwen replied, sitting up. The light returned to her eyes. "What are you planning to do?"

"If I return to the One Oak as a maid, I can search for something else of Margaret's I can use to reach her."

"Good idea," Gwen said. "I recommend adding a cap to your disguise. Some of the maids keep their hair short, but not as short as yours."

"I should be able to make one." Kay rummaged in her workbasket for suitable material.

Gwen muttered something about seeing if Jenna needed her and slipped out. *Maybe they'd be kinder to each other now that we have a plan.*

A few hours later, Kay had created a maid outfit. Kron adjusted the color and appearance of the fabric to match the uniform. Gwen knew the details of the maids' uniforms, since she was the most involved with the day-to-day running of the One Oak. Once she pronounced Kay's appearance suitable, she pulled a gold chain out of her neckline and searched through a ring of keys. "I sent most of Margaret's things to her children," she said. "But there was a journal and other papers she wanted left behind at the One Oak."

"Are you sure I should take them? They must be important."

Gwen raised her eyebrow. "More important than our current task? I don't know what's in those papers, but it must be Avatar business. There's nothing better to draw her to you."

"Are they in the Spring Study?" Kay asked.

Gwen jangled the keys as she flipped them over. "No. I didn't want them mixed up with my journals, but I couldn't send them to the Archives in Midpoint. So I had them stored in the attic."

"Before or after the lightning strike?"

At the end of a recent Chaos Season, just when Kay had thought she'd tamed the storm completely, lightning had struck the One Oak and caused a small fire. She was sure Dorian had caused it, but she had no idea what would make him attack his long-time home like that.

"Unfortunately, before. Ah, here's the key." Gwen showed her a brass key with the word "Attic" engraved on the top. "Could you take it off the chain, please? Anyway, Kron said that although the roof was damaged, the rest of the attic was fine. The papers are wrapped in white linen and sealed with red wax with the official Spring Avatar stamp."

"But you just left this cloth package out in the open?" Kay asked.

"Of course not. It's in one of Margaret's trunks. There are yellow tulips on the lid, and her initials are carved in the middle." Gwen searched through her key ring again. "Freeze it, I don't have the key with me. It's on the set of secondary household keys."

"I didn't realize we had that many locks at the One Oak," Kay said.

"Hopefully not so many secrets." Gwen gave her a wry smile. "The second set of keys is in the top drawer of my dresser, where I keep my hair pins and ribbons. I don't remember what the trunk key looks like, so you'll have to try them all."

Kay bit back a sigh. This simple errand was becoming more complicated than she'd expected.

They left the tent. Jenna and Ysabel approached Kay while Kron determined where to place a portal. "If you're going to the One Oak, could you go to my suite and bring back some more stockings?" Ysabel asked. "I could use them to help stay warm."

"I could use some more rags and unmentionables too," Jenna said.

"By the Four, I'm not even planning to visit my own suite," Kay said, glaring at them. "As soon as I find Margaret's papers, I plan to portal back here. We don't want to leave the portal open long enough for a real maid to stumble through."

Kron created a portal using the harnesses from the horses. While he stiffened them so they would stand up and form a door, Jon came over to Kay. "By the Four, why are you dressed like a maid?" he asked. "Are you going somewhere? Should I put on a disguise too?"

She shook her head. "I'm just retrieving something from the One Oak. It'll be easier if no one recognizes me."

"Do you want me to come with you?"

She wanted to tell him there was no need and that his presence would only make her errand more difficult, but she remembered how upset he'd been earlier when he thought he was useless. "Perhaps you can stand watch for me."

Kay couldn't force much enthusiasm into her voice, but Jon ignored her flat tone. "I'd be happy to do so."

"Where can we find him a footman's uniform out here?" Gwen asked.

"She's right," Kay said. "I have nothing to alter your clothes with."

"I don't think I can get all of the details exact as Kay can, but at least I can change the color of his clothes so they resemble a uniform," Kron said.

After a few alterations, Jon wore black pants with a white shirt and black vest. The poor tailoring would never fool Kay or the head housekeeper but might stand up to a quick glance by another servant. Kron even managed to create a four-colored design of an oak in different seasons to match the One Oak's insignia. Maids weren't required to wear them, but Kay had seen one on the lapel of the coachman's jacket on previous drives around Wistica.

Kay adjusted her cap. "I suppose we're ready."

Kron activated the portal, and she and Jon stepped through. Kron had found a quiet staircase in the Spring Wing. Kay glanced around to make sure they hadn't been noticed. It was mid-afternoon, a time when the upstairs servants would be finished cleaning the rooms. If the Avatars were in residence and formally dressing for dinner, the servants would be busy preparing their wardrobes. What would the servants be doing when the Avatars weren't at home?

Kay tested the air current in the hall between her and Gwen's suite. As still as a stone. She crept down the hallway, wincing as Jon's heavy steps behind her made the floorboards creak. "Stay on the carpets!" She kept her voice low.

Jon caught up with her. "What did you say?"

"I said, stay on the carpets! You'll make less noise that way."

"Oh." He looked down at the blue-and-gold carpet. "Are you sure that's allowed?"

"By the Four, of course it is! Now let's hurry."

Gwen's suite was at the end of the hall. Kay eased the door open, and Jon covered his face. "I suppose I should stay out here. You know, keep watch."

"Yes, thank you."

She darted to the dresser and yanked on the drawer. It stuck. Freeze it, why hadn't Jenna or Kron come along? Either of them could have fixed the drawer. The air in here didn't seem humid, but Kay pulled moisture out of it anyway. The dry air didn't affect the wood, so she conjured more lightning and peered through the cracks.

Something seemed to be caught between the top of the drawer and the rest of the dresser. Kay searched for something thin but sturdy enough to push the object out of the way. Gwen's comb didn't fit, and a hair ribbon forgotten on the dresser was too flimsy. Inspiration struck as Kay noticed a jug with water. She dampened the ribbon, then froze it so it was stiff as a knife. With a little maneuvering, she unblocked the drawer and pulled it open. Jeweled pins, more ribbons, and even a few hair curlers were organized into separate compartments, but she didn't see a key ring. She picked through each section in turn, trying not to rearrange everything. On the second pass through the ribbons, she found it. This key ring was even heavier than the one Gwen had worn.

Kay took the set, closed the drawer, and was about to rejoin Jon in the hallway when she heard footsteps too light to be his. She crouched down behind the dresser. No one could see her from the hallway, but she couldn't see what was happening out there either. She strained to listen.

A woman let out a little scream. "By the Four, I didn't see you! What are you doing up here? Dame H'even will have a fit. You should be downstairs helping the others."

"The butler sent me," Jon said. "I'm just checking if any of the rooms need more firewood brought up."

"By the Four Gods and Goddesses, why now? We don't know when the Avatars will be back, if ever." The maid sniffed. "Do you think they'll return? This is a good place, and I'd hate to lose it."

"Of course they'll return," Jon replied. "Why wouldn't they?"

"Then you don't believe the newspapers stories about the entire quartet vanishing overnight? It sounds like something the Artificer Avatar would do. Do you think he did it on purpose or accident? The other maids say he's in love with the Fall Avatar, so maybe he wanted to take her away and the others had to stop him."

"Dama—"

The maid continued, "Or maybe he's from another country and here to steal our Avatars away. I wish I knew what to believe. Master Pippen and Dame H'even won't let us talk about them, but I've noticed how worried they look these days."

"I swear by All Four Gods and Goddesses the Avatars are only doing what the Four want them to," Jon said.

"Oh, thank the Four! I do hope they come back soon. The cooks make much better meals when they're home."

Jon shuffled his feet. "Yes, well, I'd better check the rest of the rooms in this wing." His voice grew louder. "You didn't need anything in the Ava Spring's suite, did you? Everything seemed in order when I was in there."

Kay crouched lower.

"Ah yes, ah—you must be new here. What's your name?"

"Jon."

It was a common enough name. Maybe the maid wouldn't connect it to Kay's beau.

"Well, Jon, if you'll move along to the next room, I'll just nip in here and check if the Ava Spring left behind anything that needs to be taken care of."

"I didn't see anything out of place."

The maid's tone grew cooler. "What I need to search for wouldn't be left in plain sight."

By the Four, what did she mean? How thoroughly would she search the room? Kay glanced around, searching for a new hiding place. The closest one was under the bed. She dropped to her belly and squeezed herself under the wood bed frame, mentally cursing every pastry and cup of chocolate she'd consumed over the last several moons. Despite her thicker body, her head gave her the most trouble. As the door opened wider, she covered her face with the thick bed cover and prayed for Winter to hide her.

Inhaling the smell of wool, she peered through the weave. The maid's slippers whisked across the floor. She visited the wardrobe first, then crossed to the bed. Kay jerked her head away as the maid almost kicked her. By the Four, her sister Avatars probably heard her heartbeat all the way in Bent Hook! The maid visited a couple more spots in the room before leaving. Kay waited to make sure she was gone. Another, heavier set of footsteps approached her. She squirmed.

"By the Four, Kay, where are you?" Jon lifted the bed cover. "I can't believe you can fit under there." He offered her a hand to help her to her feet. "Did you find it?"

"I have it right here—oh, freeze it! Where'd it go?" She had to crawl back under the bed to retrieve the keys. Dust clung to her, and she gave the keys to Jon while she brushed herself off. "Dame H'even wouldn't be pleased to see this."

He chuckled. "I'd love to see you explain to her what you were doing under the Ava Spring's bed. This floor should be clear for now, but a footman will be along soon to polish and refill the wall sconces. We should hurry."

Kay nodded. "Let's go find Margaret's old trunk."

They rushed along the corridor to the Winter Wing, heedless of the noise. The staircase to the attic was at the end of the hall, behind an unlocked door. There were no sconces on the walls, so she summoned several small lighting balls and made them float above her head.

"By All Four Gods and Goddesses! Kay, I didn't know you could do that."

"It's an easy way to create light." She hurried up the stairs, keeping her face from him.

Jon clamped. "You should have used them in Rainbow River. Think of all the chals you could have saved on candles."

"Salth would have known where I was."

"But the Four would have protected you! Of course," he said thoughtfully, "If you'd used your magic, everyone would have known you were the Winter Avatar. They'd have sent you to the One Oak, and you'd been lost to me forever."

Despite the serious nature of her errand, Kay smiled. At least her magic didn't frighten Jon.

"How powerful is this Salth?" Jon asked. "Is it true she's the one responsible for Chaos Season?"

Kay nodded.

"So many storms, year after year…Is she stronger than the Avatars?"

"Stronger than all twelve of us put together, according to Kron."

"Then how can you defeat her? Wouldn't it be best to continue as you always have?"

Kay reached the top stair. She turned to look back at him. For once, they were nearly at eye level to each other. "We can't ignore her," she replied. "Her attacks are becoming less predictable, even stronger." She didn't want to tell him her suspicions about Dorian having joined forces with Salth. "If we don't put an end to Salth and Chaos Season, one day, we may not be able to tame it at all. What would happen to Challen then?"

Jon reached out to her. "But if she killed you once…."

"She's already done her worst." Kay lifted her chin, hoping if she acted brave, she'd feel braver than she really did. "It's time we showed her why the Four reign in Challen, isn't it?"

She didn't wait for his answer, but turned and cast her lighting balls into every corner, taking care they didn't set anything on fire. Kron must have repaired all the damage done by the previous fire; the roof beams were smooth and intact. Small circular windows at each end of the attic let in gray light. Heaped everywhere were forgotten things: coronation gowns embroidered with gold and draped on mannequins, broken chairs and bed frames, dented kitchen pots, a rocking horse missing its ears and tail, and trunks. Some were small and plain, abandoned by servants from another generation. Bigger ones were property of absent Season Avatars. Although Kay could smell pines and dust, the attic was cleaner than she'd expected. Perhaps Dorian's attack had blown the cobwebs away.

Jon stooped under the sloping roof as he came to her. He whistled. "All these are things the Avatars don't want anymore?"

"I suppose we should sort through everything and see what can be repaired or given away." Kay's fingers itched to stroke the gowns, though they looked old enough to disintegrate if she wasn't careful. "But that should wait for some other season. We're looking for Margaret's trunk. It has yellow tulips and the initials MgG on the lid."

"It's a good thing I'm here to help you move trunks," Jon said.

Kay nodded, though she thought that if Margaret's trunk had been used a few moons ago, it shouldn't be hard to find. She headed for the closest group of trunks. To her surprise, it wasn't there. She examined the others, trying to determine if they were from recent or older quartets. A couple of the names— Jeanne and Kylar —brought back memories from a life over a hundred years ago.

She sighed. "Jon, I think you'll have to help me look for more recent trunks. Margaret's quartet held Sophia and Charles in addition to her husband, Dorian. We need to find trunks with the initials SvE, CvE, and DgG to find hers."

He studied the group for a moment. "Maybe not." He took a few steps to the right. "I thought so! Someone arranged these trunks by order of the first initial."

"What?" She checked again as she realized she stood in front of a series of J and K trunks, including Jenna's infamous incarnation of Jacob. "Who would do that? We never organize things that way!"

"Maybe Kron did it when he repaired the roof."

Kay scoffed as she passed him. "You've never seen his workshop. No one else can make any sense of where he puts things, but he always seems to find what he needs."

Kay wished she had Kron's talent. She should be very close to Margaret's trunk, if not in front of it, but she didn't see a trunk with yellow tulips on the lid. There were two with other types of decorations and one that looked as if it had been in a fire. The lid was scorched so badly she could still smell ashes. Why had anyone even bothered to save this trunk? How could they even tell this one belonged with the Ms...

Freeze it. Kay bent her head until it nearly touched the trunk and rubbed the burned sections. Charcoal stained her hands, along with specks of yellow paint. She ran her fingertips over the center. When she found carvings, she traced them. Half of what could have been an M. Next to it, an arc.

Kay pulled out the key ring she had taken from Gwen's dresser and tried to fit the first key into the lock. It didn't fit. She tried a few more before realizing the problem wasn't with the keys, but the lock. It was partially melted. Only a lightning strike could have been so hot. It was amazing Margaret's trunk hadn't been completely destroyed. Dorian must have exercised great control to exact such specific damage, especially as a spirit acting at a distance. For a moment, some of her old self-doubt returned. Could she have managed anything like this?

No, she told herself firmly. *Not because I lack magic or skill, but because unlike Dorian, I have the decency not to do such things.* "Jon," she called. "This has to be Margaret's trunk, but the lock is damaged. Can you help me open it?"

"Let me look." He whistled as he stared at the trunk. "By the Four, it looks like someone shoveled it into the burner by mistake. What happened?"

"Dorian."

"But, if this is his wife's trunk, why would he damage it?"

Kay sighed. "I have no idea, especially since I think he did this last moon, after he died." She quickly told Jon about the attack on the One Oak, though it was hard not to blame herself for failing to stop it.

Jon let out a low whistle. "By the Four, I never realized how dangerous Chaos Season was for the Avatars. I know you can manage it," he added hurriedly. "You've been doing so for lifetimes. But you shouldn't have to do it.

"If this trip of ours is successful, we might not have to worry about Chaos Season for much longer." Kay tried to get her fingers under the lid, but her nails were too short. "Do you think you can break this open?"

"Are you sure we're allowed to?"

"The only other idea I can think of is blasting the frozen trunk with lightning."

"Then I'll do it. I just need to find something for that lock."

Jon prowled the attic; Kay set one of her lightning balls to follow him so he had enough light. If he realized what she was doing, he didn't comment. He returned with a short strip of metal.

"If we can brace the trunk, I might be able to force the lid off," he said.

They tried sandwiching the trunk between others, but in the end, Kay had to get behind the trunk and hold it while Jon pried the lid. He tore the locking mechanism out of the damaged wood. As Kay stood, he grinned at her. "Guess I was useful after all."

"You were indeed." The admission made his grin even wider, and Kay wished they had time for her to show him how much she appreciated his strength. Perhaps if they hurried, she'd find an opportunity to do so at the camp.

Jon's smile faded as he stared at the trunk. "Stowaway, what exactly were you looking for in here? I hope it was nothing flammable."

He drew back to let her open the lid. Inside were piles of charred scrolls in some ancient language, modern-looking journals with holes in the middle, and broken piles of clay statues that looked as old as the scrolls. Kay reached for a journal and flipped through the singed pages. Fragments caught her eye—"a plague swept through the land," "many people starved," "orphans were sold." She shook her head as she closed the book. Challen hadn't experienced any such calamities since she'd become a Season Avatar eight hundred years ago. Where or when had these events taken place? If they were associated with the scrolls and statues, then they were from the time before the Four. Why would Margaret hide them in an attic instead of donating them to the University for proper storage and study? Kay lifted the journals from the trunk and sorted through the clay pieces. Most of them were their natural color, but a few of them bore traces of green or yellow paint. Dark brown pieces etched with short lines looked like animal heads and legs, but she couldn't identify what kind they were. Kay emptied out the trunk, then directed lightning balls to hover over it so she could spot any tiny glittering gems on the bottom. Nothing. This entire trip had been a waste of time. How could she summon Margret's spirit with anything from here?

"Did you find what you were looking for?" Jon asked.

She shook her head, too discouraged to speak, and tossed everything back in the trunk. She ought to feel guilty for being so rough with historical items, but instead it was satisfying to watch the clay items crumble further. Something about them bothered her, but she couldn't identify what it was.

"It's all right," Jon said as he scooped up an armful of scrolls. "There are plenty of other trunks you can try."

Kay shook her head. "No. I was looking specifically for Margaret's things. Unless...." Margaret wasn't the only absent Avatar. Excluding Dorian, there were six others, including a third Winter Avatar last incarnated as Olivia ava Kalt. Maybe Kay should try summoning her spirit. They were affiliated with the same god and had taught each other in previous lives. She would be a better choice than Margaret.

Kay left the last journal out and sprang up to find a trunk labeled OaK. She smiled when she saw the word inscribed on a painting of a bare oak tree. Her smile faltered when she realized the trunk was locked, but after trying half of the keys on Gwen's ring, she managed to open it. The contents of this trunk were more promising: a formal blue gown, decorated with crystal beads, that Olivia might have worn to her wedding; clippings of fine hair tied with ribbons; and a locket that opened to show sketches of two young children. Kay claimed the locket. As she did so, the breeze outside became a gust, then a gale. For a heartbeat, Kay thought

Olivia disapproved of the locket theft. *No, she wouldn't mind. This must be Dorian.*

"We have to return to the others," she said. "It's Chaos Season."

Jon nodded and grabbed the journal. They dashed back downstairs. A couple of maids stopped to gape at them. Kay wondered if they recognized her, but she didn't ask. She raced through the portal, followed by Jon.

CHAPTER TEN

Kay Makes a Snowman

"Kron, close the portal!" Kay called as she landed back in the clearing. Lightning flashed overhead. The sky was dark gray, but there was still enough light for her to see Gwen, Jenna, Ysabel, and Lathtin gathered around Jenna's sapling. Hail fell as she ran to them, but it only took a thought to make the stones veer away from her and her sister Avatars. A tree sprouted right in front of her, forcing her to dodge. She stumbled, regained her balance, and joined her quartet.

Did you find it? Gwen asked.

Kay shook her head. *Nothing personal of Margaret's. I found something of Olivia's that might work.*

Despite the Chaos Season in progress, the others asked, *What is it? What about Margaret's trunk?* The fastest way to answer them was to share her memories of the attic. It took only a couple of heartbeats.

So, Dorian didn't just attack the One Oak, but he deliberately destroyed his wife's belongings? By All Four, why? Ysabel asked.

Kay bit down her envy at Dorian's incredible long-distance precision. *He must have thought the ancient items would be helpful to us, so he wanted to make sure we couldn't use them.*

It's a shame Kron didn't go with you, Gwen said. *Maybe he could have identified the items. Hopefully the journal will give us some clues.*

Yes, but we should tame this Chaos Season first.

Kay stretched her attention to the sky, absorbing magic and passing it to Gwen, who shared it as needed between Ysabel and Jenna. Together, the four made short work of the storm. Kay stretched her attention to Bent Hook, the One Oak, and other towns affected by the Chaos Season. Shutters had been torn off houses, a roof had caved in, and several trees had toppled over, some of them precariously close to buildings. The damage could have been much worse. Still, she was tired of having to tame storms that always happened at the worst time.

Gwen dropped the link and gave Kay a wan smile. "I think we'll all be happier if we can eliminate Chaos Season. But right now, all I want is dinner and a chance to read that journal."

"A couple of deer were killed nearby," Ysabel said sadly. "I'll bring back a haunch or two. They'll round out the beans and flatcakes."

Jenna rose. "I should be able to forage some herbs or other edible plants."

Kay clasped Olivia's locket around her own neck for safekeeping, then followed them out of the shelter. Snow had fallen, enough to cover the tops of her boots. The shadows cast by the trees told her it was already near sunset. She eyed the snow wistfully. It was wet enough to pack well. A few minutes of playing with it would allow her mind to clear.

She created a few snowballs, grinning as she targeted a nearby tree and hit its trunk every time. When this was all over, she and the other three Season Avatars could return to the One Oak. It would be a magnificent setting for a snowball fight. She doubted the other three would let her have one, since her magic gave her an advantage. It was a shame Olivia hadn't been reborn yet so they could duel each other. Dorian would make the mock fight real. Kay scowled as she thought of her tormentor. If he was here right now, she'd finally be brave enough to stand up to him and complain about his lifetimes of abuse. The snow gave her another idea, however.

She retrieved one of her snowballs and rolled it back and forth until it was tall enough to reach her waist. She left the ball at the edge of the clearing and set about making the middle part of her snow man. By the time Kay managed to lift it onto the bigger ball, Jenna returned with a woven grass basket of mushrooms and wild plants.

"By the Four, Kay, what are you doing? Shouldn't you be cooking or helping Gwen—hey!"

Kay grinned as she smacked Jenna in the face with a snowball. Jenna might be the best of them when it came to stick fighting, but Kay's knowledge of air currents—and her ability to manipulate them—gave her the edge in snowball fighting.

"You frozen fool!" Jenna sputtered as she wiped the snow from her eyes. "What do you think this is, the soltrans? I'll show you which season is best!"

"Your season can't win this time of year, Jenna."

"I don't care." She set the basket by a tree, scooped up her own snowball, and threw it at Kay, who dodged before it could land. "Cheater. Stop enchanting the snow against me."

Kay hadn't thought of it before, but now that she had the idea, it took a heartbeat to pull moisture out of Jenna's snowballs so they wouldn't stay together. After a few tries, Jenna gave up. "Never mind. I'll push you in the snow instead."

She raced after her, forcing Kay to twist and turn. Kay was surer-footed in the snow, but Jenna's longer stride allowed her to gain ground quickly. By unspoken agreement, they both stayed within the clearing. With Kron's shelter taking up most of the space, there wasn't much room left to dodge.

Jenna caught up to Kay as she cornered around her half-finished snowman. "Ha!" she cried as she jumped.

"No! Not here!"

Too late. Jenna pushed Kay into the snowman. The snow cushioned her fall even as it crept up her sleeves and into every crevice. It didn't feel cold, but the damp clothing ruined her mood.

"Freeze it, Jenna, I wasn't done." Kay brushed snow off of her clothes.

"You started it. Why are you making a snowman anyway?"

Kay sighed. "I was going to curse at him as if he was Dorian."

"Oh." Jenna stared at the chunks of snow. "He deserves it. Do you want some help rebuilding him?"

She shook her head. "I need to address him Avatar to Avatar."

"That's too bad. Snowmen are artifacts, aren't they? Maybe Kron's magic would help."

"I don't expect this snowman to walk all the way to the Dead Land. Once I'm done with it, the wind will carry my words to Dorian."

"And freeze him forever, I hope."

Jenna claimed her basket and entered the shelter. Kay repaired the snowman and finished the head. She broke up pine branches into short lengths and laid them on the snowman's head for the hair. Bark chips made a pair of eyes, a nose, and a frowning mouth. Kay didn't bother giving him arms. She stepped back and regarded her creation. If Kron were turning the snowman into an artifact, he would probably find some personal belonging of Dorian's and mold the snowman's body around it. Nothing would happen if Kay tried that. The only way she could think of to communicate with the absent Avi Winter was through the weather.

Kay glanced around to make sure no one else was listening. Then she stepped up to the snowman. Lowering her voice, she said, "Dorian, by the Four Gods and Goddesses of Challen, I don't know why your soul isn't frozen yet, but it should be. You've been cruel to me in every life as far back as I can remember. You weren't even kind to Charles and Sophia. Did you really think you made Margaret a good husband? How could you burn her belongings? Why didn't your wife invoke Fall's wrath on you? Why did Winter even choose you as one of us? I'll never understand the Four!"

The wind howled, attempting to batter her. For once, though, Kay felt strong enough to face Dorian. She narrowed her eyes and focused her will, calming the weather in the clearing.

"Now you listen to me, Dorian." She thrust a finger into the snowman's face. "If I could, I'd freeze your soul forever. I'd burn your body until nothing but ashes was left, and then I'd dance on them before scattering them in the Salt Waters. But Ysabel says we need a bone from every Avatar, even you. That includes your wife, Margaret. If you don't let us take one of her fingerbones, we'll...we'll...we'll have her journals published in the newspaper so everyone can read them."

Thunder snapped overhead.

"We will too!" she countered. "Now, you behave, for once in all of your lives. I'm the Winter Avatar now, and my sister Avatars and I won't let you hurt us any longer. I swear it by Spring, Summer, Fall, and Winter."

Kay plunged her hands into the snowman and melted it in heartbeats. If only she had dared say half that much to the real Dorian while he was still alive, he wouldn't have attacked her.

All these years I worried about dying. I never thought it would be so freeing to experience it and know I no longer have to face it with fear.

Buoyant, she examined the weather at Margaret's grave. The ice covering it was gone.

Kay returned to the shelter to tell the others. Before she could speak, Gwen grasped her by the hand and led her to a pile of blankets.

"No, I'm not tired," she protested. "We can go get Margaret's bone now."

She fell asleep the heartbeat she lay down.

CHAPTER ELEVEN

Revisiting Margaret's Grave

Kay roused herself as something soft batted her face. Without opening her eyes, she tried to knock it away, but it kept tapping at her. As she was about to tell it to leave her alone, she smelled roast meat and fresh flatcakes. Hunger pangs forced her to sit up and look around. Lathtin bounded away from her. Kron's light-producing artifacts glowed in the corners of the shelter. Her sister Avatars, along with Kron and Jon, sat on the other side of the shelter, gathered around a bowl. Ysabel was the only one absent.

Jon and Gwen came over to her; Jon had to stoop to keep his head from brushing against the ceiling. "Feel better?" Gwen asked as she passed a plate of food to Kay.

Her head still felt wool-addled, but she nodded. "I'll feel even better once I eat. How long did I sleep?"

"Only a few hours. It's close to midnight." Jon grinned as he brushed his lips against her cheek. Gwen didn't comment on the impropriety. "I feel like I'm back on the locomotives again covering the night shift," he continued.

"We decided we'd check Margaret's grave at night, when everyone in town should be sleeping," Gwen said. "Are you sure we'll be able to retrieve her bone now?"

"The ice is gone," Kay said confidently.

Ysabel entered the tent. "I wish we knew what to do with the bones once we collect them all," she said as she sat next to Kay. "Will the locket help us now that the diamond is gone?"

"I haven't had a chance to try it yet. Maybe tomorrow night." Kay wondered if her hunch was correct and Olivia would be better tuned to her than Margaret. After her previous failures, it would be nice to have something go right for once. "What about the journal, Gwen? Have you had a chance to go through it yet?"

"It would be easier to put my hand through it than to read it. All I can do is pick out fragments here and there." Gwen frowned. "It's not enough to explain why Dorian wanted to burn it."

Jenna put her plate aside and dug through their supplies for a tin of powdered chocolate. Someone must have melted snow earlier, as she mixed some of the chocolate into a bowl of water. "I'll wager a new dress it was the tale of how Dorian courted Margaret."

"I still don't know what she could have possibly seen in him," Kay grumbled.

"Then you should take a closer look at his portrait sometime. He wasn't ill-favored when he was young."

"There's more to a man than his looks." Gwen absently scratched behind Lathtin's ears before taking another bite of stew. She had to set her fork down between bites so she could use her good hand for both tasks. Kay wondered why Lathtin was spending more time with Gwen than with Ysabel.

"Yes, what would you like in a husband?" Jenna passed the bowl of chocolate to Gwen, watching her intently.

"Don't we have any cups?" Gwen set her plate aside while she rummaged through the supplies. Lathtin remained calmly in place.

"I don't think so. We'll have to share. So, share your preferences, Gwen. Fair, dark, strong arms, a chiseled jaw?"

"By the Four, it doesn't matter, does it?" Gwen sighed. "He should be able to manage the lo Havil estate and give me heirs. He doesn't need a fine jaw to do that."

Jenna waggled her eyebrows. "He might for the second half of it."

Kron nudged Jon. "I think we should start preparing to leave. We'll pack everything except what we need right now."

Once the men left, Ysabel said, "By the Four, Jenna, you're taking this conversation in an improper direction. No wonder the men left. Save this chatter for the link."

Kay glanced longingly back at the door. She still hadn't had an opportunity to find a private place and kiss Jon as if they were back in Rainbow River.

"Gwen, are you sure you want to marry a man in this life?" Jenna pressed closer to her. "Or are you going to be a Fallswoman?"

Gwen glanced at Lathtin for a heartbeat. "I just want someone whom I can talk to, someone clever enough to make witty conversation and doesn't mind listening to me talk about my patients. Someone warm and—by the Four, someone available!" She shoved the bowl of chocolate back at Jenna, sloshing it on the blankets. "Here. I'm not thirsty. I have to…to…find someplace private."

She left. Lathtin glanced at her, brushed against Ysabel, and followed her.

"By All Four Gods and Goddesses." Jenna turned to Ysabel. "Are they…attached to each other?"

She nodded, her eyes suddenly bright. "Ever since Lathtin regained his human memory, he's been able to link with Gwen as well as me. They've been spending a lot of time together on this journey. It's not as if Gwen can help much with her frozen hand."

"By the Four." Jenna's oath this time was much quieter. "But Ysabel, he's not even human anymore."

"Maybe Kron can make him human again, once we don't have to worry about Chaos Season any longer," Ysabel said. "He told me he's done so in the past. Of course, with Lathtin being my ani-link, that complicates the situation. What would happen to my magic if he does become human? You know how much Fall loathes men."

"I suppose I should apologize to Gwen for my thoughtlessness," Jenna said.

Kay nodded. "She'd appreciate that. But you know how Gwen always wants us to focus on our tasks. Maybe we should portal to Margaret's grave and retrieve her bone right away."

They devoured the last of the stew, folded up all the spare blankets, and left the shelter so Kron could dismantle it. Gwen waited near the carriage, with Lathtin curled on one shoulder. She nodded at them but didn't say anything. Lathtin jumped down and rubbed himself against Ysabel's ankles as if apologizing for his earlier neglect.

Kron broke the shelter down piece by piece until only a door frame remained standing. "Ysabel, could you please have your spies make sure no one is near Margaret's grave?"

She closed her eyes for a few heartbeats, then opened them and frowned. "An older man is keeping watch."

"Is he actually on watch, or is he sleeping?" Gwen asked.

"His eyes are open, but he's yawning."

Gwen rubbed her chin. "Ysabel, if you can ask some animals to create a distraction, I'll sneak up on him and send him to sleep."

"Is there anything I can do?" Jon asked.

"We might need you to shovel," Kay replied.

While he unpacked half of their belongings looking for a shovel—at least he didn't disturb their trunks—Kay searched ahead to see what she could do to help. The snow from the previous Chaos Season hadn't melted, and without sunlight, heating the snow would be difficult. Kay created a steady wind to blow it through cracks in the fence surrounding the grave and then out to sea. Maybe the drifting snow would make it harder for the old man to see Gwen. Once he was taken care of, Kay would find more ways to help her quartet.

"Freeze it, Kay, I can't see anything through the portal," Gwen complained. "Can you stop the wind?"

Everyone complains about the weather, even the Avatars you're trying to help. Kay obeyed, trying not to show her embarrassment.

Gwen watched the portal briefly before stepping through. As Jon finally returned with a shovel, she returned to beckon them all through. "I'll wait here and maintain the portal," Kron said.

"Is it safe to create a lightning ball?" Kay whispered.

"I think so, but make it tiny." Gwen sighed. "The way this season is heating up, someone will wake up to use the outhouse and see us."

Kay created another ball of lightning and set it to hover over Margaret's grave. The man lay sprawled in front of the gate, as if still trying to defend it. Jon dragged him off to the side, next to a bottle of whiskey. Gwen tested the gate. A simple latch without even a lock guarded it. Once inside, she bowed her head over the double grave. "Forgive us for trespassing on your rest, Margaret," she said. "You know we Avatars must serve the Four both in life and death. Dorian, we have no more reason to disturb you. Please leave us alone."

She stepped aside so Jon could enter. "Which side do I dig up?" he whispered.

Gwen pointed to the left side, where grass had grown in the moons since Margaret's burial. Jon started digging at the foot of the grave, first clearing the snow.

"Freeze it! Our footprints will be here in the morning!" Jenna said.

"Then we'd better melt them away." Gwen held out her arms, inviting them to link.

"Where am I supposed to send all of the water?" Kay asked. "I can't risk flooding the grave."

"Send it back into the clouds, I suppose."

The damp air made that difficult, but after having eaten and being able to borrow magic from the rest of the quartet, Kay managed it. She finished before Jon had reached the coffin. When he started to shovel more slowly, Gwen touched him, and he lifted dirt with more energy. Kay and the other Avatars retreated so he wouldn't fling it in their faces.

Finally, his shovel scraped wood. Jenna waited for him to clear part of the lid before gesturing him to step aside. "She's not...I mean, there's not going to be a bad smell, will there?" She wrinkled her nose in disgust.

"It's too cold for the odor to be much of a problem," Gwen assured her.

"Much of a problem? Just how much?"

Ysabel and Kay glanced at each other, then prudently stepped back. Kay found herself next to the old man. Something about his snoring didn't sound right to her. She created more light to examine him, and his face was contorted with pain. "Gwen, over here, now!"

She hurried over and swore. "It must be his heart. Oh Four, please don't take him now…Kay, Ysabel, link with me."

Kay observed as Gwen attempted to clear narrow blood vessels and coax a sluggish heart into beating regularly. Gradually the man's expression relaxed, but Gwen still frowned. "This isn't the first time he's suffered like this," she said after breaking the link. "I don't think he has more than a few moons left. He shouldn't remain outside, but I don't know where he lives."

"Try taking him back to the pub," Kay suggested.

"That's too far for us to carry him." She sighed. "Perhaps Kron can make a portal. Let me see how Jenna is doing."

While Jenna and Gwen argued over who should reach into the coffin and remove the bone, Ysabel brought Kron through to create a portal to the inn. Jon dropped the shovel and grabbed the sick man's shoes. "It's a good thing you Avas brought me along," he said, flexing his muscles. Jenna turned away from Gwen to reward him with one of her coy smiles. Kay gritted her teeth, telling herself she had no reason to feel jealous.

Gwen knelt in front of the grave for several heartbeats before climbing down into the hole Jon had made. Jenna laid down on the mixture of snow and dirt, letting her arms hang over the edge. It was difficult for her to find room in such a tiny place, and her feet stuck out of the gate. If she hadn't been wearing men's clothing, she would have caused a scandal, even close to dawn on the outskirts of a sleepy town. Ysabel and Kay hurried over to investigate.

"Help me hold onto her," Jenna said.

They braced her while she slowly slid down the hole. Loose dirt turned to mud and clung to their cloaks and boots. Kay winced in sympathy as Gwen probed inside Margaret's coffin with her good hand and tried to brace herself on her other arm. She was covered all over with mud and would need at least two baths to clean herself.

"Finally." Gwen pulled her fist out of the coffin. "Freeze it, I have no safe place to store the bone. Jenna, pass it to Ysabel."

"Is it…is it clean?"

"By the Four, yes. It's too late for you to be so squeamish."

"I volunteered to be an Avatar for plants, not bones. Especially people bones." Despite Jenna's grumbling, she took what Gwen handed to her and passed it to Ysabel. This bone appeared to be smaller than the finger bones they'd retrieved from the other Avatars. Ysabel tucked it into her reticule.

"What are you waiting for, Gwen?" Jenna reach back into the grave. "Are you getting another bone?"

"No, there was something else in her grip. I can't get it out, though. The hole's too small."

Thunder rumbled overhead. Kay glanced up at the clouds and directed the wind elsewhere. What would Margaret have taken to her grave? Dorian must have known about this.

"Maybe you should leave it there," Ysabel said.

"If Dorian tried to stop us from getting it, that makes it important." Kay braced herself for further weather challenges.

Kron came over to them. "Is there a problem?"

"Kron, could you open the coffin, please? I need to remove something else."

Jenna sighed. "I may as well see if I can rot the wood some more. I'm already a frozen mess." She pulled away from Ysabel's grasp and slid down into the hole, cursing as she landed on the coffin. A few heartbeats later, wood cracked, so loudly Kay looked around to see if anyone in Bent Hook had woken up. The air turned cold, but Kay forced the moisture to stay in the air just a little longer. They didn't need rain or snow to complicate this task any further.

"Got it!" Gwen whispered.

"Now to climb out of here," Jenna said.

Without asking, Kay froze the sides of the hole to make hand-holds for them. Kron and Jon squeezed into the fenced area around the grave to help them climb out. Gwen and Jenna brought half the dirt out with them, along with an oilcloth wrapped around a square—possibly another book. Jenna looked down at herself and laughed.

"What is it?" Gwen glared at her.

"I was just thinking this is the perfect disguise. The king would never recognize us if we portaled into his throne room looking like this."

Gwen looked down at her ruined clothes. "I suppose I should be glad my absent Aunt Gabri can't see me now. Kay, is there somewhere we can clean up? I don't want to track this dirt into the carriage."

Kay coaxed a warm drizzle out of the air, just over the two of them. Gwen shivered but didn't complain. Jenna made up for her. In the meantime, couple of badgers helped cover up the grave. Kron turned the shovel over to Jon, saying, "I have to create a portal on this side now." He selected some of the fence posts that had been damaged during the digging process and built a doorway back to their camp.

Ysabel glanced up from the badgers. "The chickens and dogs are telling me some people are stirring."

Gwen sighed as she tried to wipe the dirt off her face with an equally stained sleeve. "I don't think we'll have time to finish re-burying Margaret's grave." She turned toward the pile of mud.

"My deepest apologies for disturbing your rest, Sister Ava. Please don't be upset with us when we meet again—"

"The pub owner found the man!" Ysabel said. "They know he planned to spend the night out here. Someone will be headed out here any heartbeat."

"Freeze it," Gwen said. "Let's go."

As soon as Kron activated the portal, everyone started charging through it. Kay was one of the last to leave. As she glanced back toward Bent Hook, the sunrise starting to crest in the east, other lights came on in the village.

Only one more bone to collect, from Olivia ava Kalt, the Ava Win before Dorian. Kay didn't know for certain where she was buried, only that it was a mining town south of Rainbow River close to the Selathen border. If the native Challens of this town had been suspicious of them, the Selathens would sacrifice them all to Salth and Sal-thaath if they learned who they were.

CHAPTER TWELVE

Margaret's Journal

"By the Four, are we really going to take the carriage all the way to Black Rock?" Jenna complained. "Even if Kron doesn't know the town well enough to portal us there, isn't there a locomotive or a boat we can use? I'm going to be black and blue all over by the time we arrive!"

Two days of travel hadn't done much to temper anyone's mood. Although they'd all bathed and laundered clothes in a small lake, dirt clung to everything. Keeping the group warm was a constant drain on Kay's magic, which was slowly rebuilding after two days of sleeping as much as she could. They were between towns, so Ysabel and Jenna were foraging for food. While Ysabel was able to find them rabbits, fish, and once a deer, Jenna's contributions amounted to little more than mushrooms, herbs, and nuts. Kay was beginning to feel like she was back in Rainbow River, where she ran out of chals long before running out of appetite.

"If we don't find more grasses and hay for the horses, we'll have to walk to Black Rock," Ysabel said. "Gwen, you're our leader, so you think of a different plan."

Gwen sighed as she looked up from her journal. "There's not much to plan. We need either more supplies or a way for Kron to portal us to the final grave."

"How far is Tradetown from Black Rock?" Ysabel asked.

"It has to be closer than where we are now," Jenna muttered.

"Jenna's right; it is only a couple of days' journey to the mines," Gwen replied. "Unfortunately, Tradetown is also full of Avatar-hating Selathens."

"How can you be sure all of them hate the Four and Their Avatars?" Ysabel sat up straight. "My mother worked secretly in Tradetown for many years trying to encourage Selathen women to embrace the Four. Surely some of them would welcome us, or at least give us supplies. Kron could portal us to my family's old house in a heartbeat."

"We could sleep inside, on soft beds." Even Kay was getting tired of Kron's makeshift shelters.

"But is the house vacant, or has your father returned to claim it?" Gwen asked.

Ysabel gestured, and Lathtin rubbed his head against her hand. She closed her eyes. The horses pulling their cart slowed to a walk, but she didn't react. Abruptly she jerked her head. "Freeze it, there are people there. The crows recognize my father and some other Selathen men who aren't always kind to animals."

Kay repressed a groan, missing a proper dinner, bath, and bed more than ever.

"Kron, could you portal us to the hotel where we stayed in Tradetown?" Gwen asked. "Or the railroad station?"

He shook his head. "The hotel, maybe, but it would most likely be one of the public areas. I'd have to find some way to make us all invisible, and even that might not be safe enough."

Gwen pinched her nose. "They'd smell us instead."

Kay turned to Jon. He'd been to the railroad station several times; perhaps he knew a secluded spot where they could hide. But how could he describe the area well enough for Kron to portal there? Kron had to see a location first before he could create a portal to it. Once Gwen had sketched a farm so he could portal them there to clean up after a Chaos Season, but Jon couldn't draw as well as she could.

Kay scratched her head as she thought about Tradetown. She'd only been there twice, once when Gwen rescued Ysabel from Sal-thaath and a few moons later, when she and her sister Avatars had tried to track down Ysabel's father and the Selathens who wor-shipped Salth. She'd only been to the places the others had already mentioned, such as the train station, the hotel, and Ysabel's house. On the second visit, the Season Avatars hadn't even left Ysabel's family house. They'd stayed there while Kron had gone with the War Avatar, Charles, and Dorian to Ysabel's father's shop. The shop...

"Kron, you do know another place in Tradetown," she said. "The Honored Lathatilltin's watch shop. You could portal us there."

He stared at her for a heartbeat before saying, "But he'll be there."

"Ysabel just said he returned to their old house," Gwen pointed out. "What if we waited until nightfall and portaled there when the shop was closed? No one would see us then."

"He also had time traps scattered around the shop. If we run into one of those, we could be stuck for moons."

Ysabel smiled and put her hand on his arm. "But now that you know what they are, you can disarm them first."

Kron rubbed his chin. Unlike Jon, his beard wasn't growing in, or growing in too slowly to worry about on this trip. "Humm. Dearest, what do your little spies tell you?"

"The mice don't sense anything out of the ordinary."

Everyone looked at Gwen hopefully. "What will we do with the carriage and team of horses?" she asked. "I daresay we'll be noticed if we try to portal them into a shop."

"We'll have to hide them somewhere off road until I find a suitable place to bring them through. Perhaps there's another way to travel from Black Rock to Tradetown."

"A train?" Jenna asked longingly.

"It depends on how many chals I get when I sell off some of my family jewels," Gwen replied.

Jenna's eyes grew wide. "Are you sure you should do that?"

Gwen shrugged. "These are small pieces, not heirlooms."

What were trinkets to her would have been heirlooms for Kay's family. Still, she appreciated the gesture Gwen was making.

They drove along until late afternoon, where they found a secluded glen close to a spring and fodder for the horses. Jon and Kron unloaded the trunks, but they didn't set up the shelter. Gwen and Ysabel prepared a meal of fish and not-too-badly burned porridge. It was full dark, with a lightning ball and Kron's glowing artifacts enabling them to see, when Kron finally prepared the portal. He'd found a few boards of the proper length and already had them enchanted to stick together when he assembled them. All he had to do now to change the portal's destination was to erase the last set of chalk marks on the frame and replace them with new ones. It only took him a few heartbeats to update them. Kay, with everyone else, peered anxiously inside the portal. It was too dark on the other side to make out any other details.

Kay was about to create a lightning ball and send it through the portal when Ysabel said, "Let me have our furry friends explore the area again, just in case."

Lathtin twitched the tip of his tail, as if he planned to explore the shop for Ysabel's furry friends.

After a few heartbeats of standing in front of the portal with her eyes closed, Ysabel said, "I think the time traps are back. There are several areas the mice are avoiding, including one in front of the portal."

Kay took that as her cue to send her lightning ball into the shop, keeping it close to the floor to reduce the chance someone outside would see it. A long table with several watches in various stages of repair took up one wall of the room. Pails and bins of parts and tools were lined up next to it. Opposite the watchmaker's bench was a secretary desk similar to Gwen's back at the One Oak. A single chair stood centered between them. The only sound in the room was a chorus of *tick, tick*, as a dozen completed watches told time in unison.

Kay guided her ball up one side of the room and back down the other way, trying to see if she could identify the time traps. The air in this room was so still she was tempted to create a min-iature whirlwind in the center just to stir it up. Then she realized that a breeze and dust might help them see the time traps. The room itself was surprisingly clean, so she blew some dirt in from their side. Gradually, dust built up in several small circular piles next to the workbench and desk.

"Sal-thaath tried turning them invisible this time," Kron said. "I could have found the time traps with an artifact, but this way is faster. Thank you, Kay." Touching his satchel, he strode into the room and wrote something on each of the dust-coated watches. After the last one, he beckoned them forward. The group of six adults and a cat crowded the room as much as they did the make-shift shelter Kron built every night. Jenna glanced around, disappointment evident in her expression. "This doesn't seem like much of an improvement."

"At least we're out of the cold," Gwen said. "No offense, Kay and Kron, but I'm more comfortable with solid walls around me. We should see if we can find suitable rooms at a hotel or boarding house. Ysabel, are there any other hotels in Tradetown besides the one where we stayed?"

She shrugged. "I had little opportunity to explore the town. It was hard enough visiting the stable where Lathtin was reborn as my anilink. Selathens prefer their women to stay at home." She eyed Gwen and Kay critically. "You two are too fair to pass as Selathen women. We'll have to bundle you up so you're less no-ticeable."

"What about me?" Jenna asked.

"You don't look Selathen either, but if you can pass for a youth, they probably won't pay much attention to you."

Gwen claimed the single chair. "Maybe it would be best to have a small party go out, find us all rooms for the night, and then come back here. In the morning, we'll purchase supplies and plan how to travel to Tradetown." She pulled a couple of earrings, one with garnets and the other with pearls, from her reticule. "Do you think these will be enough?"

"Are you sure you want to sell them?" Ysabel asked. "They're so pretty!"

"The matching ones were lost years ago." Gwen cradled her paralyzed hand. "Just don't let them give you less than fifty chals each."

Ysabel weighed the jewels in her hand. "They'll try to give me less since I'm a woman. Kron, will you come with me? I can help interpret."

"Of course, Dearest."

"Hide your satchel," Gwen told him. "It's distinctive."

Kron nodded.

When they left, leaving Lathtin behind, Jenna leaned against the desk and asked, "What do we do while we wait?"

Gwen tapped her reticule. "We haven't read the journal buried with Margaret yet."

"Shouldn't we wait for them to return?" Kay asked.

"Lathtin can share what we learn with Ysabel." Gwen gestured to the cat at her feet. "He stayed behind to alert us if they run into any trouble."

Jenna glanced at Kay. "We thought about reading the journal sooner, but you seemed so drained after the latest Chaos Season that we wanted to wait until you were ready."

"You haven't peeked, have you?" They hadn't linked since recovering Margaret's bone, but for all Kay knew, they could have done it while she was sleeping.

"By the Four, I haven't." Gwen peeked over at Jenna. "I can't vouch for Jenna, though."

"Freeze it, Gwen, why would I do something like that? Besides, you're the only one who's laid a finger on either book." Jenna waved her hand. "Just go ahead and read the frozen thing."

Jon cleared his throat. "Perhaps I should go for a walk, Ava—Gwen."

"There's no need for that," Gwen said as she pulled the book out of her reticule. "You're part of the group too, Jon."

His eyebrows rose in astonishment, but he settled back against the wall and beamed proudly.

The book was a leather-bound journal, worn on the spine and along the edge. The lock had been torn out of the cover. Gwen laid the book on the floor so she could turn the pages single-handed.

"Margaret started this journal when she was fourteen," she said. "She says she saved the shopkeeper's son by healing an infected appendix before it burst, and he gave her this journal, a pen, and an inkwell in exchange. She says as a future Ava Spring, it's her duty to record all her uses of magic and any strange thing that happens to her." Gwen turned a few pages. "Most of her journal entries talk about the daily happenings of people in Bent Hook and Margaret's wish to leave the town, or at least find out more about her quartet. She says she wrote letters to the One Oak and the Hall of Records asking for information." Gwen glanced first at Ysabel, then Kay. "I hope she had better luck than I did."

Kay blushed. Then she reminded herself she'd had reason to hide and stop using magic to hide from Salth.

"This is odd." Gwen furrowed her brow. "Margaret reports she had a series of dreams about chasing a boy into the Dead Land. She always woke up before she died in her dream."

Lathtin hissed.

"Sal-thaath?" Kay asked.

"Most likely. Listen to this." Gwen's tone shifted. "'I dreamt about the boy again last night. He said, as always, that he wanted me to help his sick mother. I followed him farther into the Dead Land this time, far enough to see her. How strange she is! Her clothing looks like something out of a play. I have no idea which century she borrowed her fashion from, but no one would dare mock her for being strange. Such cruel eyes she had! She looked at me as if she planned to drain all my magic from me. I called on the Four for aid, but the woman laughed at me. "Fool," she said, "They're not what you think they are. Look for yourself, and you'll know it to be true." Then I woke, but the woman's words stayed with me. How is it we remember so little about our first lives as Avatars, or about what Challen was like before the Four showed Themselves to us? Someday, when I'm an Avatar, I must find the answers. They must be in Wistica, the oldest city in Challen.'"

Gwen looked up. "This explains why she collected the things Kay found. She was trying to understand out ancient past."

"What did she learn?" Kay asked.

"I haven't read that far ahead yet." Gwen blushed slightly. "I wonder now if I should have saved her personal papers instead of burning them. It seemed the right thing to do at the time."

"Keep reading then," Jenna said.

Gwen returned to the journal, skimming silently. Kay wished she'd read it all out loud. If Margaret had learned more about the Four, all the Avatars deserved to know about it.

"By the Four, Margaret actually wrote to the rest of her quartet and asked them if they'd dreamed of a strange boy and his mother," Gwen said.

Everyone, even Lathtin and Jon, leaned in closer to her.

"What did they say?" Kay asked.

Pages rustled in the stillness. "Sophia and Charles said they didn't have such dreams. Dorian dreamed about a woman offering him power. He said he never sees her face, and she speaks Challen with an odd accent. He asked Margaret if it was her in one of their previous lives."

Kay repressed a shudder. Even now, thinking about her past nightmares still terrified her more than a dozen whirlwinds all trying to blow her away. "And none of you dreamed about Salth and Sal-thaath before we became Avatars?"

Gwen and Jenna shook their heads; Lathtin copied them.

Kay shifted on the hard floor. "How was I unfortunate enough to draw her attention, then? And why send dreams to part of a quartet but not the entire group?"

Gwen frowned. "I'll wager Summer's bracelet Salth wanted to stop our quartets from coming together. Maybe she's behind some of our other challenges too."

Jenna rose. "Speaking of Summer's bracelet, one of the flowers just fell off." She picked it up gingerly and tried weaving it back into the bracelet. "It won't accept my magic."

"When Ysabel returns, we can link and give you more."

"It's not a question of more magic. It's…well, Summer created your bracelet. His magic is stronger than mine. If He can't sustain this bracelet any longer against your death curse, I can't." She swallowed. "Gwen, if you can send this curse into anyone else, you should do it. Soon."

"You expect a Spring Avatar to kill?" Gwen's voice broke on the last word.

"Your life is more important!"

"What about my soul, Jenna? Winter freezes murderers' souls when they die. You know that."

Lathtin yowled and rubbed himself against Gwen. Kay wished she had such an easy way to disrupt their argument or comfort Gwen. *They should have left me with the God of Winter.* But what could the three of them do without a Winter Avatar of their own?

Gwen sighed and leaned down to scratch Lathtin's head. "Ysabel and Kron found rooms for us in a pair of boarding houses— one for men, the other for women—across the street from each other. They had to take the rooms for a quarter-moon, so they spent more of the chals than I thought they would. Let's get some sleep and buy more supplies in the morning, all right?"

"That's not our biggest problem, Gwen," Jenna said in a low voice.

"I know, but it's the only one I can focus on right now." Her worried expression eased as Lathtin purred at her. "Let's trust the Four to handle the others."

As they sorted their belongings and cleaned up traces of their presence, Kay prayed the Four would do just that.

* * *

The boarding house Ysabel had found for them was comparable to the one where Kay had lived in Tradetown, though Kay thought her landlady had done a better job of keeping the rooms clean. Gwen, Ysabel, and Kay had to share the bed. Grimacing, Ysabel and Lathtin killed all the bedbugs and fleas before permitting any of them to venture into the room.

Kron used an enchantment on his cloak to become invisible and follow the women upstairs so he could create a portal between the pair of boarding houses. This allowed Ysabel to fumigate the men's quarters and Kron to repair the lopsided mattresses, so they were all equally comfortable. The sheets were harsher than those at the One Oak, but Kay was grateful for a chance to sleep soundly.

Kron didn't leave when he was done; instead, he beckoned Jon and Jenna to cross over into the women's room. Ysabel, looking grim, stood near the window as they all gathered around her. "Kron and I took a few minutes to go through my father's desk after the rest of you left," she said. "We found a secret compartment secured with another time trap. Kron disarmed it so I could read my father's letters. He's been corresponding with more Salthworshippers. They've read about the Avatar graves we disturbed and figured out we must need something from each Avatar."

"How much do they know about the Avatars?" Gwen asked. "They would have to travel to Wistica and perform some research in the Hall of Records to identify all the Avatars and where they're buried."

Ysabel hung her head. "I'm sorry. Bethany gave my father the list of names and locations we're planning to visit."

"Freeze it, freeze it, freeze it!"

Ysabel flinched at Gwen's thunderous expression. She glanced at her, and her face softened. "It's not your fault, Ysabel. By All Four, who could expect any girl to follow Salth when she could worship the Four?" She leaned forward. "But we need to know exactly what the Selathens know. Did Bethany find out Olivia's exact burial place in Black Rock?"

"I don't think so. Bethany knows the itinerary we had planned for the Grand Tour, but although it did list the hotel where we planned to stay and a stop at Olivia's grave, it didn't have the exact location."

"Good." Gwen exhaled. "Now all we have to do is think of a way to lead the Selathens off track."

"The easiest way to do that would be to send them to a different grave," Kron said.

Gwen motioned for him to whisper. "That would be ideal. Unfortunately, we should have switched the grave markers moons ago. There are Selathens already in Black Rock. They probably already have guards watching Olivia's grave night and day."

"Then we have to drive them away or divert them somehow," Jon said.

"What would they pursue besides us?" Jenna asked.

The answer seemed obvious to Kay. "What if we could create decoys of us?"

Gwen turned to look at her. "What do you mean?"

"When I was a seamstress, we sometimes displayed dresses on a mannequin. If Kron could enchant a set of mannequins to look like us, and we then put them on a cart and drove them out of the city, we would be able to sneak up to Olivia's grave and take the final bone."

Everyone grinned at her suggestion. "I'll drive the cart," Jon said. "I don't need magic for that."

"Where do we get mannequins?" Gwen asked. "Can we buy some from a seamstress shop, or do we have to make them?"

Everyone looked at Kron, expecting him to answer, but before he could, footsteps sounded outside the hall. Kron and Jon exchanged glances before diving through the portal. Jenna followed. Lathtin dove under the bed. The portal vanished a heartbeat before someone knocked on their door. "Open up in there!" the landlady called.

Since Kay was closest to the door, she answered it. The landlady, a middle-aged woman who seemed to have a permanent scowl on her face, stuck her head in and peered around. "I had a complaint from downstairs that there was talking in here." Her scowl deepened. "You're not hiding any men in here, are you? I won't tolerate a bunch of lightskirts sullying my home."

Gwen lifted her chin and assumed her haughtiest expression. "By All Four Gods and Goddesses, Dame, my cousins and I would never dream of such a thing."

"You needn't put on noble airs to impress me, young Dama." The landlady advanced into the room. The floorboards creaked under her feet. She peeked under the bed, wrinkling her nose as she stood up. Next she inspected the wardrobe. How the landlady expected a full-grown man to hide in a piece of furniture barely big enough to contain one trunk's worth of clothes was a mystery to Kay. Finally, she tried the window, even though it had been painted shut. Kay wished it did open so she could circulate some fresh air into the stale room.

"Dama Tich was certain she heard men's' voices in here," the landlady muttered. Her face contorted in a couple of sneezes. "Men don't make me sneeze, though. Has one of you been near a cat lately?"

Ysabel carefully avoided looking at the bed.

"By the Four, Dame, do you treat all of your boarders like this?" Gwen crossed her arms, hiding her paralyzed hand. "We should demand a refund."

"It's my house and my rules, Dama. If you don't like them, you can sleep in the street tonight."

"We'd probably sleep better there."

For a moment, Kay worried Gwen was going to have them evicted, but after a brief staring contest, the landlady sneezed again. "If I find a cat here, out of all you go." Watering eyes took the sting out of her threat. Scowling some more, she stomped out.

"I think she's going to be reborn as a toad in her next life." Gwen fumbled with her boots. Kay knelt to assist her.

"Maybe she'd be sweeter-tempered if you could cure her sneezing around cats," Ysabel said.

"That's one of the ailments a Spring Avatar can't cure. Even if I could, I wouldn't dare. Then she'd know I'm the Spring Avatar. I wouldn't trust her not to report us to the Watch." Gwen sighed as she pulled pins out of her chignon. "The sooner we leave this town, the better. If we're still here tomorrow, we'd better send Lathtin to sleep with the men."

Ysabel nodded agreement.

At bedtime, Kay found herself sandwiched between her sister Avatars, with Lathtin prowling guard between the window and the room. A drunkard sang loudly as he passed by the boarding house. Back at the One Oak, the main sounds outside her bedroom would have been wild animals and the wind rustling tree branches. She would have called up a wind to comfort her if she wasn't worried Dorian would steal it and create a Chaos Season.

It's odd that Salth would send dreams only to Margaret, Dorian, and me—and that she would send each of us such different dreams. Kay squirmed, trying to reclaim a pillow from Gwen. Including Dorian with herself made her uncomfortable, no matter what the context. *Best to think about what Margaret might have learned. I hope Gwen finishes reading her journal tomorrow.* Maybe then Kay would have more answers—or more questions.

* * *

The morning promised weather only a Winter Avatar could love: cold drizzle that threatened to turn to snow but wouldn't. After struggling through a bowl of weak mush for breakfast, Kay, Gwen, and Jenna met in their room and debated what they should do. Ysabel, along with Kron and Jon, would purchase supplies for the next stage of their journey. While it didn't feel natural to be separated from her, they were less likely to be recognized if they weren't together as a quartet. Hiding in their rented room would be prudent, but none of them wanted to do that. Gwen announced she wanted a pair of warmer gloves, and Jenna suggested they buy some dried herbs and spices to make their on-the-road meals more palatable. They bundled up, and Jenna portaled back to the men's boarding house so they could meet properly on the street.

Gwen gestured for Jenna to precede them. "We'd better act like typical Selathen women so we don't stand out so much."

"We look more like Challens than Selathens, though," Kay said.

"Then let's wrap our scarves around our heads so they can't tell."

Kay did so until she barely had a slit to see through. Although Selathen women were supposed to be too modest to look strange men in the eye, she stole quick peeks at the buildings as they walked to the open-air market. The stores in Tradetown, though newer than many of the ones in Wistica, were smaller, only two stories. The streets were cobblestone in some places and brick in others. The uneven wooden planks making up the sidewalk constantly threatened to trip her. Window displays, no matter if they were of furniture, pianofortes, pipes and tobacco, or just dry goods, always included one of the Honored Lathatilltin's watches somewhere in the scene, identifying the shop owner as a Salth worshipper. Gwen and Jenna didn't linger over their purchases in the dry goods store, as the sales clerk eyed them suspiciously and said something in Selathen none of them understood.

The open-air market in Prosperity Square felt more welcoming. Despite the rain, clusters of servants and several middle-class women gathered around the stalls, chatting with the stall owners and each other in a mixture of Challen and Selathen. Kay winced at the ones who complained about the weather. Most of them were content to discuss their families or fashion. As Jenna haggled over herbs, Gwen turned her head as a couple of pregnant women discussed ways to assure their children would be sons.

Kay put a hand on Gwen's arm. "You can't interfere—"

"Hush! Listen!"

One of the women said, "The Ava Spring could tell you more, if anyone knew where she was."

Kay held her breath. What were the Selathens doing discussing the Season Avatars?

Gwen edged toward the women, but Jenna gripped her arm before she could get too close. "You can't do anything," she whispered. "You'll give us all away."

"I could give her advice as a midwife—"

"No. No one would believe you. Or you would be recognized."

Gwen's face twisted in annoyance, but she nodded. As surrounding people stared at them, Jenna dropped Gwen's arm and smiled as if nothing unusual had happened.

We'd better leave before someone gets suspicious. Kay cleared her throat. "I'd like some chocolate."

"Good idea, Kathie." Gwen spoke the false name with emphasis. "I wouldn't mind reading the papers while we warm up."

Apparently half of Tradetown had the same idea, as the chocolate shop just outside the open-market district was packed so tightly no tables were free. While Jenna elbowed her way to the counter to order, Gwen searched for a paper, finally picking a few discarded pages off the floor. "Look at this!" she whispered.

Kay leaned over to read the headline: "WHERE ARE THE SEASON AVATARS?"

"Nearly a moon has passed since Challen's loveliest quartet of Avatars vanished from their house in Wistica," the newspaper proclaimed. "Their servants have been remarkably tight-lipped about where their mistresses are or what they're doing. Are they still in Challen? Have they been kidnapped by enemies of our beloved country? Or have they turned against the Four Gods and Goddesses, wantonly destroying and desecrating the remains of their predecessors?"

Kay grimaced. If she knew who the author of this article was, she'd pelt them with hail.

"In concern, His Royal Majesty, King James ro Fip-Challen, has offered a reward of five hundred chals to anyone who can provide him with information about the Season Avatars' current location. Their descriptions are as follows…"

Gwen folded the paper over and let it drop back to the floor. "Freeze it, even these disguises may not be enough. I should change our hair colors, or our complexions."

"Do you have enough magic for that?" Kay asked.

"For what?" Jenna asked as she returned with their drinks.

In whispers, Gwen explained the situation. Jenna grinned. "I already bought some walnut dye at the dry goods store. The two of us can go dark."

"Then what do we do about Kathie here?" Gwen asked. "She already has black hair." Jenna raised her eyebrows at the false name, but Gwen continued, "Maybe if I dilute the dye and apply it to her skin, she'll look like a Selathen."

"Not with blue eyes."

"No one will notice that with a casual glance. That's all we need to do to fool people."

Kay hoped they wouldn't have enough dye left over to treat her. She knew from experience how long it could take for dye to wear off of her skin. If she had to disguise herself, she'd prefer to dress as a boy.

When they returned to the boarding house, Jenna nearly walked into the women's house with them. Only a quick reminder from Gwen saved their reputation. The landlady watched Gwen and Kay with narrowed eyes as they hurried to their room. "Kay, could you boil the water in the bowl?" Gwen said as she secured the door. "I want to get this done quickly."

Jenna portaled through in time to hear her last sentence. "Normally it takes several hours to steep the dye before we can use it. Maybe if Kay keeps the water hot and I can use my magic on a plant powder, we can prepare it faster."

The dye proved more stubborn than Jenna had thought. Kay managed to keep the water boiling without losing it to steam, but Gwen had to link with Jenna to dissolve all the powder. Jenna finally pronounced the coloring ready to use. Kay cooled the solution down, but Gwen grimaced as she applied it to her hair. "It'll take me moons to strip all of this out," she complained.

"It'll fade faster than you think," Jenna said. She streaked a fingertip of dye over Gwen's eyebrows before applying it to herself. Kay was relieved to see the entire batch used up. She had to admit the pair looked quite different with dark hair.

The portal popped as Ysabel rushed through. She stared at them for a heartbeat before turning to Kay. "By the Four, I thought at first Kron had sent me to the wrong room! I'm so glad you didn't bleach your hair, Kay, or I would have been completely confused."

"Now, there's an idea…" Jenna said.

"Not now," Kay said before Gwen could. "Is everything all right?"

Ysabel's smile disappeared. "Kron disenchanted one of Salth's watches while we bought a pair of geldings, and the stable manager started screaming he was Salth's enemy. Kron had to give him about half of his chals before we could leave. He, Jon, and Lathtin are hiding behind the men's boarding house, waiting for us."

"Are we ready to leave?" Gwen asked.

Ysabel nodded.

Jenna grabbed their clothes and flung them into the trunk. Sighing, Kay removed them and folded them neatly so everything would fit.

Drunken male voices floated up from the street, chanting something in Selathen. "What's going on out there?" Kay asked.

Ysabel tensed. "That's a hymn to Salth."

Everyone dropped what they were doing and rushed to the window to look. At least a dozen men stormed up to the entrance of the men's boarding house.

"Are they looking for Kron?" Gwen asked.

Ysabel pressed against the window. "They don't know his name, but they're chanting, 'Any foe of Salth's is a foe of ours.'"

"Jon's with him," Kay said. "We should help them."

"But if they see us doing magic—"

"They don't have to. I can change the rain to snow. That might cool their temper."

Kay was cautious enough to change the weather all across Tradetown. Soon, the street below was coated with white. The mob didn't break up. As soon as someone let them in, they charged into the boarding house. Kay's stomach twisted. What would happen once the men realized their quarry weren't there?

"This might be our best chance to join the men," Gwen said. "We can leave without being seen."

Ysabel dashed through the portal without waiting for the others. Gwen sighed as she tried to shove their trunk through single-handed. Kay helped her while Jenna grabbed a few forgotten items.

Kay stumbled as she arrived in the alley, as if she'd missed a step coming down a flight of stairs. The area reeked of urine and refuse, scents she didn't miss from her days of being poor. Lathtin perched on top of the carriage, hissing as he watched the back end of the alley. Their horses were harnessed, though Kay could tell from their sweating flanks and wild eyes that they were ready to bolt. Ysabel hurried over to soothe them. Jon kept his revolver pointed at the alley exit, glancing in that direction as he helped Kay and her sister Avatars find seats among cases of tinned meat and wheels of cheese.

"They're looking for you in the boarding house right now," Gwen said. "We should leave town."

Kron took out a finder and sprinkled a pinch of dirt on it. "This will lead us on the best path."

Once Jenna and the trunk were loaded, Ysabel scrambled into the driver's seat and picked up the reins. The horses needed little urging to trot forward.

Kron guided their first few turns, but then Ysabel said, "Kron, my magic-sensing pendant is growing warm."

He said something in his ancient tongue and pulled out another finder. The stone in this one glowed red, and it pointed in the same direction as the other one.

"More bad news," he said. "They're blocking our escape route with Salth's attempts at artifacts."

"Just artifacts?" Ysabel closed her eyes even as she slowed the horses. "No. The pigeons tell me a group of Selathens with weapons are there too." She gasped and turned pale. "Oh, By All Four Gods and Goddesses, my father is with them. He looks stronger than he has in a long time."

"Salth might be turning back time for him, the way she did with Dorian before he died," Gwen said. "What else did she give him that we have to worry about?"

"Let's not find out." Kron pointed straight ahead. "Maybe we can weave our way around them."

Ysabel guided the carriage to the next turn, but more Selathens burst out of a store, screaming and waving bright cloths at the horses. The men and a few women blocked the side street where they needed to turn. Bethany stood in the front and stuck her tongue out at her sister. Others shouted in Selathen. Ysabel had difficulty keeping the horses calm as she maneuvered the carriage away from their harassers.

Kay's snow still fell. She raised the temperature a little, just enough to melt the snow and turn it into the coldest rain possible. She let the rain build to a solid downpour before releasing it on the Selathens. Several of them shrieked with surprise, and a few of them peeled away from the group.

"By the Four, Kay, that was cruel!" Ysabel smirked. "But they deserved it."

Disappointed she didn't drive more of the Selathens away, Kay made the temperature drop even more. Gwen shook her head. "Kay, we don't need ice statues blocking the path. Remember, they're still Challens, even if they are Selathen too."

Chagrined, she warmed the temperature just enough to make sure they didn't freeze to death.

Ysabel pulled the team of horses up and summoned feral cats and dogs to surround the Selathens. As the animals hissed and growled, some Selathens attempted to shoo them away, while others waved whatever they were carrying at the animals. Ysabel cocked her head at Gwen. "Do you really want me to order them to attack?"

Gwen sighed, looking older than all of them as she stroked her violet bracelet. "Maybe we should try talking to them first to see if we can reach some sort of agreement."

"Gwendolyn, they worship Salth," Kron said. "They're directly opposed to the Four Gods and Goddesses. You can't negotiate with them."

Jenna leaned forward, smiling at the Selathen men and stroking her short hair. They stared at her in shock, breaking out into Selathen that made Ysabel blush. Ignoring their words, Jenna said, "Even the Fip God of War knew well enough to leave the Four alone when He conquered Challen."

Ysabel looked up. "According to the pigeons, my father and his men are marching this way. What do we do? I don't have room enough to turn around and try a different route." She gave Gwen a pleading glance. "Gwen, are you willing to try healing him after all he's done to us? That might be the only way to convince him to let us go in peace and break Salth's hold over him."

"If your sister didn't exaggerate his illness, then I may not be able to do anything for him. But I can try—if he's willing to let me, that is."

Kron reached for his satchel. "And if he isn't....Dearest, how do you want me to handle your father?"

She sighed. "I've thought several times about invoking Fall's wrath against him, but…he's still my father. If I do anything that will lead to his death, my younger siblings will hate me just as much as Bethany already does." Her voice wavered for a few heartbeats, then firmed up. "But he can't keep interfering with my work as an Avatar. If he could be banned from Challen, or imprisoned, I'd be content."

"If I can subdue him, or trick him into a portal that leads to the Watch's guardhouse in Wistica…" Kron rummaged in his satchel. "I need time to create something."

"Kron, what do we do if they're carrying pistols?" Gwen asked.

His tone hardened. "Don't worry. They won't work."

Marching footsteps sounded behind them. Kay and her sister Avatars turned. A group of twenty to thirty men, all proudly displaying Salth's watches pinned to their coats, strode behind a man in his mid-thirties, wearing a gray coat. Ysabel and Lathtin stared at him, mouths gaping.

"He looks just like he did in his and Mama's wedding portrait, doesn't he?" Ysabel whispered. Lathtin nodded.

"Courage," Gwen told her. "He can't harm you anymore. Stand up to him like the proud Avatar you are." She reached back to Kay to link. *Kay, just in case something goes wrong, could you have some hail or fog or other distraction on hand, ready to use?*

Weather doesn't always work like that, but I'll do what I can.

While Ysabel addressed her father in Selathen, Kay thickened the clouds. She also checked to see what the others were doing so she could coordinate her efforts with theirs. Kron pulled a spool of thread from his satchel and knotted it in unfamiliar patterns. Jenna clenched her sapling pot.

You and Jenna watch our escape route, Gwen said. *Make sure the Selathens don't sneak up and overwhelm us.*

Kay nodded. As Ysabel's father spoke, she spied a smokestack belching noxious clouds. She grabbed the pollution with the wind and shaped it into a smoke bomb, which she delivered with precision to a couple of men who were stealthily approaching the nervous horses. The beasts didn't whiff a single speck of soot, but the men were forced to retreat, hacking like they'd swallowed fire. Kay exulted in her power and skill for a few heartbeats—until one of the women ran toward the men and put her arms around him. Kay drew back, suddenly remorseful. By the Four, this wasn't why Winter had given her weather magic centuries ago. Only Dorian used his magic to harm people. She was supposed to help the inhabitants of Challen, not hurt them. It didn't matter who they were; the Four cared equally for all in Challen's borders. By the Four, couldn't they stop fighting each other?

"No."

The word rang out in Challen, a male voice. Kay glanced back to look at Ysabel's farther. He stood halfway between his men and the carriage, almost as if he was daring Kron to use an artifact on him. Ysabel slumped, Lathtin in her lap. Gwen put her good hand on her shoulder—comforting, but not linking.

Kron's hand twitched, but the rest of him remained still. The horses jerked forward. A thin black line hung in the air. Kron's portal-trap. It would fall short of the Honored Lathatilltin.

Kay instinctively called another breeze to catch the thread and spread it out into a loop. With precision, she guided it up to rooftop level where Ysabel's father would be less likely to spot it.

Ysabel lifted her head. Her eyes looked wet, but she blinked furiously before shouting something back at her father.

Now. Kay didn't need anyone to tell her to take advantage of the distraction. She centered the loop around Ysabel's father and allowed it to fall. As he raised his hand, the loop swallowed him. His surprised expression seemed to linger in the air behind him.

The Honored Lathatilltin's group fell apart. Some fled, a few shouted at them, and a couple tried to fire their pistols. When that didn't work, the shooters picked up loose stones and threw them with better success. Jon blocked a stone meant for Kay with his own body.

"Are you all right?" she asked.

He grimaced. "It's going to bruise."

Gwen touched him, and the pain in his expression eased.

Cats, dogs, and birds tore into both groups of Selathens. Ysabel flung herself back into the driver's seat and grabbed the reins before the horses could panic. Gwen gestured for Jenna and Kay to link with her before she touched Ysabel's neck. Kay slipped her hand over Gwen's wrist, and Jenna brushed her cheek. Together, they sent magic into Ysabel, enough to help her guide the animals as they drove the humans off of the street.

The carriage surged forward. A few stragglers rushed to get out of the way; Kay forced them aside with a stiff wind. One man grabbed onto the back of the carriage and dragged his heels as he tried to slow them down. Before anyone else could react, Jon whacked the man's hands with his revolver until he finally let go. Gwen winced as he fell backwards, but she didn't protest. She sent a wave of healing energy back to take care of the injured Selathens.

Ysabel gradually coaxed more speed out of the horses. Still linked with her sister Avatars, Kay felt the jouncing of the carriage distantly. More Selathens on the sides of the street threw things at them. Kron scrambled from one side of the carriage to the other as he set up an invisible barricade. Just as they did during Chaos Season, Kay concentrated on using her magic to help them. Although Ysabel required the most magic to handle both the horses and her animal guides, Kay swept away obstacles whenever she could find them.

Again and again they turned until the gate leading to the main road waited for them. Two men pulled at the iron gate, trying to close it. Kron waved his hand, and it froze in place. Ysabel didn't slow the horses as they drove through. Kay let a fog build behind them as they continued their flight.

CHAPTER THIRTEEN

The Four's Secret

"There's no signs of pursuit," Ysabel reported as they pulled off the road into a grove of trees. "But I have several pairs of birds watching the town and road, just in case."

"Thanks, Ysabel," Gwen said. "Well done back there, everyone." Her words came out in a whisper, alarming enough that Kay looked at the violet bracelet before Gwen could hide it. The deep purple flowers had faded to lavender, and the leaves were spotted with brown.

Jon unloaded a few supplies, and Kron paced the perimeter of the grove, placing artifacts in several locations. Jenna coaxed the dead grass behind them to grow and hide their tracks. Then she approached Gwen and seized her arm, exposing Gwen's bracelet. Jenna touched it, scowled, and stomped out of the clearing. "Fetching wood," she called back belatedly.

"What was that about?" Kay asked.

Gwen covered the bracelet with her cloak. "At the rate it's fading, I'll be lucky if it lasts until the winter solstice."

Kay and Ysabel exchanged worried looks. If Gwen couldn't heal her hand now, what would happen when Summer's bracelet no longer shielded her from the death inside the shard?

Ysabel set out bedrolls while Kay conjured rainwater for chocolate. Gwen sat with Lathtin, eyes closed as if she was too exhausted to help. Her mouth twitched occasionally. Whatever they were discussing must have been quite amusing if it could make Gwen smile in these circumstances.

Jenna returned and dropped a small pile of dead wood in the center of the grove. She stalked over to Gwen. "You can't go on like this, Gwen. We should portal back to Wistica and beg the Four to heal you."

Gwen opened an eye. "We're so close, Jenna. We only need one more bone and a way to summon the other Avatars' souls. Then you can shake all the dead trees you want at Salth and Salthaath. By the Four, I never thought you'd back away from that fight."

"Is it really worth it, if we lose you?" Jenna twisted the edge of her coat.

"Spring Avatars don't die easily." Gwen opened her other eye and looked around. "Ysabel, Kay, what do you think? Are you ready for Black Rock and Salth?"

"Maybe we're not ready yet, but we will be soon," Ysabel replied.

By the Four, I hope she's right. We still don't know what's in the rest of the journal or how to pull Margaret and the other souls from Winter's world to this one—

"Kay? How do you feel about going on?" Gwen's voice was raised. She must have asked the question more than once.

Kay swallowed. "We have to do it. The Four and Challen are depending on us."

"Then it's settled. Onward we go." Gwen straightened herself, as if their decision had given her strength. "But not without dinner."

Kay smiled as she stirred the chocolate to make it frothier. Some things never changed.

Ysabel and Lathtin continued to monitor the road through their animal connections, but everyone else relaxed as the evening darkened to night. They prepared a stew flavored with wild garlic and other herbs Jenna found. Dessert was dried fruit and honey moistened with water—an unusual combination, but it helped to restore Kay's energy.

Kron set up a shelter as before, with a blanket wall between the men and the women. This time, Jenna joined Kay and the other Avatars on their side. "Now we can make plans for facing Salth," Gwen said.

"What about Black Rock?" Ysabel asked. "We still have to retrieve the last bone, and we'll have to go through Challens and Selathens alike."

"I've been thinking about that," Gwen replied. "We could have Kron portal a message to Lex and ask him to explain to his brother that we have a task to perform for the Four and the Watch needs to let us go about it in peace."

Jenna shook her head. "I know Lex can't wait to use his All-weapon against Salth, but even if he does explain everything to the king, he might not listen. You always say the crown doesn't like how much power we have. His Majesty could use this as an excuse to seize the One Oak and banish us forever from Wistica."

"He wouldn't dare." Gwen didn't sound so certain.

"He couldn't do that, not without causing an uprising," Ysabel said. "Our people know how much we do for them."

Kay sat up and conjured a small lightning ball so they could see each other. "Then...what if we send a message to the Challens as well?"

"How would we do that?" Jenna asked.

"Send a letter to the newspaper in Wistica," Gwen said. "They would print it if they know it's from us."

Ysabel frowned. "But are you sure that's safe? Even if Kron portals it to them—and he probably doesn't know where their office is—everyone will know where we are."

"Couldn't Kron leave the letter with someone in the University?" Gwen asked. "And all we have to do is say we're venturing into the Dead Land. No one will come after us."

And no one would expect us to come back. Kay thought of her parents and siblings. After a series of nightmares, she'd fled her family in a panic and hadn't contacted them for years, hoping no one would force her to become a Winter Avatar. Leaving them again after only a few moons seemed cruel.

"We should also send letters to our families too," she added. "Just in case..." She couldn't say the final words, but they all nodded. No one needed to link to know what she was referring to.

"We can write them but not have them sent unless absolutely necessary," Gwen said. "If we figure out how to bring Margaret and the other absent Avatars back to Challen, we won't need the letters. Hopefully." She yawned. "I'll read the rest of Margaret's journals tomorrow as we travel. Let's pray the answers we need are in there."

Gwen settled back on her pile of cloth, and Ysabel and Jenna copied her. Kay extinguished her lightning ball first before preparing herself for sleep. She had another job ahead of them tomorrow. Hopefully she would finish it before arriving in Black Rock—and hopefully Kron could use the artifacts they created.

* * *

The next morning proved to be cloudy and cold. Kay drove a snow shower eastward, both to be out of their way and to interfere with any pursuers. No one had a detailed map of this region, so Ysabel followed random roads leading either south or west. Gwen and Jenna, with occasional input from Kron or Jon, debated whom they should ask for better directions and whether it was safer to stop at an isolated farmhouse or at a small town. Kay didn't bother joining the conversation. Instead, she sewed dolls.

These weren't dolls that Kay would have played with as a child. Each of them was about half the size of the Avatar they were supposed to represent and made from spare clothing supplemented with other fabric. The stitching was uneven due to the rough road. Kay would have preferred a chance to work somewhere more stable, preferably a cozy room with good lighting and plenty of refreshments. Even an opportunity to sit on a stable surface while creating tricky portions such as the face would have been helpful. But as days passed on the trip—surely they'd crossed this particular bridge before, or seen this particular view of the land rising into foothills and mountains—and no one was any surer how close they were to Black Rock, Kay grew restless, wishing the journey was over. At least creating the dolls, each one sewn with several strands of her Avatar's hair, helped pass the time. Besides, Kron wanted them complete before they arrived in Black Rock so he could use them immediately. As soon as Kay sewed the basic shape and added features to the face, Jenna stuffed the doll with crumpled leaves or whatever else she could find. Kron then added objects from his satchel, usually something in the Avatar's color

or something else related to the Avatar. Once he judged a doll finished, its features shifted to match the Avatar, though the dolls
remained creepily still. Jenna posed a few of the dolls in Gwen's
bed or peeking out of the men's sleeping area. During a lunch stop,
she put Kay's doll under the carriage wheel. Ysabel shrieked when
she saw it, half-convinced Kay had died again.

"By All Four, Jenna, that's enough." Kay gave Jenna her
strongest glare, her stomach still queasy from seeing her double in
pretend danger. "We need something else to do. Gwen, do you
need any help with the journals?"

Gwen shook her head as she closed the book from Margaret's
grave.

"You're done? Finally! I thought you finished ages ago." Jenna
prepared a sachet of tea leaves. "So, why haven't you told us what
you learned?"

Gwen stared at the fire. "I'm still not sure what to make of it
all." She drew in her arms, as if afraid of accidentally triggering a
link.

"Did Margaret learn something about the Four, then?" Kay
poured water into the kettle, then sat down next to Gwen. Kron,
Jon, and the rest gathered around to listen.

"It's hard to tell. Once Margaret was recognized as the Spring
Avatar, she spent much of her free time talking to history profes-
sors at the University and looking at artifacts from the pre-
Annexation period. She even learned to read Old Challen so she
could do her own research." Gwen glanced up. "I didn't find any
of her books or research papers in the Spring Study, so either she
didn't keep them there, or else the other members of her quartet
cleared them out quickly once she went to the God of Winter."

"Why would they do that?" Jon asked.

Gwen shrugged. "From offhand comments in her main journal, the one buried with her, Sophia and Charles didn't approve of her research. Dorian supported her, even after she dug into the foundations of the house in Wistica."

"By the Four, it's a good thing she didn't tear down the house too," Kron said. "It looks like it was altered over the centuries, but I still recognized some of the walls and rooms."

"Did it have any secret compartments in the foundation?" Gwen asked.

Kron raised his eyebrows, then shook his head.

"Well, she found one. It had some old documents from pre-Annexation Visticha." Gwen took a deep breath. "Four documents from a time of great upheaval. One showed a picture of a blonde healer who treated plague victims without getting sick—the city-state king wanted her to work for him, but she refused. Another one has a poem about a youth eating bark and grass in a time of famine. One is a bill of sale for a nine-year-old girl to something called a pleasure house, with a note at the bottom saying she was carted off three years later by a wolf and a cougar." Gwen grimaced. "Margaret adds a note saying none of the historians she talked to wanted to explain what a pleasure house was, or how you could sell a person. Do you know anything about that, Kron?"

He sighed. "A pleasure house is a place where women they…they meet with men and…."

Gwen stared at him. "Are they lightskirts?"

"Is that what you call them? Wait, how do you know about them?"

Now Gwen sighed. "This isn't my first life as Spring's Avatar. Women who sleep with men for chals come to Spring Avatars so they don't catch an illness—or an unwanted child. But lightskirts generally work in a tavern serving drinks or entertaining customers, and usually there are only one or two in a tavern. Why would they agree to all go to a single place? Wouldn't they compete with each other?"

Kron flushed. "It's to give the men a choice."

"And the women too?"

"They don't get a choice. Many of these women don't choose to be lightskirts."

Kay and her sister Avatars stared at him in confusion.

"But Fall would protect them..." Ysabel said. "Unless...Gwen, did you say they sent a nine-year-old girl to such a place?"

Gwen nodded, her face pale.

"By All Four Gods and Goddesses, I wouldn't do such a thing to Bethany no matter how she betrayed me! And she's older! A child, a poor child..." Ysabel hugged herself. Gwen reached out to her; so did Jenna and Kay. The link formed. Beneath it ran the thought Ysabel didn't want to share out loud: Fall was always shown as a girl becoming a woman, the same age as this girl when she escaped with the help of animals.

It couldn't be. It couldn't be. Could it?

The healer could be Spring, and the starving youth Summer, Gwen said. *I didn't even tell you there was another record about an old man who lost his entire family in a severe storm.*

Winter. Kay tried to imagine her God as a mere human, but it seemed as impossible as a rainbow at midnight.

Gwen broke the link and stared at Kron. "You have to tell us the truth, Kron Evenhanded. Were the people Margaret described real? If so, how are they connected to the Four?"

Kron glanced away to poke at the fire, which had dwindled to embers. "I'd have to handle the historical papers she mentions to determine how old they are. That wouldn't tell me if the words on them are true or not."

"So…these stories could have been based on the Four?" Gwen asked. "Do you think our ancestors wrote them to explain Spring, Summer, Fall, and Winter?"

"It has to be that way," Kay said. "The Four never explained where They came from, so someone made up stories about Them."

Ysabel shook her head. "I can't believe anyone would make up something so horrible about Fall. Why didn't She send insects to chew such lies to shreds?"

Kron let the stick clatter to the ground. "I don't know how or when the Four came to Challen. They were already divine when I first encountered Them." He let out a breath that turned to fog. "But from what They've hinted at, it's possible They were born human and somehow Ascended to godhood."

"Ascended to godhood? What do you mean?" Gwen leaned forward. "By the—" She put her hand over her mouth. "Please explain."

Kay couldn't help adding, "It's not fair you know so much more about Them than we do, when we're the ones who have served Them for centuries."

Kron shrugged. "They never confirmed that They Ascended. All They said was Salth couldn't Ascend, but I could with more star magic."

"Where could you Ascend to?" Gwen tilted her head to look up. "The clouds? The stars?"

"I know clouds, and the Four don't live in them," Kay added.

"It's not a literal Ascension. I think it's some sort of test humans with enough magic can take to become gods." Kron's hand stilled, and he glanced around in every direction—even up—before continuing, "In my time, there was a night when magic came from the stars. Salth is the only person I know of who saw it coming. She and I each absorbed some of the star magic, and it enhanced our abilities. I think The Four may have started as ordinary men and women, maybe even the same people listed in the ancient documents you mentioned. They might have had some magic of Their own, but if They did, They didn't come to the Magic Institute where I studied. When the star magic came, They absorbed some, passed whatever test is required to Ascend, and became the Four you know."

Everyone was silent for a moment, absorbing his information. The forgotten water for tea hissed as it boiled over the pot. Kay hastened to cool the water magically, just to prove her magic still worked as it should.

Lies, all of this had to be lies. The Four were as eternal as Their seasons. If They weren't, if They could change, then maybe she'd given Them so many lifetimes of service for nothing.

If humans can rise, can Gods fall? After all, if the Four hadn't managed to eliminate Salth after centuries, maybe They weren't as powerful or as capable protectors as Kay had always thought. She froze the disquieting idea deep in her mind, so deep she could pretend it had never appeared in the first place.

Tea leaves fluttered out of Jenna's hands. "By the—freeze it, Kron, you're not saying we could become like the Four, are you? Their magic is far beyond ours."

He nodded. "The Four are similar in some ways to the magicians I used to work with, but Their magic is a level beyond mine. I don't think there is enough free star magic for you and the other Avatars to Ascend to the Four's level." Kron's mouth quirked. "I don't think Salth and I have enough star magic to try it either. That's why the Four claim she's only a demigoddess. But if one of us could claim the other's magic—"

Ysabel clenched his arm. "She can't have yours."

"No, but...I don't want to Ascend." He smiled at her. "Everything I want is here."

Their romantic words didn't warm the chill Kay felt inside.

"This is all very astonishing," Gwen said. "How do we explain this to the people of Challen?"

"We can't do that!" Kay jumped up so quickly she nearly knocked the water over. "They'll lose faith in the Four!"

Ysabel used a stick to pull the pot out of danger. "I don't understand. I thought Margaret's journals were supposed to help us discover how to work with the absent Avatars. How does knowing the Four were once human help us with that?"

"Maybe it's not supposed to," Kay said. "Maybe it's a trick. Maybe Salth had something to do with it."

Before the others could ask more questions, she ran into the woods. A fire must have come through here within the last few years, burning off the undergrowth and clearing the path for her. Too bad a lightning strike couldn't clear her head of all the thoughts whirling around inside her mind.

The Four lied to us, didn't They? Did They claim to be Gods from the start? Well, They were already divine when I first met Winter, I'm almost certain of that. I would be if I remembered that life in any detail. Freeze it! She tripped on a tree root but managed to catch herself before falling. *The ancient tales of the Four never say where They came from, only that They performed many miracles, both separately and together, before They gathered the twelve people who would become Their Avatars. Then, after They gave the Avatars magic, They spoke to the inhabitants of Vistichia and disappeared.* Kay sighed. *What am I supposed to make of that?*

She halted at a riverbank. Little more than a creek, the water flowed despite the cold weather. Kay knew instinctively it wasn't cold enough to freeze moving water, but she envied the creek's ability to continue fulfilling its purpose no matter how the Four challenged it.

She stared at her hands as she summoned a lightning ball and made it split into four smaller ones spinning around like juggler's toys. After making the balls vanish, she created a cloud, then decided against making it rain and allowed the cloud to settle around her, a comforting blanket of fog. All but the closest trees became invisible, and sounds of snapping twigs echoed. Despite the years she'd hidden her magic, despite the doubt she felt now, Winter still saw fit to let her keep her weather magic. Then again, He hadn't punished Dorian for attempting to kill her. Why was that? Didn't He care what His Avatars did in His name? Or were the Four as powerless as Their statues in the Temple?

"Kay? Stowaway, where are you?" Several sticks crunched, then came the deeper sound of something hitting a tree. "Ow! Freeze it, Kay, could you please banish the fog before I—" Jon yelped. "By the Four, that's cold."

"Jon?" She'd expected one of her sister Avatars to come after her—Gwen, most likely, to show her logically why she shouldn't behave like this, or Ysabel, so worried about other people she sometimes forgot about herself. Kay had thought Jon would want to avoid discussing the Four. She let the water vapor return to the creek she'd borrowed it from. The cloud thinned, then disappeared. He stood on the bank, shaking his leg as if trying to get water out of his boot. She sent a gust of warm air at him to dry him off.

"What was that? Kay? There you are!" He held his hands out as he carefully felt his way toward her. "Why'd you run off like that?"

She shrugged, not ready to talk.

Jon halted several feet from her. "Is it really true what Lady Io Havil and Kron Evenhanded said back there, about the Four being human before They were gods?"

"I don't know. I don't remember that life well enough to be certain. But you would think the Avatars should know, shouldn't they?" She stamped her feet, suddenly wishing for snow she could flatten or form into balls and throw at trees. "Why didn't the Four tell us anything?"

"Does it really matter what the Four were before They started watching over Challen?" Jon asked. "I'm no Avatar; I'm only a simple locomotive engineer trying to make a better life for me and the girl I love. I don't know as much about gods as you do, but I suppose you can judge Them like people, by their actions. And the Four have made Challen prosperous and fertile."

Kay crossed her arms. She and her sister Avatars were the ones who directly used their magic to aid Challen. Even though the Four had given them that magic in their first lives as Avatars, it seemed unfair for the Four to get the credit now.

Jon smiled sheepishly. "I mean, you and all of the other Season Avatars through the years have made Challen prosperous and fertile."

"But…but we thought we were serving Gods, not people!" she cried out.

"Isn't that what you do, serve the people of Challen with your magic?"

"That's not what I meant, and you know it." A few snowflakes drifted down, not enough to pelt him with a snowball. "It's … more noble to think our masters are above humans."

"Yes. Humans can be quite common," he said bitterly.

"Jon! By the…you're just complicating things! Go away and let me think."

She stomped off further downstream, but he followed her.

"Kay ava Seltich, has running away ever solved a problem?" His voice echoed strangely in the forest, deeper and more resonant than she'd ever heard before.

She halted in mid-step and turned toward him. Something about his posture seemed unnatural. Her knees flowed like water to the ground. Her mouth was a desert, too dry to let words escape.

"You ran from your magic, only to put yourself in Salth's clutches. When your sister Avatars forced you to take up your magic again, you let Dorian intimidate you even though your magic is equal to his. And when Salth and Sal-thaath attacked you with the ancient animals they resurrected, you didn't resist." Jon—if it was just him—shook his head. "It's time for you to show your courage, Kay. If you fail your final test, Challen and your sister Avatars will suffer along with you."

Hope and dread flurried within her. "Winter? Is that You?" she whispered.

Jon shook his head and blinked. "What?"

A bird chirped in the distance, restoring the atmosphere to normal. Winter's presence lingered for a few heartbeats. Kay remained stock still, absorbing His traces, until she felt she could breathe again. "Are you all right?" She wanted to approach Jon and check for herself, but she felt far too profane to touch him.

"I'm fine. It's you I'm worried about."

"I...I need to pray. Privately." Before he could be hurt, she added, "But could you stay close by and watch out for me, please?"

Jon smiled tenderly at her. "Of course, Stowaway."

She cast around for a suitable glade. A lone willow guarded a sharp bend in the creek. Though its leaves were gone, thin branches offered a curtain of privacy. Kay gestured at the tree, then followed a narrow path to it. Jon trailed her at a distance.

Kay parted the branches as respectfully as Jenna would have and knelt on the bare soil. All animal sounds faded away, replaced by an expectant silence. Kay drew in several deep breaths, feeling renewed energy and calm as the air warmed inside her.

"God of Winter," she whispered into the silence. "I know I haven't always been a worthy Avatar. I fled for my life when I should have faced Dorian and froze when I should have confronted Salth's creature. But even all the years when I pretended I was nothing more than an ordinary seamstress, even when I shut myself off from the weather, I still loved You with all of my heart. I know that while everyone else in Challen hates winter, Your season is necessary. You give the whole world a chance to rest and prepare for Spring's renewal. There is beauty in every snowflake of Yours, in every cloud. I know You have to be far wiser than us humans." She took another deep breath, as if she could only use the purest air for her next words. "But I always thought You were more than human. You have to be. We're so puny and short-lived, and we're not always kind to each other. We need something greater than us to believe in. We need to believe in You and the rest of the Four Gods and Goddesses, so how could You have ever been human?"

She stopped talking and wondered how Winter would answer—or if He would. What else did He need to say after speaking through Jon? A breeze stirred the willow branches, as though they were fighting a soltrans ceremony with each other. She listened to them tapping, but they didn't spell out any message for her. Neither did the water sluggishly churning against the shore. Perhaps she should have stayed with Jon. His odd words were the closest she'd had to a response from Winter.

She sighed. "Maybe it's not important what You were before You called me to be an Avatar. I have a task to do. I suppose I should go back to my sister Avatars so we can continue our journey. I'm sorry for bothering You with my doubt and fears. I'll try to do better."

She rose, brushed off her skirt, and pushed aside the willow branches. As she emerged, she gasped. The ground before her was carpeted with winter roses that hadn't been there a few moments ago. They didn't smell like true roses, but that didn't matter. Seeing them in bloom a moon too early made Kay realize her prayer had been heard. She raised her head and murmured "Thank you" to the clouds. When she looked down again, the flowers were wilting and disappearing to wherever they had come from. They vanished before she could pluck one.

Jon stood at the edge of where the flowers had been. "Kay? Was that real?"

"You saw the flowers too?" Perhaps it was good that someone else had seen this miracle. "We should rejoin the others and tell them about this."

They walked hand-in-hand back toward the clearing. Halfway there, a crow circled overhead, then followed them by flying from tree to tree. *Ysabel must be worried about me. I shouldn't have run off like that. This revelation must be difficult for them to accept too. I'd better apologize to them as well when I see them.*

Ysabel was the only Avatar waiting for them when they reached the camp. The fire was out, and the supplies put away. All that needed to be done before they left was harness the horses. Ysabel cut off Kay's apology with a wave of her hand. "After you left, Gwen and Jenna decided to head separately into the woods to pray too. I stayed here and listened to Kron's stories of meeting the Four. Fall didn't seem to like him much; I hope She doesn't object when we marry." Her smile became more pensive. "I wonder if the reason we don't remember much about our first life is because the Four worried we'd figure out the truth of where They came from."

"Maybe. Where are the others?" Kay looked around. "Did you receive a sign from Fall?"

"No. Did you?" The green flecks in Ysabel's eyes seemed brighter for a moment. "How lucky! What happened?"

"Something Jenna would like. Will she be back soon?"

"I sent crows after both of them. They'll return in a few heartbeats."

Kron looked down from the top of the carriage. "I hope so. We should keep moving before someone finds us."

A few moments later, branches rustled as Gwen and Jenna emerged separately. They looked dazed, but they didn't speak. Ysabel and Jon hitched up the horses, and soon all of them were back on the road.

They clustered by the window next to the driver so they could link with Ysabel. The road was clear and the horses cooperative, so she was able to keep control with her magic alone. Gwen cautiously extended the link. *I think we must keep going with our quest despite what we learned.*

Kay nodded eagerly. *The Four sent me a sign.* She shared her memories of her prayer and the Four's response. The other three shared memories of their prayers too, with all of their thoughts shuttling back and forth as if they were weaving a giant cloth together. To Kay's shame, she was the one who had questioned the Four most severely. Gwen had been more interested in the history of the Four, and Jenna had wondered why the Four had wanted her to marry her first husband if They knew he would die before Gwen could help him. Ysabel, kind soul that she was, wondered what had made Fall so sad and if she could comfort Her. Next to them, Kay felt selfish—until Gwen opened the link to a deeper level. *I wanted to know why They didn't tell us long ago,* she said.

Me too, Jenna and Ysabel added. Their thoughts made it clear that they had been thinking about their respective gods instead of Spring.

Someone had to ask the Four, Gwen said. *I wish They'd given us all a sign, though.* She glanced down at her violet bracelet. *It would have been nice if you'd been able to bring back flowers for all of us.*

Winter roses are poisonous, so that's probably why Summer took them back after you'd seen them, Jenna said.

Kay wordlessly sent her relief to the others. *There's something I still don't understand, though. Why did the other Avatars keep this information hidden, and why did Dorian try to destroy it?*

I didn't share the rest of the journal with you, did I? Gwen recalled images of paper with faded ink. Other pages were full of crossed-out sections and angry exclamation points. *Margaret wanted to share the news with the ordinary people of Challen, but the rest of her quartet, particularly Dorian, felt it should stay hidden.*

Kay grimaced. She would have chosen to keep this information secret too. It troubled her that she and Dorian would agree on anything.

If there's so much disagreement in one quartet, will the twelve of us be able to work together when we face Salth? Ysabel asked.

Gwen sighed. *I don't know. We need to contact the absent Avatars before we enter the Dead Land. Could you try it tonight, Kay?*

Kay felt Olivia's locket. She'd been putting off using it, but they were running out of time. Gwen was right; she had to be certain she could contact the other Avatars' souls before the winter solstice. Salth wasn't going to give her time to practice.

Tonight, she agreed.

Gwen broke the link. Kay watched the trees pass by for several minutes, letting everything she'd learned soak in. Winter still accepted her as His Avatar, despite her doubt and anger. So did her sister Avatars. They were all depending on her to create the spirit-portal.

She'd better be ready.

* * *

Before they camped for the night, they came across a signpost indicating Black Rock was less than ten miles away. They'd reach it tomorrow. Ysabel took extra care finding a campsite, driving them well off the road until Kay wondered if they'd ever come out of the forest.

"The animals report there have been more people traveling into the town recently than leaving it," Ysabel said. "One group from the east, a larger group from the north, and then a big carriage drawn by six horses."

Jenna dropped her armful of firewood. "Lex?"

"Maybe. I can't be sure. The animals couldn't describe the carriage to me."

"Well, do you think they could find him?"

Ysabel sighed. "I can search for the team of horses, but if he doesn't have frequent contact with them, they may not recognize them."

"If you're going to spy on him, please make sure he doesn't suspect," Gwen said. "He doesn't know yet why we're collecting Avatar bones, so he may be here on his brother's behalf, not ours."

Jenna shook her head. "Once War explains everything to Lex, he'll listen to us."

"How can you be so sure War will support the Four against Salth?" Kron asked quietly. "It would be more like Him to keep the two sides evenly balanced so They battle each other forever."

Gwen sighed. "I've had enough lives filled with Chaos Season. I'd be happy to see that end." She glanced up at the sky. Geese flew overhead in a vee, black against the dark blue sky of twilight. "So after supper, let's pay a call on our absent Avatars."

Kay took her turn at cooking—fresh fish, mushrooms Jenna had gathered, and the last of the bread they'd brought from Tradetown—with some nervousness about how the summoning would work with so many people present. Her sister Avatars shouldn't be a problem; all of the Avatars had met before in other incarnations. Kron and Jon might be distractions. She made sure to brush against Gwen as she served the fish. *Could we keep the summoning among the four of us?*

Of course. I planned to do it that way all along.

Kay had to force herself to eat, each bite a struggle to swallow. She told herself she was overreacting; there was no need to worry. She'd always worked well with Olivia. Margaret's spirit had never harmed her, at least not physically. But would Kay learn everything else she'd believed in for lifetimes was wrong?

She took a deep breath and looked around her. Gwen sat across the fire from her, her plate braced in her lap. Gwen had gained some skill at using her off hand, but she still bent forward every time she took a bite. Lathin lay between Gwen and his sister. Ysabel smiled at something Kron said, then broke off a piece of fish and offered it to Lathtin. Kron finished his meal, scraped the leftovers into the fire, and spun his plate on one finger. Kay couldn't help grinning, and next to her, Jon squeezed her hand. Past him, Jenna piled more mushrooms onto Gwen's plate before helping herself to more.

I can have faith in my sister Avatars, Kay told herself. *No matter how many lives we've been through, no matter what we've experienced or how often we have words with each other, we still care for and support each other. By the Four, I think they would have saved me even if they didn't depend on my magic.* Warmth bloomed in her chest. If she could trust her sister Avatars completely, maybe she could trust the other two quartets as well. The warmth faded. *Except for Dorian. I can never accept Dorian. Charles and Sophia were kind enough to me, as well as Dorian's wife, but him? Never.*

"Something wrong, Stowaway?" Jon asked when she refused dessert, apples and nuts Jenna had gleamed along the road.

"Just worried about this next summoning," she said. "We need advice from the absent Avatars."

Jon made the sign of the Four. "If Winter gifted you with the magic to contact them, then you must trust He gave you enough magic to do what needs to be done."

"I'm worried they'll have more disturbing news. I keep thinking I've already been through the worst, and then something else happens."

"And each time you passed through it. You can do so again and again if need be."

She sighed. "The seasons always circle around again."

"That's a good thing, Kay. We know what to expect and when it will change."

Gwen climbed to her feet with Jenna's assistance. "Ysabel, Kay, are you ready?"

Kay nodded. "But not at the campsite. Let's find a clearing."

"Are you sure you don't want us to guard you while you work?" Jon looked woeful, as if they were about to run off to the Dead Land and never come back.

"They'll be fine." Kron touched his shoulder. "Lathtin will stay with us and let us know if they need our help. I have some artifacts to show you."

Jon only seemed to be mollified when Kay boldly kissed him in front of everyone else. Blushing, she wondered if they would have to announce their engagement when they returned to Wistica. She hoped planning a wedding would be their only worry by then.

Surprisingly, Gwen gestured for her to lead the way. It took Kay a heartbeat to move into position. She was used to always being last. The unexpected promotion terrified her more than thrilled her, but she conjured four balls of lightning to help them all find even footing. Jenna and Ysabel came next, with Gwen last. Jenna whispered a few directions to Kay, directing her to a clearing in the middle of pine trees.

Kay set the lighting balls floating over their heads, oriented in each of the cardinal directions. She positioned herself in the north, Winter's direction. Then she unclasped Olivia's necklace. She whispered to Winter, "Please let this work," before sketching a circle in the air similar to the portals Kron created but smaller. As an afterthought, she touched the center of the circle with the stone.

Kay nearly dropped the locket when the air fell away—she had no better way to describe it. A circle of solid black blotted out the pines. Then the circle flashed to white. The air, already brisk, became even colder. A few snowflakes drifted out, melting instantly despite the chill. When they cleared away, a white-haired lady in an ice-blue dress nodded at her. Kay knew her from memory and a portrait back at the One Oak. Olivia ava Kalt, the third Winter Avatar, stood before her.

"Kay, so good to see you again." She smiled. "Such a daring hairstyle you have this time."

Kay nervously brushed her hair out of her eyes. "Olivia?" When she thought back to her most recent life, she remembered this woman as an awkward adolescent who let winds scatter out of control, not the polished and poised older woman in front of her who wouldn't let a hair in her wig stir. For a moment, Kay wished she could let Olivia be in charge of facing Salth; she seemed better suited for the challenge. Then she reminded herself she'd already survived facing Salth, and Winter had picked her for this task, not Olivia. She met Olivia's gaze straight on, surprised to see kindness in her eyes. Dorian had never shown her kindness in any life. Kay smiled. "Olivia. It's good to see you again too."

A second woman appeared next to Olivia. Like Gwen, she had blonde hair. Her features were vaguely familiar, but she stared at Kay warily.

"Margaret!" Gwen pushed her way up to the portal. "At last, we can finally talk! I have so much to ask you!"

"A moment, sister Ava." Margaret's mouth thinned as she stared at Kay. "We ended on the wrong note last time. Olivia told me a little about what she's seen between you and Dorian. I wish things were better between you two. But I still stand by him."

Kay nodded. Dorian should be the one apologizing to her, but she'd sooner expect mercy from Salth.

Margaret turned her attention to Ysabel and Jenna as they came up to the portal. "I see your entire quartet is with you this time. May the blessings of the Four be on you."

"And on you as well," Gwen murmured, her blue eyes bright.

"Is that them?" another woman's voice asked.

Ysabel started. "Sophia! By the Four, are you there?"

"Of course I am, child." Sophia pushed up against Margaret. She looked exactly as she had the morning of her death. Her soul had the vitality her body had lacked at the memorial. "Charles too, of course."

Although Kay hadn't been close to any members of Dorian's quartet, seeing them again, walking and speaking as if nothing had happened at the fall soltrans, made her wish she could touch them to prove they were real.

"Hello." Charles appeared behind the women, bending down to peer between them. "I say, can't you make this window any bigger? There's more of us behind me."

Gingerly, Kay stuck the locket into the edge of the portal and tugged it. At first, the portal shifted over, hiding the other Avatars. Then it halted as if it had snagged on a hidden nail. Kay pulled on the portal, stretching it into an oval instead of a circle. Three more people, vaguely familiar but in old-fashioned clothing, appeared. *Tylon, Frederick, and Helene. Eleven, of us, not twelve.*

Gwen, Jenna, and Ysabel came closer to the portal, exchanging greetings with their counterparts. They had two each, while Kay had only Olivia. The other Ava Win glanced around, then lowered her voice. "Are you certain Dorian is no longer among the living?"

She nodded. "We saw it happen. We were there at his memorial service, the same one for Charles and Sophia."

"Then why isn't his spirit here with the rest of us?"

"He doesn't deserve to be with Winter." Kay wanted to spit any mention of him from her mouth. "He betrayed all of us, Olivia. He's joined forces with Salth. Chaos Season is ten times worse than before now that his spirit is driving it."

Olivia shook her head. "You must change that, Kay."

"By All Four Gods and Goddesses, how?"

"The Four haven't told me that." Olivia leaned closer, as if she wanted to cross back to the living side. "What They have told us is that we will work with the Avatars of our own seasons this time, not as quartets."

CHAPTER FOURTEEN

Decoy Dolls

"You mean, link with each other, instead of through our Ava Spring?" Kay knotted her eyebrows as she stared at her older counterpart. "We've never been able to do that!"

Olivia smiled. "And how often has your Ava Spring pointed out that your quartet has had to face many difficulties we've never faced before, such as the shard she carries, or your return from Winter's realm? You have a tie to His domain now, Kay. You can use that to bring me and the rest of the Avatars to you when you're at the right time and place."

The right time had to be the winter soltrans; the place, the Dead Land. "So, once we arrive, all I have to do is open the portal again?"

"I don't think it's that simple. You have to draw us through it to you." Olivia gave Kay a stern look. "All of us."

Only Dorian would still trouble me so much after his death. "Even if Dorian was with you, he won't listen to me," she told Olivia. "He's hated me since our first life together. Now that he's working with Salth, he's turned his back on the Four."

"I can't believe that." Olivia shook her head, but her hair didn't move. "I always thought he was one of the Four's most fervent defenders."

"What makes you say that?"

"He was one of the Avatars who wanted to keep The Four's former identity as humans a secret. He thought it might weaken the Challens' faith in Them."

Kay stepped back from the portal. She and Dorian had too much in common for her liking.

"Sophia thought Margaret should publish her findings," Olivia continued. "Dorian came up with the compromise that Margaret should keep them safe instead."

Kay still wanted to argue that it was all a sham. Before she could, the portal shrank. Jenna and Ysabel stepped back as their counterparts vanished. Gwen exchanged a few final words with Margaret and Tylon before yielding as well, leaving Kay face-to-face with Olivia and Margaret.

"Think about what I've told you, Kay." Olivia stretched out her hands, but she didn't break through the portal.

Margaret gave her a sad smile. "Dorian has his faults—"

"Trying to kill me is more than just a fault!"

Margaret winced. "I'm sorry. I know my husband wasn't always kind to you, but he wouldn't have gone to such an extreme if I'd been there. And I can't believe he's truly turned against the Four. He still serves Them, I know it."

The portal disappeared before Kay could tell her how wrong she was. Frustrated, she sent a wind to rattle the pine trees.

Jenna approached her cautiously. "It doesn't do any good to be angry at Margaret. She was absent when Dorian attacked you. We were there. We know better. Now, could you please stop tormenting the trees?"

"Sorry." She looked away as the wind died.

"Does this mean all of our efforts will be for nothing if we can't persuade Dorian to come back and serve the Four?" Ysabel asked.

"We still have a chance to do that." Gwen came over to them. "When Kay opens the portal in the Dead Land, Margaret will be able to contact her husband. He may not listen to any of us, but he'll listen to her." She sighed. "But first, let's retrieve the final bone. In the morning, we'll ask Kron how he plans to use the decoys Kay created."

* * *

"I've never done anything like this before, but there's no reason why it shouldn't work," Kron said the next morning as they packed supplies. "I'll require some assistance from the four of you, though."

Wonderful, Jenna commented through the link.

Let's hear him out before we decide his plan will fail, Gwen said. "What kind of assistance?" She directed the question to Kron.

"First, I have to key each decoy to the matching Avatar. You're closest to me, Kay, so would you like to go first?"

She jerked out of the link before Gwen and Jenna could comment. "Do you need an artifact from me?"

"You mean, like blood? By the Four, no, that won't work." He stroked his chin as he looked back and forth between her and the doll she'd created. "I think it would help if you breathed on it, though."

Kron often said he created his artifacts by instinct, often not knowing what parts he needed until he saw or handled them. Kay closed her eyes and blew on the doll, wondering if his instinct was true.

"Again," Kron said. "Four times in all."

She obeyed. As soon as the last breath ebbed away, the doll moved, trying to twist out of her grasp. Startled, Kay nearly dropped it.

"Oh, my! Can we keep these when we're done with them?" Ysabel asked. "Francie would love playing with living dolls!"

Kay opened her eyes to look at her doll. Its features had now shifted to match hers, down to the eyes and hairstyle. It was unnerving to see her own face on something other than a mirror's surface. She blinked, and the doll copied her.

"How do I make it stop?" she asked.

"How do I make it stop?" the doll asked.

Kron grabbed it from Kay's hands and removed a scrap of cloth. The doll reverted to its lifeless state, still with Kay's face. She grimaced and turned away. No matter what the doll did or didn't do, it reminded her too much of what she must have looked like when she had died.

"Do we really have to use these dolls?" Jenna, who had been studying the one that was supposed to be her, put it down. "How will they fool anyone? They're too small."

"I'll use them as the basis of an illusion." Kron pulled a clock hand, a ball of string that Lathtin stole, a pencil stub, and a few more items out of his satchel before coming across a button. "This should do the trick." He put back everything except the string. After persuading Lathtin to relinquish a length of it, he attached the button to the back of the doll's dress. "Now when I tuck this in...yes." He looked up at Kay. "Now you'll be able to control what your doll does."

Suppressing a grimace, Gwen picked up a yellow-gowned doll. "What exactly should we make them do?"

"Just...talk to each other normally. Let everyone see that you're the Season Avatars. Maybe drop some false clues about what you're doing and where you're going. When the dolls are trained, I'll put them somewhere where they can fool the Watch and the Selathens. While they're distracted, we'll sneak into Black Rock and take the final bone." Kron's face hardened. "Then we can finally confront Salth and Sal-thaath. Any questions?"

After all their setbacks on this journey, Kay doubted this plan would proceed as smoothly as Kron thought it would. Nevertheless, she picked up her doll and twisted the button to the right. "Hello," she said.

Nothing happened.

Frowning, turned the button the other way and repeated her greeting. This time, the doll copied her, frown and all.

Gwen, Jenna, and Ysabel breathed a semblance of life into their dolls after Kron attached buttons. After the women spent several minutes learning how to handle the dolls, they brought them together to stand in a line, from spring to winter. The dolls flopped over, and Kron had to enchant them so they could stand up straight without falling.

Once they were ready, Kron gestured for them to begin.

"Sister Avas," Gwen said, "I'm so glad we've reached Black Rock, the last point on our Grand Tour. I'll be very busy checking all the coal miners and their families, making sure they aren't ill."

Jenna spoke in an unnaturally loud voice. "I'll study the trees to see if the coal dust in the air is affecting them."

"I'll do the same for the animals," Ysabel added.

Kay's throat suddenly seemed dry. What could she say? She couldn't hint at a visit to Olivia's gravesite, even though the Season Avatars had announced they would be visiting their predecessors' graves during their Grand Tour. As she looked up at the mountains, the answer came to her. "I haven't had a chance in this life to study how mountains affect the weather. I'm looking forward to experiencing mountain winds in person."

"May the Four bless our tasks," Gwen said, and the others repeated her words.

Kron gestured for them to stop, so they did. "Excellent. That should work. Now let me see what else I have to adjust...."

He pulled a few more items out of his satchel and studied them. Finally, he pulled several small metal rings out and slipped them onto the dolls. As each ring stuck onto the doll's body, she spoke her line. Kron sewed a mark on each doll's foot; Kay was impressed by the tiny stitches he made. When he was done, the four dolls came to life and spoke the same lines over and over.

"By the Four, I hope we don't have to listen to that all day," Jon said. "I'd want to stuff my ears full of wax."

Lathtin yowled and walked off as if he agreed with Jon.

Ysabel smiled. "Don't worry. I already have four crows willing and waiting to fly them over to the road." She looked over at Kron. "Any other adjustments you have to make?"

He shook his head. "Once the dolls are in place, the illusion I've worked into them will make them appear as tall as real people."

"That's a good thing," Jenna said. "Even Kay looks like a giant next to the dolls now."

Kay wanted to stick her tongue out at her, but it was more fun—and perhaps more fitting—to send a gust of wind at her face. Jenna's hair tangled.

"Freeze it, Kay! Can anyone lend me a proper brush?" Jenna sighed as she pulled a comb out of the pocket of her jacket. "I miss having a reticule."

Ysabel's crows flew down to take food from her hands before snatching the dolls and flying off.

"Well then," Gwen said. "Let's make ourselves look as ordinary as possible and hope we can sneak into Black Rock while our decoys draw off our pursuers."

* * *

A few hours later, Kay wrapped herself in a cloak she didn't need as they approached the outskirts of Black Rock. The air itself seemed black to her as she tried in vain to refresh it. Ysabel guided the horses down a stretch of road sloping into a valley. Below them stood a hundred tiny homes, so ill-made Kay worried a slight breeze would topple them. Along the main street of town she could see a few bigger buildings, perhaps a hotel or general store, probably some saloons as well. On the other end of the town, several wooden mills pumped water into a nearby river. Here and there, Kay could make out laundry drying on a line, or smoke from a fireplace, but the town itself seemed deserted.

"The workers must all still be underground," Gwen said quietly. "Perhaps we should go straight to Olivia's grave while there are fewer people about."

"Where is it?" Ysabel asked.

"Close to the river, on the bank opposite Black Rock. Apparently Olivia liked to sneak off to play in the woods when she was a girl."

"Can't say I blame her." Jenna stretched and peered off in the distance. "The woods are the prettiest part of this place, even if they're ailing."

Many of the pine trees were missing branches or had brown-tinted needles. Even the birds called less often than they did back at the One Oak.

"Where are the dolls?" Gwen asked. "This looks like the only road going in and out of Black Rock. How could we have missed a group of Selathens or the Watch?"

"The crows left the dolls about five miles farther out from Black Rock," Ysabel replied. "There's a group of about twenty horses with riders heading toward them."

"Selathens?"

Ysabel nodded.

"I can keep them distracted for a little while longer," Kron said. "This might be our best opportunity to retrieve Olivia's bone."

"We're not even going to stop for a meal first?" Jenna held up an empty basket that had once held bread. "How will we perform our magic on empty stomachs?"

"You can hold out a little while longer, Jenna." Gwen gripped the carriage door as Ysabel coaxed more speed out of her team. "Especially since you were the one who ate the last roll."

"Not me! Ysabel gave it to the birds!"

"Perhaps both of you can save your arguing for later?" Kron fumbled in his satchel. "I wonder if I can make us invisible..."

Gwen shook her head. "Now he thinks of it."

Ysabel said nothing until she reached the outskirts of Black Rock. "The animals tell me there's a footbridge not far from here, but we'll have to leave the carriage hidden somewhere."

"I'll take care of it," Kron said. He jumped down and hung several tiny objects on the sides of the carriage. "Go on, hurry. We still have to find a hidden place where I can create an artifact to take us safely to Salth."

Jon looked first at Kron, then at Kay, before saying, "I know you Avatars can defend yourselves and don't need my help at the gravesite, but I'd be happy to come along. I can lift heavy stones for you if necessary."

Kay glanced at Gwen and was secretly happier than she expected to be when the Ava Spring nodded permission.

Jenna led the way over a rickety bridge and then down a path so narrow even Kay had trouble squeezing through. Jon, following her, cursed as branches poked through his cloak. If they didn't have the Summer Avatar with them, they would have gotten caught in brambles before proceeding twenty paces.

"Gwen, do you know what Olivia's grave looks like?" Ysabel asked as they scrambled over giant tree roots.

"I think it's similar to Frederick's grave, another stone mausoleum. Why do you ask?"

"Because I asked some blue jays to scout ahead, and there's a man already at the 'stone box,' as they call it."

"What does he look like?" Jenna asked, her voice breathless.

"All they're telling me is that he's big," Ysabel replied, "but from their perspective, all of us are big. He talks of eagles."

"It must be Lex." Jenna hurried forward, forcing all of them to match her or be lost.

"Jenna, that doesn't mean he's here to help us," Gwen said. "He might be here to defend the grave from the 'robbers.'"

"But once he knows it's us—"

"You'd better flirt with abandon." Gwen sighed. "Thank the Four you're already pledged to each other."

Jenna turned her head back to face Gwen. "Freeze it, Gwen, are you ever going to accept him? Just because Lex never brought you flow—what!"

A spear hurtled toward her. She stumbled and fell.

CHAPTER FIFTEEN

Reunion

Jenna's shrieks of pain drove birds out of their perches. Kay, near the end of the line, pressed forward to see what had happened. The spear had struck Jenna near the hip. Her brown cloak turned dark with blood as the spear pulled itself out and hurtled back the way it had come.

Freeze it, that's the Allweapon. Lex had to be nearby. What would he do when he learned what happened?

"Let me see." Gwen knelt next to Jenna, heedless of the dirt. "Ysabel, link with me. Kay and Jon, watch for more attackers." Her voice hardened. "Kay, you have my permission to shock the War Avatar if you see him."

Lex rushed forward, his bloody spear at the ready. "Hold! Who are you…" He halted, his spear still aimed at Jenna. "Eagle's Talons, the Season Avatars? Where's my intended?"

"Bleeding, thanks to your frozen Allweapon," Gwen retorted.

He gaped, and his face turned white. "Jenna? Is that you? I swear by the War Eagle I didn't recognize you!"

"You weren't supposed to." She gritted her teeth.

Gwen pushed the torn cloth aside, touched Jenna, and closed her eyes. Ysabel pressed her hand on Gwen's cheek. Kay wondered if they would need her to link as well, but the pain in Jenna's expression eased after a few heartbeats. Gwen continued to touch her a little longer before finally pulling away. "There. You may be a little stiff and achy still, so move slowly as you stand up." Gwen's mouth quirked briefly. "No thrashing your intended either."

"I think he owes me an emerald necklace after that." Jenna held onto Gwen for support, but Lex came forward to claim her. She scowled at him for a heartbeat before accepting his aid. "Or maybe an eight-course meal."

"I have something you'll like even better, my brave one. But what are you and your sister Avatars doing here?" Lex shook his head. "Please don't tell you it was you at all the other graves."

Jenna looked down coyly, scraping the dirt with a foot. Lex's expression didn't change. Gwen gave Jenna a let-me-handle-this expression and strode forward to face the man who had once wanted to wed her.

"It was us." Her good hand trembled, but she met Lex's stare with one of her own. "The Four Gods and Goddesses gave us a sign that They wanted us to recover a bone from each of the other Avatars. It's the only way the twelve of us can unite to face Salth."

Lex's gaze unfocused as his eyes silvered over. Kay looked away, waiting for the God of War to possess His Avatar and speak through him. To her surprise, the God remained silent. After a few heartbeats, Lex's expression returned to normal. He frowned as he studied Gwen.

"War says it is true, you are following the Four's wishes." He frowned. "But you are still breaking the law of the Fip Empire."

Gwen lifted her chin. "Then what do you intend to do about it, Your Royal Avatarness?"

"By all rights, I should turn you in. My brother will think I am shaming our family otherwise." Lex closed his eyes as he reverently tightened his grip on the Allweapon. "But War says I should not. The time we have waited for is almost at hand." He grinned, and Kay shivered. *War. Battles and killing, everything we Season Avatars have worked so hard to avoid.* Her hand traced the scar on her chest. *But some things must be faced.*

"Are you with us, then?" Gwen asked. "Will you join us?"

"It is War's will." Lex lowered his Allweapon. His expression shifted, showing weariness and lines under his eyes. For the first time, he looked not regal, not an Avatar of a powerful God, but merely human. "War is not an easy God to serve, and I suspect you find your Four difficult as well."

No one spoke. Kay wouldn't give the War Avatar the satisfaction of agreeing with him. Yes, she had never expected to die and be resurrected in Winter's service. But she wouldn't have chosen to lead a normal life instead.

"Please, Royal Avatar." Kay used the title with respect, unlike Jenna or Gwen. "If you plan to join us, then let us collect the last bone from Olivia, one of the Winter Avatars. We need it to—"

He shuddered and raised his hand. "I prefer not to know the details of what you plan to do or be involved in any way. Your task may be necessary, but back in Fip, we believe the dead should rest in peace."

"We don't take pleasure in this task either," Gwen said, "But as you say, it must be done."

Jenna stepped forward, "Lex, we haven't seen each other in so long." She stared boldly at him. "It would be lovely to stroll through this thin excuse of a forest with you. I daresay you owe it to me."

"Let us hope no one else sees you in that scandalous outfit." His gaze traveled up and down her body. "Most shocking." He grinned, this time in a hungry fashion. "And yet, very intriguing." He returned the Allweapon, which had shrank down to a dagger, to his belt. "Come, my rose in winter, and show me these woods. You probably scouted them out already, I will wager. And I owe you my heartfelt apologies…"

Jenna hooked her arm in his in a forward fashion. Heads together, they sauntered to the edge of the clearing.

Gwen waited for them to disappear before saying, "I'm certain Jenna will keep him occupied for a while, even if she's not completely healed, but I'd like to finish this final grave robbery. Kron, will we have any trouble breaking into the tomb? How do you suggest we do it?"

Compared to some of the other tombs Kay had seen, this one was simple. No stone mausoleums or iron fences guarded the body. Someone had created a sculpture of a snowflake out of broken shovels and other tools and mounted it on top of the grave. "I'd like to find the artist who made this," Kron said.

"Imagine what he or she could do at the University in Wistica with proper supplies," Gwen said.

Kay came up to study the grave. It was covered with an iron slab with Olivia's full name, dates of birth and death, and the words, "Twenty-Second Winter Avatar of Challen." That would make her the twenty-fourth. It was a good omen that their quartet's number was divisible by four. Omens, however, weren't going to make the slab disappear. Ysabel had joined Kron at the grave and now knelt in the dirt, studying the soil.

"This slab is deeper than I thought," she said. "I haven't recruited any burrowers yet to tunnel into the coffin. I think it might be metal, though. Can you tell, Kron?"

He shook his head. "It's not just metal. The outside of the coffin is pine, and the inside is lined with an alloy. Whoever crafted it did an excellent job. It'll be a shame to damage it."

Gwen paced back and forth in front of the grave. "Do we have time to dig it up?"

Kay shook her head. "The ground is too hard. The permafrost level is higher than it is back in the middle of Challen, so the grave is shallower than what we're used to, but at the same time, the soil here freezes sooner than it does back home." She did have a rapid way of heating not just the soil, but the iron block protecting the coffin. However, if she used it, she might cremate the very bones she was trying to collect.

Gwen stopped in front of the grave, smiling. "If cold is the main problem, then all we have to do is add heat."

"A lightning strike would be far too much heat. I'd not only melt the metal but burn the bones."

"You don't need a lightning strike, just balls of lightning." Gwen held her good hand at waist height. "Suspend a few small ones around the grave so they slowly heat the ground and the grave covering."

"Oh. Yes, that might work." Kay could have chastised herself for not thinking of that. She crafted four small balls and set them to hover at each corner of the grave. Gwen, Ysabel, and Kron retreated to the edge of the clearing.

"Ysabel, can you tell if it's working?" Kay asked. "Do your burrowers feel any difference in the ground?"

"There aren't any close by here. I'll have to rouse one from hibernation."

Ysabel closed her eyes, then opened them as Lathtin hissed. A wind swept through the pines, releasing a calming scent that lulled Kay as the wind battered her lightning balls away from the grave. Alarm roused her, and she fought to bring them back under her control.

"Lathtin says we have another Chaos Season," Ysabel said.

Gwen shook her head. "Salth is a master of bad timing for us."

"There's more bad timing." Ysabel looked up at a blue jay sitting near the top of one of the pines. "The Selathens discovered our decoys."

They had to delay the Selathens or find a faster way of recovering Olivia's bone—preferably both. Kay would need more magic to accomplish that. She reached for the magic in the Chaos Season, but it pulled back before she could claim it.

Gwen and Ysabel stepped up to her and arranged themselves so Gwen was in the middle. They linked. The increased power enabled Kay to catch the Chaos Season. She recreated the lightning balls, this time closer to the ground. Kron poked at the metal slab with a carved stick he pulled out of his satchel. She steered the lightning away from him so he wouldn't get burned, then focused her attention on finding the Selathens.

She found a couple of farmers bringing supplies into Black Rock, but she left them alone. Smoke guided her to the Selathens. There were nearly twenty of them. Four or five of them herded the dolls off to the side while the others probed the side of the road, most likely searching for the real Avatars.

She needed fog to shroud the road back to Black Rock. Kay grabbed all the moisture she could find, most of it on the other side of the mountains. She forced it to rise over the peaks and then descend, slowing it so it wouldn't drop out of the air as rain. She spun the water out through the air, thinner than the finest silk, creating a fog centered on the Selathens. It was thickest around them and faded away before reaching the outskirts of town. Hopefully that would keep them away from Olivia's grave until Kron was able to retrieve her bone.

Creating the fog didn't use up all of the magic in Chaos Season, so now Gwen seized it and visited the miners and their families. In one house, a pregnant woman sighed as the aches in her body faded; in the mines, the workers breathed easier as Gwen cleared their lungs. Then she sagged, leaning her weight on Ysabel. *By the Four, I'm so tired, even with Chaos Season to draw on.*

In the link, it was impossible to conceal the concern Kay and Ysabel felt. *Frozen shard,* Ysabel offered sympathetically.

Do you need our energy? Kay asked.

No. Gwen's automatic refusal didn't hide her desire to accept. She firmed up her mental voice. *Let's just get this bone, and then we can all rest. Where's Jenna? Why isn't she here by now? Ysabel, send an animal or a bird after her. Please.*

As Ysabel obeyed, Kay returned her attention to the grave. Kron and Jon had used a pair of stout branches to pry up one corner of the metal slab. Partly molten, it bulged like a misshapen cocoon. Jon's arms strained with the weight. They wouldn't be able to lift the entire slab. Was there any way their magic could help?

The ground is softer now, Ysabel said. *I found an assistant to dig the coffin out, but Kron will have to use his artifact magic to break it open.*

I'm sure he'll manage that—

Gwen, the Watch! Ysabel mentally shouted as she showed them what her avian spies had seen. Ten yellow-jacketed members of the

Watch, both men and women, marched from Black Rock. Each of them carried a revolver and a quarterstaff.

Delay them! Gwen ordered.

Kay started a blizzard, but they'd already used up most of the magic in the Chaos Season. Even with howling winds blowing in their faces, the Watch wouldn't give up. She might buy them five or ten extra minutes at most.

"Work faster!" Gwen shouted at the men.

"By the Four, we're trying!" Jon shouted back.

Help is almost here, Ysabel announced. *We need to give him room.* She pointed in the direction of Black Rock. *Kay, douse your lightning. I don't want to risk you singing his fur or paws.*

Kay did so. As they broke the link, she realized dusk was approaching. Hopefully that would help them hide from the Watch. Ysabel waved Jon and Kron over, and the group retreated from the grave.

All five of them held their breath as a bear shuffled into the clearing. He ambled as if he'd just woken up from hibernation. Kay hoped he'd had pleasant dreams and that Ysabel hadn't promised Jon to him as a meal.

Jon and Kron had created a gap at one corner of the grave. The bear dug this out with surprising speed. Before Kay realized it, the light-colored wood of the coffin gleamed against the soil. The bear swiped at it a couple of times, growling as a claw got stuck. Ysabel and Lathtin calmly walked over to him. Gwen and Kay clutched hands slick with sweat.

Ladies aren't supposed to sweat, Gwen thought distractedly, still watching Ysabel.

Kay ignored the comment. *Should we go with her in case she needs the link?*

I don't think so. She has Lathtin, and she must feel confident that she can handle the bear on her own. Gwen nodded at Jon and Kron, both of whom were reaching for weapons. "Don't interfere," she whispered to them.

"Poor bear." Ysabel circled around the beast before approaching his head. "Does your paw hurt? Let me see."

She held out her hand, and the bear laid his paw, more than twice the size, over it. Ysabel laid her other hand over the paw for a heartbeat, reached up to pat his head, and stepped away. He shambled back through the trees without paying any attention to the others.

As Gwen let out a shaky breath, Kay struggled to remain upright on legs that felt as if they'd melted.

"By the Four, Ysabel, you could have warned us exactly what animal you were summoning," Gwen said.

"What for? All he wanted was the honey I promised him." Her gaze became unfocused. "Now I have to make sure he doesn't take too much honey, or else we might lose the hive over the winter. Jenna and I need to decide at some point if we need more flowering plants in this region to support more bees."

Jenna and Lex finally stepped out into the clearing, their garments and hair neater than when they had left. Lex stared at the hole in the ground. "Are you finished here?"

Gwen curtseyed to him as properly as if they were back in the palace. "Your Highness, I must report that a bear damaged the grave. We will inspect it to make sure it's still intact."

Lex made a sour face and turned his back. "I see the claw marks. That's all I wish to see."

Kron darted in and, with Jon's help, scrambled halfway into the hole, with Jon holding onto his boots to make sure he didn't tumble in. Kron grunted a few times, then called for Ysabel to toss down his satchel. When she didn't respond, he summoned Gwen over.

Kay turned her attention to the Watch. Freeze it, they were only a few turns of the path away! As if that wasn't enough, she'd been so distracted by the bear that she'd let the fog burn off. Now the Selathens were returning to Black Rock. What to do with them?

"Gwen?" Kay called.

"I have it!" Kron said. "Pull me up."

Jon hauled Kron up all by himself, as Lex still ignored them. The sounds of the Watch tramping through the woods, however, were too loud to ignore.

"Scatter!" Lex gave Jenna a fond look before brushing past Kay to take up a fighting stance at the head of the path. The Allweapon shifted into a sword as he drew it. "I'll handle this."

"What about the carriage?" Jenna asked.

Ysabel shook her head. "The Selathens are investigating it now."

Lex gestured at them to leave, so Jenna ran back the way she'd come. Kay followed her, as did everyone except Lex. The Season Avatars were stronger together than they were apart, so Lex's advice didn't make sense.

"Quiet!" Jenna whispered as Jon snapped a twig underfoot. Then again, maybe bigger groups had their disadvantages.

"What should we do?" Ysabel asked.

Gwen glanced at her. "I don't suppose you could bring the bear back, could you?"

She shook her head. "He's too busy devouring the honey. I might be able to bring in a pack of wolves, but they're too far away to get here before dark."

Kay had an idea. "What if you have them howl, and I use wind to carry the sound so it seems as if they're closer than they really are?"

"It's worth a try," Gwen said. She held her arms out in an invitation to link. "Let's see if there is anything else we can do from here. Kron will have to disarm their weapons before I can send them to sleep."

Ysabel's pack was small, so Kay bounced their howls around to make them seem like a larger pack and to make the Selathens feel as if they were surrounded. However, they were focused on wrecking the carriage and ransacking their food supplies.

Kron could portal us to the carriage, Ysabel said. *But we'd be at risk from the Selathen guns.*

I can target them with lightning once we step through, Kay said. *I'd have no problem at such close range, and I'll make sure the bolts are small enough not to kill, only to disable.*

Kron can destroy the guns too, Ysabel pointed out.

They can destroy all the guns in Challen as far as I'm concerned, Gwen said. *Let's drive the Selathens away before Lex finds us and attempts to give us more orders.*

Kron always seemed to come up with new materials to use every time he created a portal. This time, however, he must have been in too much of a hurry to improvise. He pulled a ball of yarn from his satchel and shaped it into a door, pinching it in spots to make it keep its shape. Then he laid his hands on it. The instant the carriage appeared, Jenna dashed through the portal, a stripped pine branch at the ready. Kron darted through next. Gwen followed, leaving Ysabel, holding Lathtin, and Kay to bring up the rear.

They arrived to find the others already in action. Jenna had plunged into a crowd of Selathens, bashing them with her stick. In the confusion, none of them dared fire their guns, although a couple of the men attempted to use their weapons as bayonets. Gwen darted from man to man, sending each of them to sleep with a single touch. Kron and Jon acted as her bodyguards. Jon wrestled with anyone who tried to attack Gwen, and Kron crumbled their weapons to dust.

Two men holding the dolls dashed towards Ysabel and Kay. Lathtin jumped out of Ysabel's arms while Kay summoned lightning balls. Before she could throw them at the men, Lathtin pounced on the closest one, slashing his leg just above his boot. The Selathen cursed and drew a knife, but Lathtin darted out of reach. Kay took the opportunity to lob the lightning at the men. The first ball flew straight to the soldier's arm. He screamed, and the smell of roasting flesh filled the air. Nauseated, Kay summoned a breeze to blow away the odor. Nonetheless, she continued with the attack on the other Selathen. He stared at the lightning with wide eyes before turning and bolting, dropping the dolls. Kay let the bolt pursue him even as Ysabel called something in Selathen after him.

Lex charged through the portal, his sword raised high. He looked around and slowed, since there was no one left to fight. "Close the portal, Artificer," he said.

As Kron did so, Gwen circled around, touching the men again to make sure they remained unconscious. "Are we just going to leave them here?" she asked.

Lex shrank the Allweapon into a dagger and thrust it into a sheath on his belt. "Did you finish your task at the grave?"

They all nodded.

He grinned. "Are we ready to face Salth now?"

Kay shook her head. "We have to wait for the winter solstice."

"That's less than a quarter-moon away. But if you're going to portal to her—"

"No." Kron didn't look sorry for interrupting the king's brother. "The Dead Land has changed too much since I was last there. Besides, Salth would sense a portal immediately. I plan to build another artifact to bring us to her in a way she'll never expect. But it'll take some time to assemble it. We need to find a place to hide and rest while Kay and I work."

"Me?" Kay asked.

Kron turned to her and said, "I'll explain once we find a suitable place."

Jenna's cheeks flamed red as she mumbled something.

Gwen cupped her ear. "What was that, Jenna?"

Flushing even more furiously, she replied, "Lex and I found a woodman's shelter while we were walking in the forest. It's very small, though. It won't even hold our quartet, let alone the entire group."

"That shouldn't be a problem." Kron flexed his fingers. "Jon and I can make it bigger."

"But should we stay so far out of town?" Gwen asked. "What about food?"

"I can help you restock," Lex said. "I have to return to town, or else they'll raze Challen to the ground looking for me, just like the Watch is looking for you." He studied the battered carriage for a moment. "Do you need your carriage for the artifact?"

"I might need some of the fabric from the seats," Kron replied, "but no, we won't be taking it into the Dead Land."

Lex smiled grimly. "Take what you need, then burn the carriage. It might cover your disappearance."

"The horses—" Ysabel said.

"Send them on the road to Black Rock. I'll have the Watch take care of them."

Ysabel looked dubious, but she released them. Kron stripped the cushions and made sure nothing useful was left behind. He even started the fire so Kay didn't have to. It felt much better to put out the flames with a small storm after the carriage frame was consumed. While Kay worked, Jenna and Ysabel gathered around Lex, talking in low voices. Kay wondered what Ysabel was doing before she remembered the king still held the children hostage. They must be seeking news of them.

Ysabel detoured to collect the scattered dolls before returning to Kay. "Do you think you can salvage them?" She frowned and put a hand to her chest. "By the Four, I feel so warm all of a sudden…my pendant!" She pulled it out from under her neckline. The pendant was glowing. Something in the area had hostile magic. The closest things were the dolls Kay had made.

That can't be right. I'm the only one who made them, and Kron's the only one who has magic that can affect them. "Are you sure the pendant's working properly?" Kay asked. "The dolls were fine before, weren't they? There must be something else around here that's affecting your necklace."

Ysabel picked up her own doll and held it up against the pendant. The jewel flared with red light. Kay closed her eyes, but she heard Ysabel cry out in pain.

"Freeze it! That can't be right" Kay said.

Gwen hurried over. "What's wrong?"

"The dolls have been cursed!" Ysabel dropped hers, a look of disappointment on her face. Each of them had been fitted with a black-and-silver watch.

Gwen knelt to examine them, while Jenna came over, followed by Lex and Kron. Even Lathtin sniffed one of the dolls. He hissed, fur rising along his spine as he swiped his claws across a doll head. Kay shuddered as she realized it was the one with her face. What was going on? How had this happened?

"You shouldn't touch them until I've had a chance to inspect them," Kron said. "The Four alone know what they might do."

Gwen jerked away and put her bad hand behind her back.

Kron extracted white gloves from his satchel. "Dearest, let me see your pendant, please?"

He grimaced as he fiddled with the watch strap on Ysabel's doll. The gloves scorched, emitting a nauseating smell. Kron leaned closer and after a few more heartbeats of fiddling, he removed the watch. He held the pendant next to the doll, then the watch. "Freeze it, it's too late. The curse already transferred to the doll."

Lex fingered his Allweapon. "Maybe we should just destroy them."

"Not until I figure out what this is supposed to do. This would be a bad time for the entire quartet to age to death, don't you think?"

Jenna shuddered. Kay wished Kron was exaggerating, but she had too much experience with Salth to doubt Kron's words.

He pulled a finder out of his satchel, removed the gem in the corner, and pressed various small items—a piece of blue cloth, a stone, a chunk of wood, and several other things Kay didn't see well enough to identify—to it. Once he was done, he held the finder above each doll and spun the arrow in the center of the finder. Each time, it switched back and forth between a pinch of sand and a white strip of cloth.

"What does it mean?" Jenna asked.

"There are two parts to the spell," Kron replied. "There's a time component that triggers the main part of the spell at some point in the future."

Gwen drew her eyebrows together. "And the second part?"

"Something to do with death."

At that, everyone except Kron retreated to the other side of the road.

"Are you certain we can't just destroy the dolls?" Gwen demanded in a high-pitched voice.

"Not until I understand exactly how this enchantment works." Kron sighed as he pulled a silk shawl out of his satchel. "We'd better take them with us so no one else gets hurt."

He wrapped the dolls in the shawl and looked around for somewhere to stow them. Shrugging, he gripped the bundle in his hand. Apparently even his satchel ran out of room. *Or, maybe they're too dangerous to put in there.*

Lex bade them farewell with a promise to leave messages and supplies by Olivia's grave as often as he could. "Be ready to join us soon," Kron told him. "You'll know when."

As the sun set, they trudged back into the pines. Jenna hadn't come this way before, but Ysabel was able to orient them thanks to some songbirds. The pair of them seemed happy, so Kay supposed Lex must have had good news that they would pass on later.

The shelter Jenna had described wasn't much bigger than a lean-to with a fire pit out front. A tattered blanket covered a pile of crushed pine branches still giving off a pleasant scent. Kron frowned as he studied the building. "This is smaller than I thought it would be. I'll need a lot of wood to make this comfortable for all of us."

Jenna sighed. "I'll see what I can find."

Ysabel also entered the woods to gleam food, leaving Kay and Gwen to handle other chores while Jon split dead wood—smaller pieces for a fire, bigger ones for extending the shelter. Kron retreated to the edge of the clearing and dug a hole for the bundle of dolls, buried them, then built a shelter of sticks over the site. Kay swallowed and prayed that would be enough to protect them from Salth's magic.

Jenna returned with herbs and some edible roots, while Ysabel carried a string of fish. Together with hard bread and some wine starting to turn into vinegar, it was a less than satisfying meal. No wonder no one was celebrating the retrieval of bones from all eight Season Avatars. Yes, they'd accomplished one goal they'd been pursuing ever since the other Avatars died, but now their biggest task in eight hundred years was nearly upon them. Were they ready for the challenge?

Kron set his empty bowl down. "I haven't had an opportunity to work on the artifact that will take us to Salth's crystal house." He looked at Kay. "Since you did such a good job creating those decoys, would you mind taking on another sewing project?"

Her heart raced. "What sort of project?" *What could he want me to sew now? I hope it's not another blanket like the one we flew on back in Summerton.* Her stomach already churned at the thought of such flimsy support.

"It's not another blanket," he said, as if he was linked with her and could read her thoughts. "It's a balloon."

Kay and everyone else in the clearing stared at him. "A balloon?" Gwen asked. "A child's toy?"

"Not a toy balloon, a giant silk one, like the kind they make in my home country of Delns. I read about it in the paper." Kron gestured at the clearing. "One as big as this clearing. I'll make it float above the ground." He grinned. "Salth is so obsessed with the past that she doesn't pay attention to the present. She'll be so busy watching the river for us, the way we traveled eight hundred years ago, that she won't know we're attacking her until we arrive at her doorstep!"

Ysabel shook her head. "Kron, my heart, I fear you've forgotten something. How are we supposed to use a balloon to travel? Are we all going to ride on it, like the carpet?"

"By All Four, I don't want to do that again!" Kay exclaimed. Jon put his arm over her shoulders. Some of her fear drained away.

Kron smiled. "I remember how much all of you disliked the carpet. This time, I plan to attach a wagon or basket to the balloon, one with high sides so you don't have to worry about falling out."

Gwen raised both eyebrows. "A basket big enough to carry all four Avatars?"

"And Jon, Lathtin, myself, and the War Avatar as well." Kron nodded. "I can enlarge a basket so that it's big enough to carry all of us. Knowing Salth, she'll find or create monsters even stranger than the ones we faced last moon. We'll defend you while you create the portal to the God of Winter's domain and link with the absent Avatars."

Jon nodded. "I'd better get some target practice with that revolver, then."

"Where am I supposed to get the silk for the balloon?" Kay asked.

"Well…" Kron flushed as he studied the ground. "I was hoping you ladies wouldn't mind donating some of your dresses to the effort. Silk will be the best material for the balloon, but even I can't conjure it from nothing."

"By the Four, are you serious?" Jenna knocked over the last bottle of wine as she leapt up from her log seat. "Just when we've finally obtained clothes fit for a queen, we have to give them up?"

Gwen shook her head as she gave Jenna stern look. "The Avatars' wealth isn't ours to keep. We may use it during our times as Avatars, but it's to maintain all twelve of us and to help Challen."

"That's easy for you to say when you have wealth of your own!"

Gwen sighed.

Before she could respond, Ysabel said, "Well, at least we can order new dresses when we return to the One Oak."

Assuming we return, Kay thought. Other objections came to mind. "Our dresses are tailored to each of us, and we all have very different bodies. The dresses will turn into silk pieces of very different sizes once I take them apart. What if there isn't enough material? I doubt we'll find many dress shops catering to nobles in Black Rock."

Kron drooped as if he was deflating like a leaky balloon. "I don't choose parts for my artifacts randomly. While your dresses aren't magic, the fact that you've worn them gives them a certain…holiness, perhaps, an association with the Four Gods and Goddesses. I can search for more material, but your dresses will be key to the balloon's success."

Gwen sighed. "Very well. Take whatever you need." She looked Kron straight in the eye. "However, I ask something in return."

"What is that?" he asked warily.

"When we finally face Salth and Sal-thaath, we do it wearing our Avatar colors." She smiled, but her eyes didn't sparkle. "I never thought I'd say this, but I miss wearing yellow. I don't feel like myself without it."

"I agree," Ysabel said. "We have to make sure Salth knows who we are, especially since we've been reborn."

"I'm confident she'll recognize you no matter how many centuries it's been or how different you look now," Kron answered wryly. "What I'm more worried about is whether your magic skills have developed enough to face her. She was one of the most talented magicians I knew back at the Magic Institute, and that was before she had the life force of an entire country to draw on."

The communal mood plunged as instantly as if Kay had changed boiling water to ice. Ysabel shifted closer to Kron and conversed with him in whispers, while Lathtin climbed to the top of the lean-to and disappeared. Gwen exchanged glances with Kay and Jenna.

"I was about to propose a group prayer with all of us, but I think some people are getting more comfort as couples instead." Gwen sighed. "We'll pray in the morning before Kay starts her latest sewing project."

Kay took a seat near Jon and took his hand. Despite feeling slightly guilty about choosing his company over her sister Avatars, the warmth from his hand steadied her. They exchanged wordless glances and sat like that until bedtime.

CHAPTER SIXTEEN

Kay's Largest Sewing Project

"By the Four, Kron, we should take rooms in Black Rock," Kay said. "The middle of the woods is hardly a proper place for a sewing workshop."

It was a couple of hours past sunrise, but the pines around them were still edged with frost. Gwen and Ysabel sorted through the trunks they'd salvaged from the carriage, picking out dresses and other suitable garments while hiding the unmentionables from the men's sight. They moved slowly, as if they needed another night's sleep. Gwen, Jenna, and Ysabel had all had nightmares. It was almost enough to make Kay feel guilty for sleeping soundly, but she'd already suffered enough sleepless nights thanks to Salth. Kay winced as Ysabel laid another dress on the ground. It would be dirty and full of pine needles before she even had a chance to work on it.

"The birds saw the Watch leaving the town early this morning, but the Selathens haven't given up," Ysabel said. "They've taken over a floor at the inn and are inquiring after us at every boarding house. I don't know how we'd stay hidden in Black Rock."

"And I don't know how I'm supposed to keep the silk smooth under these conditions," Kay snapped.

"You don't need to worry about that," Kron said. "I can repair the fabric if necessary. Just having you put it together is a big help. It allows me to focus on finding the right materials to create the rest of the artifact." He frowned. "I'm not sure how to find the special lighter-than-regular-air gas that the Delns used. I can use magic if necessary, but the less magic I use, the less chance Salth has of detecting us."

Winter, give me strength to handle these tasks, and to do so without feeling the burden is all on me this season. If only she could take her worries and make them float away like smoke....

"Smoke!" she said. "Smoke floats in air!"

The others stared at her with puzzled expressions on their faces. Kron was the first to understand her idea. "You mean to use smoke to lift the balloon and us? Will it work for such a long distance?"

"Not smoke, but warm air. Even in the middle of winter, I can keep the air inside the balloon much warmer than the air outside."

"But that's using your magic," Gwen pointed out. "Won't Salth sense that?"

"She wouldn't if we could somehow attach a steam engine to the balloon," Jon said. "It would require a lot of coal and water, but it wouldn't be magic."

"Yes, I've seen your locomotive engines, and they're very big." Kron beckoned Jon over. "Come tell me what you know about steam engines. There may be a way to make them more efficient, like an artifact, so there's no magic use once we're in the Dead Land."

As the men left, Gwen and Ysabel brought Kay the dresses and laid them out, Gwen tugging at them with her good hand. The dresses were still in the colors Kron had changed them to back in Wistica: pink, purple, brown, and gray. Kay identified their owners by the cut and sizing of each gown. She took one of Gwen's and studied the stitching and embroidered flowers on the sleeve. Kay sighed a final time. It seemed a shame to waste some other seamstresses' work by sewing it up into a balloon where the details would never be seen, but the dresses were serving a higher purpose now.

Kay carefully deconstructed the first dress, taking care to preserve as much material as possible. As she continued, Gwen and Ysabel laid the pieces out, constantly rearranging them as if they couldn't decide what the final puzzle should look like. Kay let their murmuring fade into the background. When Gwen and the other Season Avatars had taken her away from the dressmaker's shop, she'd thought she'd never have to sew all day, just enough to clear her workbasket and occupy an hour or two. How long would it take her to sew all of this material together, especially if she had to make her stitches as tiny as she could? Kay repressed a sigh. It was barely noon, and already her eyes ached and her hand cramped.

Gwen sat down next to her. "Perhaps Salth will be so blinded by our balloon's many colors that she'll be too distracted to fight."

"Is that what you think we're supposed to do? Fight her?"

"Well, not just by ourselves. We'll have the spirits of the other Avatars to help."

"Except for Dorian," Kay said sourly.

"Do you think he'll change his mind once he senses Margaret?" Gwen asked. "Remember, we didn't know him when his wife was still alive. Grief may have driven him to do things he wouldn't normally do."

Kay set her scissors down and flexed her hand. "I've endured his abuse for too many lives to excuse him. He's not worth defending, Gwen. Have you forgotten he tried to kill me?"

"By All Four Gods and Goddesses, of course not. Set your hand down. Right there." Gwen laid Kay's hand in her lap and massaged it. Her aches eased. "I can't forget that Dorian wanted to destroy our quartet," Gwen continued, "To me, he's lower than horse manure, and I'd rather shovel out our stables in my best ball gown, using only my bare hands, than let him ever become an Avatar again."

Kay smiled at the image. "Please don't treat your dresses like that," she said. "They don't deserve it."

"I doubt I'll have any spare dresses by the time we're done with this balloon," Gwen said. "But that's not important. What is important is that no matter how twisted Dorian is, no matter what he's done by breaking his oath to Winter and harming other Season Avatars, he's still less evil than Salth. Only the Four know how many lives she's taken over the centuries to preserve her son's."

Kay half-wished for her hand back so she could slash something with her scissors. "That still doesn't excuse Dorian's behavior."

Gwen released her. "I know, but if we have to deal with one or the other, Dorian might be the better choice, don't you agree?"

"Gwen, we can't trust Dorian anymore!"

"I never said I would." Gwen's voice hardened. "I just trust him— or Margaret—a little more than I do Salth." She stood. "Let's find something to eat. I'm sure the wind won't blow any pieces away while we take a break."

Kay, still worried something would happen to the fabric, finished her share of stale bread and dried beef as quickly as she could swallow it. When she was done, she studied the layout Gwen and Ysabel had come up with, walking around the pieces and rearranging them slightly for better fit. She ran out of pins, so she used twigs and pine needles to join some of the pieces. By the time Kron brought her more thread, she was ready to start sewing, even though only a couple hours of daylight were left.

"Here." Gwen surprised Kay by linking with her. *Let me help.*

How? There's no magic involved in sewing.

I can give you stamina and help you see better so you can continue sewing longer.

Gwen's magic proved to be more useful than Kay had expected. Even without bringing Jenna and Ysabel into the link, Kay's hand felt steadier with Gwen joined to her. Her eyes didn't burn with dryness, and no matter how long she sat, her legs didn't become numb or her body demand refreshment or release. Pieces of fabric and spools of thread appeared exactly when she needed them, and she didn't even have to pause to snip thread. Dimly she was aware of Ysabel and Jenna assisting and singing hymns to the Four Gods and Goddesses, of Kron and Jon hammering at the shelter, but they seemed curtained off from her awareness.

When Gwen finally broke the link, it took Kay several heartbeats to return to the normal world. She blinked several times, thinking she'd sewed herself blind, before realizing it had grown dark. Various parts of her body—shaky legs, grumbling stomach, dry mouth—sent her their complaints. Gwen helped her to her feet while Ysabel offered her a mug of weak cider. Kay stretched out each finger and rolled her head on her neck for a few heartbeats before taking the drink. She wasn't as stiff as she normally was after a day of sewing, but the ritual from her seamstress days made her feel spiritually complete.

She drained half of the cider before saying, "By the Four, I can't remember when I've had such a smooth day of sewing! How much is done? I feel like I must have assembled all the fabric by now…"

She summoned more lighting balls to view her handiwork more clearly. Fabric scraps of various colors melded together like a segment of orange peel, but beyond them lay more scraps than had been there this morning. They poured out of the shelter—which held two more beds and had a longer roof—and stretched into of the clearing, covering all of it except for the spot where Kron had buried the dolls.

Kay shook her head, but the untouched fabric didn't disappear. "Freeze it, where did this all come from? I know we didn't bring along a dozen trunks each!"

"Kron did it," Ysabel said with pride. "He found scraps of torn flour and sugar bags and transformed them to match our dresses."

"Couldn't he have done that without us having to rip them up?" Jenna asked.

"Unfortunately not," Kron replied as he left the shelter. "I needed models. But I think we finally have enough fabric now. All I have to do is figure out how to warm the air."

He left the clearing while Kay gaped at all the work to be done.

* * *

Assembling the balloon took Kay exactly four days, one for each of the Four Gods and Goddesses. They all passed very much the same as the first day, with Gwen supporting Kay through the link. Occasionally Jenna or Ysabel contributed magic to the link, but most often they seemed to be busy foraging for food or gathering supplies. Whatever they were doing, they weren't sleeping well, judging from the dark circles under their eyes. Jon and Kron finished expanding the shelter by the end of the second day and then disappeared into the forest to work on the balloon engine. Every time Kay emerged from her sewing trance, she expected that they'd been surrounded by Selathens or that the dolls' curse had taken effect. It wasn't like Salth to allow Challen a quiet season. Maybe the Four were arranging for Their Avatars to have some peace for once.

At the end of the fourth day, Kay tied the final knot, snipped the thread, and stood to stretch and survey the completed project. Although she'd been aware of the fabric becoming heavier and more awkward to stitch as she joined pieces to it, she hadn't seen the full shape until now. As she'd predicted, it filled their shelter and covered the clearing. Although patches clashed with each other, the overall effect was of muted colors. Kay hoped the colors would blend into the sky so Salth wouldn't see them approaching.

"Where's the basket we're supposed to travel in?" she asked.

"Under the balloon." Gwen pointed to a circular hump in the middle. Next to it was another, taller lump flailing around.

Kay grinned. "Is that Jenna?"

"Yes. She's been helping Kron enlarge a laundry basket by weaving branches into it."

"I hope it will be safe." Kay shivered. She'd been so focused on assembling the balloon she hadn't thought about what it meant—another terrifying trip in the sky to confront the woman who'd haunted her dreams for years. "It wouldn't do to fall out before Salth has a chance to kill us."

"Or figure out how we're supposed to work with the other Avatars for our seasons," Gwen said thoughtfully. "Will we do it individually, or linked? I don't think there's ever been a link involving all twelve Avatars, at least not that I can remember."

"By season." Kay scowled, thinking of Dorian. If she had to link with him—if it was even possible—she'd rather have her sister Avatars with her to cushion the link.

Jenna pushed the balloon off her. Her short hair was mussed, and her cheeks were red. "Freeze it, Kron, this isn't the right type of branch for what you want me to do."

"It doesn't matter," he said. "I'll make it work."

"You'd better. If any of us fall out on the way to confront Salth, The Four will be very displeased with you."

Kay gulped.

Kron appeared undisturbed by Jenna's threat. "If this basket breaks, then I'll stop calling myself an artificer. The basket isn't half the problem the steam engine is." He paced, casually kicking the fabric. "A locomotive engine is far too heavy and requires too much coal and water. I'm modifying it, but I'm still missing a key component...or something."

"May we see it anyway?" Gwen asked.

"You may as well." Kron abruptly left the clearing. Kay and the others followed him. The short walk was more exercise than she'd had in days, and it felt good to stretch her legs.

The path led to another, smaller clearing dominated by a chunk of iron in the center. Kay wasn't familiar with any of the engine parts. Jon, however, seemed quite at home with it as he unscrewed the cover. He looked up and grinned at her, causing her to grin back.

"Where did you get that?" she asked.

"Kron and I went to the locomotive station here and bartered for an old engine that didn't work anymore," Jon said.

"I've enhanced it so we'll get more power out of it—once I figure out how to make it run on as little magic as possible," Kron added. "There has to be a better source of energy than coal!"

Jon shook his head. "If there is, it isn't here."

This didn't seem like a subject that Kay knew much about. Jenna and Ysabel shrugged, then retreated, perhaps to find more food or take care of some of the chores. Gwen lingered, so Kay did too. She hadn't had much time to spend with Jon while sewing the balloon, and it made her happy to see Kron treating him as an equal.

Kron reached into a bucket and pulled out a piece of coal. "I wish my magic could make it burn without consuming it," he murmured. "That would make it so much easier to use this engine."

"Can't you enchant the engine to run on its own?" Jon asked.

"By the Four, I would if I could. I'm missing something…something obvious, I fear." Kron emptied out his satchel. One by one, he placed things like chalk, gems, and coins close to the piece of coal, shook his head, and returned the rejected item to the bag. The only thing he saved was an antique flint and steel set for starting fires. That made sense. Kron still didn't seem satisfied, though.

"I'm missing something," he said. "What else does fire need?"

"Air," Jon replied. "If you close a fire off from air, it dies."

"That's it!" Kron leapt up so quickly he startled Kay. "Something for air, and something to make the fire last. And maybe some things to hide our presence from Salth. Now to determine exactly what those things are…"

He dashed off before Kay could suggest using a fan for air. Perhaps she could make one from leftover fabric scraps. For now, she wanted to spend some time with Jon. He was so intent on the engine she had to tap his shoulder to get him to look at her. But when she whispered in his ear, he nodded eagerly.

Gwen cleared her throat. "I suppose we should see if there's anything we need to do back at camp…"

Kay deliberately turned away and kissed Jon.

Pine needles burst open as Gwen walked away, muttering, "I hope Lathtin will have time for me."

Kay felt a tinge of guilt, but as Jon put his arms around her, she set it aside.

***

When Kay and Jon returned to the shelter at sunset, Kron wasn't there. Maybe he was still looking for items he needed for his artifact. Beneath a string of glowing lights, she searched for flat sticks and scraps of leftover fabric. It didn't take her long to sew them together into a small but functional fan.

Kron returned from only the Four knew where after dinner with an abstracted look on his face. He missed Ysabel's cheek when she came up to him for a kiss, had to be coaxed to eat the leftovers she had saved for him, and immediately set out for the engine. Kay followed him with the fan. She didn't catch up with him until he'd arrived at the engine and emptied out his satchel, holding up one item at a time to the engine, the piece of coal, and the flint-and-steel set. Over and over he cursed in his ancient language and scattered his belongings on the ground.

Kay waited until he had run out of items, then stepped forward. "Here. Will this work?"

He stared at her for a moment with dark eyes before accepting her fan. As soon as he touched it to the other items, he laughed harshly. "By All Four, I portal all over Challen looking for items, and of course the Winter Avatar had what I needed all along."

He made it sound like an accusation. "I made it just now for the balloon."

Kron sighed. "Perhaps that's what I should be doing as well, making new things. But nothing feels right to me. Have I lost my artifact magic just when we need it most?"

Shrieks rose from the clearing. Kay whirled and ran toward them, lighting welling up in her fingertips. Kron passed her, but she joined him heartbeats later to a scene of chaos.

The balloon had been pushed to the side, but Kay immediately spotted several long rips she'd have to repair. It took her a couple of heartbeats to spot the culprit: her own doll had stolen her scissors, even though they were almost as long as the doll, and was undoing her work.

Fury rose in Kay's throat. She wanted to blast the doll with lightning, but she didn't want to risk setting the balloon on fire. She switched instead to creating hail, which was trickier. She had to cool the air directly above the doll while drawing moisture to the spot at the same time. The doll didn't oblige her by remaining still; it ran from one end of the balloon to the other. Kay groaned at the thought of having to so much to repair, but she willed a hand-sized chunk of hail into existence. A well-timed wind flung it onto the doll and smacked it onto its back. Kay nodded in satisfaction. Before she could pick her way over the fabric to claim the doll, the hail holding it in place melted. It stood up, dropped the scissors, and glared at her. Then it opened its hand, and a tiny lightning ball flickered as it sped toward Kay.

Freeze it! She smothered the lightning before it could burn her, but she was stunned her doll had magic of its own. Or was it borrowing or copying hers?

"Kron!" she called. "The dolls have our magic!"

"We know," Gwen replied in a strained voice. "Come here and link with us!"

Kay glanced back at the shelter. The other three dolls had attached themselves to their Avatars. Gwen held her dead hand above her head while trying to thrust her decoy off of her skirt with the other. Jenna's doll had grabbed a scaled-down fighting stick and was whacking Jenna's boot. Jenna hopped around cursing while she reached for a suitable staff of her own. The only one who held the upper hand over her doll was Ysabel. Lathtin had her doll pinned down and hissed at it, drowning out its cries for mice to swarm over the cat.

Another spark zapped Kay, and she rubbed her stinging side as she tried to figure out what to do. Lightning was too dangerous, freezing not effective...maybe a wind to sweep the doll away. That didn't seem likely to destroy it, however.

"By All Four Gods and Goddesses!" Gwen trapped her doll against the table. "It has an aura!"

"An aura?" Jenna asked.

"Some sickly mustard color, like a corrupted yellow." Gwen shuddered. "Yours is a nauseating shade of green, and Ysabel's looks like blood. I can't make out the aura in Kay's doll very well. How could I have missed them earlier?"

"They might have been masked," Kron said. "Or maybe the dolls weren't possessed until just now, when we're nearly ready to face Salth herself."

"But what do we do with these dolls?" Ysabel asked.

Kay stared at hers. She couldn't see auras like Gwen, but she was even more reluctant to destroy the doll. Were these souls evil and worthy of eternal freezing in Winter's domain, or innocents tortured by Salth? Either way, Winter Himself should deal with them, not her. Unless...Kay fingered the locket around her neck. "Kron, if I opened a portal to Winter's domain, could we send the souls there?"

"Perhaps." The lack of enthusiasm in his voice made her think her idea must not be very good. Footsteps crunched as he approached her. "But let's try it on your doll. It's farthest away from the others, but it's also the most dangerous."

With that, Kay approached her doll, lifting her feet with care as she was forced to cross over the balloon. The doll continued to jolt her. Its strikes became more powerful as she closed the distance between them.

"I think they draw on our own magic!" she called back to her sisters. "Stay away from the one that matches you!"

"Easier said than done," Jenna muttered.

Kay ignored her and unfastened Olivia's locket. Wind gusted toward her, but remembering what had happened to Margaret's diamond, she wrapped the chain around her wrist. Clutching the locket for good measure, Kay closed the gap between her and the doll. With every step, her stomach twisted. *By the Four, how close do I have to get?* Once she was within arms' reach, she drew a circle in the air, keeping it small so only the doll would fit. The doll scooted away. Kron was waiting with a pair of white gloves. He caught the doll, and it screamed in a tiny voice and flailed its limbs. He held it as far away from his body as possible.

"Are you ready, Kay?"

She nodded, then made the sign of the Four over her heart.

Kron stepped up to the blacker-than-black circle and tossed the doll through.

Kay sank to her knees as a wave of nausea overwhelmed her. The doll tugged at her soul as if it wanted to drag her with it to Winter's domain. *I won't go,* she told herself. *I'm needed here.* The Four would save her, just as They had before—

Kron slashed a silver knife through the air, between her and the portal. The nausea ebbed, though it took several heartbeats before it completely faded.

The Four preferred not to intervene directly, she reminded herself. Perhaps Kron was Their agent, just as her sister Avatars were.

Gwen rushed over to her and laid a concerned hand on her arm. The contact made Kay feel better immediately.

After that, taking care of the rest of the dolls was simple. Kay's weather magic was back to normal, so she trapped the dolls with freezing rain. Kron severed the links between the dolls and their counterparts before tossing the dolls through the portal. Kay felt a tinge of envy that they didn't have to suffer—not that she would have wished her illness on them. They all breathed easier once the dolls were gone. Not even the cloth that Kay had used to make them remained behind.

Kay stood among the wreckage of her greatest sewing project, ruined by another sewing project of hers. She picked up a scrap of silk and rubbed it between her fingers. Wasted, just like all the years she'd spent fearing Salth and hiding her magic. Here Kay had thought Salth could do nothing else to hurt her, only to see all of her hard work destroyed. Salth had tried to destroy her bodily, and now she was attacking the soul Kay put into her projects? Kay wadded up the silk. Anger seethed, boiled, then abruptly froze into ice-hard determination.

"By All Four Gods and Goddesses, I swear we will travel across the Dead Land to face Salth on the winter solstice." She took a deep breath. "Even if I have to carry us there in the center of a whirlwind."

The others stared at her with shock and a little fear in their eyes.

CHAPTER SEVENTEEN

Repairs

"Perhaps it's not so bad the balloon was torn apart." Kron walked through the frosted clearing the next morning, rolling up sections of the balloon. "It'll be easier to move this way."

"Move it?" Kay asked incredulously. "You mean after having me spend days sewing here, you were going to use the balloon somewhere else?"

"I didn't realize how big it would be. If we inflated it here, it would get stuck in the tree branches." He shrugged his shoulders. "Then we really would need your whirlwind. But I'm not giving up on repairing the balloon, even if I have to hold it together with enchanted string."

Jenna crossed her arms. "You're not making me feel enthusiastic for this trip, Kron, and I always love the chance to leave the One Oak."

"I wish we were back there, or Wistica, and had nothing else to worry about besides the soltrans. I suppose we'll miss it. It'll be the first time in the history of the Season Avatars." Gwen sighed as she stared down at her dead hand. The violet bracelet had become completely white, as if it had been transformed from living flowers into ice. "Very well, let's get this done. How should we move it? We don't have a carriage anymore, or even a team of horses."

Kay collected strips of balloon and folded them with Jenna's help. Ysabel clutched Lathtin and peered toward the path. After a few moments, she said, "All of the wild animals nearby that are big enough to help are skittish. It's as if they sense a Chaos Season, but Lathtin says we should have a couple of hours before it starts."

"That should be enough time to move the balloon, if not the entire camp," Kron said. "But we also need to bring the engine along, even if it's not complete."

"Where are we moving them to?" Jon asked. "By the river where the Selathens ambushed the carriage? That doesn't seem like a safe spot to work."

"But it's the closest open area. I'll just have to ward us." Kron paced off toward the engine. "I'll meet you there."

He left, but Jon remained behind. "What can I do?" he asked.

"If you could help us gather everything…" Gwen headed back to the shelter, found a carpetbag, and tossed the remaining food supplies inside.

Jon and Jenna stacked the balloon pieces, then tried lifting them. "Maybe we can carry these on our own," Jon said.

"I think we could use another assistant," Jenna said. "Ysabel, if I wrote a note to Lex, could Lathtin bring it to him?"

"You think he should come now?" Gwen called. "By the Four, we're not ready!"

"But we have to be ready soon, Gwen. Tomorrow is the solstice!" Jenna turned toward Kay. "And Kay's birthday."

Kay flushed. It didn't seem like her birthday. They had far more important things to think about than that, like facing Salth.

Lathtin hopped down from Ysabel's arms and strolled over to Jenna as if he was ready to carry the message this instant. He, along with everyone else, stared at Gwen.

"Freeze it. I suppose we don't have much choice." She nodded permission.

Jon hauled off the first load of fabric—Kay winced, thinking how much damage it would receive—while Jenna scrawled a note on a page from Gwen's sketchbook. Lathtin gripped it between his teeth. He padded over first to his sister, then to Gwen, who knelt to scratch behind his ears. "Travel safely, dear one," she murmured so quietly Kay wouldn't have caught her words without the wind.

He bounded off.

Jenna and Ysabel struggled with the next load, so Kay helped Gwen pack the rest of their meager supplies. They followed the others down the narrow trail to the river. Kay blinked at the empty road. Their carriage was gone as if it had never been. Snowflakes drifted down, but Kay sensed they wouldn't last long. They covered everything, but they seemed to cluster in random places in the air....

"There!" She pointed.

Gwen's mouth quirked in a smile. "Kron, your invisibility wards don't fool the weather."

"I've never come up with a way to account for that." Kron popped into view, along with the others. The carriage frame was still there, but the doors, seats, and even the wooden trim had been removed. Gwen scowled but said nothing.

Jenna had piled the other parts of the balloon off to the side, so Kay set her load down next to the carriage's skeleton and started arranging the fabric back into position. Although several sections had been completely separated, they weren't as big as she thought they would be. Maybe she could manage this repair job on her own without help...

The wind taunted her by blowing a strip away so it tangled in reeds. Kay scowled. While she hadn't been consciously directing the wind, she wouldn't permit it to interfere with her work. She reached out with her magic to quiet the wind, but it tore away from her with power of its own.

Freeze it! Why does this always happen at the worst time? "Chaos Season!" she called to the others.

"My sapling!" Jenna turned her head wildly. "It's still back by the shelter!"

"And Lathtin's already halfway to Black Rock," Ysabel said. "Kay, how widespread is the storm? Is it safe to call him back?"

Kay probed the storm. It was local but building in strength. Both cold and moisture were combining overhead to form freezing rain. Instead of answering, she held out her hands, inviting the link. The other three joined her as she pulled magic out of the clouds. No matter how much she pulled, there seemed to be more. While she worked, Ysabel searched for her brother. Dimly, Kay felt Ysabel call to Lathtin and heard him refuse to return. He bounded along as if Fall had put springs in his paws, evading falling branches with ease. He would reach shelter at Lex's hotel faster than if he returned to them.

If this storm is just a small one, maybe we can tame it without him, Ysabel said hopefully.

But the trees are...growing, Jenna said. *They're adding growth rings as if every heartbeat is a year!*

Kay sent her more magic to halt the unnatural tree growth. Meanwhile, mayflies exploded into existence and died in a heartbeat. A doe gave birth to a fawn, which developed into a stag and died while Ysabel watched in horror.

Salth's doing more than mixing up the seasons, Gwen said. *She's speeding up time.*

Speeding up time? The others chorused. Kay could feel them sharing her uncertainty that they could restore the natural order. They'd never handled a Chaos Storm like this before.

Will Lex get older if he ventures out into this? Jenna asked. *There's already an age gap between us.*

He's an Avatar. Maybe the God of War will protect him.

If Salth harms one of Lathtin's whiskers, I'll ask Fall for claws so I can shred that frozen woman myself.

All of them paused, taken aback by the fierceness in Ysabel's thoughts.

Lathtin must have heard his sister, for he twisted and dodged as if Salth was targeting him with bolts of time magic. All Kay could see was weather magic, so she cleared snow and dried mud before he could get caught in it. He made it to Black Rock, which was deserted after the coal miners had descended for their shift. Lathtin raced to the hotel, then halted at the entrance, waiting for someone to open the door so he could sneak in. One of the servants, a stableman, left the building. He saw Lathtin and grabbed for him, but all he could catch was the cat's tail. Lathtin yowled so pitifully Kay wanted to hurl ice at the man. Before she could, Lex appeared to grab Lathtin and the note he'd carried. He studied the note, then grinned.

"Saddle my stallion," he told the stableman.

As the man ran for the stables,. Lex chucked Lathtin under his chin. "Well, little friend, looks as if I'm about to face a foe worthy of my skill. Are you joining me?"

Lathtin yowled.

"You must be the Fall Avatar's anilink. I wasn't sure at first. Come, let us pack." Lex brought Lathtin inside the hotel. Ysabel withdrew her attention from them. *Now that we know he made it there safely, let's finish taming this Chaos Season so they have safe travels here.*

Kay examined the storm again, looking for some flaw that would allow her to unravel it. Nothing. Even the connection to Salth was wrapped in time magic that spun dizzyingly when Kay approached it. Then, just for a heartbeat, the connection frayed like a worn thread. She pounced and severed it. Without additional power, the storm would be more manageable. Giving thanks to Winter, she worked at the edge of the Chaos Season to weaken it. She stilled a wind, and abruptly, the entire storm fell apart as if someone had snipped a thread holding everything together. Only a single gray cloud remained, dormant.

Kay sniffed. That had been far easier than she expected. Dorian must be playing a trick on her; any heartbeat now, the Chaos Season would return with four-fold strength. She waited for a few moments, but nothing happened.

Kay, share the magic with us, Jenna said. *If Chaos Season returns, we'll just take care of it again.*

It'll be worse—

Maybe not, Ysabel said as she stopped a pair of deer from mating out of season. *Maybe Dorian is getting tired of helping the enemy. Or maybe he realizes Margaret is on our side and is going to behave for her.*

Kay started to deny it, but as Ysabel and Jenna focused on their tasks, she wondered if they were right. Maybe Dorian had repented of his foolish decision to side with Salth. Did it matter? He'd been cruel to Kay over so many lifetimes that nothing he could do would ever redeem him in her mind.

Kay, Chaos Season is over, Gwen said. *Let's eat something while we wait for Lex and Lathtin to arrive.*

That sounded like a good idea. Her stomach rumbled like the Jon's locomotive.

Kay ate a quick meal of bread, cheese, and melted snow before returning to the balloon. As she stitched the first strip back into place, the others finished bringing the rest of the supplies from the clearing. Ysabel seemed anxious as she paused every few minutes to look around, but Kay bent her head to ignore her sister Avatar and sew as fast as she could. As she snapped her thread, Ysabel announced, "The animals are aging again."

"By All Four!" Gwen dropped what she was holding. "I thought we'd eliminated that time storm with the regular Chaos Season. How did it return?"

Kay probed the weather, searching for an answer. The weather on the ground was normal. She looked upward. The gray cloud from before held the answer: buried in the water droplets was a knot of magic Kay couldn't undo. Time magic, not weather magic.

"Kron!" she called. "How do we stop time magic?"

He stood up and blinked as if the engine had mesmerized him. "Time magic in Challen? Where?"

She pointed upward. Kron shaded his eyes as he stared at the cloud. Finally he said, "I'd need an artifact, but I can't reach Salth's magic from here. Once the balloon is ready...."

Kay gestured at the ripped balloon. "Are you certain I have to do all of the repairs myself?"

Gwen approached them and asked, "What if I linked with you again?"

"It's still slow work."

"I could try sewing one-handed, but it never was my most impressive accomplishment." Gwen turned to Kron. "Are you certain you can't use your magic to help her?"

He studied the balloon for a moment. "Could I see your sewing supplies?" he asked.

Kay brought over her sewing kit while Gwen, Jenna, and Ysabel linked. Kron selected several needles and pulled his own spool of thread from his satchel. He threaded her needles with more skill than she'd expected. Then he held them out to her. "Blow on them."

She complied, but nothing happened. Kron rubbed the needles against silk and wool before burying them in the balloon fabric, one at the start of each ripped seam. Finally, he placed lodestones at the ends. The needles whipped through the fabric, their stitches as wild as a beginner's.

"You'll have to control them yourself," he said as he handed her a candle stub. "I still need one more item for the engine."

He started off. Kay called after him, "What do I do?"

"Guide them!" he called back. "Take a few stitches with each to show them what they should do. If you need to start over, take them out and put them at the start of the bad section. Use the wax to make the stitches airtight."

Kay wished he'd told her that before setting the needles free. Some stitches were as broad as her hand. Some needles grabbed so much fabric it flapped back and forth. She had to remove all the needles, then set them to work one at a time. But once she taught each needle how to sew properly, it continued without her. She sighed with relief as a repair job that would have taken her hours was finished in a few minutes. Rubbing the candle over the seams took longer, but she didn't run out of wax.

Hoofbeats plodded wearily on the road. Kay tensed as a rider came into view, then relaxed as she realized it was the War Avatar, cradling something he braced against his body while guiding his horse one-handed. Lex and Lathtin sat proudly on a horse that appeared on the verge of collapse. Ysabel rushed out to stroke the horse, who snorted at her.

"Eagle's Claws, what's going on?" Lex said as he halted the horse. "My horse was in his prime when we left the town, and now Crusher looks like he's going to fall over."

"This Chaos Season had time magic mixed in it. Thank the Four it hasn't spread to Black Rock—yet."

"It's tied to us," Kron said. "If it weren't for my artifacts, we'd all be piles of bones by now."

Jenna shuddered.

"If I had known about that, then I would not have brought this precious burden." Lex beckoned Jenna over and offered her a blanket—and their son Robbie.

"Robbie!" She cradled the baby, who babbled at her excitedly. "You never said you had him here? How did you rescue him?"

"And why is he here?" Gwen asked.

"War willed it, though He would not explain why."

"What about my brothers and sister?" Ysabel asked. "Are they here too?"

Lex shook his head. "They are still in Wistica. I persuaded my brother that they are more useful in Challen than back in Fip. They were well as of my general's last report."

Ysabel sighed and took charge of the horse.

"But why isn't Robbie with Ysabel's family?" Gwen asked. "Why would the God of War tell you to bring a baby here when we're about to visit the Dead Land?"

Jenna drew him closer to her. "We can't just leave him here."

Gwen nodded. "Kron can send him to the One Oak. The servants will find him and take care of him."

"But maybe the War God sent Robbie to me for a reason," Jenna said.

Gwen rolled her eyes. "By the Four, why would you trust the Fip God with your child's safety?"

"He's my child too, Ava." Lex glared at her. "Do you think I will fail to defend him, no matter what War wishes?"

"Salth would love to claim an infant's life," Gwen said darkly.

Fear shone in Jenna's eyes. "But Kron can protect him with an artifact." She pressed her own altered watch against her child, as if it would be enough to protect both of them.

As if hearing his name had got his attention, Kron left the engine and came over to study the War Avatar. His eyes gleamed. "What's the oldest piece of jewelry you're wearing? Is it your ring? I need to borrow it."

"My signet ring?" Lex cupped his other hand over his ring. "Eagle's Claws, are you mad, artificer?"

"I need something to keep the engine running during the trip, something that endures. I can sense your ring will work."

Lex shook his head. "It belongs to the Fip family. Unless... you would be willing to guarantee my son will be protected from Salth and Sal-thaath?"

"I need threads from your clothes and Jenna's," Kron replied. "I'll weave camouflage so Salth and Sal-thaath won't even realize the child is there." He glanced at the cloud. "But I can do that while we travel. We should get the balloon off the ground before Salth figures out how to break through my defenses."

As they walked off, Lex said, "You plan to confront the demigoddess of Time with a child's toy? That doesn't sound promising."

Kay tuned out the men's conversation as she joined with Gwen to lend her strength to Ysabel. Unfortunately, the stallion had exhausted himself, and the only way Ysabel was able to help him was to end his suffering. Tears hung in her eyes as she broke the link. "Freeze it, Salth has no reason to put animals through such pain!" She clenched her fists. "This has to be the last animal that dies because of Chaos Season."

"May the Four make it so," Gwen said.

The four of them linked to share their resolution, then turned to final preparations.

For Kay, that meant monitoring the weather as Kron and Jon finished assembling the balloon. The cloud had turned an ugly shade of gray-green, and the wind whipped the treetops around as if they were sticks. Kay diverted the wind so it wouldn't steal the balloon. The others held the balloon fabric out of the way while Kron started the engine. As the air warmed, Kay directed it into the balloon and made sure all the stitches were tight. Soon, the balloon towered above the trees again. Jon hurried to lash the basket down with a couple of ropes tied to trees before the artifact could fly off without them.

Gwen hurried to the basket, then stopped. "How are we supposed to climb in?" The basket rose past her waist.

"Freeze it, I didn't make a door." Kron touched the wicker basket. "If I added one now, it would take too much time and materials to make the rest of the basket strong enough to carry us."

"Use a stepping block, Avas." Jon pushed an empty trunk into position.

One by one, they climbed in with the help of the men. Lathtin leapt in and scrambled up into his sister's arms. Kay was the last of the Season Avatars to board. Jon hoisted her in, then followed her. Kron boarded next. Lex cut the ropes holding the balloon down with his Allweapon and jumped aboard to much muttering from everyone else. With everyone aboard, there was barely enough room to move. Kay wiggled until she managed to fish the scrap of silk from her reticule. "Please tie it around my finger," she said to Jon. "So I remember to be brave."

He secured it around her smallest finger, sealing it with a kiss. Then Jon adjusted something on the engine. Hot air blew out a funnel on top into the balloon. After a few moments, while everyone tried to find a comfortable position, the basket rose off the ground. At first, it only lifted a couple of feet, not enough to bother Kay. Sooner than she expected, it shot higher, first above the cabin, then to treetop level. She shuddered and pushed her way to the center of the basket, near the engine. Surrounded as she was by the others, she couldn't see past them to the edge of the basket. That helped steady her nerves, as did looking up into the interior of the balloon. The patchwork colors and airtight stitches cheered her. She summoned her magic to blow more warm air into the balloon.

"Perfect." Kron rummaged in his satchel and pulled out what appeared to be a ball of wadded-up paper. He flattened it out, placed a stone arrowhead and a steel one in the center, and wrote words around them in multiple languages using a quill already filled with ink. The others bent away from him to let him work. When he was done, he blew on the paper, then crumpled the paper around the arrowheads. "I'm ready. Kay, kindly steer us toward the cloud."

"How accurately can you throw your artifact?" Lex asked.

Kron gave him a cool look. "They always connect with their target. It's part of the built-in enchantment."

"Then would I be able to use it? War's magic might provide additional power."

Kron shrugged and handed the ball to him. "Very well. Aim for the center of the cloud."

"Hold a moment," Gwen said. As they looked at her, she continued, "This time storm must be destroyed, but will this artifact alert Salth to our means of travel?"

"Not unless she has a magical eye or telescope to let her see us," Kron replied. "If anything, letting War's Avatar lead the attack might confuse her. She'll think he was able to reach the cloud from the ground because of his God's magic."

"Then what are we waiting for? Hold this contraption steady, Ava!"

Kay stilled the wind. The balloon hung in the air like a raindrop ready to burst out of a cloud. She grimaced and tried not to think about

Kron's flying carpet, or the ancient flying creature that had scooped her up and deliberately dropped her.

Lex leaned over the side of the basket and threw the artifact. The basket rocked, causing Kay's sister Avatars to cry, "Freeze it!" and clutch onto whatever they could. Jon wrapped his arm around her waist to steady her.

"Did he make it?" she asked.

"Of course I did." Lex sniffed with an annoyed air.

"You could move over here to see better," Jon said.

Before she could respond that she was happier where she was, the sky grew lighter. Kay could tell by the way the cloth of the balloon glowed.

Jenna clutched Robbie and the branch from her tree to her chest. "That's done it. The trees have stopped aging."

Gwen signaled for a link. Kay gathered as much residual magic as she could from the air and fed it to Jenna and Ysabel. Much of the forest plants and animals had already aged beyond their ability to restore them. The best the Avatars could do was make sure the survivors were as fit as possible to survive the upcoming winter.

"We've done all we can here," Kron said once they unlinked. "Time to find Salth in the Dead Land and make sure that was the last storm she ever creates."

Heart racing, Kay called up another wind to blow them west toward their ancient enemy.

CHAPTER EIGHTEEN

The Dead Land

The border between Challen and Selath appeared sooner than Kay had expected. Even though they were well above the earth and she couldn't see past the others crowding around her, she could sense the change magically. The sense of connection to her country and her God faded. In its place rose a feeling of dread, along with fatigue. If she had had room, she would have slumped to the bottom of the basket. She looked at her companions, and all of them, even Kron, seemed ready to collapse. Jon moaned and put his hand to his head. "By the Four, I never knew being up in the air could make one so ill."

"It might be Salth's magic. Here." Kron's hand crept toward his satchel and pulled out one of his modified watches. "Put this on. Quickly."

Jon fumbled as he attempted to strap the watch in place, so Kay helped him. "Thanks, Stowaway." He kissed her on the cheek.

Kron reached out and touched everyone else's watches. As he did so, the pull on Kay's vitality ebbed, still present, but distant, as if muffled under many layers of cloth.

"Which way should I take us, Kron?" she asked.

He pulled out one of his finders, this one with a bit of crystal embedded in the wood base and a gold wire spinning freely. "Keep us heading west for now. When we reach the river, we'll need to head north."

"There's a river below?" Jenna asked. "By the Four, I could use something to drink."

"I did manage to bring some refreshment with me." Lex attempted to remove his pack, but he didn't have enough room to reach it. Ysabel took care of it as Jenna entertained her son with a strand of beads. Lex continued, "But it may not be enough for all of us."

"It will have to do," Gwen muttered, sliding down toward the bottom of the basket.

"Are you all right, dear heart?" Jenna bent down as if she'd grown a third arm to tend to the Spring Avatar.

Behind her, Lex raised his eyebrows.

"My hand aches." Gwen covered her scarred hand with the other one.

"Can you move your fingers?" Jenna asked.

Gwen shook her head.

"Then let us know if you need to borrow strength from us."

Kay knew Gwen would hold out as long as she could. For now, all of them needed to conserve their magic for the task ahead.

Lex's idea of provisions turned out to be dried meat and hard bread, along with a few bottles of cider. He didn't have enough for each of them to have their own bottle, and Kay longed for something else to drink, even water, to wash down the food. Every bite required so much chewing her mouth was sore before she finished her portion. At least the food filled her stomach. She wondered if there was a way to collect moisture from the air but was too tired to try it.

When the sun set and the balloon darkened to the point where she couldn't tell one color apart from another, she leaned against Jon and drowsed, trusting to Kron to keep them on course. But it was hard to find genuine rest with everyone else shifting about, crushing her with their limbs or pinning her in an awkward position until her muscles cramped. Even their breathing seemed more distracting tonight than it had at any other point on this journey. Other than the wind rustling the balloon, there were no other sounds. No trees tapping out secret messages on windowpanes, no night birds or animals calling to each other, no sounds of any other humans anywhere near them. Only death below them…

"Freeze it!" Gwen sat up, dislodging Jenna and Lathtin. "We need proper rest before we face Salth tomorrow, especially with limited supplies." She reached out with her good hand. "Go to sleep, Jenna. You too, Lathtin, Ysabel, Kay…"

As soon as Gwen touched Kay, she immediately felt as sleepy as if she were back in the One Oak, happily cocooned in soft blankets and pillows. She knew there were things she should worry about, but she couldn't put them into words. She rested her head on Jon's chest and slept.

"Freeze it!" Kron's voice shocked her into wakefulness. Fabric smothered her. "Kay, we need a strong wind right now!"

Startled, she grabbed the first current she could find and blasted it at the balloon. It rocked, making the others cry out as they woke up, then sped along. The bottom bumped against something. *The ground? Where are we?* Kay struggled to stand so she could see past everyone. She realized that the engine next to her was silent. Kron readjusted the fan, then slammed the cover in place.

"I didn't have a chance to set it before Gwen forced us all into sleep." His normally calm voice had an irritated edge to it that didn't disappear even when Ysabel clutched his hand. "Thank the Four I woke up when I did. There's no telling how long we were grounded. Another gust, Kay, now!"

She pushed as hard as she could, trying to escape the mental image she had of them all ageing and dying in their sleep. The balloon lurched. Her magic couldn't affect the engine, but as it began to chug, she collected the warm air and directed it upwards, back into the balloon. Its colors lightened as it swelled. The basket rocked again as it rose. It didn't scare her as much as it had the first time.

Kron sighed. "Kay, I think you're blowing us back toward Challen."

"Oh, By the Four!" Feeling herself blush, she stole power from the westerly wind and fed it to its opponent. The balloon slowed and hung in the air for several suspenseful heartbeats before finally heading back. Kron pulled out his finder and nodded.

"I could swear I saw a line of green back there," Jenna said mournfully.

Kay hoped she hadn't taken them too far off course. It wasn't long past sunrise, but even Kron didn't seem sure how far they still had to travel.

"You know it's not a day for green, Jenna," Ysabel said. "It's the winter solstice, a day for blue."

"Well, the ground doesn't look very blue either. All I can see is bare, cracked dirt."

Ysabel shook her head. "Happy Birthday, Kay," she said loudly enough to drown out Jenna's complaint.

The others echoed Ysabel. Lex presented her with a wizened apple in addition to another portion of dried meat and hard bread. She cut it into wedges with scissors, wiping the blades well afterwards, and insisted everyone one else take a piece before she ate her share. Despite it being dry, it was the best apple she'd had in a long time.

After their meager breakfast, there was nothing to distract them. For a time, they entertained themselves by sharing stories of their childhoods. Kron, constantly watching the finder, described what Wistica had been like in pre-Annexation days when its name was still Vistichia. Even Lex unbent to describe growing up in the capital of the Fip empire and some of the worst combat training sessions he'd endured as a boy. Towards midday, they ran out of cider. Gwen suggested they stop speaking as much as possible. Lex took Robbie from Jenna and played a game of peek-a-boo with the delighted child, even allowing him to handle the Allweapon, currently a dagger. Jenna grimaced the entire time, but Robbie didn't suffer a single cut.

Around noon, Kron looked over the basket side and said, "That's the river down below. Kay, see if you can shift the wind so that we're going north as well as west."

"A river?" Jenna raised her head. "Is there any way we can scoop up some water?"

"It might not be safe to drink," Gwen said.

Jon had already emptied out a coal bucket and wiped the inside with his jacket. "Would you know if it was safe, Ava?"

"Probably." She licked her lips but kept her arms crossed.

Kron adjusted the engine, and the balloon slowly descended. "We won't touch down," he said. "All we have to do is go down a little farther so we can lower the bucket on a rope. Kay, could you kindly keep the balloon steady above the river?"

Winter should have told me the most important task I had to learn wasn't how to bring rain where it's needed or spin tornadoes down to gentle breezes, but steering a basket and a bag made from our clothes over the Dead Land.

Kay hadn't meant to share her complaint with the others, but Gwen gave her a wry grin. Then she shared Kay's thoughts with Jenna and Ysabel, who had to stifle their amusement.

"Something funny?" Kron asked after attaching the bucket to a thin rope and lowering it.

"There's nothing funny about the Dead Land," Jon said. "I see a lot of abandoned houses and yellowish bones like the ones on display at the University."

"Maybe that's where Salth got the idea to turn them against us—"

Ysabel hadn't finished speaking before Lex handed Robbie back to Jenna and edged past her to the side of the basket.

"What is it?" Jenna asked.

"I felt enemies stirring."

Jon bent his head close to Kron and whispered something. Kron nodded and impossibly pulled a revolver out of his satchel.

Gwen narrowed her eyes. "Don't you normally destroy guns, Kron?"

"Even they have their season, Ava," Jon said.

"That's it," Jenna said, "It's not a satchel; it's a portal to Kron's storage closet. If he could turn our reticules into portals like that, we wouldn't need trunks the next time we set out on a Grand Tour."

"Who's going to haul up the water?" Jon asked as he loaded a bullet and powder into his revolver.

Jenna passed her son to Ysabel and took the rope. Kay thought of helping, but she decided her task of keeping the balloon steady was more important.

Otherworldly cries like nothing Kay had ever heard filled the air. She couldn't help peeking between the others. Two flying skeletons, like the ancient creature that had killed her but smaller, ascended, circling the balloon.

Kay shook with fear, but she focused on keeping the balloon steady. She wished she dare summon lightning or a tornado to strike the skeletons, but they were too close. She could damage the balloon or hurt the other Avatars if she wasn't careful.

"Get down," Lex told them. "I need room to draw my bow." The dagger was no longer visible. Instead, the War Avatar held a crossbow. Jon stood next to him, aiming his revolver.

The other Season Avatars huddled on the bottom of the basket. Kay used the engine as a shield so she could see what was happening.

One after the other, the men shot their targets. Jon's bullet passed through an eye opening in a skull, but his creature didn't slow down. Lex's arrow chipped off part of the second skeleton's beak. That didn't deter the ancient birdlike thing from swooping toward the balloon.

Kay eyed the creature's pointy beak and imagined it tearing through the fabric of the balloon. Maybe Kron had enchanted it to resist damage, but she couldn't take that chance. Lightning would be hot enough to burn the bones, but guiding even a tiny ball of lightning out that far would be risky. Unless...

Lex had conjuired another arrow out of nowhere, so she pushed past Ysabel toward him. "Can you...can you shoot lightning?"

"A lightning bolt? Eagle's Claws, Winter Avatar, the Allweapon wasn't created for that!"

"I mean, if I put a tiny ball of lightning on the tip of your arrow, could you still shoot it? Would it burn the arrow before it reached the target?"

Jon's revolver barked again, jolting the basket. This time he connected with a wingtip on one of the skeletons. A couple of small bones fell off, but the animal pumped its meatless wings harder to gain altitude. Kay wondered how much magic it took to allow bones to fly by themselves.

"If we let those creatures rise past our basket, Jon and I won't be able to shoot at them for fear of damaging the balloon," Lex said. "Let's try it."

"And while you try that, I'll make sure they don't damage our craft," Kron said.

Kay touched Lex's arrowhead with a tiny ball of lightning. The steel tip wouldn't sustain a fire, so Lex shot his arrow as soon as she drew away. As the arrow sped toward its target, she concentrated on keeping the lightning from dying out. Once the arrow struck a rib, the lightning ball flared to consume the skeleton. Flaming bones hung suspended in the air for a few heartbeats before falling.

"I have the water!" Jenna cried.

"Kay, speed us out of here!" Kron pointed to the northwest. "That way!"

She hadn't waited for his command. The wind sprang up, shoving the balloon so hard Jon almost lost his revolver overboard. Kay watched the second bird fall behind, then gain additional speed. Should she cast lightning at it or increase their speed? One look at how her sister Avatars clung to the basket convinced her they shouldn't go faster.

Kron and Jon stumbled to the far side of the basket. Kron touched an unlit match to the side of the revolver before Jon shot. Kay never saw where he struck. The second creature exploded into fragments.

Gwen let out a breath. "All that for half a bucket of water."

Jenna groaned as she looked into the bucket. "And my sapling is even thirstier than Robbie."

Robbie was smellier, but Kay didn't want to mention that. None of them smelled as clean as new-fallen snow by this point.

Gwen reached for the bucket and sipped the water, pursing her lips before nodding. Everyone scooped out a handful of water; Ysabel claimed an extra handful for Lathtin. After Jenna took portions for herself and Robbie, she stuck her tree branch into the bucket.

"I suppose Salth knows we're here now," Gwen said.

"Yes." Kron sighed. "We should make final preparations to face her and Sal-thaath."

"I'll stand watch for more of those unnatural beings," Jon said.

Kay gave him a grateful glance.

Kron only need a few moments to change their clothes back to their traditional colors. Kay kept the wind blowing at a steady speed. After an hour or so without further attack, Ysabel, standing at the rim of the basket, pointed to something. Gwen struggled to her feet and leaned against Jenna to look. Curious, Kay craned her head around Jenna to see for herself. Still nothing but sky. Trembling, she released her grip on the engine mount and approached the edge of the basket. Gwen and Jenna steadied her by gripping her arms. At last, she had her own good view of the Dead Land.

As the others had already mentioned, there was very little of interest in the scenery. Rock-hard dirt, so dry the soil was covered with a web of cracks, stretched across the horizon. No sign of anything living, not even a weed, broke the monotony.

Jon pushed his way through the group while keeping his revolver pointed outward. "It's not as bad as it looks," he said. "See that glint over there? That could be metal ore. And minerals make up those striped bands in the hillside over there. There's so much potential in this land—"

"If only it didn't sap your life the heartbeat you step on it," Gwen said.

"Did you catch that spark of light over there on the horizon?" Ysabel asked. "That could be Salth's crystal house."

Kay shaded her eyes. Near the setting sun was a white speck of light, like a star fallen from the sky but still burning.

"By the Four, that's the prettiest thing I've seen all day," Jenna said.

Lex smiled. "What about me, dear heart?"

"'Pretty' doesn't even begin to describe you."

Kay shook her head and adjusted the wind to take them straight toward the white light. Kron glanced down at his finder, nodded, and returned it to his satchel. Starting with Jon next to him, he inspected the watches they all wore and brought out another set of artifacts for all of them to wear. These were loops of string in the various colors of the Four. Even Robbie, Lathtin, and Jenna's tree gained additional protections.

"Will these protect us against Salth's ancient monsters, Kron?" Lex asked.

"No, just direct time attacks. I'll leave the creatures to you and your weapon."

"Maybe she doesn't have any more creatures left," Jon said. He didn't sound very hopeful.

Ysabel shuddered. "Lathtin says she does. They're waiting for us up ahead, at the light."

"Freeze it," Gwen whispered, her face nearly as white as the violets on her bracelet.

Kay stretched her awareness upward. Maybe if she unleashed a downpour, then shocked the skeletons, they'd all fall apart at once. But this land was dry. Even the river far beneath them was a mere trickle of what it used to be. To create a storm, she'd have to pull water from the

Salt Waters at the other end of the Dead Land, and at their current rate of speed, they'd arrive before she was done.

She slowed the wind down, trying to keep the balloon aloft as she did so. But before she could draw water into the air, the others asked, "What are you doing?"

"We need a storm…"

Lex shook his head. "Avas, I don't know exactly what your Gods and Goddesses have instructed you to do, but you should save your strength for your task." He took a deep breath and stuck out his chest. "As the Avatar of War, it is my duty to defend you as you face the Demigoddess of Time."

Kron narrowed his eyes. "Well, you won't be doing it alone. I was here the first time the Season Avatars faced Salth, and I'll be here the second time to help them."

Hopefully there won't be a third time. Kron had been reluctant to share details of their first encounter, no matter how much Gwen begged for them.

Lathtin yowled. Ysabel clutched him tightly, looking at the rest of them with a troubled expression. "I'm going to need my brother to be my anilink, yes?"

"Of course," Gwen replied, wrinkling her forehead.

"Because he wants to join the others and fight the creatures. He says as an anilink, he might be able to understand them in ways Kron, Lex, and Jon won't."

Gwen shook her head. "That's probably not a good idea. How can he defend himself?"

Laththin extended his claws.

"Yes, but even sharp claws can't scratch bone."

The anilink sulked. Before Ysabel could translate more of his speech, Kron said, "Kay, bring us up again, please. We have to find a safe spot to land."

She sent more power to the wind, hoping Kron wouldn't ask her to circle around. Changing the direction of the wind so much would be a waste of magic at this point.

The light gradually grew larger and larger, becoming rectangular instead of a point. Lex leaned over the side of the balloon, watching the ground. "It's all very flat here," he said in disgust. "Where are we supposed to make our stand?"

Gwen let Jenna pull her up, then made her way to the basket's wall as well, though she kept some distance between herself and Lex. "The colors," she whispered.

"Colors? What colors?" Jenna asked.

"In the crystal structure. It's…it's a mass of colors swirling about, all blue and red and yellow and green…" Gwen gripped the rim. "By the Four, the colors of souls! Salth must be keeping countless souls prisoner!" She turned to the others. "Sisters, I think I see part of what the Four want from us. We must free those poor souls so they can be reborn."

"Salth is drawing on their magic for additional power," Kron said. "It's what she uses to keep Sal-thaath alive."

"Then we should be next to that crystal house when we summon the absent Season Avatars," she said.

"All we have to do is cut a path through that army." Lex grinned as if looking forward to the prospect.

Ysabel and Jenna shifted about so they could link with Gwen and Kay. Once all four of them were connected, Kay saw what Gwen did.

Surrounding the crystal house were rows and rows of the strangest creatures any of them had ever seen. They looked like mixes of everything that lived in Challen: trees with human arms, birds perched on twigs or other animals' legs, deer heads—complete with antlers—stuck on wolves' bodies, even fish fins replacing ears on people and horses. Those were just the ones the Avatars recognized. Other crawling things had oddly-shaped mouths or too many joints in their legs or extra-long spines. There were even a couple of the wooly tubenoses and reptiles that reminded Kay of the extra-large one with puny forelimbs that had attacked them at the Avi Spring's grave. She gave thanks to Winter that nothing resembled the giant flying reptile-bird that had carried her off. A few of the creations had skin or fur of some sort, but most were only bones held in place by magic. Some of the disjointed beings looked as if they would fall apart in a breeze or were too weak to be harmful, even to Lathtin. Others had enough teeth or claws to make her want to keep her distance. There had to be at least a hundred creatures for each Avatar. Even the Avatar of War would require a miracle to slay them all.

Lex turned back to face them. "Perhaps the safest place for us to land is directly on top of the crystal structure."

"By the Four, are you serious?" Kron said. "That's the storage place for Salth's stolen magic. She'll have more protections on that house than you have hairs on your head!"

"But it's the highest place anywhere, and it would put us out of reach of most of those creatures—"

A harsh cry Kay had hoped never to hear again sounded behind them. She broke out of the link to see for herself. Another one of the winged gliders headed toward them, carrying a humanlike figure with a spear.

Freeze it! For an instant, the fear she'd felt the first time she'd encountered one of them flooded through her, making her want to throw up the water and scant meals she'd eater earlier. *Where'd she find another one of those? What if it's the same one, and she brought it back to life to kill me again?* She touched the scrap of silk on her finger. By the Four, she wasn't going to die twice.

"Let me through," she said, pushing her way to the back of the balloon. The others cleared out of her path—at least, as much as possible in the cramped quarters. When she reached the basket wall, she clenched it with one hand. With the other, she directed lighting at the flying creature. The creature tried to dodge, but she followed it, feeling as calm as if she stood in the eye of a hurricane. After several heartbeats, her bolt connected. Both creature and rider shrieked, and the smell of scorched skin and bone blew toward her. It only goaded her into putting more energy into her lightning. With a last cry, the creatures came apart and fell to the Dead Land. *Good riddance.* She scanned the sky for more flying attackers, but for the moment, none were present.

Lex sighed. "If we can't land on the crystal structure, then we need some way to divert the creatures from one spot so we can establish a base. We need bait."

"Kay just roasted the flying thing," Ysabel pointed out. "If we could convince the other creatures to eat it—"

"Except none of us are cooks," Jenna said. "I didn't bring any fresh herbs with me."

"Kron, could you create an artifact to lure them somewhere?" With visible effort, Gwen turned to look at him. "Maybe something moving to make them give chase?"

"By the Four, I wish I'd brought more materials with me." Kron shook his head as he examined his satchel. They all watched him for several heartbeats, expecting him to triumphantly pull something odd— or several odd things—out of it. He pulled out a salt shaker, frowned, and passed it to Ysabel. Kay glimpsed more items—string, a cat carved out of bone, a box Kron hastily pushed back out of sight—before he settled on a knife, a quill full of ink, and a sheet of paper.

"Salth's creations won't attack each other," he said as he wrote in his ancient script. "They're enchanted to follow the Avatars. So any lure will need a bit of blood from all four of you."

Gwen scowled, but she held out her good hand to be pricked. Blood beaded out, a drop at a time. Kron blotted the wound with the paper until a quarter of the sheet was red. He repeated the process with the other three Season Avatars. Kay had jabbed herself many times with needles and pins, so she didn't flinch as she bled. When the entire sheet was covered in blood, Kron waved it about a couple of times to dry. Then he folded it into a hollow ball and sprinkled salt inside before sealing it.

"Are you ready, Kay?" he asked. "As soon as the creatures follow the ball, blow the balloon closer to the crystal house. Jon, turn off the heat so we start to descend."

Once, nothing would have made Kay happier than to leave this balloon. Now, she wasn't sure she wanted to. She readied the air for another gust anyway.

Kron tossed the ball. It tumbled as it landed, a red speck in the dirt. At first, Kay thought the trick wouldn't work. Nothing seemed to happen. Then a creature with a neck so long it nearly reached the basket sniffed toward the ball. It took one, step, then another. Other things followed it, some of them falling apart as they gained speed. Several rows of the beasts still surrounded the crystal house, but when Lex nodded at Kay, she blew the balloon toward it.

"Send us to the left," Kron suddenly said.

"Eagle's Claws, man, we should head right!" Lex glared at Kron. "The enemies on that side are much weaker!"

"But the house itself will be weakest on the other end When we— well, the Season Avatars and I—confronted Salth eight hundred years ago, I managed to insert a thin gold wire into the crystal. Someone with very keen vision might be able to see it."

"If it's still there," Lex said, tilting his head up as if it wasn't worth his time to check.

Gwen sighed. "I'll look." She swayed as she rose to her feet, her good hand covering her violet bracelet. Jenna supported her as the Ava Spring studied the crystal house. Kay hoped she would settle the matter quickly, before the creatures returned.

"There is a faint line in the crystal," she reported, "and a slight bulge where it ends."

Kay didn't wait for Kron and Lex to resume arguing. She followed her Ava Spring, not the men. The wind obeyed her, shaking everyone as the balloon lurched into position in front of the army. Jon caught Kay with an arm around her waist. His other hand gripped a valve to release air from the balloon.

"For luck, and the Four's favor," Jon said, then kissed Kay fiercely, as if he had to put a lifetime's worth of love into his lips. Kay squeezed him back. Lex and Kron grabbed their partners too. Lathtin hopped onto Gwen's shoulder, purring loudly.

"Wait! The bones," Gwen said. "Jenna, Ysabel, Kay, you should take them now, before—"

Before we descend into that madness and get separated, or worse, Kay thought.

Gwen pulled a drawstring bag out from under the neckline of her dress. "Could someone hold the bones while I sort them?"

Jenna grimaced, but Ysabel thrust her hand forward. Gwen shook the bag awkwardly, and Kay had a horrible thought of one of the bones falling out of the balloon and being lost in the dirt below—or even Salth turning the bone and the absent Avatar against them. But Ysabel caught all eight bones safely. They filled her hand like pieces in a macabre game.

Gwen grasped each of them, turning them about before identifying them. "Frederick." She gave the first bone to Jenna before she could protest. "Sophia—take it in your other hand, Ysabel. Kay, here's Olivia. Margaret I'll take later.... Charles. Helene. Tylon, he's mine...." She stared at Kay before picking up the final bone. "Dorian."

Kay wished she could toss this bone overboard. Dorian was already on Salth's side, so what did it matter if his bone was part of the ceremony? She didn't owe him a chance to escape the God of Winter's domain—but she owed it to her sister Avatars to do her best to stop Chaos Season. So she forced herself to pluck the bone out of Ysabel's hand. It felt slightly warm, but that must have been due to Gwen carrying it next to her skin; Olivia's bone had also been warmer than she expected. His bone was bigger than Olivia's, so Kay wouldn't have trouble telling them apart.

"Are we ready?" Jon asked.

Everyone nodded.

He turned the valve all the way open. The balloon fell. Kay kissed Jon back, borrowing courage from his strength. At the last moment, she remembered to pull back and ease their landing with controlled winds. The balloon draped over them, completely deflated. Cursing in Fip, Lex slashed the balloon and hurled the silk rags away from them. He kicked a hole in the basket and charged at the creatures rushing forward to meet them.

"By the Four..." Jenna's voice turned husky. "I hope the Four watch over him, even if he isn't one of Theirs."

"Follow me!" Lex called.

They hurried out of the basket. Only Jon remained behind. "I'll use this for cover," he said as he aimed his revolver at a charging woolly tubenose. It seemed like an ineffective weapon against a huge beast, and Kay worried Ysabel would have to destroy all the creatures individually. A pair of shots struck both eyes, and the woolly tubenose bellowed as it dropped.

"Poor thing," Ysabel whispered as they passed the corpse.

"Save your pity for us," Jenna retorted. She brandished a branch from her sapling. "I'll guard this side. You and Gwen stay in the middle."

Kay found herself toward the back of the group. Lex cleared the way for them, chanting in Fip as he brandished a two-handed battle axe left and right. It tore through bones and flesh as though they were paper. Skeletons fell apart and tried to reassemble themselves. Flesh-and-blood creations continued to drag themselves towards the Avatars even with their intestines hanging out of their bellies. The stench inspired Kay to push the creatures away with more wind. Kron threw exploding artifacts in their midst. The resulting mess shuffled about as the parts reconnected. This time, they joined together to create one huge beast. Its body, as big as Kay's suite back at the One Oak, sagged despite being supported by a hundred legs of various sizes. The head of a fanged lion bit the ear off an enormous wolf, and the two heads attacked each other.

"Blasphemy," Ysabel muttered.

"Keep going!" Lex shouted in Challen. He tossed a leg at the growing creature. "The more we feed it, the sooner it will collapse so we can dodge around it!"

Kay wondered at his advice. The creature was so long it could block their way to the crystal house simply by laying down next to it.

Lathtin struggled out of Gwen's hold and dashed toward the creature.

"No!" she screamed, right before Ysabel could.

Lathtin bounded right up to a bird leg ending in talons, then jumped away before it could catch him.

"Lathtin! Come back here this instant!"

"He gives you time, Ava," Lex said. "Do not waste it."

Gwen nodded grimly, her skin as white as her violets. She made the sign of the Four as they continued toward the crystal house. Shots sputtered behind them, and Kay worried the monster would crush Jon. But fewer and fewer creatures blocked their path.

They crossed a line drawn in bone. Time seemed to slow; each stroke of Lex's weapon lasted a hundred heartbeats. Every step cost a thousand heartbeats of life. The house retreated, and Kay knew they would all die of old age before they could reach it. Then Kron, muttering, dropped something from his satchel and smashed it underfoot. The spell broke, and time returned to normal. *Just one hundred more paces till we reach the house. Ninety-nine...*

"Kay, I'm hurt!" Jon screamed. "Help me!"

She froze. Jon needed her; she had to go to him. But why would he call to her for healing when that wasn't her type of magic?

"It's not him." Ysabel sounded shaken, but she pointed to the artifact Kron had made for her. "It's a trick, Salth's doing."

"Season Avatars, take hold of each other!" Gwen ordered.

Even though the link didn't form, Kay drew strength from her sisters. All of them had courage. She had to have it too, if she was their equal. And she was, she reminded herself. It didn't matter if she was the smallest or youngest or had the least amount of magical practice in this life. She'd been with them since the very first Chaos Season. Now, she and the rest of her quartet would put an end to them.

They pressed forward, inch by inch, as slowly as if they were plodding through knee-deep snow or heavy sand. The sounds of combat ebbed. The crowd of defenders surrounding the crystal house thinned, then disappeared. For a heartbeat, the way in front of them was clear. The crystal house gleamed in front of them, a wall of pure white—except for a single dull dot in the center. Gwen reached forward as if to touch the dot, but before she could, a woman and a boy appeared in front of them.

Kron had said Salth came from a faraway place and a long-ago time. She fit the part with her red-brown skin and dark hair coiled on her head. She wore a linen shift embroidered with metallic thread at the hem and neckline. Deep red garnets dangled from her ears, and bracelets of tiny skulls clattered on her wrists. Her body seemed frail, as if she would shatter with a single touch. But who would touch someone with such power in her stance and with eyes as red as blood? Kay gripped the silk around her finger, reminding herself to stay strong. She couldn't let this woman terrorize her or anyone else anymore.

The boy beside her was just as intimidating, for all that he appeared to be only seven or eight years old. His eyes held no innocence, only malice and cruelty. Like his mother, he wore bones for decoration. As he advanced on Ysabel, Lathtin sprang forward to defend his sister. The boy's eyes watered, and he sneezed several times.

Ysabel grinned. "Allergic to cats, are you? Fall must have known!"

Sal-thaath glared at her. He waved his hand at Lathtin, but the cat sat down and washed his front paws, not even glancing at the boy.

Salth spoke in harsh syllables none of the Avatars could understand. Her son smiled, exposing pointed teeth. "My mother thanks you for coming. Your magic will give Me many more years of life. Once your souls are Ours, We will be able to invade your country and take its riches."

Jenna scowled and tried to run at him with her upraised sapling, but Gwen blocked her. Meeting Sal-thaath's gaze, she said, "The Four Gods and Goddesses will stop you, even if we can't."

"Foolish mortal! Do you really think your gods are that powerful? They're still weak from giving you so much magic—magic We'll take for Ourselves."

Kron stepped forward, artifact in hand, before Sal-thaath could finish speaking. Lex positioned himself between Salth and the Avatars. Instead of bearing a sword or axe, he had a shield with a spike in the center. Kay wondered if the Allweapon could fight magical wars as well as physical ones.

Salth sneered at him. Raising her hand, she rubbed her thumb and forefinger together. Gwen gasped.

"Gwen!" Jenna cried.

Gwen's violet bracelet fell to the ground, withered to dust, and blew away.

CHAPTER NINETEEN

The Summoning

Gwen sank to the ground, her face contorting with pain. Her arm jerked around.

"Gwen!" Jenna, Ysabel, and Kay shouted simultaneously. They couldn't link with her fast enough.

It's my death she's experiencing, Kay thought to them. Gwen and the Four had performed a miracle to bring her back to life. It was another miracle that Gwen had been able to hold death at bay for so long, even with the God of Summer's bracelet to shield her. How could anyone, even a Spring Avatar, survive when death invaded her entire body?

You should give the death back to me, Kay said.

By the Four, no! The others chorused. *We can't lose any of us now.*

But if we could share the death, spread it out among us... Gwen thought.

We could use the death to draw the absent Avatars through the spirit-portal! Ysabel finished.

They knew each other so well they didn't need to discuss the idea. Instant agreement flashed among them. As death raced towards Gwen's heart, Jenna offered herself up to receive it. All four of them felt her love for Gwen burning like a star, strong enough to briefly overcome her desire to live. Surprisingly, Gwen sent yearning back, but she closed off her private thoughts before Kay and the others could learn anything else.

Ysabel smiled as she accepted her share of the death. *Friends. We're all friends, loyal to each other life after life—oh!*

Kay had no time to wonder what made Ysabel exclaim so before Gwen turned her attention to her. With Gwen was an inky shadow, ice-cold that even Kay's weather magic couldn't defend her from. Kay gulped. Her first death had come so suddenly, just when she thought she was out of danger, that she didn't remember what it felt like to die. Now that they were in the middle of the Dead Land, in front of Salth's fortress, would the Four be able to resurrect Their Avatars if they truly died?

I have to have faith in the Four, no matter what or who They were. Kay reached forward and accepted a portion of her own death back. It sank into her as if it hadn't left. Her body felt heavier, older. Not so old as to bring illness, stiff joints, or complete loss of youth, but enough to weigh on her. The link gained strength to make itself felt over the omnipresent shadow of death. Gwen, Jenna, and Ysabel all felt older than they had been heartbeats ago.

It's part of the price we must pay for bearing this death, Gwen said.

We can worry about that later, Jenna said impatiently. *Kay, open the portal!*

Freeze it, she'd almost forgotten that part. Kay dropped out of the link to grasp Olivia's locket. The others gripped their bones tightly in both hands. For a moment, Kay was tempted to let Dorian's bone slip out of her grasp, but she shifted it to her other hand, with Olivia's bone.

The jewelry glowed softly, the light protecting them. Kay sketched the biggest circle she could manage. White blinded her for a moment. When she could see again, seven of the absent Avatars waited on the other side.

Gwen awkwardly curtsied to them. "Our season is here. Does it matter in what order we summon you over?"

"It's got to be the proper season order, Gwen," Jenna said.

"But do we do it by quartet or season?"

To Kay, it seemed obvious. Even dead, the Avatars grouped themselves by quartet, not season. She turned away so she wouldn't have to face the incomplete trio of Margaret, Charles, and Sophia. What would happen when they crossed over without Dorian? Would this work at all? Kay suppressed a twinge of guilt.

"Quartet and season, Ava," Tylon said. "Best hurry."

"I hope this works," Gwen muttered. She extended her good hand, palm up, with a single bone displayed on it. "By the Goddess of Spring, I summon Her Avatar, Tylon fi Vort, from the God of Winter's domain into the world of the living!"

Tylon stepped forward but halted at the portal. "I can't pass through. My soul has nowhere to go."

"But your bone…" Gwen's hand trembled.

"It's not enough. I need a whole body."

Margaret leaned forward. "We need to share our magic with you as closely as possible, Gwen."

"If you were any closer, you'd be inside me…." Gwen's eyes widened. "By the Four, is that what you mean?"

The bubble surrounding them quivered as if struck.

Gwen took a deep breath and popped the bone in her mouth. After a few heartbeats, Gwen straightened, extended her hand until she almost touched the portal, and repeated her command, changing the final words to "into me, Gwendolyn lo Havil, Ava Spring."

Tylon stepped closer and held his hand up to hers. The portal shone as they touched. Gwen staggered backward, with Jenna reaching out to catch her.

"Gwen?" she asked.

"By All Four Gods and Goddesses," Gwen replied in a double-toned voice, "that feels odd."

Jenna said Gwen's name again, this time as if she wasn't sure who would answer.

"I'm here," Gwen said, her voice sounding normal for a moment, "and so is Tylon." Her tone deepened. "I'm only here to aid her and loan her my magic."

Jenna gaped. "And…each of us has to host an Avatar?"

"Not just one. Two."

"By All Four Gods and Goddesses." Jenna shook her head as she stared at the portal. The Summer Avatar on the other side approached it. "I guess it's my turn." She stared appealingly at Gwen-and-Tylon. "Do we really have to eat it?"

Gwen shook her head. A slight bulge was noticeable in her cheek. She must be holding the bone in her mouth. *If I do that with Dorian's bone, he'll probably choke me,* Kay thought.

Jenna stared at the bone in her hand for a few heartbeats. Her son, strapped to her chest, reached for it. He wailed as she placed the bone in her own mouth and garbled the words Gwen had said earlier. As Frederick disappeared into Jenna, Robbie quieted. The combined Summer Avatars crooned an old song at him as he stared into Jenna's face.

Ysabel performed her own summoning of Helene so quickly Kay didn't even realize it had happened until her sister Avatar stepped away from the portal and gestured for her to approach it. Kay did so warily despite Olivia's welcoming smile. What would it feel like to have someone else in her body? How well did she really know the other Winter Avatar? Would Olivia betray her the way Dorian had? *Winter, protect me.* She placed the smaller bone in her mouth. It tasted dry and smelled of dirt. Even that was enough to make her gag. She struggled not to spit the bone out. Trying to speak around it made her tongue want to tie itself into knots. She focused on saying one word at a time. "By the God of Winter, I summon His Avatar, Olivia ava Kalt, from the God of Winter's domain into me, Kay ava Seltich, Winter's Avatar."

Olivia flowed through the portal and into her skin, filling her body as if she meant to push Kay out of it. The other spirit flexed Kay's fingers and toes and took several deep breaths. Then Olivia said, *Thank you for hosting me*, and pictured herself taking a seat in a quiet corner of Kay's mind. Control of her body returned to her.

I share my magic and knowledge with you, Olivia said.

Clouds spun between them. A gentle breeze blew from Olivia to Kay, refreshing her. Power built in her until she felt like she could control all of Challen's weather without draining magic from Chaos Season. A second store of knowledge presented itself next to her own, supplementing it in places but not as deep as hers in others. Kay didn't know how long she would be able to use Olivia's magic, but she hoped to keep the knowledge. *Thank you,* she sent back. So far, linking with the other quartet wasn't as bad as she had thought it would be. Then she glanced at the portal, where Margaret, Charles, and Sophia still waited to cross over. *Thank the Four I won't have to summon Dorian. He'll be impossible to reach.*

But we'll still be short an Avatar, Kay. The quartets won't be balanced.

He was never balanced, Olivia. He never treated me like an equal. Was he any better with you? Did he ever try to send lightning at you?

He only does that to test our skill. It's never harmed me.

Frustrated, Kay showed Olivia the memory of how Dorian had threatened them.

Olivia sent Kay a mental image of her as she had been in the prime of her life, only frowning and shaking her head. *By The Four, that is serious.*

Even after all he's done to me, I'm still supposed to accept him into my body and treat him as a welcome partner? He might not even want to do that! He's aligned himself with Salth.

Olivia sighed. *It's not our season yet. Let's see what happens when your sister Avatars summon the other members of Margaret's quartet into them.*

Gwen had already taken her place at the portal. She seemed healthier than she'd been ever since she'd taken Kay's death into herself. She stared at Margaret with the joy of meeting an old friend unexpectedly, and Margaret's expression held nothing but welcome. Gwen spoke the words of the ritual, and Margaret stepped through the portal and into Gwen. Gwen's face contorted, and she staggered away from the portal. Jenna followed her with her arms out as if to catch her. Gwen waved her away.

"Three in one…this was never meant to be done." Her voice shifted. "It doesn't have to last very long. Surely we can work together without harming our host." Gwen's voice. "But what am I supposed to do with the pair of you afterwards?"

Jenna edged away from her, not looking at the portal where Charles peered impatiently toward Jenna.

"It's your turn again, Jenna," Ysabel said.

"I know, but…." She looked back and forth between Ysabel and Kay. "What if this is wrong? What if we fail, and all of the Avatars' souls are lost? Or what if we're all mixed up with each other afterwards, and we're never the same again?"

Kay had been wondering the same thing, though she'd been trying to hide it from Olivia. She exchanged glances with Ysabel. It had been the Fall Avatar's idea to use the bones to replace the absent Avatars, but no one had anticipated consequences like this.

Gwen continued to talk to herself, her voice switching among three different pitches. Tylon apparently thought he should be the dominant personality, even though Gwen and Margaret disagreed with him. With dread pressing on her heart, Kay realized what she had to say, though she wasn't sure if it was true.

"Jenna! Listen to me." Kay pointed at Gwen. "We definitely can't leave her like this, but we don't know how to return the other Avatars to the God of Winter's domain."

"I can make a guess." Jenna approached the portal, but her legs stiffened. She grimaced. "Freeze it! Frederick says he refuses to leave until we've faced Salth."

Kay nodded. "That's right. The only way out of this is for all of us to complete the summoning. We have to do it—for Gwen, at the very least."

Jenna glared at her. "Then By the Four, you'd better get us Dorian." With that, she marched to the portal and spoke the summoning so quickly Charles was gone before Kay realized it. Jenna's body shook as she cleared the portal, but Ysabel didn't hesitate to take her place and summon Sophia over. Kay shadowed Jenna.

"Do you need to hold on to me?" Jenna was the tallest Avatar, while Kay was the shortest and slightest. If Jenna fell, she'd probably bring Kay down with her.

Jenna clutched her fists and took a few deep breaths. "I'm fine," she told Kay, her voice also complete with its own three-part harmony. "It's up to you now. Find Dorian's soul."

If Gwen and Jenna struggled so much with their counterparts, Kay wondered what would happen if she did find Dorian and allowed him inside herself. He'd probably try to electrocute her from the inside out.

I'll act as a buffer, Olivia volunteered.

Thank you, but I'm going to have to confront him first. Before she could even do that, she had to locate where he was. The portal to the God of Winter's domain was empty, but she'd already known he wouldn't be there. He was aiding Salth and Sal-thaath now, so he had to be somewhere in the Dead Land, most likely in the crystal structure. How could she find one soul among the countless ones in there?

"Well, we can't do anything in here, where we can't even see or feel the crystal house," she said.

The others studied her, the weight of nine people concentrated in their gazes. Olivia's presence wasn't enough to balance them.

"Let us link," Gwen and her chorus said.

Kay hesitantly touched her. The link was overwhelming with the presence of so many other voices she didn't know, like a bolt of cloth with an ill-woven pattern. She focused on the threads she knew. Together, all of them pushed past the bubble of darkness protecting them.

Kay felt a slight pressure in her ears, but otherwise she wasn't sure what had changed. The horizon split the red-gold sun in half, but around them night had already fallen. Flickers of movement indicated where Kron, Lex, and Jon still fought their opponents. Kay and the rest of her quartet longed to check on them, but their guests urged them forward. They only managed a couple of steps before the crystal house's soft gleam flared with white heat. Kay and Olivia grabbed most of the energy and flung it out of the way. They would have preferred to block the heat with cold, but that was harder to summon.

"Wait," Gwen said. Her voice shifted, becoming throatier, more alluring. "Dorian, it's me, Margaret. Gwen was kind enough to let me link with her. For the love of the Four, please stop working with Salth and link with Kay. It's the only way we'll ever be together again."

A blue light, stronger than the rest, flickered excitedly and approached the knob of crystal covering a darker spot in the wall. Perhaps that spot was the gold wire Kron had inserted into the wall hundreds of years ago.

Go on, Olivia urged, forcing Kay to step ahead of the others. She was so close she could feel waves of heat still flowing from the crystal. Abruptly the heat faded away, and the blue light bobbed up to the inner edge of the wall.

Kay stared at it for several long heartbeats. Behind her, the other Avatars were silent. Even Olivia tucked herself into a corner of Kay's mind, as if trying to have as little as possible to do with the other Winter Avatars. It felt as if she and Dorian were the only two souls left in the world, and for once she was ascendant over him. Memories of every time he'd insulted her or attacked her flooded her mind. Anger surged in her. Nothing else mattered but expressing her hate and showing him what it felt like to be a victim.

"Dorian!" Kay spat on the ground. "Dorian gran Garnell, I can't even fathom why the God of Winter ever chose you as an Avatar. Maybe you're skilled at controlling the weather, but you always fail at working outside of your quartet. I don't even know how you manage to work with anyone else other than Margaret. You and Salth deserve each other. Why do we need you for this anyway? The eleven of us should be powerful enough."

The blue light came closer, growing bigger and shaping itself into something resembling a human. If it was Dorian, he had changed a great deal. His face and body were thinner, almost razor-sharp, with a blue-gray cast to his complexion. His eyes were as hawkish as ever. He touched the gold wire protruding into the crystal. As he spoke, his words traveled through the wire so she could hear them.

"Margaret is here?" He asked. "Where is she? Let me see her!"

Kay was glad Gwen wasn't close enough to hear him. "You can't see her," she said maliciously. "You don't deserve to."

Dorian's face contorted for a heartbeat. He sneered. "Still think you're the best Winter Avatar, don't you?"

"By All Four, what do you mean?"

"Don't play coy, Kay. I remember our first life as Avatars quite well. After we failed to defeat Salth, your quartet was chosen to lead the sol-transes. You went around all day singing!"

Funny, she wasn't much of a singer in this life or any of her most recent ones. "Why did that bother you so much? Was I badly out of tune?"

"You were flaunting your new status all over the place! You were the lowest-born of all of us, and suddenly you were supposed to be my equal! Me, nobly born in every life!" Dorian raised his chin. "If that's not proof Winter loves me more than you, I don't know what is."

It did seem as if Winter favored Dorian, but Kay knew that wasn't true. Avatars were supposed to be reborn into many different lives to understand the needs of all Challens. "I think all Winter did for you was allow your head to swell," she retorted. "Better dry it out and shrink it, you faithless one."

Dorian's face grew solemn. "I serve the Four more devotedly than you can ever understand, Kay."

"Then why are you in Salth's crystal house? Why do you help her send Chaos Seasons to Challen?"

"She was supposed to spare Charles and Sophia!" Dorian said. "I only wanted her to hurt your quartet, so you'd be forced to give up your role. I thought I could use her, but she was more powerful than I expected." His expression grew sly. "But she's not infallible, you know. Help me, Kay. I know her weakness now."

She narrowed her eyes. "What is it?"

"You have to release me from this prison before Salth destroys me."

Kay wanted to refuse. Dorian had already betrayed his God, his country, and his own quartet of Avatars. She wasn't sure what the crystal house was supposed to do, though from the colors of the lights Gwen reported seeing inside the structure, it seemed somehow linked to souls. If it trapped them, Dorian couldn't harm anyone.

Are you sure about that? Olivia asked. *What if Salth is using these souls to increase her power?*

Was that possible? No one else besides Avatars had magic. How could Salth squeeze magic from ordinary people? Still…. Kay frowned, trying to remember what Kron had told them about Salth's power. Like Kron, she possessed her own magic, but she'd gained more power than him—he'd never explained that clearly. All Kay knew was that Kron's magic had been boosted, and he aged very slowly now, if at all.

The Four never age, either.

Freeze it! Kay hadn't wanted to think about what she'd learned about the Four being human once. They had gained power from the stars—that was where Kron and Salth had gained extra magic too.

If Salth has her own magic and star magic, why does she need soul magic too? Kay asked Olivia.

It's not for her. It's for her son. He's born of magic itself, so he needs magic to live. Kron killed him accidentally a long time ago by draining power from the boy to punish him. Salth now uses the lives of others to keep her son alive.

It all now made sense to Kay. The crystal house didn't just take magic from people, but their time to live. If there were souls trapped inside, they couldn't be reborn. No wonder this land was so barren.

And as long as Dorian is in there, he can't be reborn? Margaret's quartet can't become Season Avatars?

I don't know that for certain, but I believe so, Olivia replied.

Kay stared at Dorian, who watched her silently, making no more pleas for release. Maybe he deserved to suffer, but the rest of his quartet didn't. And if Sal-thaath drained Dorian of his weather magic in addition to his time, the result would be a catastrophe. An evil, undead child using weather to harvest Challen souls directly and starve others with poor harvests...no, she couldn't allow it to happen. No matter how much she despised Dorian, she couldn't leave him in there.

She sighed. "What do we have to do to free you, Dorian?"

He tapped the dark dot in the crystal. "This gold wire is the only weakness I can find in the crystal. If we melt it with lightning, maybe I can escape—"

He glanced back over his shoulder. Kay followed his movement. The other soul lights bounced around, as if they floated in a pot of boiling water. As they collided with each other, unlike colors recoiled. Those of the same shade stuck together.

Kay doubted the dead souls could gain magic by joining together. However, as they grew, their shapes became more human-like. What would they be able to do as they grew bigger? She and the other Season Avatars couldn't afford to find out.

CHAPTER TWENTY

The Crystal House

Dorian frowned as he studied the four shapes assembling themselves inside the crystal house. However, he made no move to attack them.

"What are they?" Kay asked. "What are they meant to do?"

The blue one, about half the size of a man, floated toward him.

"Stop me from leaving Salth's crystal, I think." He placed both hands over the gold wire and thrust lightning at it. A flash of light traveled a third of the way through the crystal before dying out. "What are you waiting for, child? Destroy it on your end!"

It would be harder for her than it was for him. A crystal knob had grown over the end of the wire. Kay extended her hands toward it, careful not to touch it but hoping she could gain some clues about how to destroy it. She cast her own lightning at it, but the crystal remained unchanged.

Any ideas? She asked Olivia.

Try extreme cold to shatter the crystal, Olivia replied. *If necessary, we can cycle between extreme cold and extreme heat. If you'll let me, I'll help.*

Kay nodded, then lowered the temperature. This was trickier than warming an object, as when chilling something, she had to find someplace to store the extra heat. Ice frosted the knob, but it remained unaffected. Before Olivia could suggest it, Kay heated the knob with the warmth she had stolen from it and more besides. Still nothing changed.

We'll have to make it even colder, Olivia said. *Should we link with the others?*

There are limits to what we can do, no matter how many Avatars are joined.

Well, we have to do something soon, before the other souls tear Dorian apart.

Kay focused on what lay beyond the crystal wall. Dorian was surrounded by four human-like figures that towered over him. He flew up and down, darting like a hummingbird as he evaded their clumsy movements. What would they do if they managed to corner him? For a heartbeat, Kay imagined a world without her eternal tormentor. Every life after this would be a peaceful one…NO! Without Dorian, without all twelve Avatars, they could never defeat Salth. At best, she would continue to plague Challen with more Chaos Seasons; at worst, she might be able to overcome the Avatar's defenses and bring starvation to the country. Kay thought of her family in their cramped, unheated quarters in Wistica; of Jenna's family in the country; of Ysabel's sisters and brothers in the One Oak. Even nobles like Gwen's family would suffer; she'd already lost her aunt. She couldn't let them all down because of her hatred of one Avatar.

"Give me strength!" she cried.

Gwen took her arm, and Jenna and Ysabel followed suit. Power from nine other Avatars flowed into her. She boldly grabbed the knob with both hands and pulled heat away from it. Her hands burned, though she couldn't tell if it was from heat or cold or both. They seemed clamped in place, bonded to the crystal. *I'll be here forever,* she thought in panic, as Gwen sent her a wave of healing and reassurance. Even that wouldn't be able to save her this time. She would die, and all that would be left of her would be her bones.

Even my bones will serve the Four, should They wish it.

She gave herself over to Winter and His cold. She was nothing but coldness itself, down to her core. She would become a living ice sculpture, so cold even her blood would stop flowing....

Crack.

The faintest of sounds brought Kay back to herself. Crystal shards pierced her hands in hundreds of places. Her fingers still moved, though, and beneath them, the knob broke off and fell out of her grasp.

Thanks be to the Four. It took Kay a moment to remember why she'd wanted to remove the knob in the first place. Once she did, it took her more time to banish the cold that had possessed her so she could summon lighting. Power flowed into her, though she didn't recognize its source.

I'd say freeze it, Kay, but you have to unfreeze your brain! Jenna snapped. *Melt that wire so we can save Dorian!*

Anger drove away the last of her numbness. Kay concentrated lightning into a thin but powerful jolt and whipped it through the gold. As it sizzled, cracks formed in the crystal, only to heal before she could take advantage of them.

Dorian had been chased to the other end of the crystal structure. He feinted up, then dropped down before the green soul-mass could catch him. The blue one reached for him, but he blasted an ice barrier in front of its hand. He darted toward the gold wire, but the yellow and red soul-masses pressed themselves against the wall, blocking his path.

Gwen, Margaret, and Tylon sang out, "Goddess of Spring, call Your lost children home!"

The scents of lilacs and violets freshened the air. Kay forced a stream of it into the gap. The yellow soul-mass quivered, and parts of it broke off, back into individual souls. Some of them ventured toward Dorian, but others battered the crystal wall.

The Summer Avatars called for their God, evoking fresh grass, roses, and ripe strawberries. Kay sent those smells toward the green summer-born souls. Next, Ysabel led the Fall Avatars as they cried for their Goddess, She of apple cider, fall leaves, and smoke. The combination of odors seemed to make the soul-masses break down faster. Only the blue one remained intact.

Kay surfaced from the link long enough to chant with Olivia, "God of Winter, call Your lost children home!" A heartbeat later, Dorian joined them.

Smells of pine needles and fresh snow assured Kay her God still answered her in the middle of the Dead Land. The final soul-mass exploded into blue dots of light. Dorian shrank down into a slightly larger dot and zoomed for the hole in the crystal. Was it Kay's imagination, or did the hole seem even narrower? How was that possible? Somehow, Dorian managed to penetrate it. Kay held her breath as he traveled through. By the Four, he seemed to be slowing down. She pressed both hands on either side of the exit. Raw pain flashed through her hands before Gwen stopped it. Kay forced more heat through the narrow opening, hoping to keep the crystal from sealing Dorian inside.

Keep a link with me open, Dorian thought. *I'm going to need all of the magic.*

Why? What are you doing?

Just trust me, Kay.

She didn't have any reason to trust him, but at this point, she didn't have any choice. How could she maintain a link with Dorian if the wall closed? *Why don't you just come here, to me?*

His bone, Olivia said suddenly. *It could help you link with him.*

The bone was too thick to push into the hole, but Ysabel simply said, *Make it thinner and longer.*

Gwen and the other two Spring Avatars passed magic through Kay and into Dorian's bone, shaving it into strips so thin Kay feared she would choke on them. She pushed them out of her mouth one at the time, and Gwen joined them end-to-end as she did so. Kay fed the bone through the tiny hole in the crystal until only the very end stuck out of the crystal. Dorian darted to the other end.

Before touching her end, Kay asked the rest of the Avatars, *Are we sure we want to give him all of our magic? What if he turns it against us?*

He won't, Margaret said confidently.

But are you sure?

He did try to protect us when those clawfeet attacked, Charles said.

Kay remembered that moment. Dorian still cared for the other members in his quartet. She hoped that since their souls were linked with her sister Avatars, he would protect them all.

Gwen, Margaret, and Tylon gathered a final surge of magic from everyone and passed it to Kay. If only she could use it on this side of the wall—but she'd already tried that.

Dorian, if you let us down now, I swear by All Four Gods and Goddesses to see your soul frozen forever.

I need magic, not threats.

Kay took a deep breath, then allowed the magic to flow through the bone to Dorian. His soul spark blazed up like a star fallen to the ground. The crystal glowed with heat that made Kay and the others stagger backward, squinting against the light.

CRRRR-ACCKKK!

The crystal wall fractured.

CHAPTER TWENTY-ONE

Salth and Sal-thaath

The crystal spilt first horizontally and vertically along the thin hole Kron had made centuries ago, then additional cracks formed in a spiderweb pattern.

The souls. Gwen scarcely breathed. *Look at them.*

A yellow soul bounced into a crack and passed through the wall. It hovered in front of them for a moment, as if drawn by the Spring Avatars. Then it sailed over the Dead Land toward Challen. Other lights of all four colors battered against the crystal. Every heartbeat, more of them escaped, streaming into the darkness. Kay couldn't help but be awed. After centuries of imprisonment, all these souls would be able to rejoin the Four and be reborn. The Dead Land would become alive once again.

Dorian? Margret's voice was pure worry. *Where is he?*

I...I don't know, Gwen replied. *I lost track of him.*

He didn't destroy himself, did he?

"You've destroyed him!" Salth shrieked.

At first, Kay thought she was referring to Dorian. But as the Avatars shifted their attention to their enemies, she saw Kron step away from Sal-thaath. The child had lost the feral expression he had earlier and now looked scared. Ysabel felt sorry for him, but the others drowned out her sympathy. All of them were shocked as Sal-thaath turned pale, dried up, and blew away.

"Sal-thaath!" Salth dropped to her knees, keening in her ancient language. She reached toward her crystal house, but it had gone dark.

Kron stepped forward, one hand concealed in his satchel, and spoke sharply to her. She threw back her head and replied only to him.

How rude of her not to include us in the discussion, Jenna complained. The older Avatars all agreed with her.

Only fools want spring to last all year, Gwen retorted. *She'll remember us soon enough and attack again. See?*

Salth turned away from Kron, but to Kay's surprise, she didn't attack the Avatars, but instead gestured at the remnants of the crystal structure. Souls of all four colors arced backwards, falling into it.

What is she doing? Jenna asked.

By the Four, I think she's turning back time to before the house was destroyed! Gwen replied.

Will that bring Sal-thaath back as well? Ysabel's voice held only a little bit of fear.

We can't let that happen, Margaret said, *especially now that we know what's keeping that frozen child alive.*

What could they do? Their magic wasn't strong enough to halt time or change its course. Even Dorian wouldn't be able to stop Salth. She would just lock his soul inside the crystal again. But if they were linked with him, maybe their hold on him would be stronger than hers. If Salth couldn't put everything—or everyone—back exactly as it had been earlier, maybe it would weaken her.

None of the other Avatars were sure Kay's idea would work, but they all agreed it was their best course of action. The Spring Avatars searched for his bright blue soul, with Margaret calling for him using Gwen's voice.

What if his soul was torn apart? Jenna asked.

A soul can't die, Gwen said. *The Four wouldn't allow it.* She didn't sound certain.

If something had happened to Dorian's soul, where would it be? He belonged in the God of Winter's domain. Maybe he had slipped through the portal. Kay had a hunch it was the only way for him to hide from Salth as she turned back time.

Kay, you control the portal, Gwen said. *You have to protect Dorian.*

Kay dropped out of the link to check on the portal. She hadn't done anything with it since she first realized Dorian wasn't on the other side. She checked it now. Dorian hovered on the edge of the portal, frowning as if unsure which side of the portal was safer. Kay smirked for a moment before she realized the danger he was in. She wanted to warn him, but he wasn't part of the link yet. If she called out to him, Salth might discover where he was.

Summon fog, Olivia suggested.

Kay searched for water, but the ground was so hard she wouldn't be able to draw it into the air quickly. Clouds were also very far above her. *We need another idea,* Kay told the other Avatars.

More lightning balls, Gwen said. *Make them small enough so they look like souls.* She sent Kay enough magic to generate a field of souls. Colored lightning was hard to create, but Kay hoped it would look yellow enough to make Salth think they were Spring Avatar souls. She seemed greedy enough to claim all of them and forget about Dorian. Perhaps that would give Kay a few moments to bring Dorian into the link. Kay created a hundred balls, then edged for the portal. Dorian glanced at her, then drifted in her direction.

All of Kay's lightning balls vanished in an instant. Salth screeched.

"Dorian!" Abandoning all attempts at secrecy, Kay ran to him with her arm outreached.

He stared at her, not moving.

"Link with me!" She called. "For the love of the Four, link with me!"

An uncertain look crossed his face, but he reached for her. Just as their fingertips touched, a wind that wasn't a wind pulled Dorian back toward the crystal house. Kay raced as fast as she could after him. Dorian created a strong gust to slow him down. Kay leapt forward and grasped at an insubstantial hand. It sizzled like lightning but didn't burn her. The link surged between them, yet he resisted flowing into her.

About time you joined us, Dorian! Olivia said.

Olivia, give us some privacy for a few heartbeats.

She scoffed. *That's impossible when we're linked.*

Then try not to listen to us. Dorian turned to Kay. *Winter was right. You are a better Avatar than I am.*

He couldn't lie outright in the link, so she knew how much he grudged having to admit that to her. Despite that, she couldn't help taking his praise to heart after all these centuries. *You're very skilled with weather magic,* she told him.

Yes, but even after all the torment I've inflicted on you, you're still willing to link with me...Margaret! Dorian ignored Kay as the link deepened enough for him to sense the rest of the Avatars. Instantly all the suppressed feelings of jealousy and bitterness disappeared, leaving nothing but radiant love. It wasn't directed at Kay, but it warmed her anyway, along with the rest of the Avatars. *Finally, a complete set of twelve.* The link wove them together....

Salth screamed in fury. The crystal house was nearly complete, including scores of soul lights they'd worked so hard to free. She tugged at Dorian, but she couldn't pry him loose.

Salth stamped her feet and gestured wildly as her face darkened. A force pulled Kay and the rest of her quartet toward the crystal house. Apparently Salth wasn't going to settle for just one Avatar when she could have the entire collection.

Attack her. Now.

Kay raised her hands and directed the largest bolt of lightning she'd ever created toward Salth. Kay's hands and eyes burned, but Salth still stood. She beckoned the group toward her, and they slid toward the crystal house.

Again! Gwen said. *Wait for the others!*

As Kay's vision cleared, she saw Lex with the Allweapon as a long pike, Jon with his revolver, and Kron holding an open box. Even Lathtin was there, bearing no weapons but his natural ones.

One...two...three...now!

With the last of their magic, Kay struck Salth with another lightning bolt. At the same time, Lex and Jon attacked the crystal house, which still displayed cracks. Kron and Lathtin bounded toward Salth from different directions. She sneezed several times. Her gestures halted, and the crystal house exploded again. A brief wail rose above the noise. Salth sank to her knees, suddenly looking like a woman of eighty winters.

Light streamed out of Salth. It was cool white light, not any of the Four's traditional colors. Most of it clustered around Kron and his box, but some flowed toward Jon and Lathtin, covering them so they were no longer visible. A few sparks floated toward the Avatars, then turned away.

Kay and her sister Avatars collapsed, but the smell of violets and lilacs kept her from passing out and gave her new strength.

"You've done so much, My daughters," a woman's musical voice said. "It would be a shame for you to miss the end now, wouldn't it?"

CHAPTER TWENTY-TWO

Of Gods and Avatars

"Spring!" Gwen, Margaret, and Tylon said in their chord of voices.

A woman with long blonde hair—a color so rich as to wash out Gwen's honey-colored chignon—and a yellow dress appeared behind Salth, who didn't look up. In quick succession appeared a thin green-skinned youth, a twelve-year-old girl in a red dress, and a white-haired but still vigorous man. Spring, Summer, Fall, and Winter; the Four Gods and Goddesses had shown Themselves at last.

Kay was already on her knees, so she bowed her head. She couldn't stay in that position for long, not when she hadn't seen Winter in eight hundred years. She stared at Him in awe, studying the way his suit in the most current style fluttered in breezes of His own making. He didn't even glance her way. No one was able to look one of the Four in the eyes, it was said, so perhaps that was a blessing.

The Four surrounded Salth and said something to her quietly.

"Sal-thaath," she replied, grabbing at the rock-hard dirt.

"He is safe with me," Winter said, both in Challen and in whatever language Salth originally spoke. "Will you not join him?"

After several heartbeats, she nodded.

Something shimmered in the air, but Fall blocked Kay's view of it. Whatever it was, it was something Salth must have wanted. She lunged for it. As she wrapped her arms around the shimmer, she turned translucent. The Four stepped away from her, revealing the figure of a mother embracing a young child. Both of them looked delicate enough to be spun from spider webs as clear as glass.

Ysabel sighed. "Mother and son. How touching."

"If Salth had been half as attentive to her son before he died the first time, maybe none of us would be here today," Kron muttered.

Winter gestured. A portal swallowed the frozen soul-statues and took them with it.

Gwen cleared her throat. "Are we safe from them now, O Four?"

The Four nodded in unison.

"And…is Chaos Season over forever?"

"Yes." Spring's smile warmed them all.

"Praise to the Four!" Kay said, the others joining in.

At that, Spring's grin widened further. "We should be thanking you, Our sons and daughters. Even though the Demigoddess of Time had not fully Ascended to Our level, We were not allowed to attack her directly. Only you could have done this task for Us." She nodded at Kron and Lex. "We appreciate your assistance as well, Artificer and Avatar of War."

"But where is the star magic?" a male voice boomed. A tall man clad in dazzling red armor appeared. He had to be the God of War. "What did you do with it, Artificer?"

Kron's arms trembled as he held the box, but his voice was steady. "I've put it away for safekeeping."

"WHAT?"

As the five deities spoke, Ysabel flinched. Kay wanted to cower as well, even though Their anger wasn't directed at her.

Kron raised his chin. "We've seen what can happen when too much power gets into the hands of those who would use it for their own ends. I intend to shield this box in such a way so that only a selfless person can claim this magic."

"You would keep it even from Us?" Spring asked. "Haven't We shown Ourselves concerned about Challen's welfare, Kron Even-handed?"

"Yes." Kron swallowed, still keeping hold of his box. "But Spring...you and the rest of the Four don't need it. Even I don't need this star magic I picked up. It keeps me from aging, but it also means I won't be able to give Ysabel what she most desires: children of her own."

"If you wish to become mortal, Artificer, I'm happy to oblige." War stepped toward him.

"Leave him alone, War." Winter held up His hand. "He's been very helpful to Us and Our Avatars."

"And You're not supposed to be here!" Fall looked ready to spit at him.

"Neither am I, dear children, yet here I am." An old woman with skin darker than walnut stepped out of the air. She leaned on a cane made of some type of wood the Summer Avatars didn't recognize.

"Grandmother of Stories." To Kay's surprise, Spring, the rest of the Four, and even War bowed Their heads to Her.

Kay and her sister Avatars were still kneeling, so all they could do was lower their heads for a heartbeat, then stare at the newcomer. Her brightly patterned dress was more suitable for summer than winter, and She had tucked a fuchsia blossom behind an ear. Despite Her wrinkles, She smiled as if She alone knew the end of a very funny story.

"You're very far from Your own islands, Grandmother," Spring said.

"I can be everywhere where stories are told," She replied, "And I've been following this story for quite some time. My people can't stay hidden in their archipelago forever, You know." She shaded her eyes as she looked around. "This land is very different from where my people live, but it's neutral, clear of all other Gods and people. I hope to send some of my people up to the coast where they can found a village."

The other gods stared at her. While it was hard to read Their expressions, They seemed shocked.

Selathens lived here before it became The Dead Land, Ysabel told the others. *Shouldn't they be allowed to resettle it?*

Would they want to? Gwen replied. *How long will it be before anyone can grow crops here?*

"Spring, Summer, Fall, and Winter," the Grandmother of Stories continued, "You may think this land belongs to Challen, but it doesn't. It was always meant to be separate. And War, I know you want to conquer it, but there's nothing here for You. Let this land draw people of every nation and every deity—or none of Us, if they choose."

Ysabel fidgeted with her sleeve hem before saying, "Grandmother—if I may address You by that name—Selath is where the Selathens used to live hundreds of years ago, before Salth killed the land. By all rights, they should have the first chance to return once the land is restored."

"You would speak for them after the way they treat women?" Gwen asked.

Fall frowned, and a pair or wolves appeared, flanking Her.

Ysabel glanced at her Goddess, then nodded. "Some of the Selathens—the ones that don't worship Salth—blame her for ruining this country. They use that as an excuse to disdain all women. They can't do that anymore, can they?"

"Unfortunately, daughter, humans are not always as reasonable or forgiving as We wish," Spring said.

"Then perhaps it would be best to let them leave Challen," Gwen said.

"Only those who want to leave," Ysabel hurriedly added. "Fall, remember the work my mother did for You, spreading word about the Four to Selathen women. Some of them, and their families, will want to stay in Challen. If You've seen fit to have me be part Selathen in this life, how can You turn away from the rest of the Selathens now?"

The Four exchanged glances with each other but didn't speak.

"The Selathens should choose another God—or Goddess—to serve before being granted their own province," War said.

"Province?" Grandmother asked.

"Naturally, this land will become part of the Fip Empire."

Gwen narrowed her eyes.

"First You have to conquer it, War," Grandmother said. "You may not find it as easy as You think, when Your tidy rules for distributing magic have already been disrupted." She looked past the Avatars and beckoned with her finger. "You two can come out now."

Jon came forward. He wasn't wearing his suit jacket. He seemed unharmed physically, but from the way he stared at the ground, not looking at Kay or anyone else, made her worry he'd been hit in the head. He halted, then squatted and laid his hands on the ground. It crumbled away, revealing a sparkle. "Opal," he said as he picked it up. He looked up and seemed to notice for the first time the Gods and Goddesses watching him. His eyes widened. "Begging your pardon...."

His aura's brown now, Gwen said.

"He stole star magic from Us!" War unsheathed His own All-weapon.

"Magic goes to whom it wills," Kron said quietly.

"Earth magic." Spring turned to the rest of the Four. "He will be useful in making the Dead Land live again."

"What about Ysabel's anilink?" Fall asked, eyes narrowed. "He'll cause all sorts of mischief if We let him keep his magic!"

Lathtin? Where is he? Gwen asked.

I can't feel my link to him! Ysabel broke the Avatar link and looked wildly about. "Lathtin! Brother, where are you?"

"Here, Sister," a strange yet familiar tenor voice said. "By the Four, don't look at me! I'm not fit to be seen."

Kay couldn't help turning, along with the others. A young, part-Selathen man resembling Ysabel peeked around a mound of bones.

"Lathitn!" Ysabel ran to him, followed by Gwen. "You're...you're human? How? Is this a miracle from Spring or Fall or both?"

"I don't know." He shrugged. "I felt itchy all over, like I had fleas, even though they never come near me, and then I sneezed and swallowed something in the air. The next thing I knew, I was back in my human body." He ducked back behind the pile. "But not much else."

Gwen halted, blushing.

"Kron!" Ysabel called. "Don't you have any extra clothing in that satchel of yours?"

"I can create some." A few scraps of cloth grew into pants and a shirt. Kay hoped Kron wouldn't single-handedly put all tailors and seamstresses out of business. Kron brought them over to Lathtin, and a few moments later, Ysabel's brother emerged from his hiding place. He hugged his sister fiercely, but he watched Gwen the entire time.

"Lady Gwendolyn," he said as he approached her, "you're even more beautiful in person. I mean, when I'm a person."

She stifled a laugh. "You were more eloquent in the link, Lathtin. But you do have a beautiful aura, all swirled with red and yellow." She said it kindly, peeping at him under fluttering eyelashes in a matter that would have done Jenna proud.

"I had no hope as a cat, so I was free to say what I pleased."

She drew back. "You didn't mean what you said?"

"By All Four, I did!" He blanched, as if suddenly realizing They were physically present to witness what he said. "But what do I have to offer you? My father thinks I'm dead, and even if I showed myself to him, he wouldn't pass his watch shop on to me." He looked down. "You deserve so much more than that."

Gwen drooped. It pained Kay to watch her, as Gwen hadn't shown any interest in other men.

Whispers from behind her made Kay turn around. Fall and the Grandmother of Stories stood next to each other, arguing about something. When Spring joined in, Fall scowled, disappeared for a heartbeat, and reappeared carrying a wooden box. She chewed Her lip for several heartbeats, rocking back and forth. Seeing a Goddess so nervous reinforced the fact that She must have been human once. Kay glanced away, ashamed of seeing her deities appear less than perfect. A deep growl made her look up. Flanked by wolves, Fall advanced, a step at a time, toward Lathtin. Ysabel and Gwen drew off to the side, clutching hands.

"Here." Fall stopped several yards away from Lathtin and set the box down. "These trinkets are for you, as a reward for your service."

She backed away. Lathtin let her return to Her place beside the rest of the Four before bowing and retrieving the box. Gwen and Ysabel hurried to his side as he opened it.

"Oh my...." Ysabel fanned herself. "Only a Goddess could have created these."

Gwen took the box—with both hands, Kay noticed—and tilted it so Jenna and Kay could see the contents. It was filled with little balls of every color.

"What are they?" Kay asked.

"Pearls." Gwen sounded stunned. "Lots and lots of pearls, finer than any I've ever seen." She handed the box back to Lathtin. "The Goddess has been very generous to you."

"I...I thank You, gracious Goddess. May Your season always be praised." Although he addressed Fall, Lathtin kept stealing glances at Gwen. He searched through the casket until he pulled out a bright yellow one. Setting the box down, he knelt and extended the pearl to Gwen. "Lady Gwendolyn lo Havil, you are more priceless than all these pearls put together. All I can give you are these and my undying love. Will you...will you marry me?"

The color rose again in Gwen's cheeks. She stared at him, her hand on her heart. "If I could choose for myself, I would. But my duties as a lo Havil...."

"Freeze your duties, Gwen!" Jenna said. "By All Four Gods and Goddesses, make yourself happy for once. You deserve it."

"But the lo Havil estate...."

"Can be managed by someone else. Hire someone. Freeze it, sell the land off if it's that much of a burden."

"Sell it? Are you mad, Jenna? Still...." Gwen stepped closer to Lathtin, glancing at her sister Avatars. "Should I accept him?"

Ysabel grinned. "You'd better. I think he became human just for you."

"Then...yes." Gwen took Lathtin's hand. "Most assuredly yes."

He rose, and they joined their free hands, smiling broadly as they stared into each other's eyes. Kay thought they wouldn't have noticed a Chaos Season if it covered them in snow. How wonderful for Gwen that she had finally found the one she'd longed for for several moons. Kay risked a glance at Jon. What would happen to the two of them now that he had magic of his own?

Jon studied her for several heartbeats, one hand clenched around the opal he'd found. His clothes were torn, but he appeared unhurt. Kay realized, astonished, that she had recovered her strength as well. He jerked his head toward another pile of broken crystal, barely wide enough to give the two of them some privacy. Kay felt her cheeks grow warm as they both stepped around the other side. The face she'd loved for so long had been subtly altered. New confidence shone in Jon's eyes, as if he'd finally acknowledged the strength she'd sensed in him all along.

"Well, this has been quite the adventure, hasn't it, my Stowaway?" His dark brown eyes became more intense as he stared into her eyes. "I don't know what's in store for us next, but I hope we can face it together. Will you, Kay?" He held out the opal to her. "Will you be my wife, side by side, no matter what season we face?"

Kay didn't need to consult with her sister Avatars to decide. She'd only been waiting for him to be ready for her. "Yes," she whispered. "For always."

She stood on tiptoe to kiss him. Never had it tasted so sweet.

Kay could have stayed there until spring returned to the Dead Land, but the Goddess of Spring called out, "Couples, will your accept Our blessings on your unions now?"

"Not yet, Spring," Winter said. "Some souls need to return home first."

He summons us, Dorian. Olivia and Dorian had been so silent Kay had forgotten about them.

He summons you, maybe. Dorian sounded resigned. *At least let me see my Margaret's soul before Winter freezes me forever.*

Once, Kay would have urged Winter to freeze her hated rival. Now, the thought filled her with fear for him. Maybe the Season Avatars were no longer needed with Chaos Season over, but it still didn't seem right to dispose of Dorian permanently.

Another portal opened, and Kay found herself drawn to it. One by one, Gwen, Jenna, and Ysabel approached it and held both hands up to the portal. Each of them seemed relieved as they left, especially as they were joined by their intendeds. Finally, it was Kay's turn. As she paced toward the portal, she did her best to keep her thoughts shielded from Olivia and Dorian. Should she say something to Winter? What kind of punishment did Dorian deserve that wouldn't harm the rest of his quartet? Sadly, she couldn't think of any. Perhaps it no longer mattered, since they would never have to tame a Chaos Season again.

Farewell, Kay, Olivia said as she slipped out of the link. *May you and your quartet have a long and peaceful reign before Winter summons you back.* Her soul appeared briefly as a blue-edged form that waved to her before passing through the portal.

Kay took a deep breath. "Great and glorious God of Winter, what do You have planned for Dorian? Will You punish him?"

"That is My decision, Daughter." His breath swirled around her, a frost she couldn't shield herself from.

"Yes, of course, but … may I speak?"

Silence.

Kay hurried on, fearful He would freeze her even after all she'd done for Him. "Winter, You know Dorian and I have hated each other ever since we first both became Your Avatars. He's treated me horribly whenever we encountered each other. Not only did he try to kill me this summer, but he betrayed all of us to support Salth, even if he claims that was a ruse. But for all of Dorian's crimes, I don't think You should freeze him. Instead, take away his weather magic, even if just for one life."

Her sister Avatars stared at her as if her hair had turned to icicles.

Are you trying to help me or get revenge? Dorian demanded.

She didn't respond to him. "He loves magic best, or at least almost as much as he loves Margaret. But he thinks it makes him superior to everyone else. Maybe if he has to do without it for a while, he'll learn to behave better."

Winter raised a shaggy eyebrow just enough to be noticeable. "What would you have Me do with the rest of his quartet?"

She sighed. "They should go without magic as well. It might not seem fair, but they could have done a better job of keeping him in line."

The Four exchanged glances. "We will consider your suggestion, Kay," Winter said. "For now, Dorian, your season here is done."

The God untwined Dorian from Kay. Before his soul passed through the portal, he flung a handful of snow at her. She flinched, expecting a trick.

"Take it," he said. "It's my knowledge of weather patterns in Challen."

She guided the flakes to her with a breeze and touched one to her tongue. New memories of wind patterns along the Chikasi River bloomed in her mind. Dorian had spoken true. A way to make amends? Maybe it wasn't enough, but it was still welcome.

She met his gaze. "Thank you."

Winter sent Dorian through the portal before he had a chance to reply. Kay stood up straight and breathed deeply. It felt good to have her body all to herself again.

"And now that that's done," Spring said, "perhaps Our Avatars can now exchange vows with their partners."

The Grandmother of Stories cackled. "A quadruple wedding! What a wonderful way to end this story."

War snorted. "Not My type of ending at all. If You're actually going to let that renegade magician keep star magic from Us, then there's no reason for Me to be here." He turned to Kron. "But I'll be watching you, Artificer. Remember, you aren't as immortal as you think you are."

"I never said I was," Kron replied.

War scowled at him and disappeared. Kron was too busy with Ysabel to notice.

The Grandmother of Stories chanted in a musical language Kay didn't recognize. The dry soil turned to fine sand; the broken crystal house became a moonlit sea. As the other couples assembled next to the water, Kay noted her sister Avatars now wore flowing gauzy dresses, each in the appropriate color of their God or Goddess. Her own clothes felt unchanged, but when she glanced down at herself, she saw ocean blue fabric embroidered with silver swirls. She didn't have a dress like that, nor did Jon own a silk suit with a blue shirt.

"Grandmother is graciously using illusion to make this Dead Land appear more suitable for weddings," Spring said, amusement in her voice. "But I think We can provide a few real touches of Our own."

Garlands of holly branches with red berries appeared next to Jon and Kay. They crowned each other, Jon stooping so she could reach his head. The simple act made this ceremony seem real. Kay and Jon stared at each other for a long time, letting Gods and Avatars and everything else fade away.

"I pledge myself to you, Kay Seltich, Winter Avatar," Jon whispered. "Through the promise of Spring, the growth of Summer, the bounty of Fall, and the death of Winter. In all the seasons of our lives, I will walk by your side. I will wear your initials on my arm so we will always be a part of each other. Together we will raise any and all children the Four give us and teach them to be thankful for the Four's blessings. By the Four Gods and Goddesses, I promise you my love in this life, and, if They will, in other lives to come."

Kay swallowed. "And I pledge myself to you, Jon Stunstrug, Avatar of Earth." With his new magic, it seemed right to name him an Avatar and equal to her. As she finished reciting the rest of her vows, her arm tingled. Jon's initials appeared on her arm in an iridescent ink only Spring could have created. She and Jon kissed as a chorus of birds sang a hymn to the Four. When the music died away, the foreign Goddess and Her illusions had disappeared. Dazed, Kay glanced around to see

Gwen with Lathtin, Jenna with Lex, and Ysabel with Kron, all of them wearing appropriate seasonal garlands and displaying marriage tattoos on their arms.

"I don't think even my father can question this marriage," Gwen said as she examined her tattoo.

"Do you think he'll like me?" Lathtin asked.

"He'll like it when we give him grandchildren." Gwen's eyes widened. "By the Four, there's no more reason to wait, especially since we've … aged."

The signs of it were subtle, particularly in Gwen. Kay had to look hard to see how Gwen's face had become narrower. Jenna bore a few creases around her eyes, as did Ysabel around her mouth. Kay wondered how aging had changed her.

"There's a streak of white in your hair, as if Winter touched you," Jon said. "But it doesn't matter."

"Challens will recognize you as their Season Avatars," Winter said. "And they're still waiting for their soltrans."

"The soltrans!" Today, in addition to being Kay's birthday, was also the day where she would debut in the soltrans. She hadn't even thought about the ritual combat with Ysabel. Hopefully memories from other lives would be enough to help her make a decent showing.

As Kron collected materials to build a portal, Spring said, "Take a piece of Salth's house with you to show Our people. It will prove to them that Chaos Season is over."

Jon nodded and selected a chunk of dull crystal almost as big as Robbie. As he staggered over with it, Robbie reached a hand toward the crystal and burbled at it in baby talk. Jenna absently pulled him away.

"Eagle's Claws, the child's bloody!" Lex frowned. "Why were we commanded to bring him with us if he was going to be injured?"

"The bleeding's stopped, Your Highness." Even if they were now all in-laws of a sort, Gwen was obviously going to maintain a formal relationship with Jenna's husband. She crouched down to peer at Robbie. "I don't see a wound. But his left eye…it turned gray."

Jenna clutched her son tightly enough to make him wail. "Goddess of Spring, please don't let my son become blind!"

"He's not, Jenna," the Goddess said mildly. "Just the opposite. We hope his new vision will be useful to Us later."

"What kind of new vision?"

Spring didn't reply.

Lex's hand moved to his Allweapon. "It seems You're gaining new types of Avatars, Challen Gods and Goddesses. War will not be pleased."

"They're not Ours, War Avatar. They belong to Selath, which, thanks to Kron, doesn't belong to any God." Winter crossed His arms. "The Dead Land will be very interesting to watch over the next few centuries."

Kron didn't take long to set up his portal. Darkness on the other side made it difficult to determine exactly where they were going. Kay thought she saw the outline of the Fours' altars in the Temple in Wistica. Light glimmered from far off, and a crowd chanted a prayer to Winter. Gwen frowned, but she curtseyed to each of the Four before passing through the portal with Lathtin. Jenna and Ysabel followed suit with their new spouses. Jon set the crystal down long enough to make his bows.

"Go through," Kay told him. "I need a few heartbeats here first."

He gave her a concerned look, then nodded and stepped through.

Alone with the Four, Kay studied the dirt, unable to look at Them or ask the question burning in her heart.

"You want to ask if We really are divine or if We're human," Spring said.

Kay nodded, throat swollen too much to let her speak.

Spring sighed. "It's true that We were human centuries ago, in a time much harsher than today. Plagues, poor harvests, harsh weather, and wars all took away Our loved ones and caused Us personal suffering. When We gained the ability to do something about these problems, We chose to work together to solve them." She spread Her hands. "How could We help others if We didn't have Our own experiences with pain? We wouldn't understand human problems properly."

Kay let out her own sigh, this one of relief. The Goddess made sense. The Four were more divine for having been human once.

"Thank You, thank all of You." She made them the deepest curtseys she could manage before racing through the portal.

Gwen had already left the altar room and stood on the Temple porch. Kay hurried to the storage room to select a fighting stick, but she peeped out from around a corner. Thousands of candles indicated where Challens gathered in the street and across the way, waiting for their Avatars.

"People of Challen!" Gwen called. "Today is a wondrous day! With the help of the Four Gods and Goddesses, as well as His Royal Highness Lex voy ro Fip, Kron Evenhanded, Lathtin s'Ivena Lathatilltin, and Jon Stunstrug, we have ensured Chaos Season will never return! As proof, we have brought a crystal from the Dead Land. It was part of a larger one that was causing Chaos Season. After the soltrans, you are all invited to look at it!"

Kay wondered why Gwen had chosen to present the story this way. Perhaps it was best to avoid all mention of Salth and Sal-thaath so that they could be forgotten.

It took many moments for the cheering to die down. "My brother can't take action against you Avatars now," Lex said, "No matter what he accuses you of. It would mean revolution."

Gwen spoke for a few more minutes before returning to the altar room. "Ysabel, Kay, are you ready?"

"Not yet. No one will be able to see us." Kay sent several lightning balls ahead of her to illuminate the corners of the temple porch.

Gwen quirked her lips. "I remember when I met you earlier this spring, how you were so afraid to use your magic you wouldn't even heat up a room. Now look at how far you've come."

"We've all changed this year," Jenna said.

"That's because we're stronger together." Ysabel graced all of them with a smile. "We bring out the best in each other."

Kay twirled her fighting stick. "No matter what happens to Challen and to the Season Avatars now that Chaos Season is done, I pray the Four allow us to continue working together."

"May it be so," her sister Avatars chorused.

They exchanged glances, linked without a physical link. Ysabel saluted Gwen and Jenna as she exited to start the soltrans. Kay followed, ready to usher a new season into Challen.

Author's Note

Thanks for reading my work; I hope you enjoyed it. If you did, please consider leaving a review. Reviews help other readers decide if a particular book is for them, and many advertisers require a certain number of positive reviews before accepting a book.

As always, thanks go out the beta readers listed in previous books and Maria Zannini of *The Book Diva* for creating the cover. I thank my husband, Eugene, and Alex for putting up with my constant reading and writing.

This series has been in my head for over twenty years, and I'm glad it's finally complete. That doesn't mean the story is over for our Fem Four. They will face new challenges as they work to make Selath habitable, and Challen will be changing as well. I plan to write a spin-off series tentatively called Selathen Avatars to chronicle these events. However, it'll take some planning. In the meantime, I'm drafting a children's book and an urban fantasy series. Please check my blog or website often to learn more about my projects. Better yet, sign up for my newsletter for announcements of new works and sales. You can do that through the blog or website; however, if you go through Instafreebie, you can download a free story of mine.

Thanks again for reading!

Best,

Sandra

The Season Avatars

(Names in parentheses are from the Avatars' first lives as shown in *Seasons' Beginnings*.)

Quartet 1

Gwendolyn lo Havil (Galia)—Spring

Jenna dor Treve (Janno)—Summer

Ysabel ava Sivena (Bella)—Fall

Kay ava Seltich (Caye)—Winter

Quartet 2 (all deceased)

Margaret gran Garnell (Magstrom)—Spring

Charles vin Estcher (Carver)—Summer

Sophia vin Estcher (Sylva)—Fall

Dorian gran Garnell (Domina)—Winter

Quartet 3 (all deceased)

Tylon fi Vort (Tylan)—Spring

Frederick min Jole (Flilya)—Summer

Helene ava Hartfut (Hala)—Fall

Olivia ava Kalt (Ocul)—Winter

Other Works By the Author

Science Fiction: Catalyst Chronicles Series

Lyon's Legacy
The Mommy Clone
Twinned Universes
Seasonal Stories from the *Sagan*

Non-Fiction

Life at Seventeen Syllables a Day: A Journal in Haiku
SF Women A-Z: A Reader's Guide

Fantasy: Short Stories

Letters to Psyche
Silver Rain

Fantasy: Season Avatars Series

Seasons' Beginnings
Young Seasons: A Season Avatars Short Story Collection
Scattered Seasons
Chaos Season
Fifth Season
Summon the Seasons

About the Author

Sandra Ulbrich Almazan started reading at the age of three and only stops when absolutely required to. Although she hasn't been writing quite that long, she did compose a very simple play in German during middle school. Her science fiction novella *Move Over Ms. L.* (an early version of *Lyon's Legacy*) earned an Honorable Mention in the 2001 UPC Science Fiction Awards, and her short story "A Reptile at the Reunion" was published in the anthology *Firestorm of Dragons*. Other works include the science fiction *Catalyst Chronicles* series, the fantasy *Season Avatars* series, *SF Women A-Z: A Reader's Guide*, and several science fiction and fantasy short stories. She is a founding member of Broad Universe, which promotes science fiction, fantasy, and horror written by women. Her undergraduate degree is in molecular biology/English, and she has a Master of Technical and Scientific Communication degree. She is currently a QA Representative; she's also been a technical writer and a part-time copyeditor for a local newspaper. Some of her other accomplishments are losing on *Jeopardy*! and taking a stuffed orca to three continents. She lives in the Chicago area with her husband, Eugene; and son, Alex. In her rare moments of free time, she enjoys crocheting, listening to classic rock (particularly the Beatles), trooping with the Midwest Garrison of the 501st Legion, and watching improv comedy.

Sandra can be found online at the following links:

Website (www.sandraulbrichalmazan.com)

Blog (www.ulbrichalmazan.blogspot.com)

Twitter (@ulbrichalmazan)

Facebook (https://www.facebook.com/SandraUlbrichAlmazanSffAuthor)

Goodreads (http://www.goodreads.com/author/show/5282664.Sandra_Ulbrich_Almazan).

Newsletter (http://eepurl.com/cbvrfX)

www.ingramcontent.com/pod-product-compliance
Lightning Source LLC
Chambersburg PA
CBHW060534180626
46817CB00002B/559